HOUSECAT TROUBLE
LOST AND FOUND

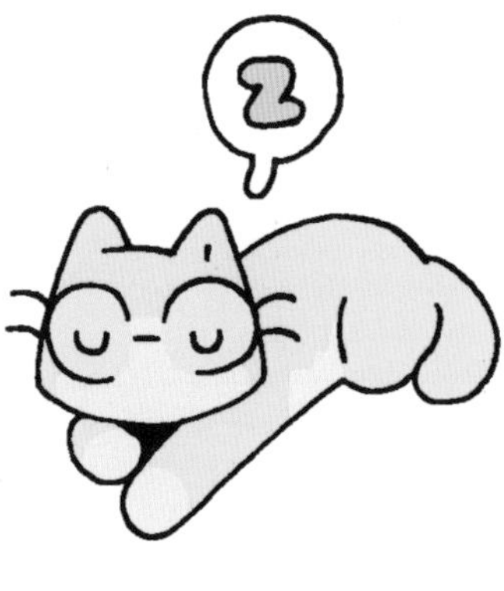
z

HOUSECAT TROUBLE: LOST AND FOUND
WAS DRAWN ON 8.5" x 14" 110LB
INDEX PAPER WITH SAKURA PIGMA
MICRON PENS AND THEN COLORED
DIGITALLY WITH CLIP STUDIO PAINT.

Copyright © 2023 by Mason Dickerson

All rights reserved. Published in the United States by RH Graphic, an imprint of Random House Children's Books, a division of Penguin Random House LLC, New York.

RH Graphic with the book design is a trademark of Penguin Random House LLC.

Visit us on the web! RHKidsGraphic.com • @RHKidsGraphic

Educators and librarians, for a variety of teaching tools, visit us at RHTeachersLibrarians.com

Library of Congress Cataloging-in-Publication Data is available upon request.
ISBN 978-0-593-17348-0 (hardcover) — ISBN 978-0-593-17349-7 (library binding)
ISBN 978-0-593-17350-3 (ebook)

Designed by Patrick Crotty

MANUFACTURED IN CHINA
10 9 8 7 6 5 4 3 2 1
First Edition

A comic on every bookshelf.

HOUSECAT

TROUBLE

LOST AND FOUND

MASON DICKERSON

CHAPTER 1

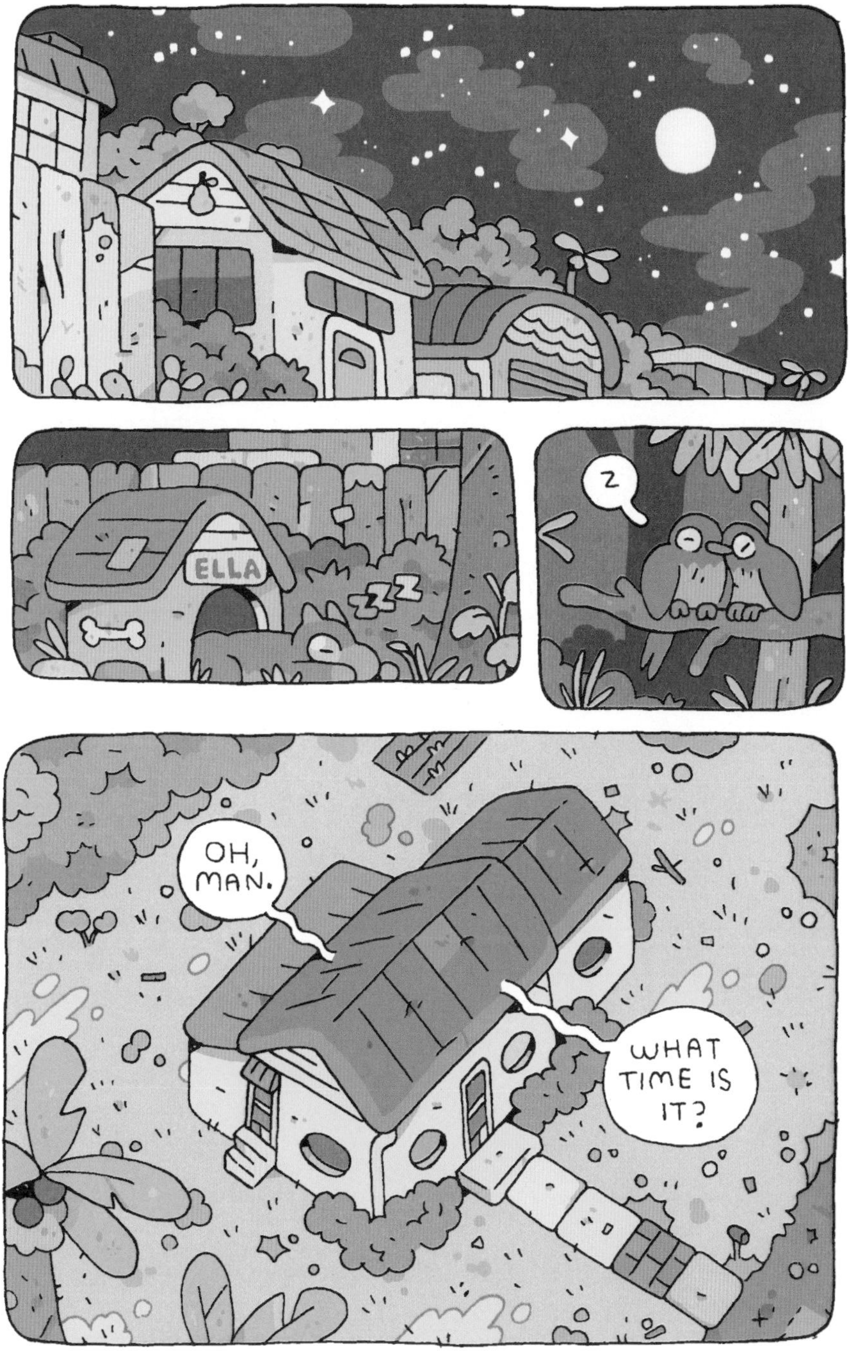
ELLA
ZZZ
Z
OH, MAN.
WHAT TIME IS IT?

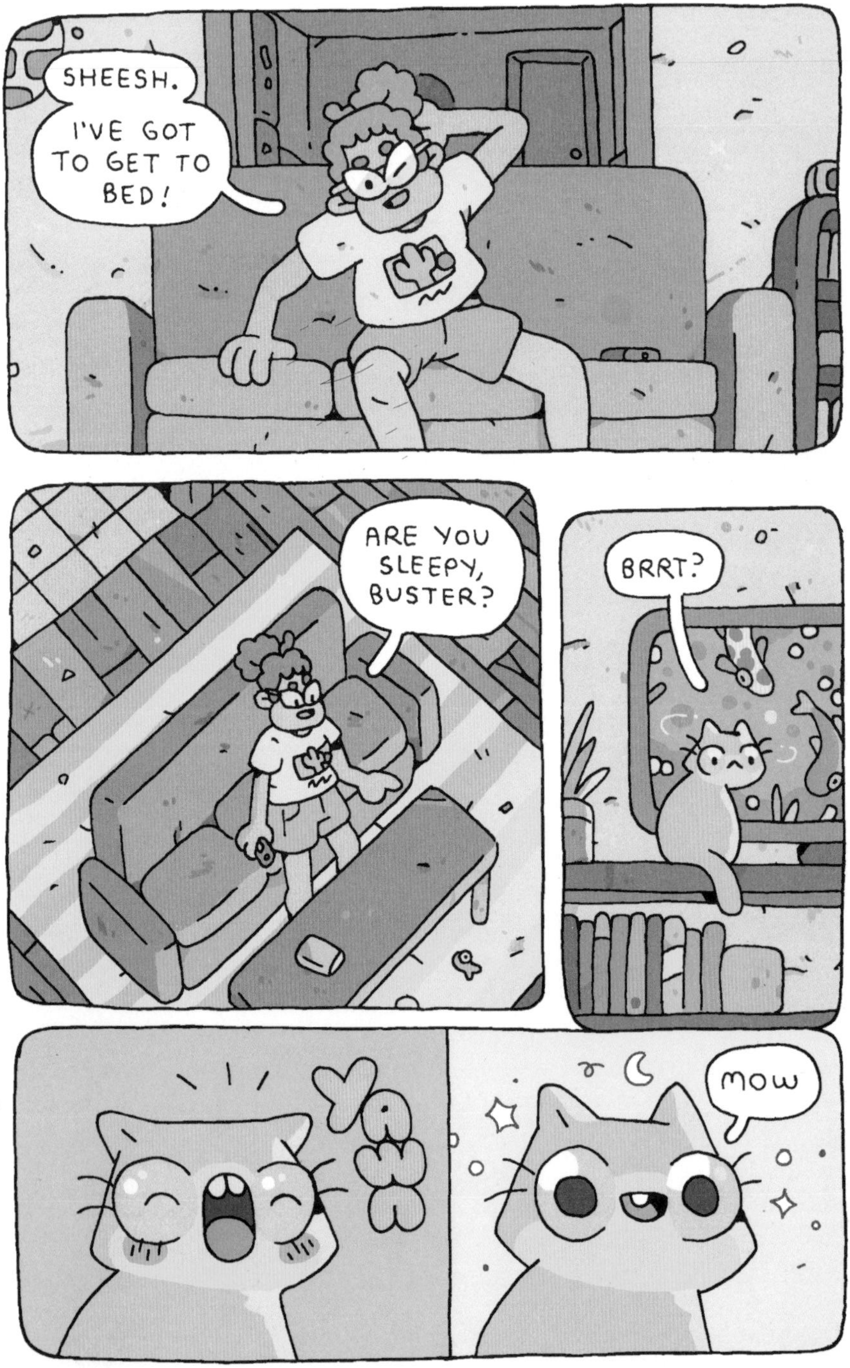
SHEESH.
I'VE GOT TO GET TO BED!
ARE YOU SLEEPY, BUSTER?
BRRT?
YAWN
mow

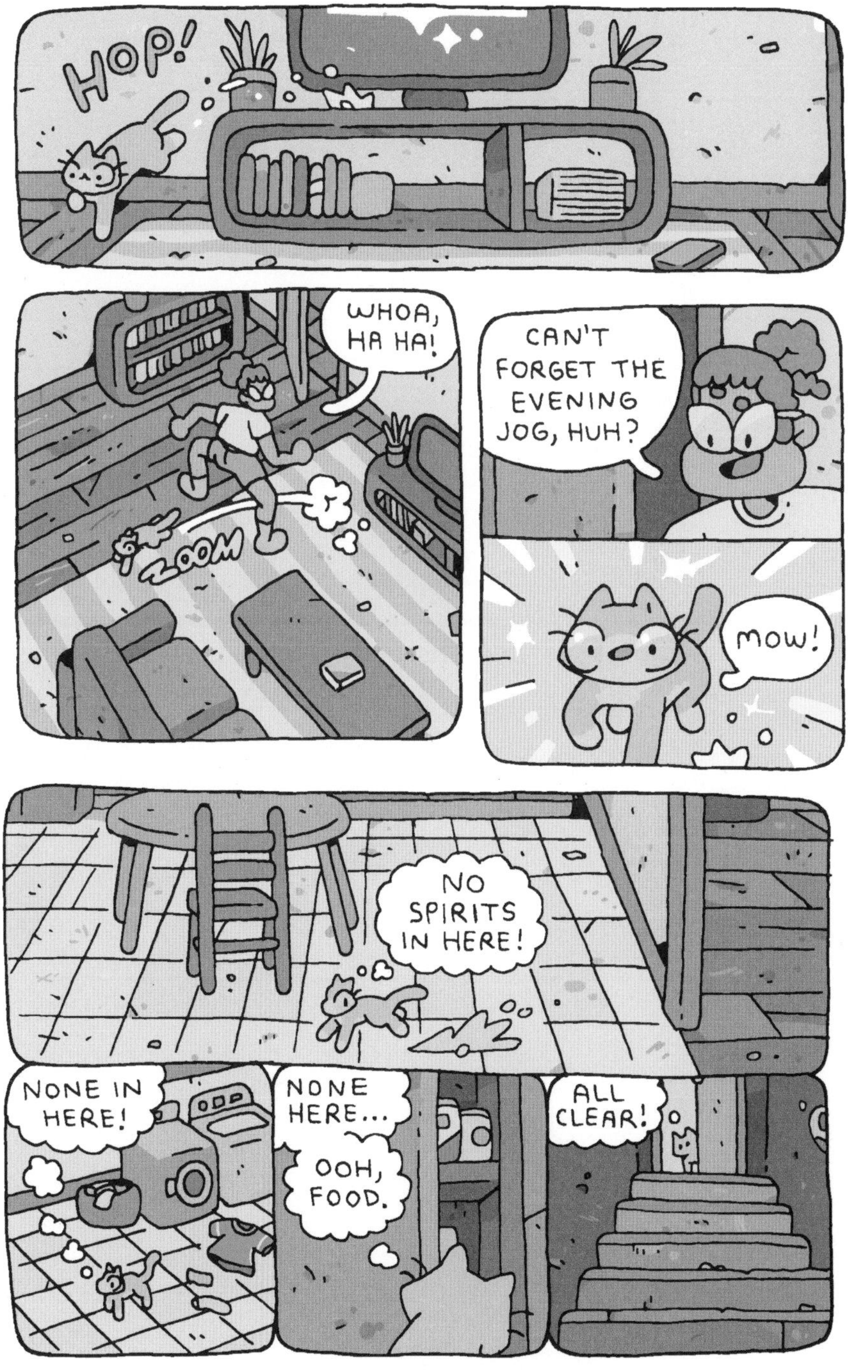
HOP!
WHOA, HA HA!
ZOOM
CAN'T FORGET THE EVENING JOG, HUH?
MOW!
NO SPIRITS IN HERE!
NONE IN HERE!
NONE HERE...
OOH, FOOD.
ALL CLEAR!

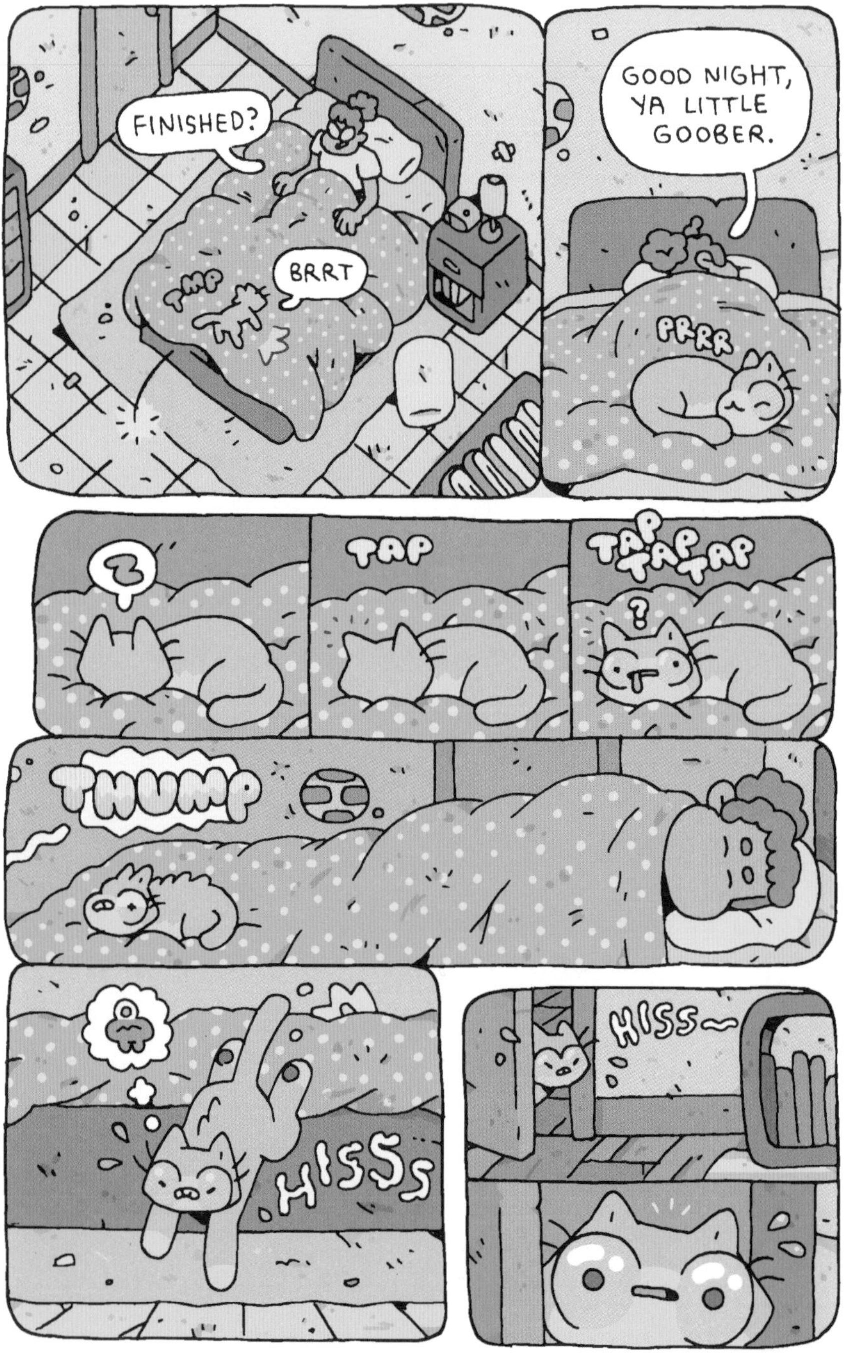
FINISHED?
TMP
BRRT
GOOD NIGHT, YA LITTLE GOOBER.
PRRR
TAP
TAP TAP TAP
?
THUMP
HISSS
HISS~

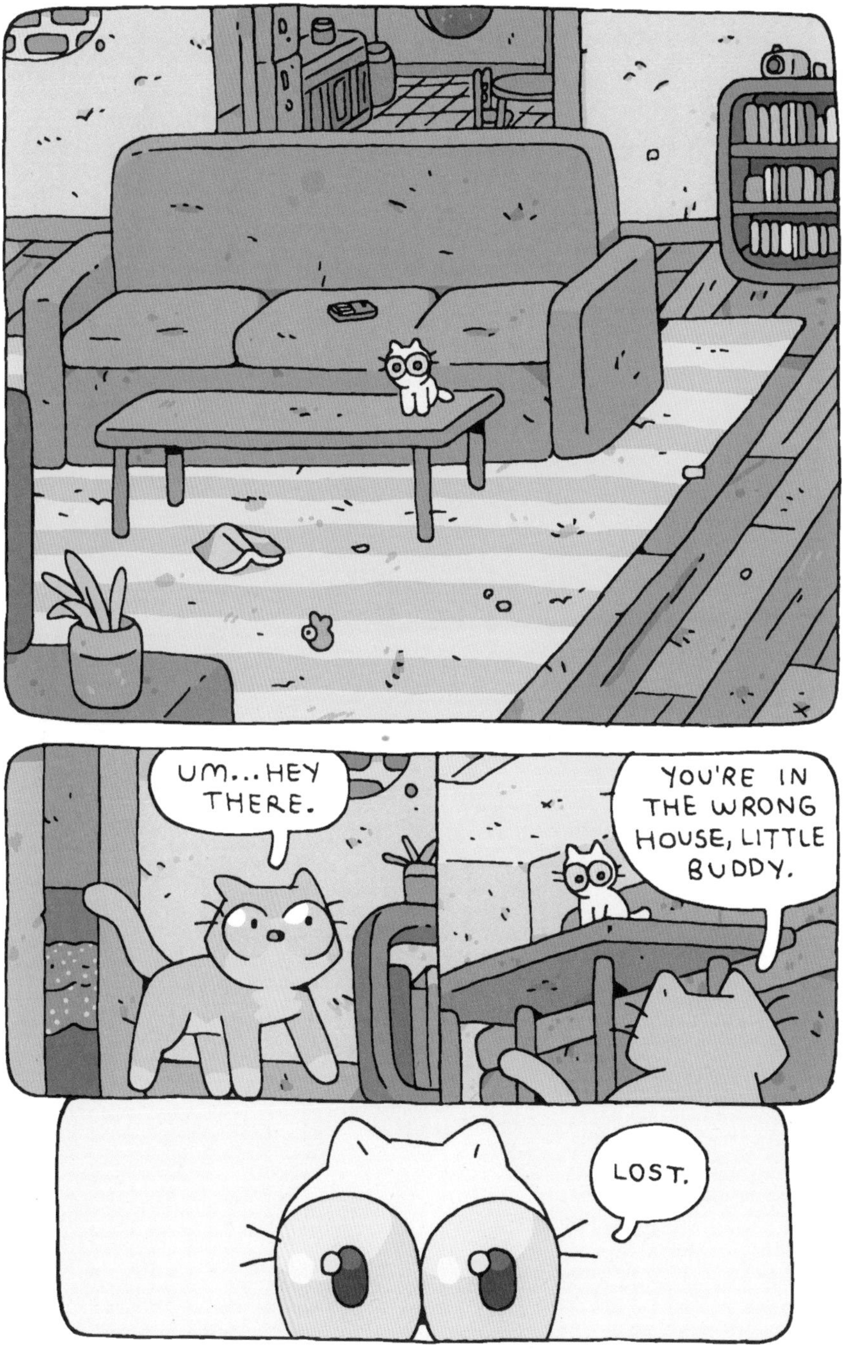
UM...HEY THERE.
YOU'RE IN THE WRONG HOUSE, LITTLE BUDDY.
LOST.

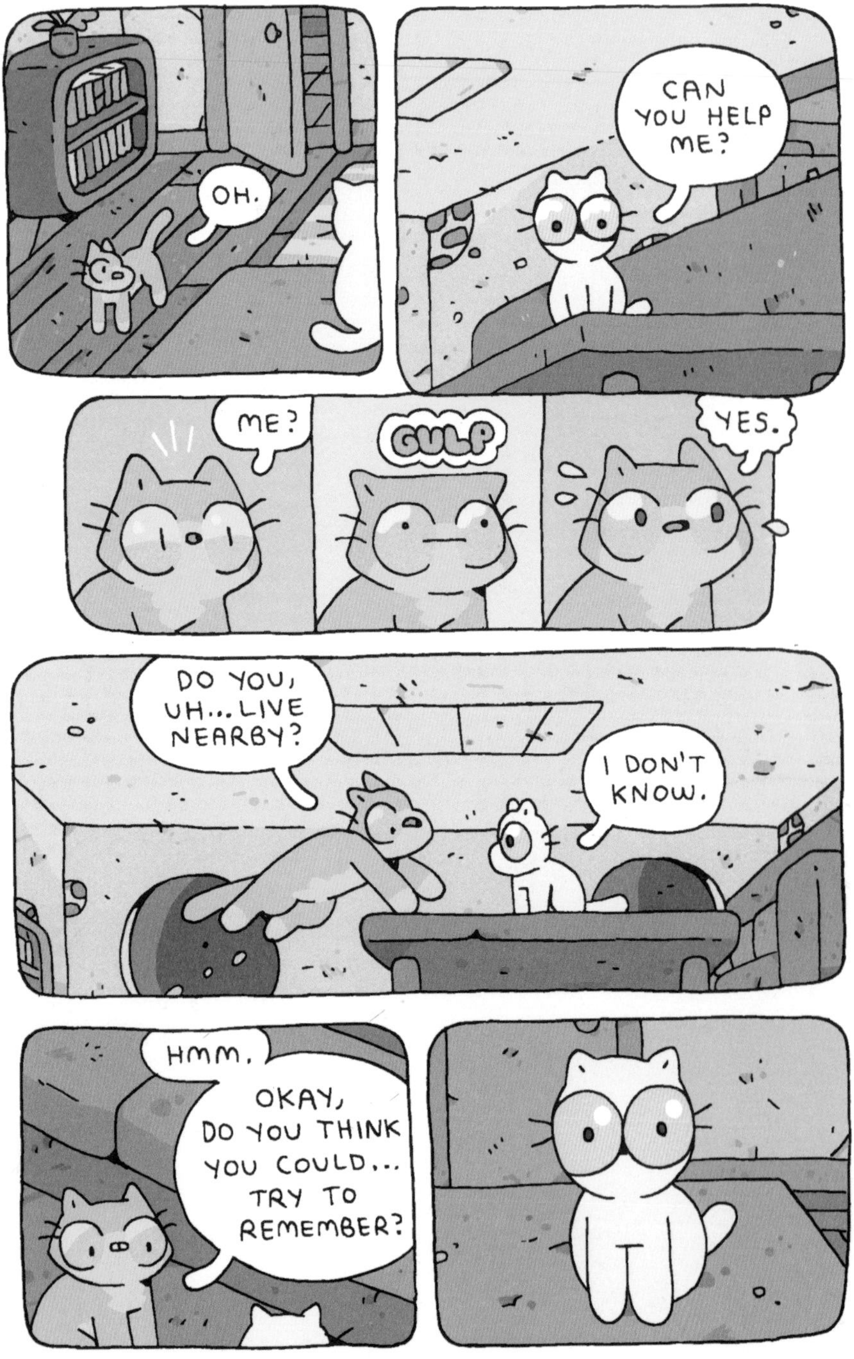
OH.
CAN YOU HELP ME?
ME?
GULP
YES.
DO YOU, UH...LIVE NEARBY?
I DON'T KNOW.
HMM.
OKAY, DO YOU THINK YOU COULD... TRY TO REMEMBER?

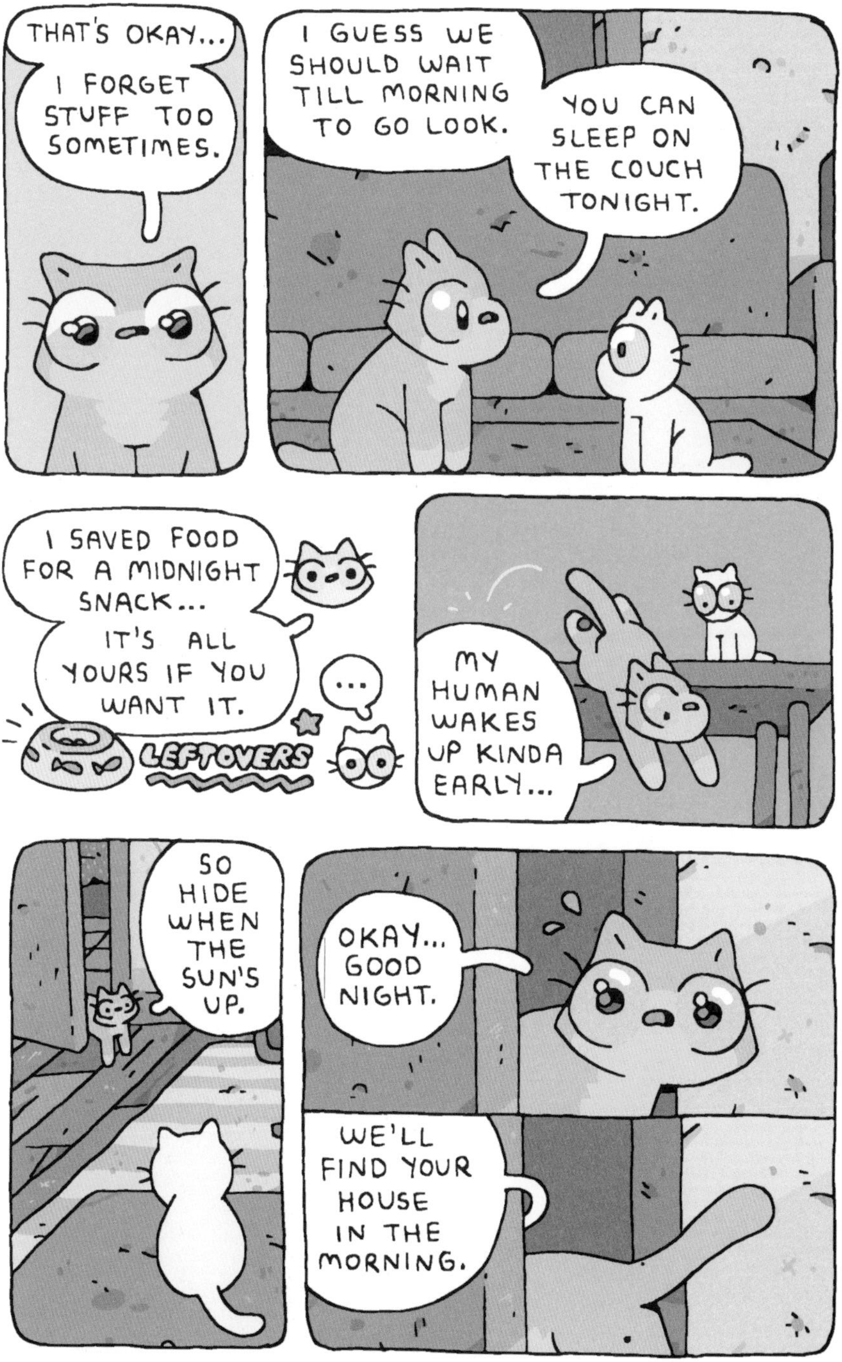
THAT'S OKAY...
I FORGET STUFF TOO SOMETIMES.
I GUESS WE SHOULD WAIT TILL MORNING TO GO LOOK.
YOU CAN SLEEP ON THE COUCH TONIGHT.
I SAVED FOOD FOR A MIDNIGHT SNACK...
IT'S ALL YOURS IF YOU WANT IT.
...
LEFTOVERS
MY HUMAN WAKES UP KINDA EARLY...
SO HIDE WHEN THE SUN'S UP.
OKAY... GOOD NIGHT.
WE'LL FIND YOUR HOUSE IN THE MORNING.

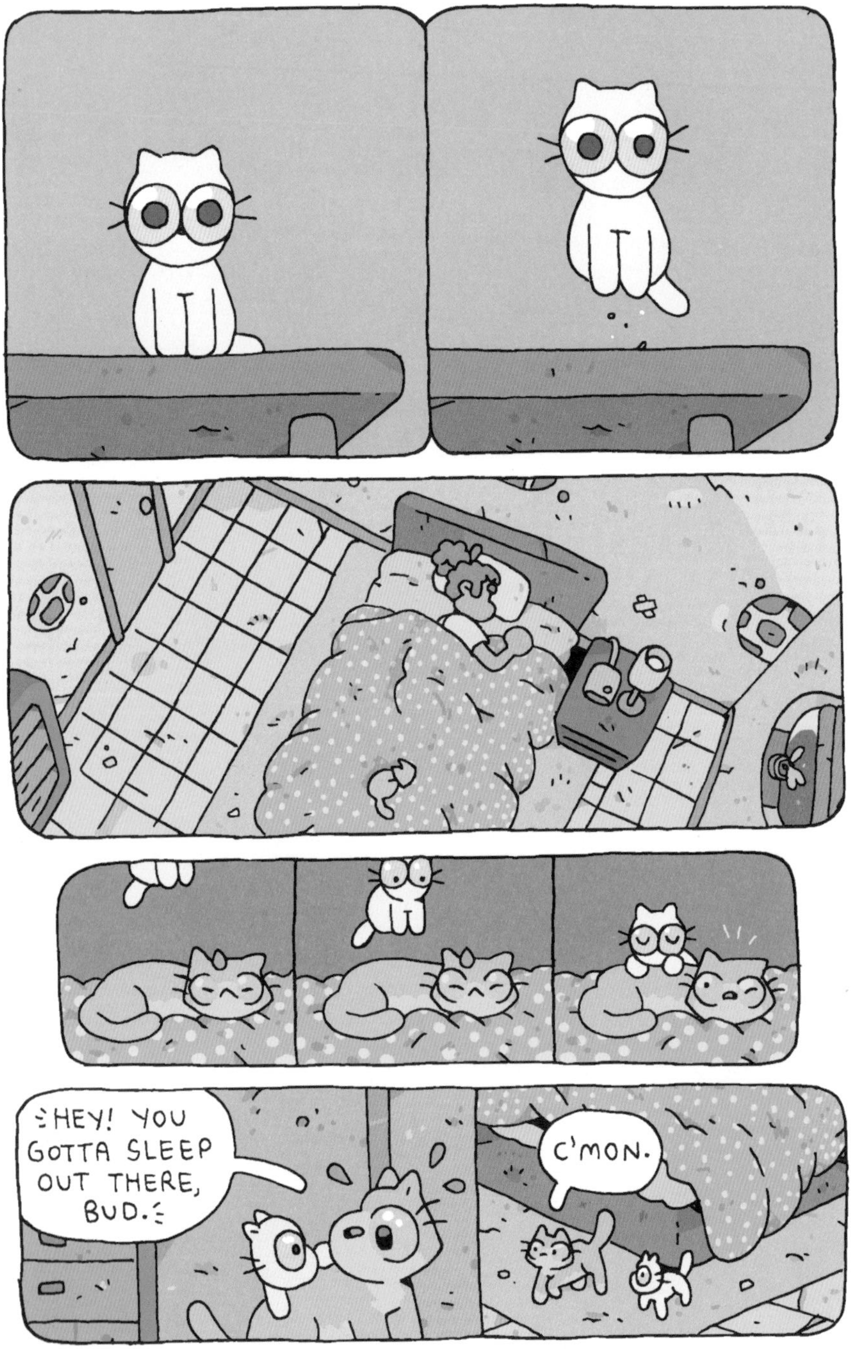
HEY! YOU GOTTA SLEEP OUT THERE, BUD.
C'MON.

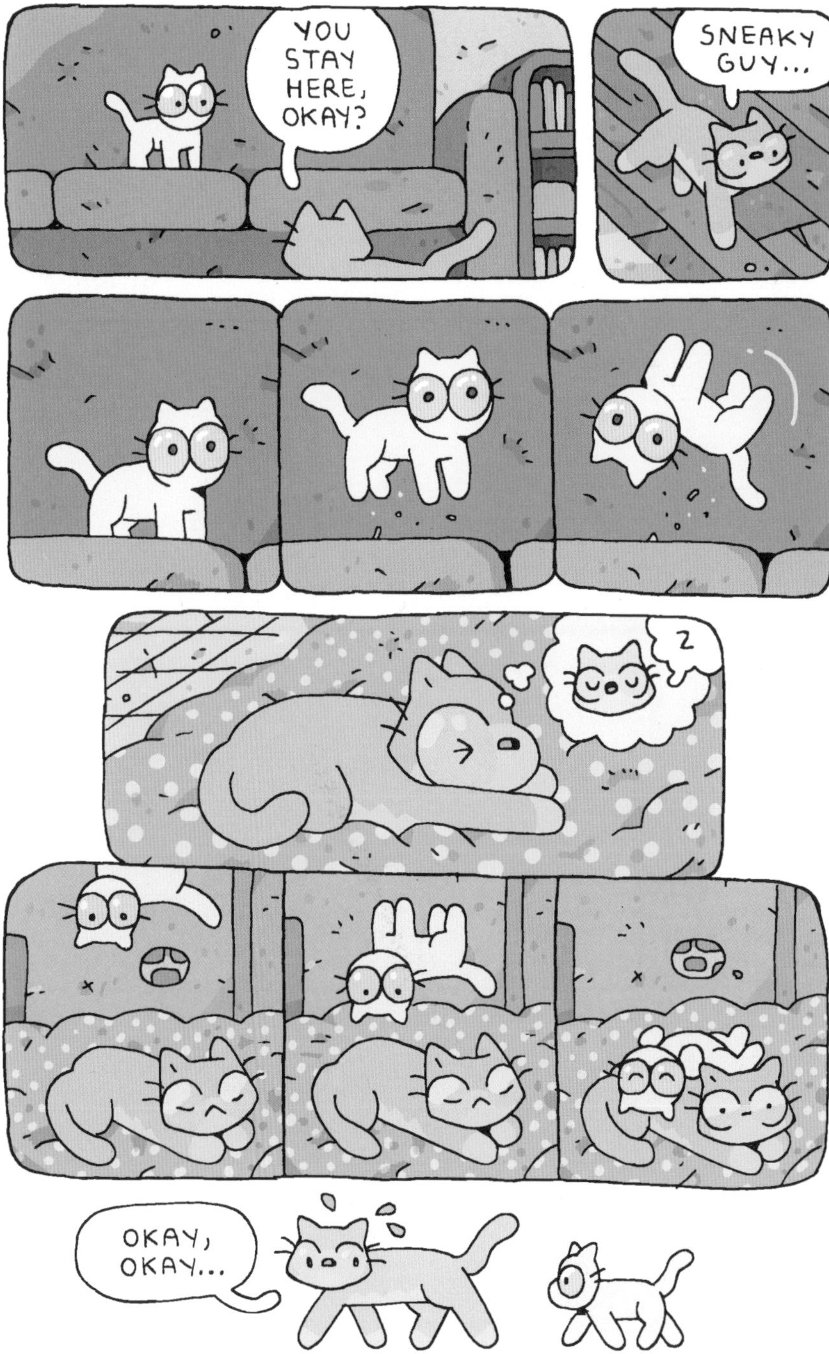
YOU STAY HERE, OKAY?
SNEAKY GUY...
Z
OKAY, OKAY...

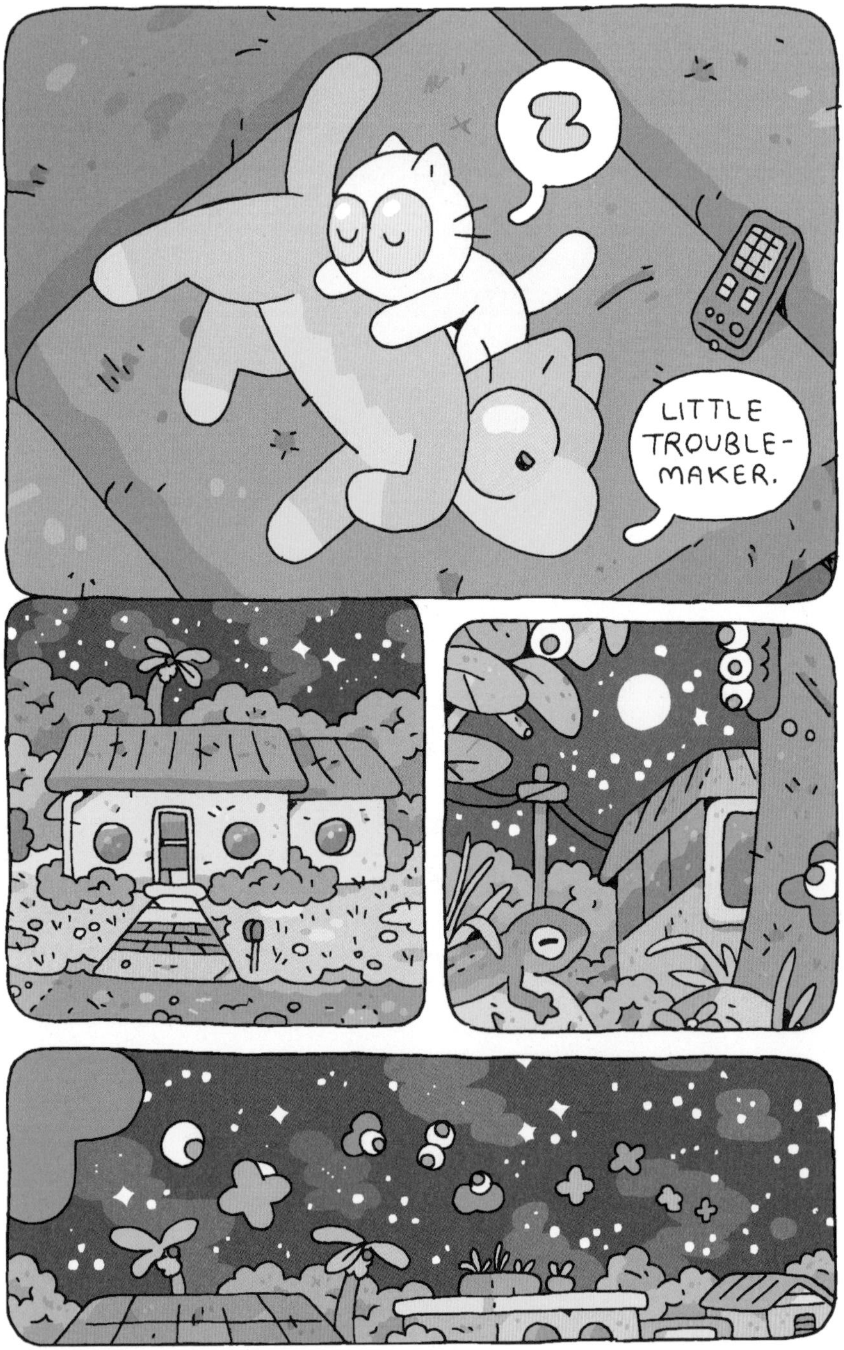
Z
LITTLE TROUBLE-MAKER.

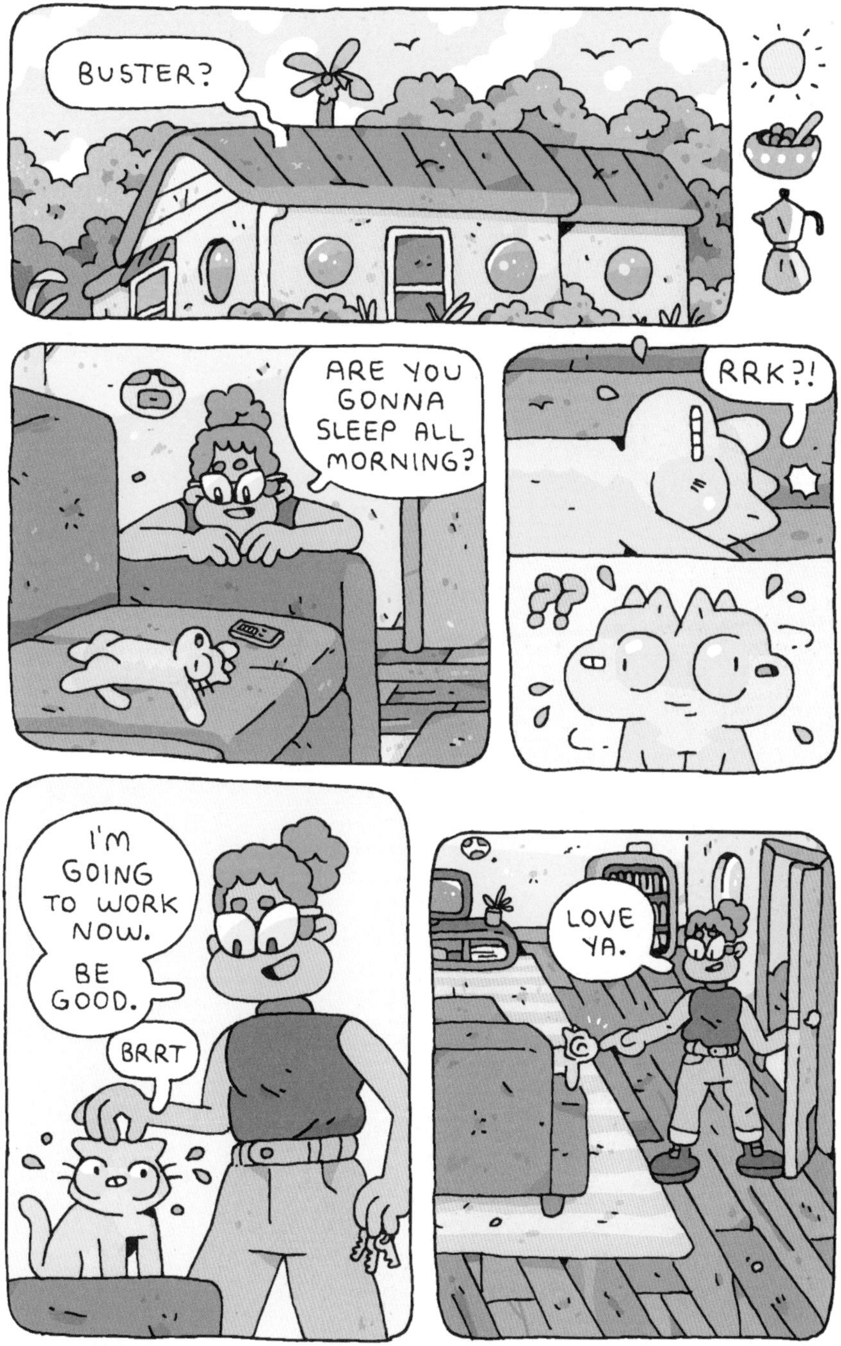
BUSTER?
ARE YOU GONNA SLEEP ALL MORNING?
RRK?!
I'M GOING TO WORK NOW.
BE GOOD.
BRRT
LOVE YA.

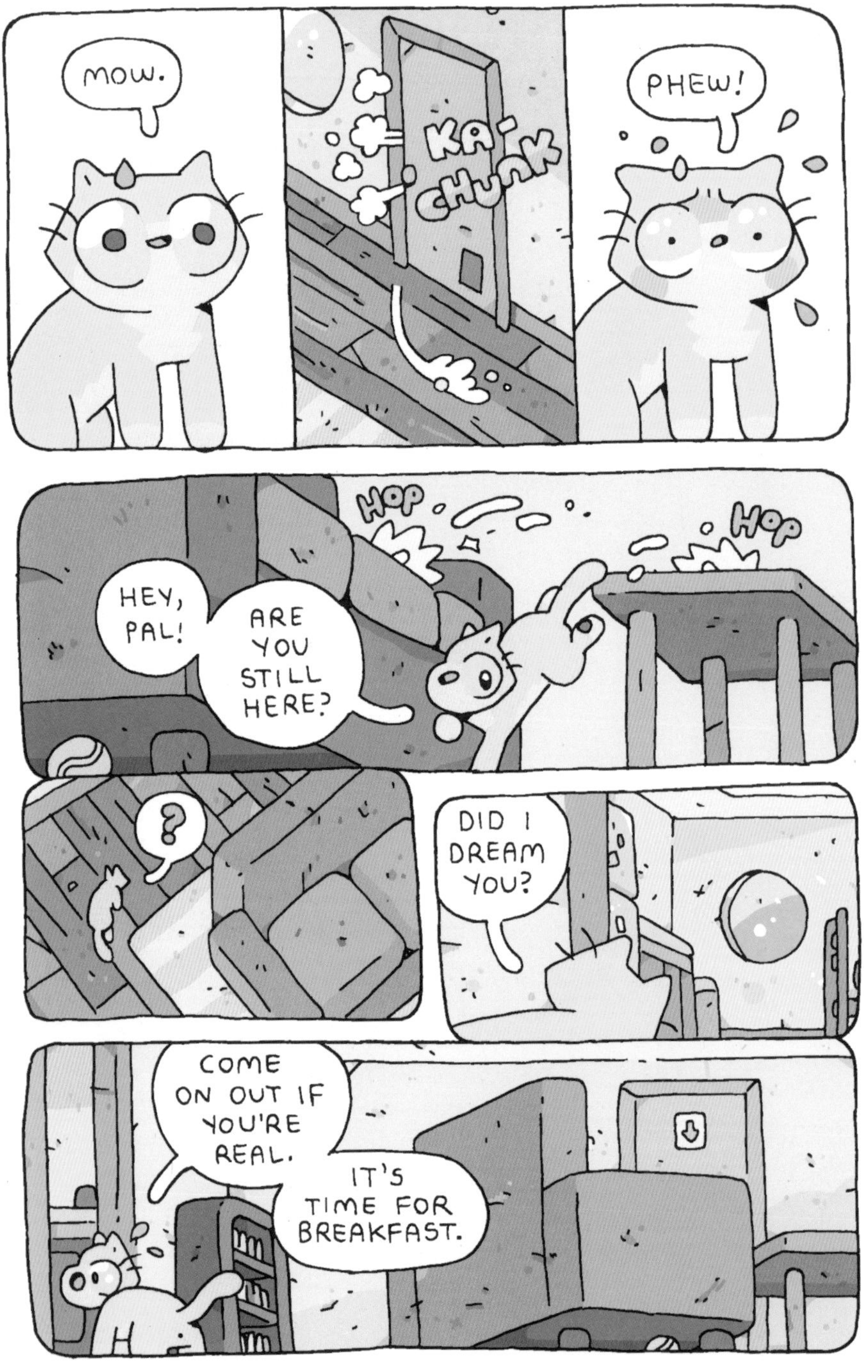
MOW.
KA-CHUNK
PHEW!
HOP
HOP
HEY, PAL!
ARE YOU STILL HERE?
?
DID I DREAM YOU?
COME ON OUT IF YOU'RE REAL.
IT'S TIME FOR BREAKFAST.

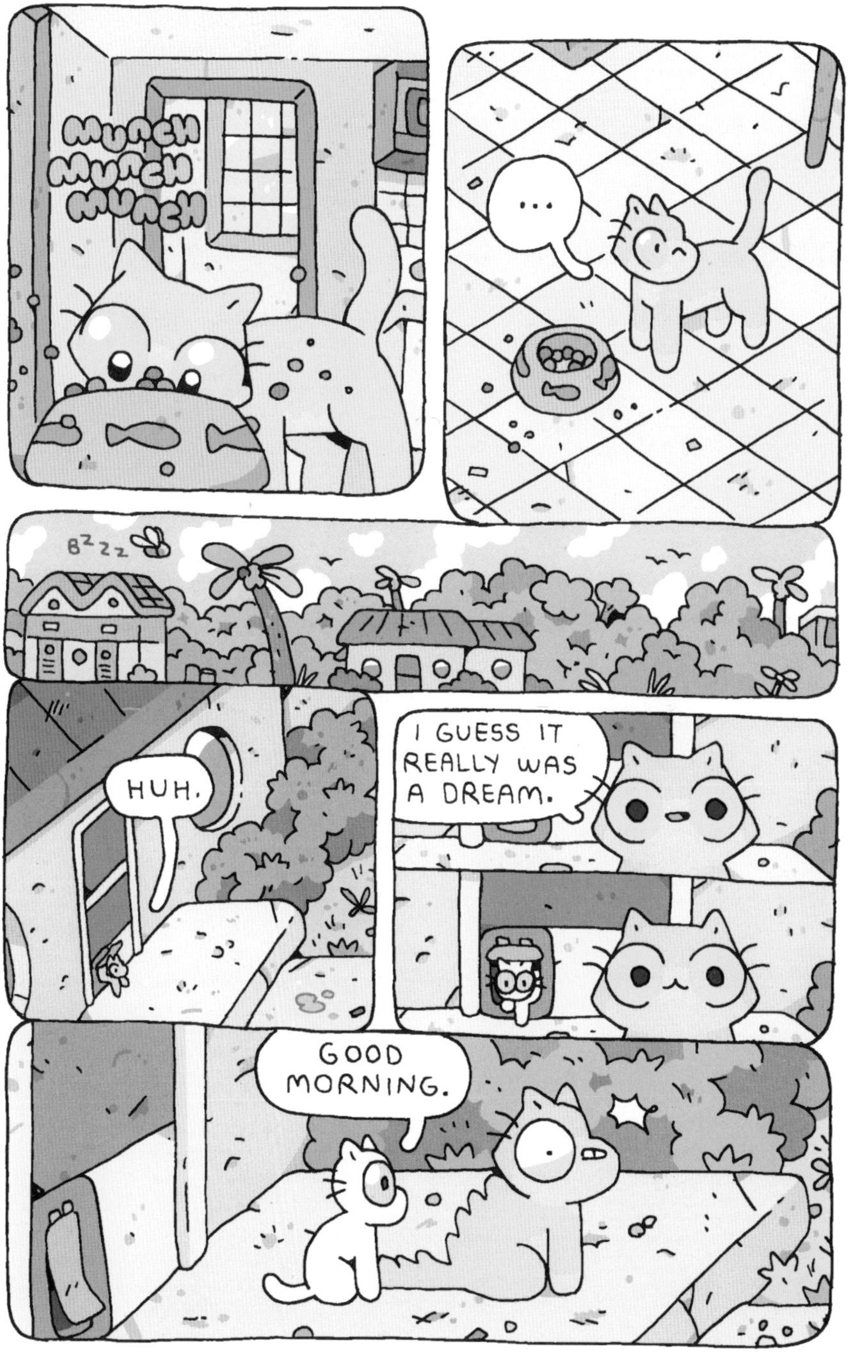
MUNCH
MUNCH
MUNCH
...
BZZZ
HUH.
I GUESS IT REALLY WAS A DREAM.
GOOD MORNING.

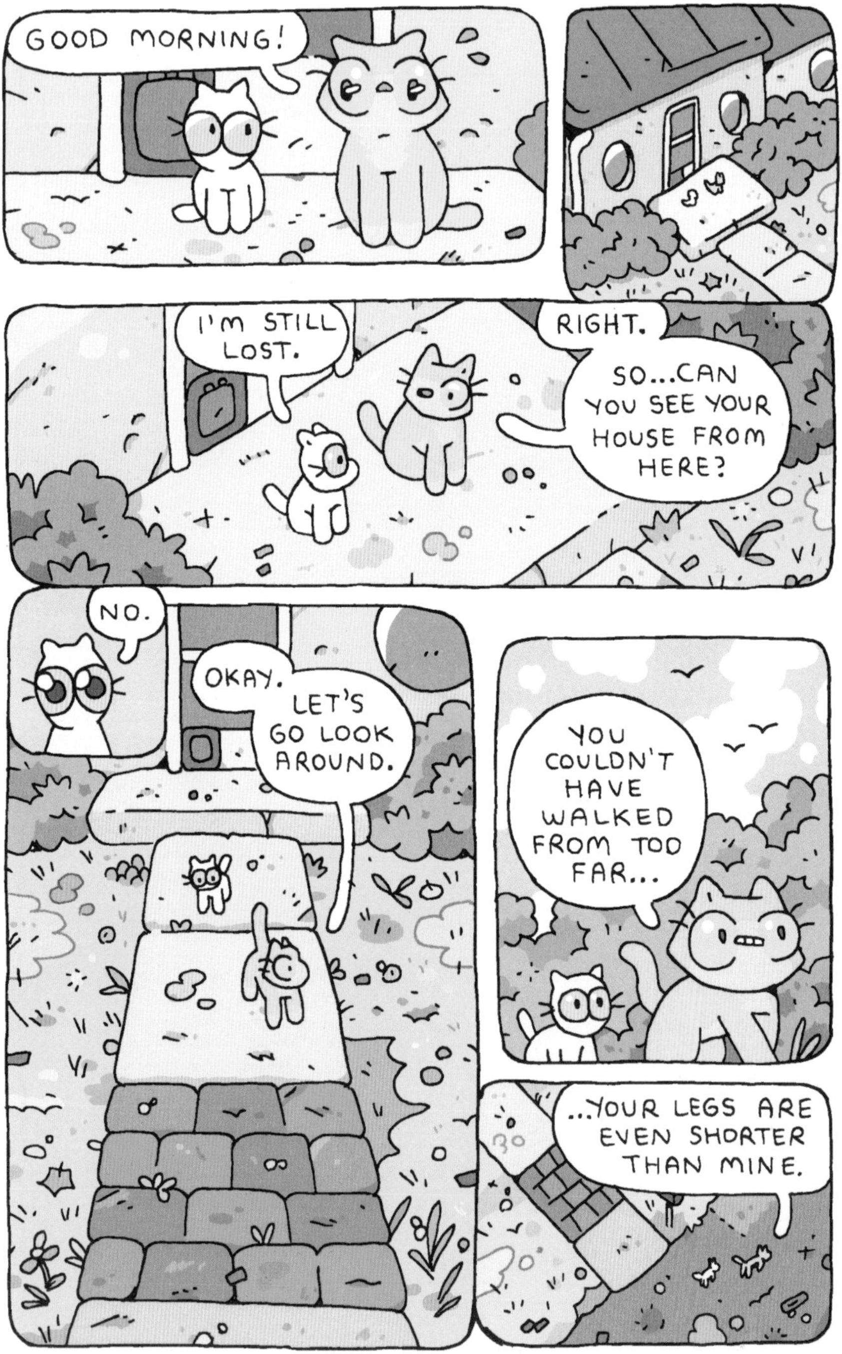
GOOD MORNING!
I'M STILL LOST.
RIGHT.
SO...CAN YOU SEE YOUR HOUSE FROM HERE?
NO.
OKAY.
LET'S GO LOOK AROUND.
YOU COULDN'T HAVE WALKED FROM TOO FAR...
...YOUR LEGS ARE EVEN SHORTER THAN MINE.

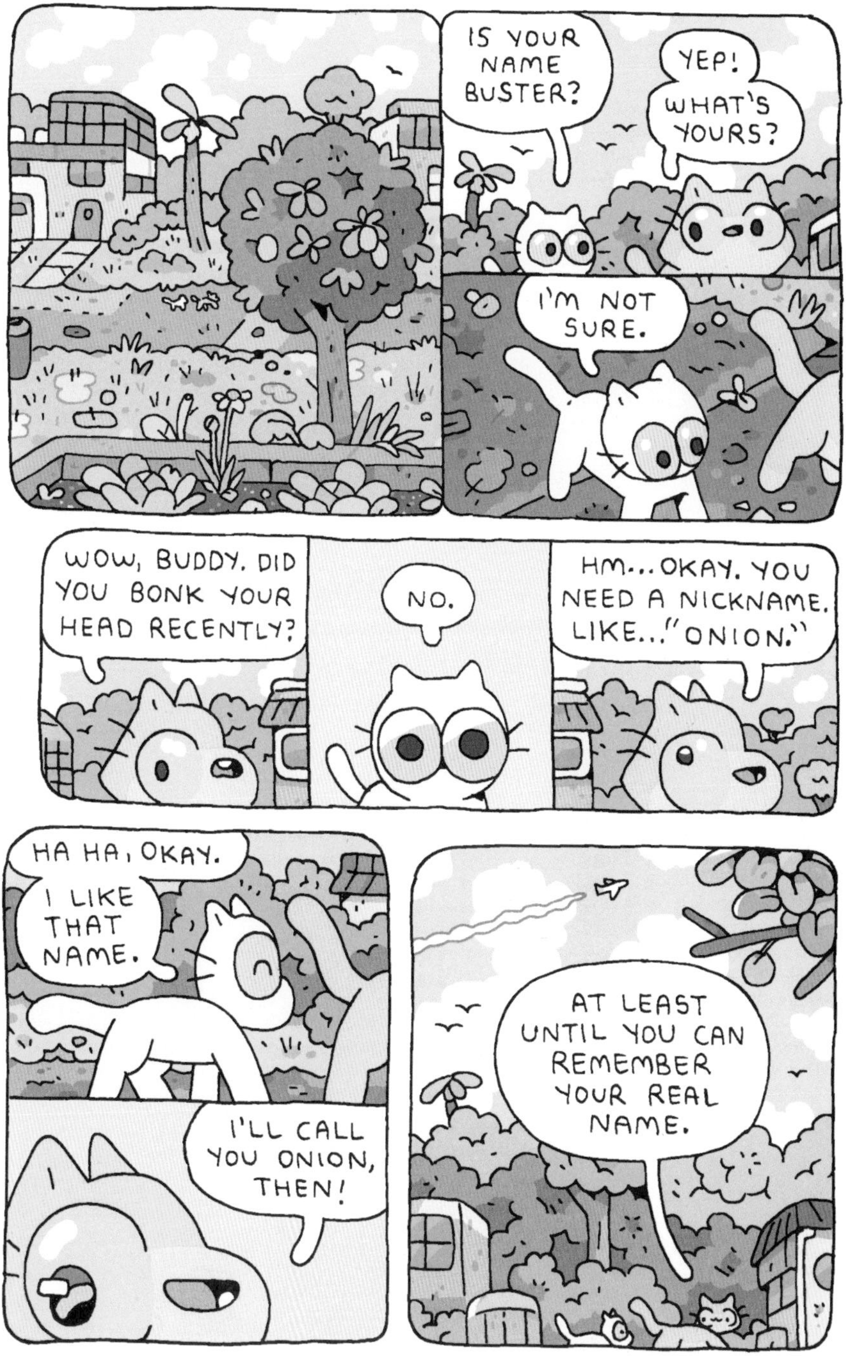
IS YOUR NAME BUSTER?
YEP!
WHAT'S YOURS?
I'M NOT SURE.
WOW, BUDDY. DID YOU BONK YOUR HEAD RECENTLY?
NO.
HM...OKAY. YOU NEED A NICKNAME. LIKE..."ONION."
HA HA, OKAY.
I LIKE THAT NAME.
I'LL CALL YOU ONION, THEN!
AT LEAST UNTIL YOU CAN REMEMBER YOUR REAL NAME.

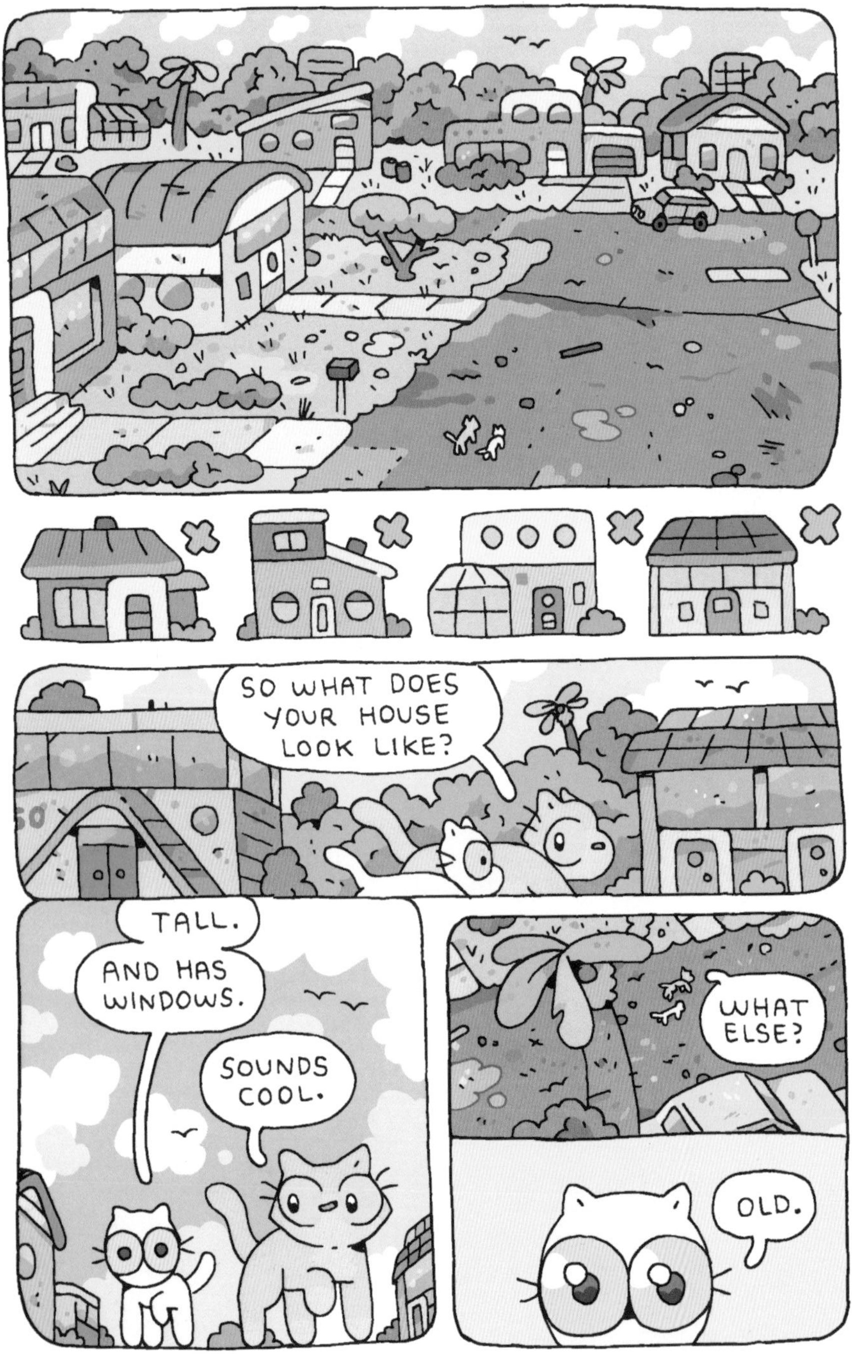
SO WHAT DOES YOUR HOUSE LOOK LIKE?
TALL.
AND HAS WINDOWS.
SOUNDS COOL.
WHAT ELSE?
OLD.

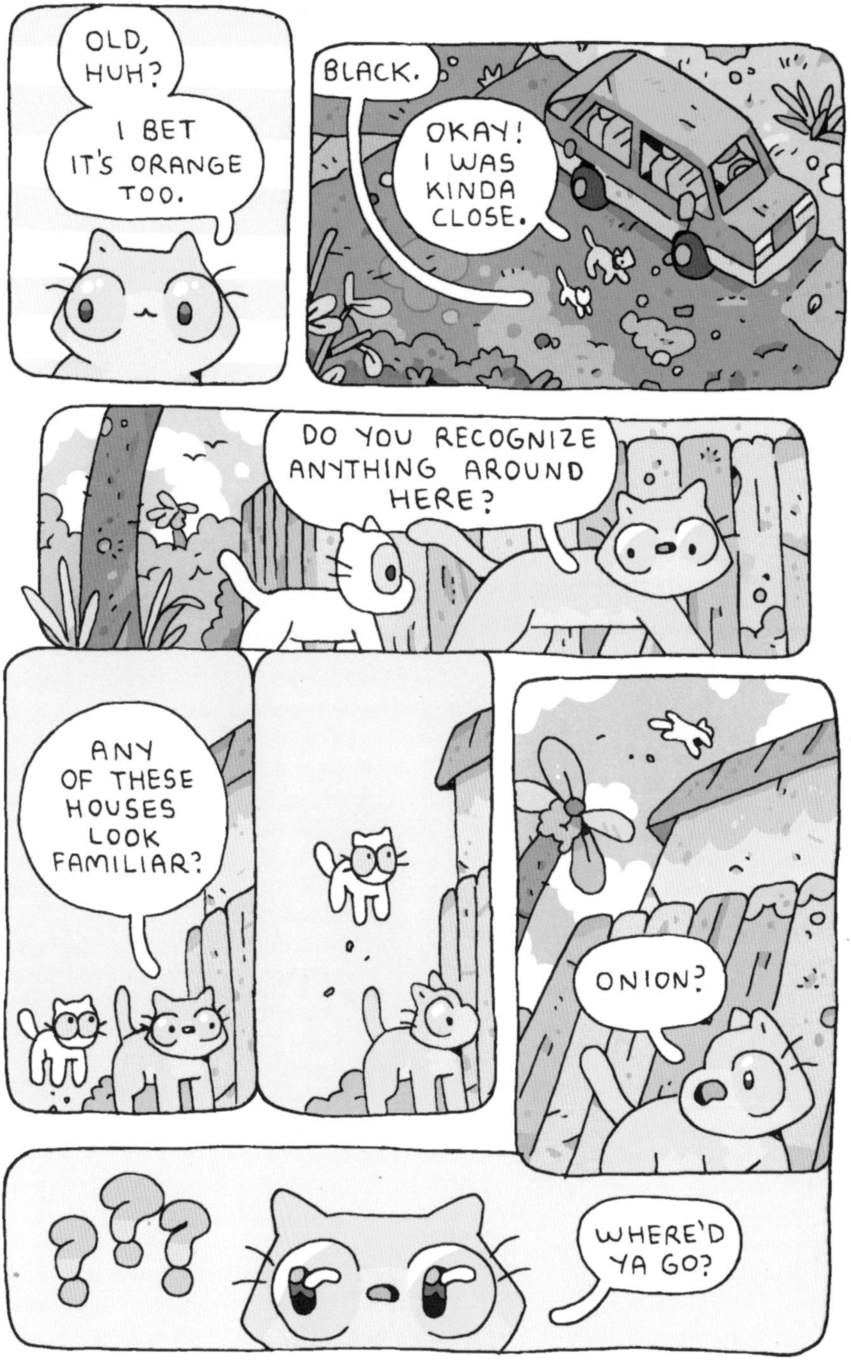
OLD, HUH?
I BET IT'S ORANGE TOO.
BLACK.
OKAY! I WAS KINDA CLOSE.
DO YOU RECOGNIZE ANYTHING AROUND HERE?
ANY OF THESE HOUSES LOOK FAMILIAR?
ONION?
WHERE'D YA GO?

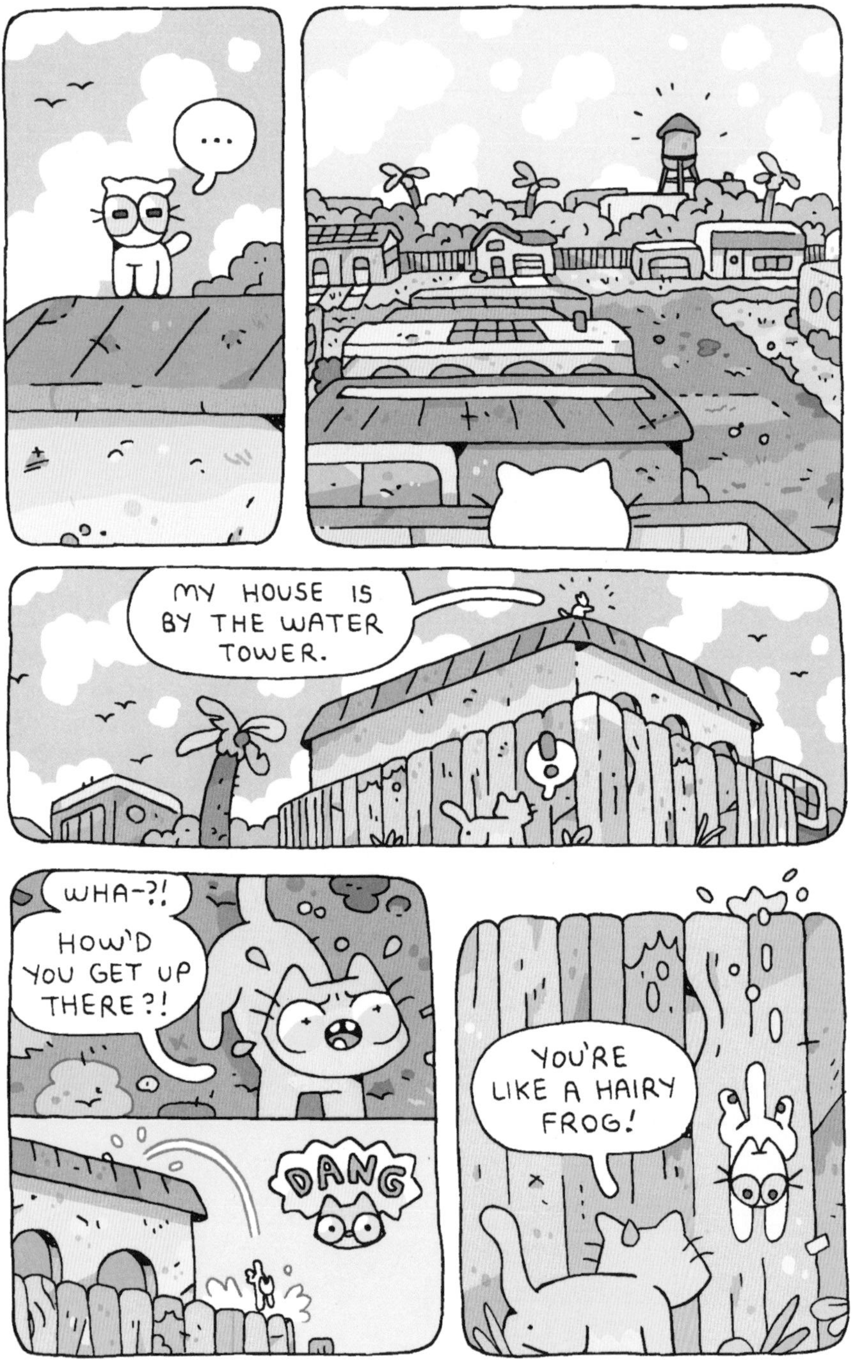
...
MY HOUSE IS BY THE WATER TOWER.
WHA-?!
HOW'D YOU GET UP THERE?!
DANG
YOU'RE LIKE A HAIRY FROG!

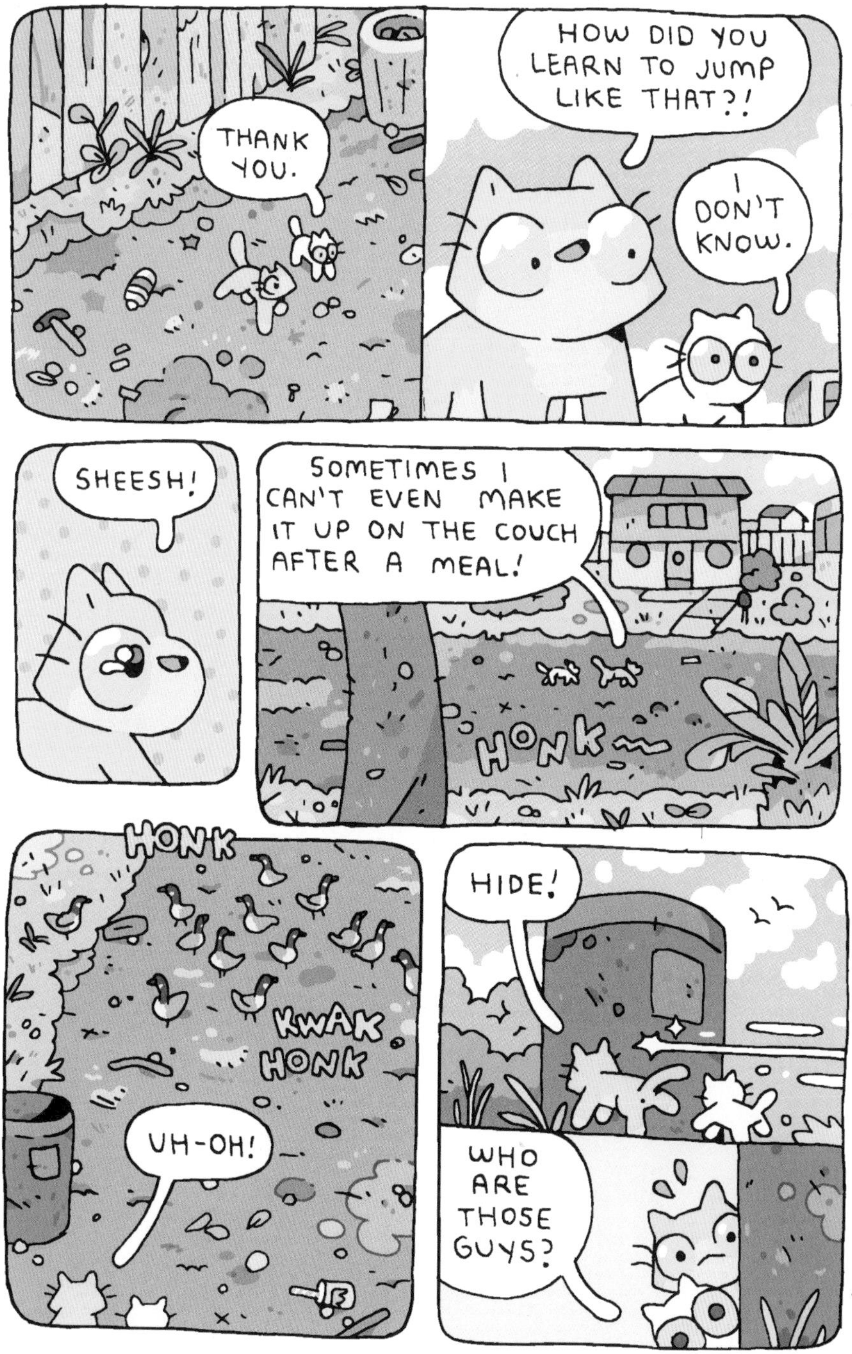
THANK YOU.
HOW DID YOU LEARN TO JUMP LIKE THAT?!
I DON'T KNOW.
SHEESH!
SOMETIMES I CAN'T EVEN MAKE IT UP ON THE COUCH AFTER A MEAL!
HONK
HONK
KWAK
HONK
UH-OH!
HIDE!
WHO ARE THOSE GUYS?

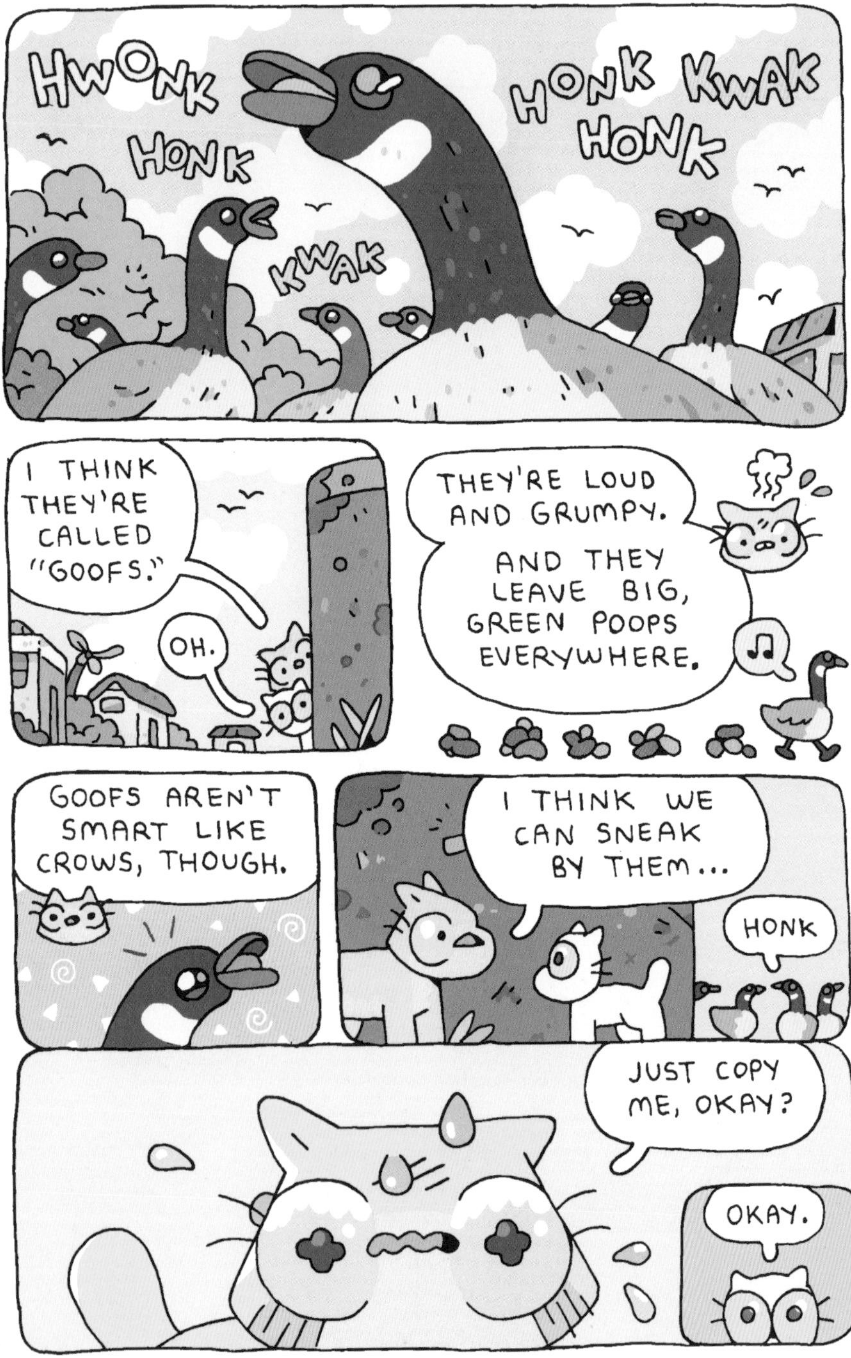
HWONK
HONK
KWAK
HONK KWAK
HONK
I THINK THEY'RE CALLED "GOOFS."
OH.
THEY'RE LOUD AND GRUMPY.
AND THEY LEAVE BIG, GREEN POOPS EVERYWHERE.
GOOFS AREN'T SMART LIKE CROWS, THOUGH.
I THINK WE CAN SNEAK BY THEM...
HONK
JUST COPY ME, OKAY?
OKAY.

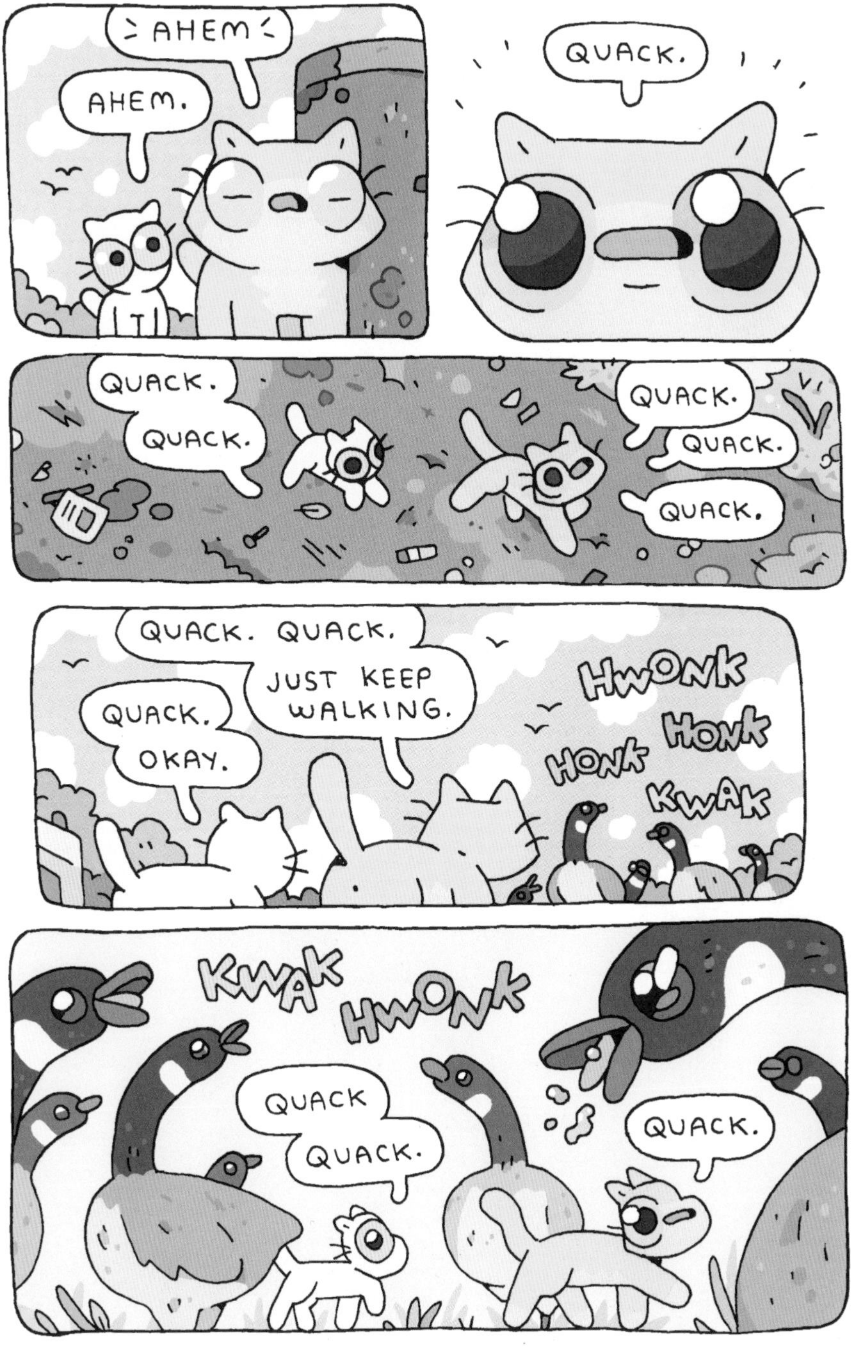
AHEM.
AHEM
QUACK.
QUACK.
QUACK.
QUACK.
QUACK.
QUACK.
QUACK. QUACK.
JUST KEEP WALKING.
QUACK.
OKAY.
HWONK
HONK
HONK
KWAK
KWAK
HWONK
QUACK
QUACK.
QUACK.

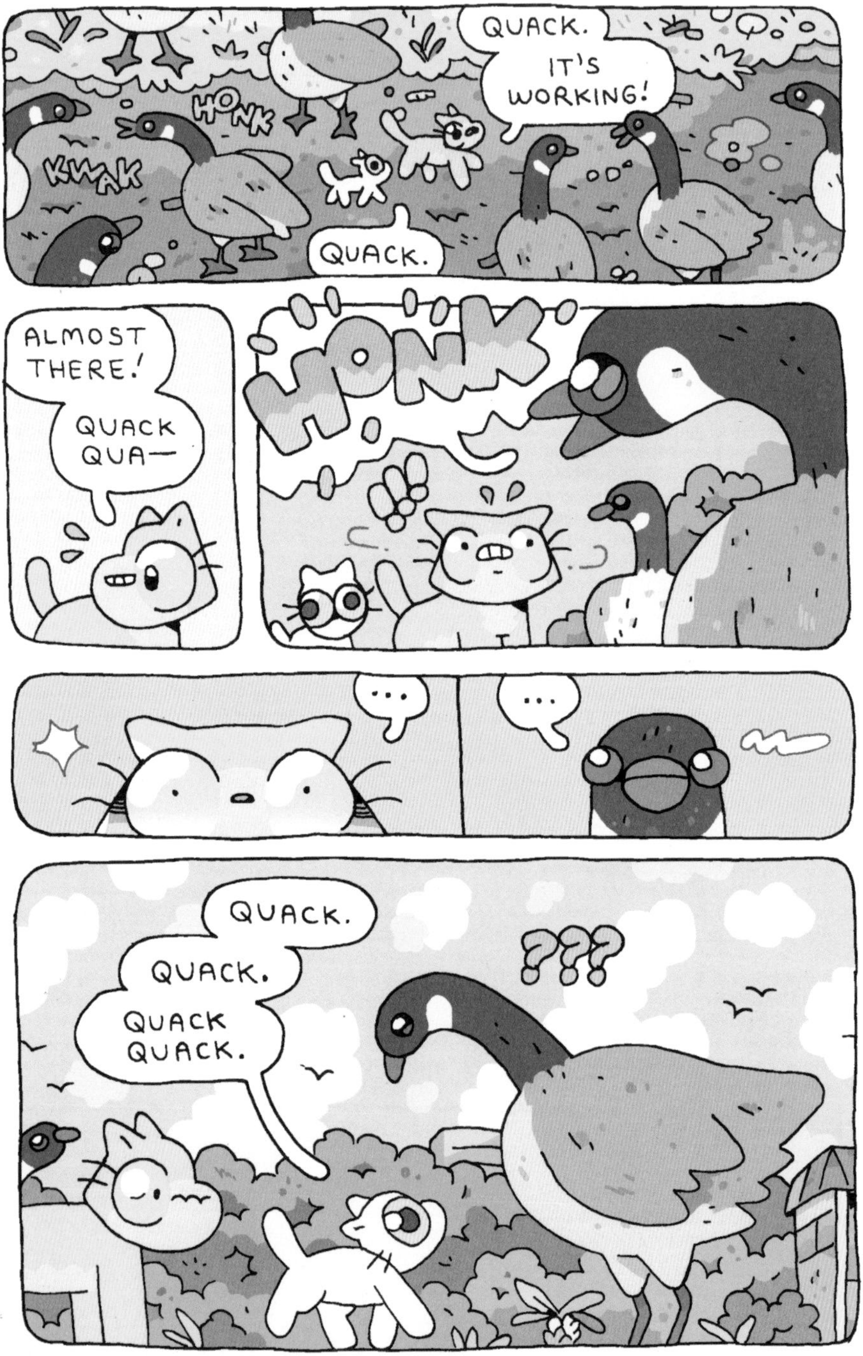
HONK
KWAK
QUACK.
IT'S WORKING!
QUACK.
ALMOST THERE!
QUACK QUA—
HONK
...
...
QUACK.
QUACK.
QUACK QUACK.
???

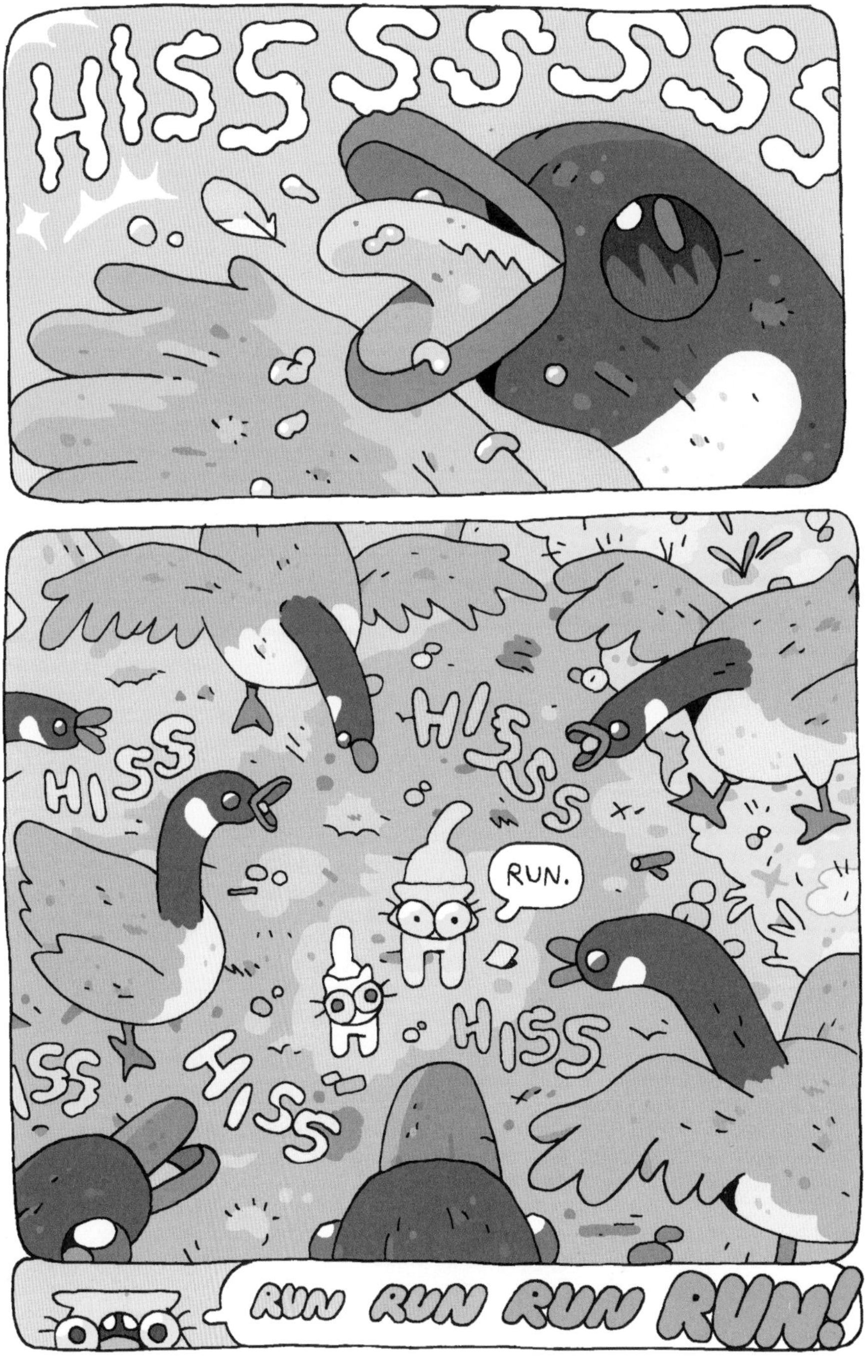

HISSSSSSS
HISS
HISS
HISS
RUN.
HISS
ISS
HISS
RUN RUN RUN RUN!

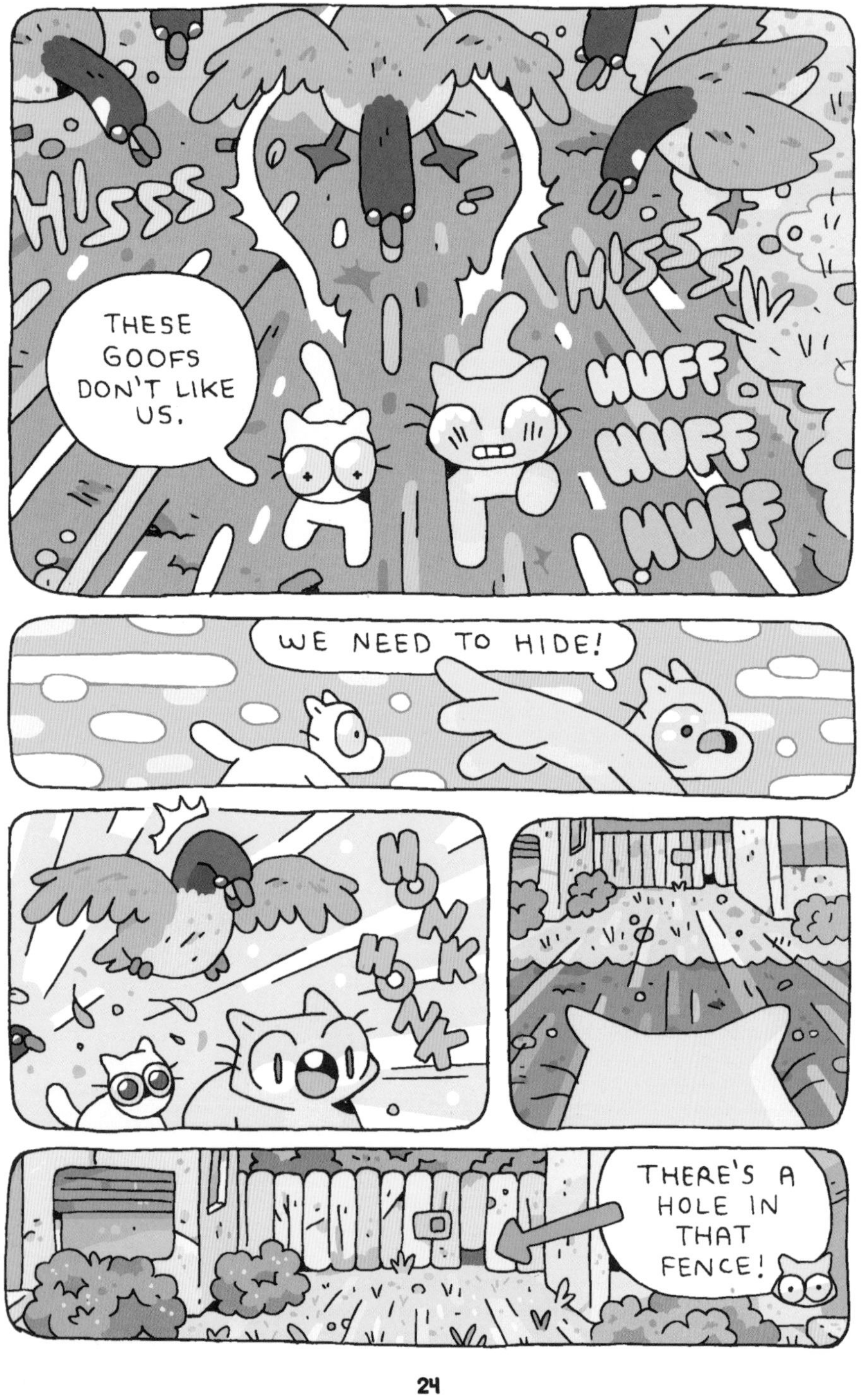
HISSS
THESE GOOFS DON'T LIKE US.
HISSS
HUFF HUFF HUFF
WE NEED TO HIDE!
HONK HONK
THERE'S A HOLE IN THAT FENCE!

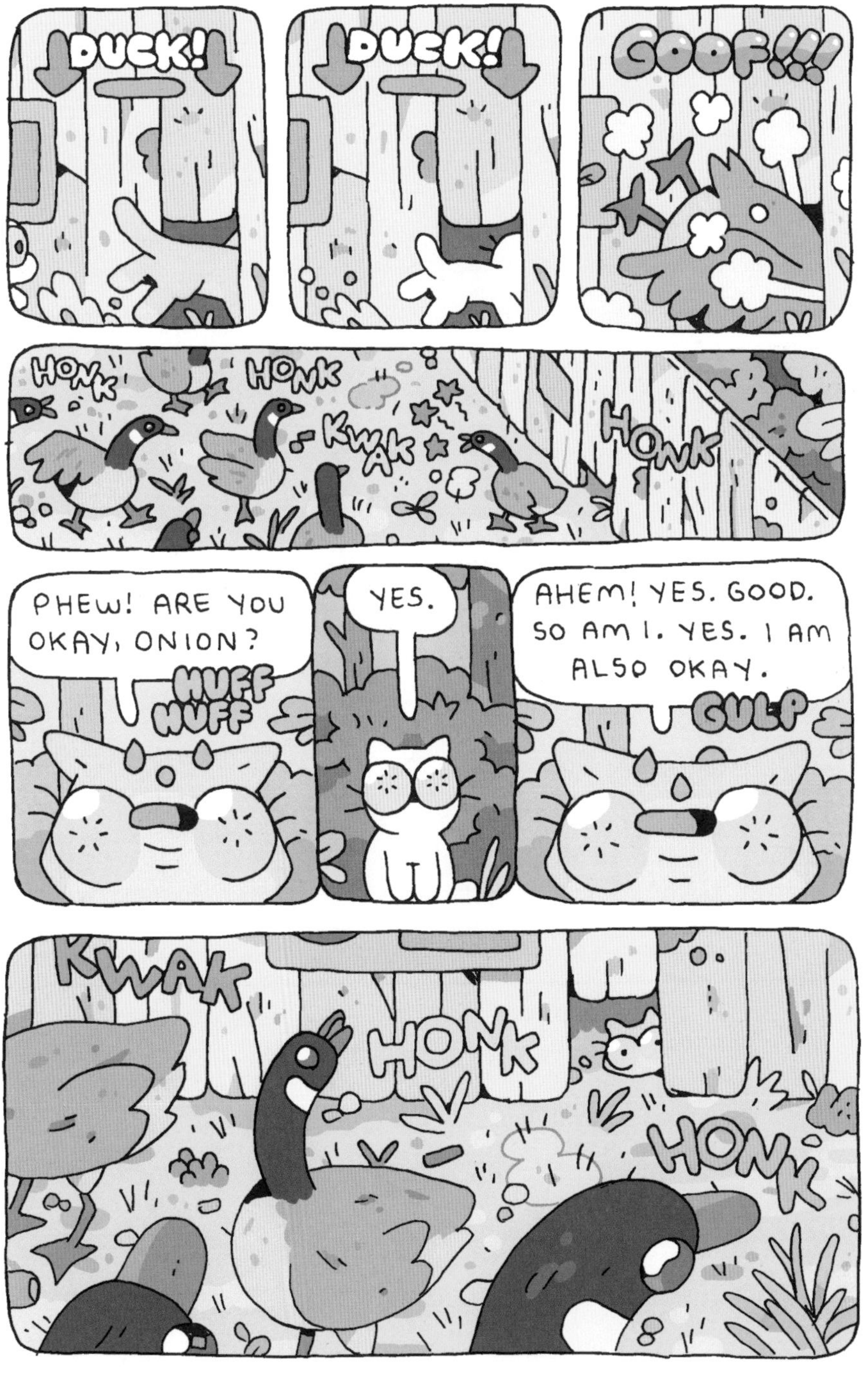
DUCK!
DUCK!
GOOF!!!
HONK
HONK
KWAK
HONK
PHEW! ARE YOU OKAY, ONION?
HUFF HUFF
YES.
AHEM! YES. GOOD. SO AM I. YES. I AM ALSO OKAY.
GULP
KWAK
HONK
HONK

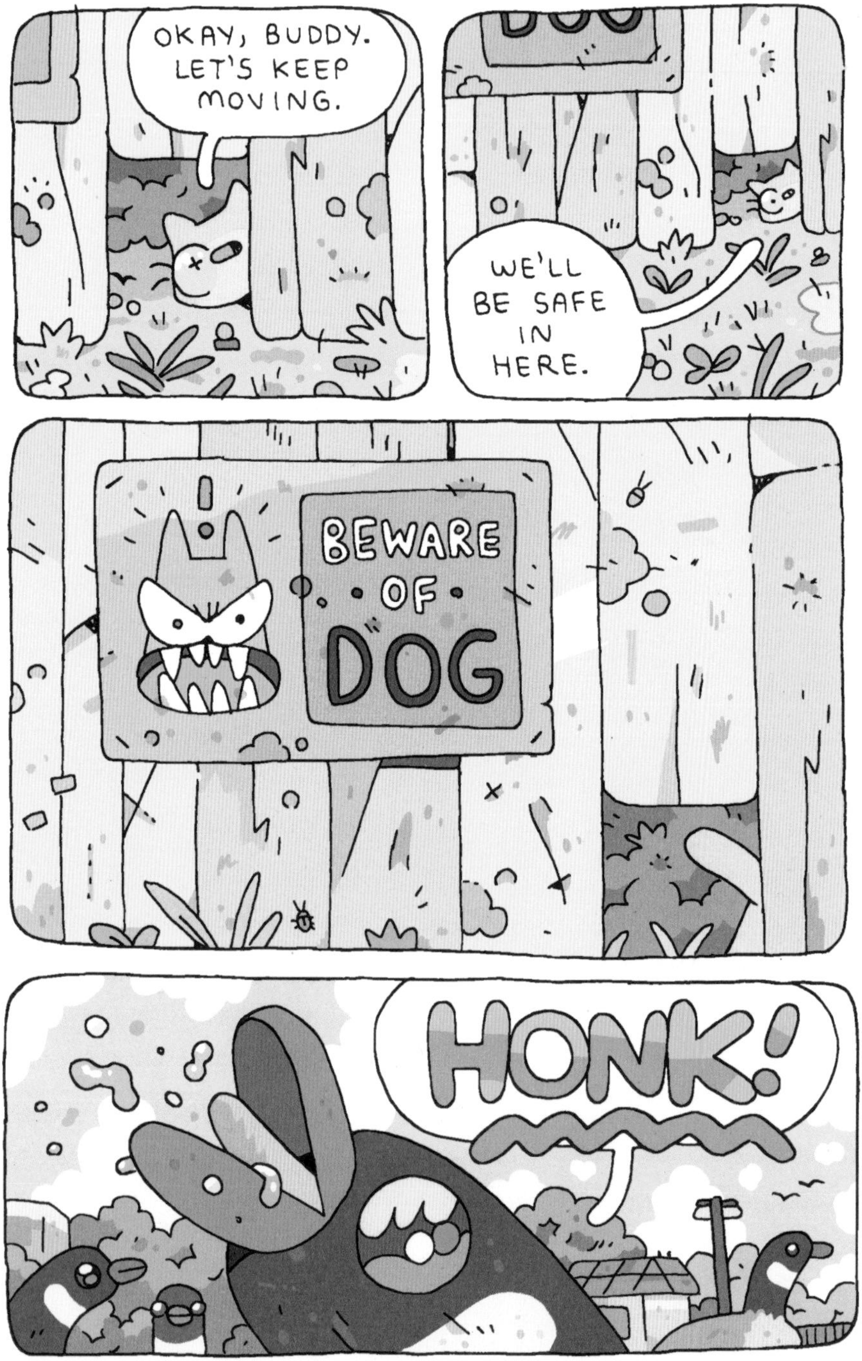
OKAY, BUDDY. LET'S KEEP MOVING.
WE'LL BE SAFE IN HERE.
BEWARE OF DOG
HONK!

CHAPTER 2

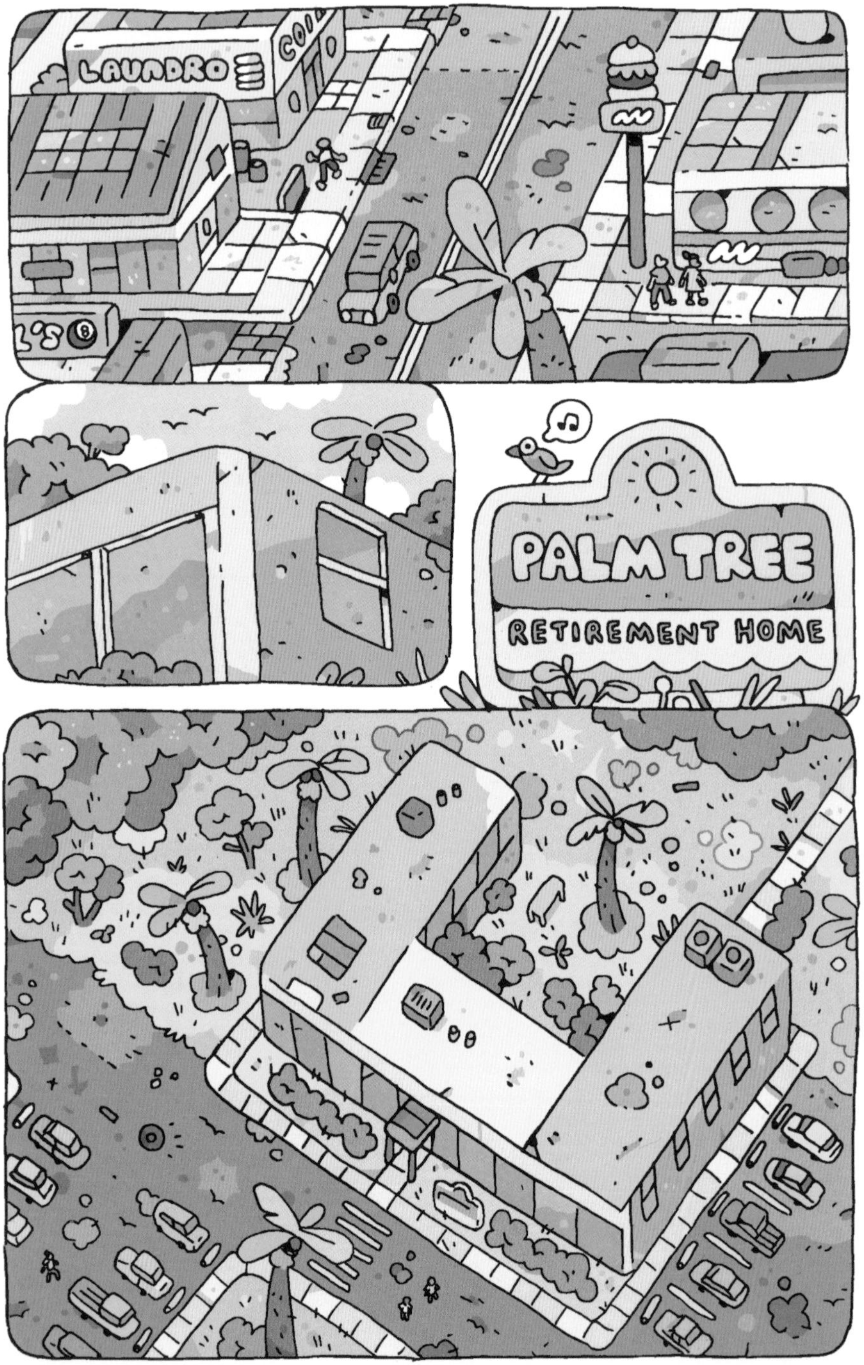
LAUNDRO
PALM TREE
RETIREMENT HOME

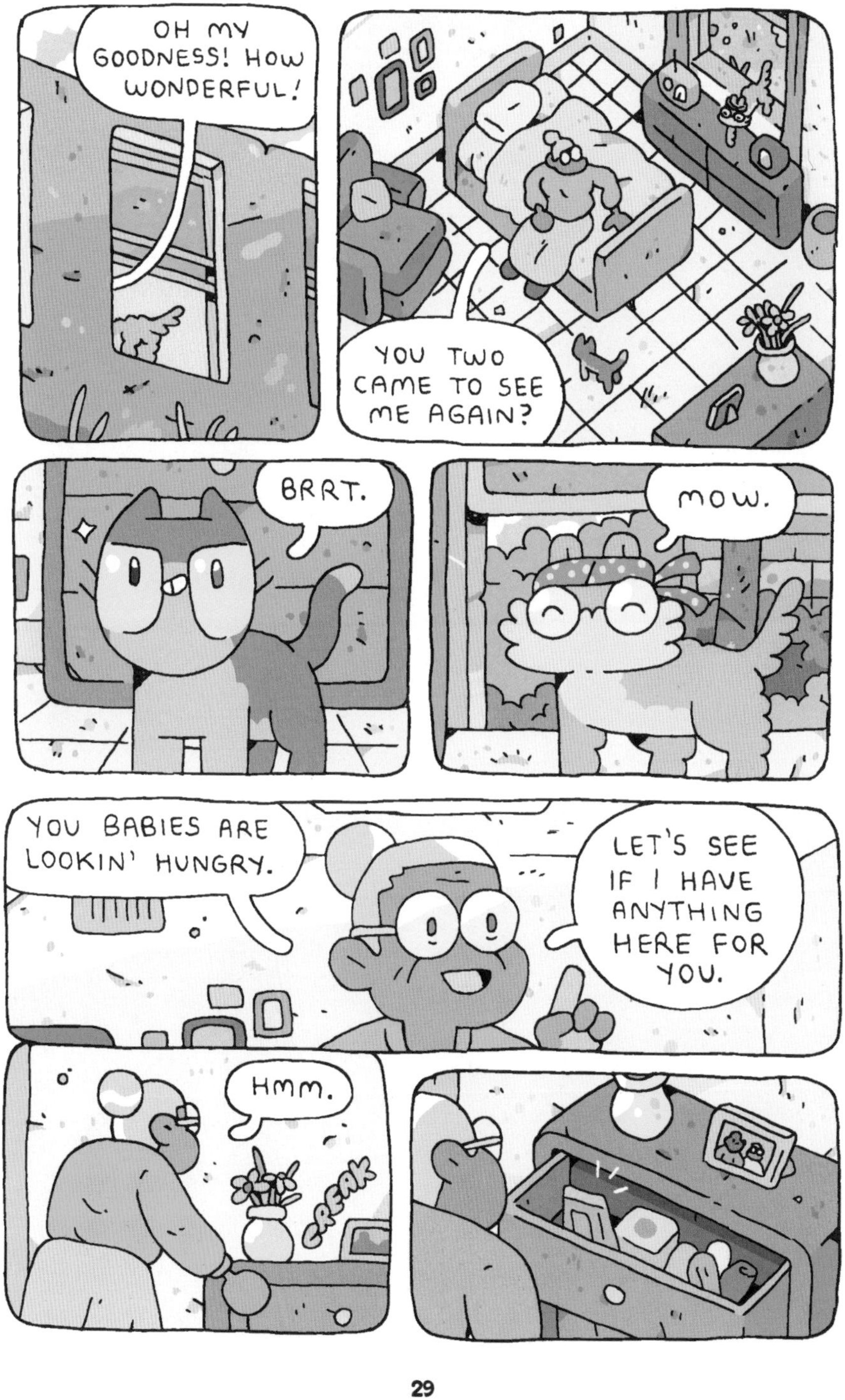
OH MY GOODNESS! HOW WONDERFUL!
YOU TWO CAME TO SEE ME AGAIN?
BRRT.
MOW.
YOU BABIES ARE LOOKIN' HUNGRY.
LET'S SEE IF I HAVE ANYTHING HERE FOR YOU.
HMM.
CREAK

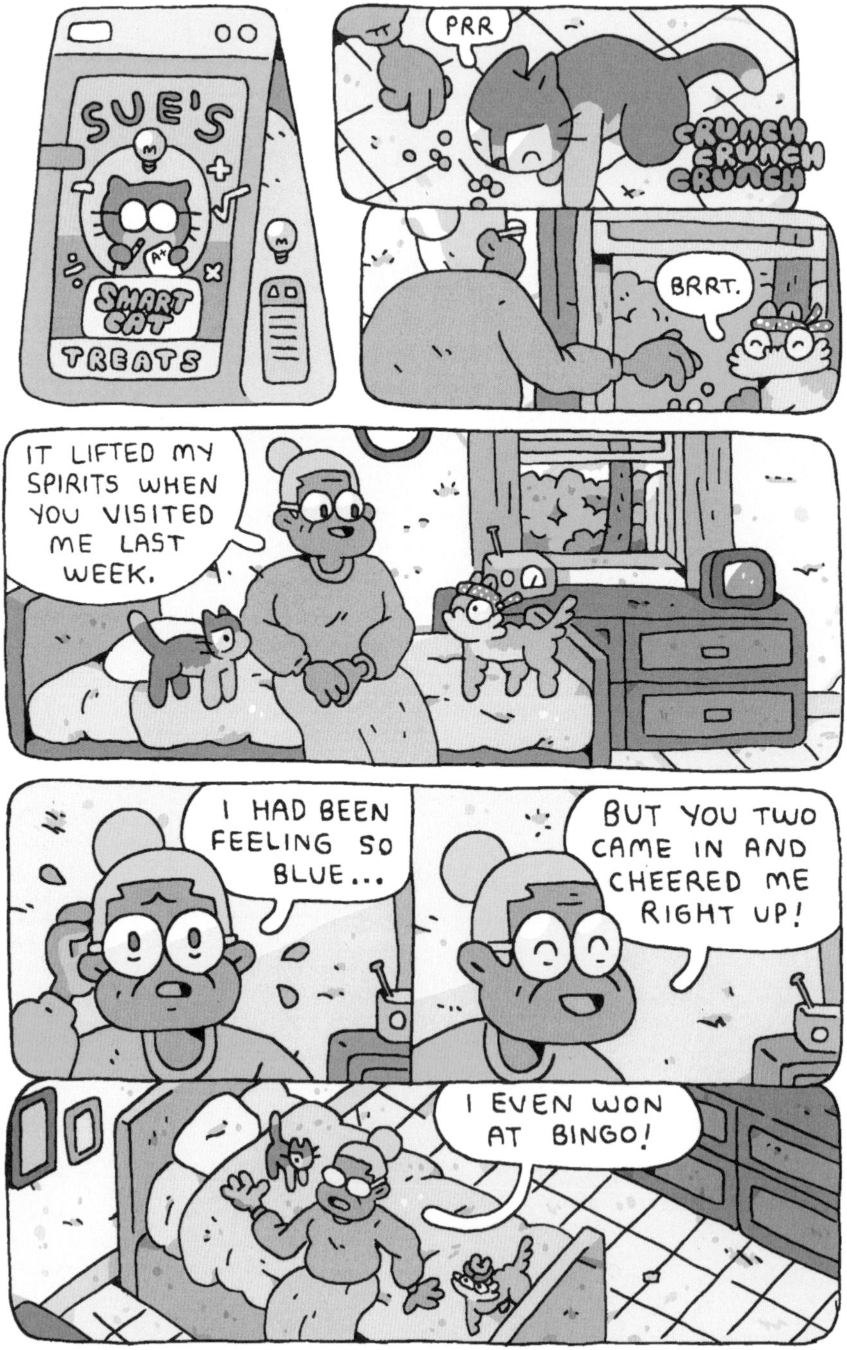
SUE'S
SMART CAT
TREATS
PRR
CRUNCH
CRUNCH
CRUNCH
BRRT.
IT LIFTED MY SPIRITS WHEN YOU VISITED ME LAST WEEK.
I HAD BEEN FEELING SO BLUE...
BUT YOU TWO CAME IN AND CHEERED ME RIGHT UP!
I EVEN WON AT BINGO!

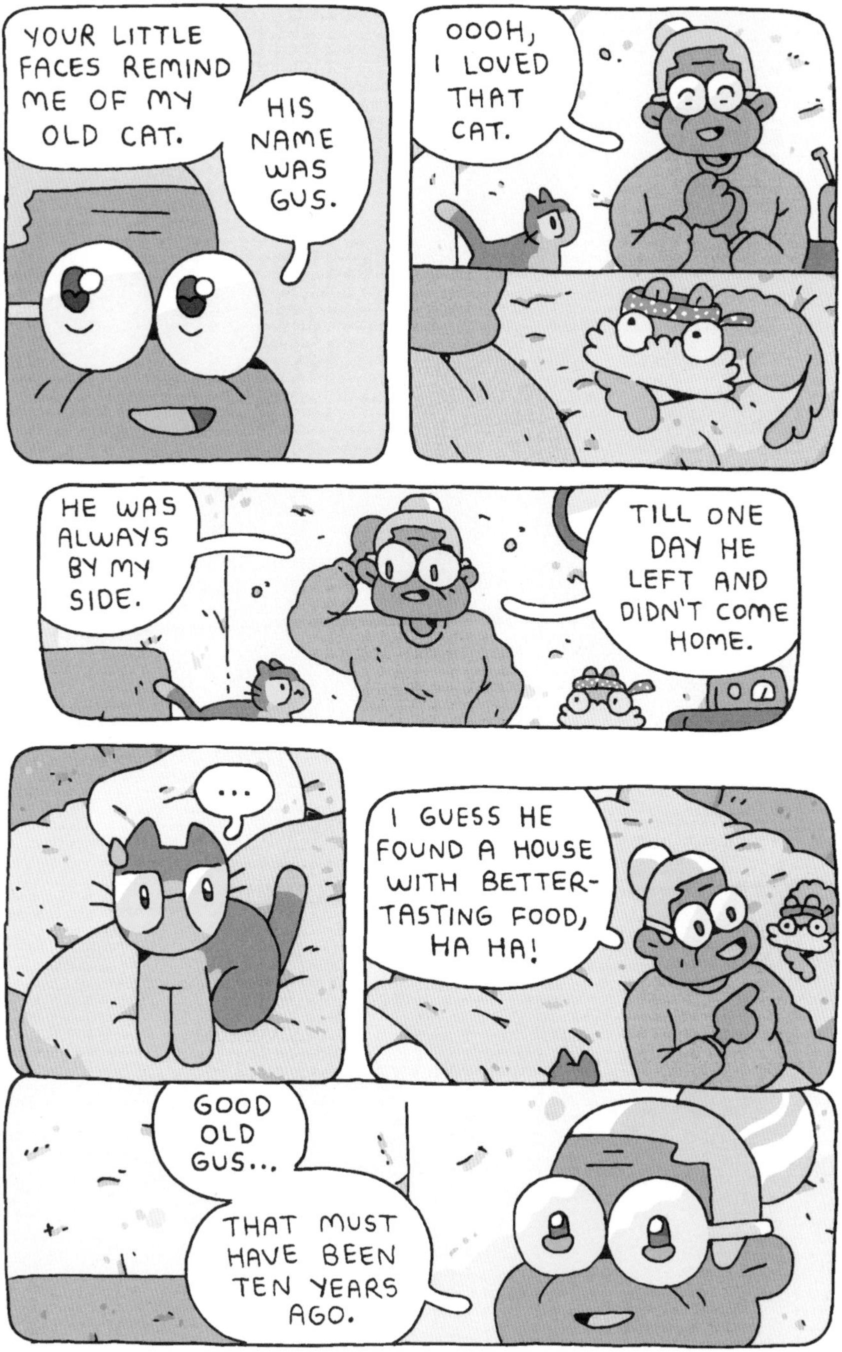
YOUR LITTLE FACES REMIND ME OF MY OLD CAT.
HIS NAME WAS GUS.
OOOH, I LOVED THAT CAT.
HE WAS ALWAYS BY MY SIDE.
TILL ONE DAY HE LEFT AND DIDN'T COME HOME.
...
I GUESS HE FOUND A HOUSE WITH BETTER-TASTING FOOD, HA HA!
GOOD OLD GUS...
THAT MUST HAVE BEEN TEN YEARS AGO.

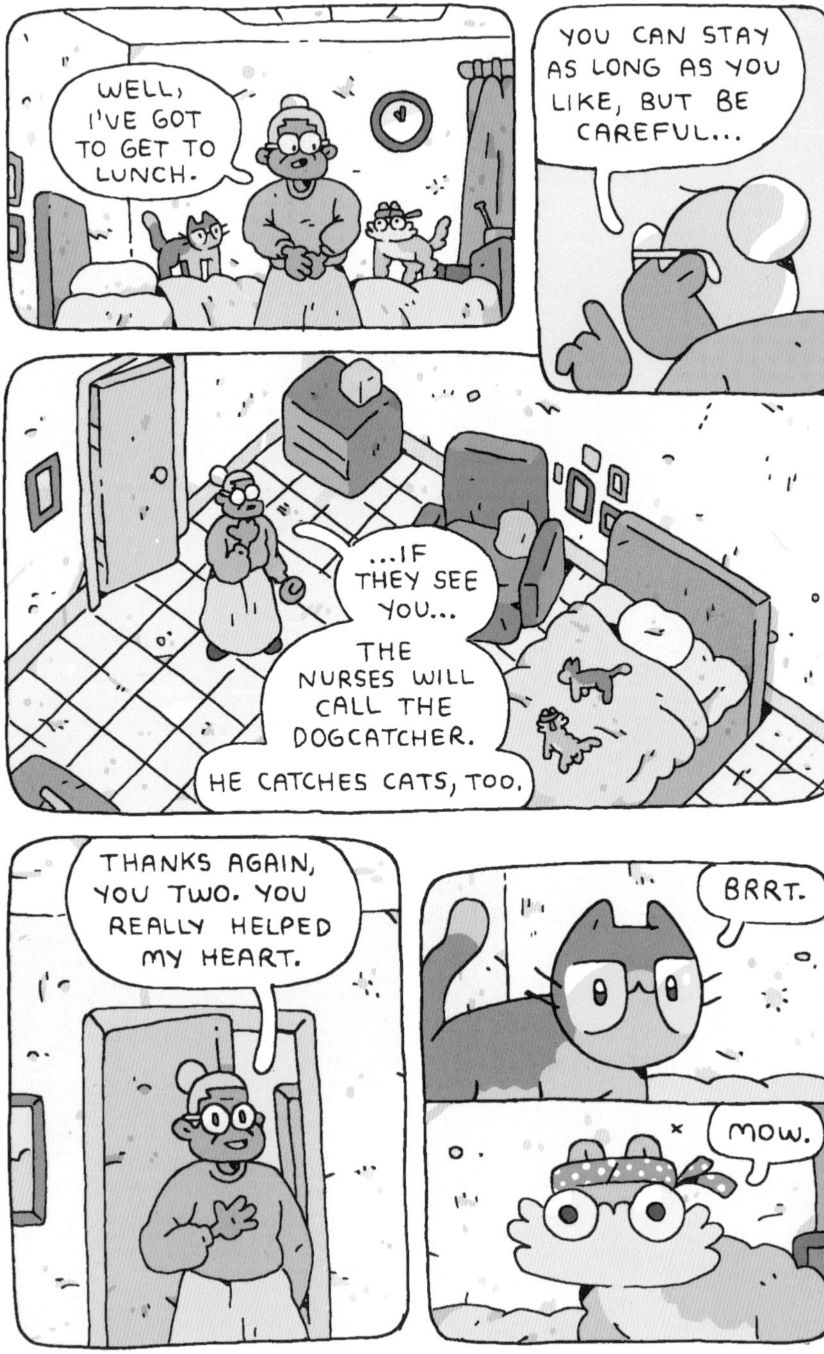
WELL, I'VE GOT TO GET TO LUNCH.
YOU CAN STAY AS LONG AS YOU LIKE, BUT BE CAREFUL...
...IF THEY SEE YOU...
THE NURSES WILL CALL THE DOGCATCHER.
HE CATCHES CATS, TOO.
THANKS AGAIN, YOU TWO. YOU REALLY HELPED MY HEART.
BRRT.
MOW.

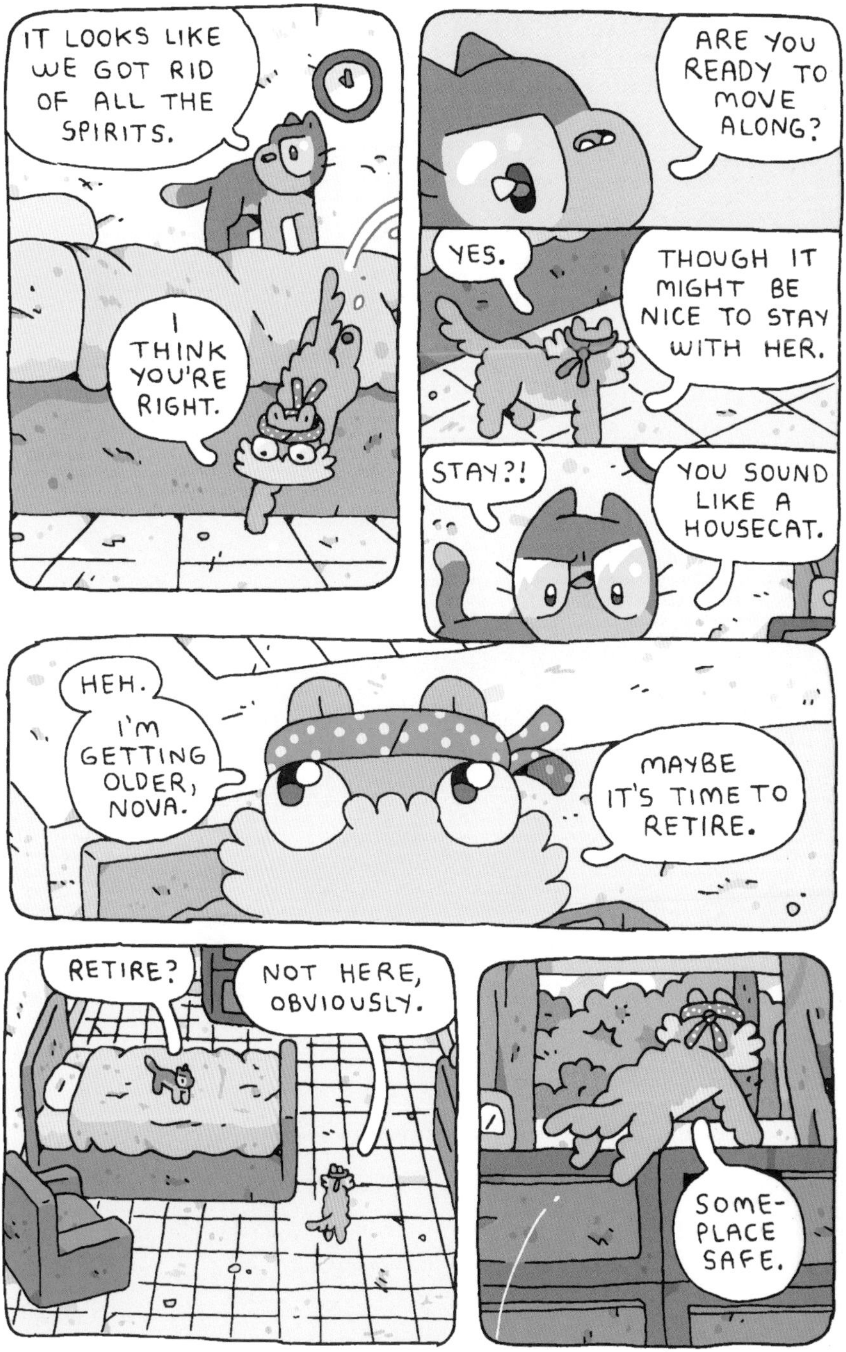
IT LOOKS LIKE WE GOT RID OF ALL THE SPIRITS.
I THINK YOU'RE RIGHT.
ARE YOU READY TO MOVE ALONG?
YES.
THOUGH IT MIGHT BE NICE TO STAY WITH HER.
STAY?!
YOU SOUND LIKE A HOUSECAT.
HEH.
I'M GETTING OLDER, NOVA.
MAYBE IT'S TIME TO RETIRE.
RETIRE?
NOT HERE, OBVIOUSLY.
SOME-PLACE SAFE.

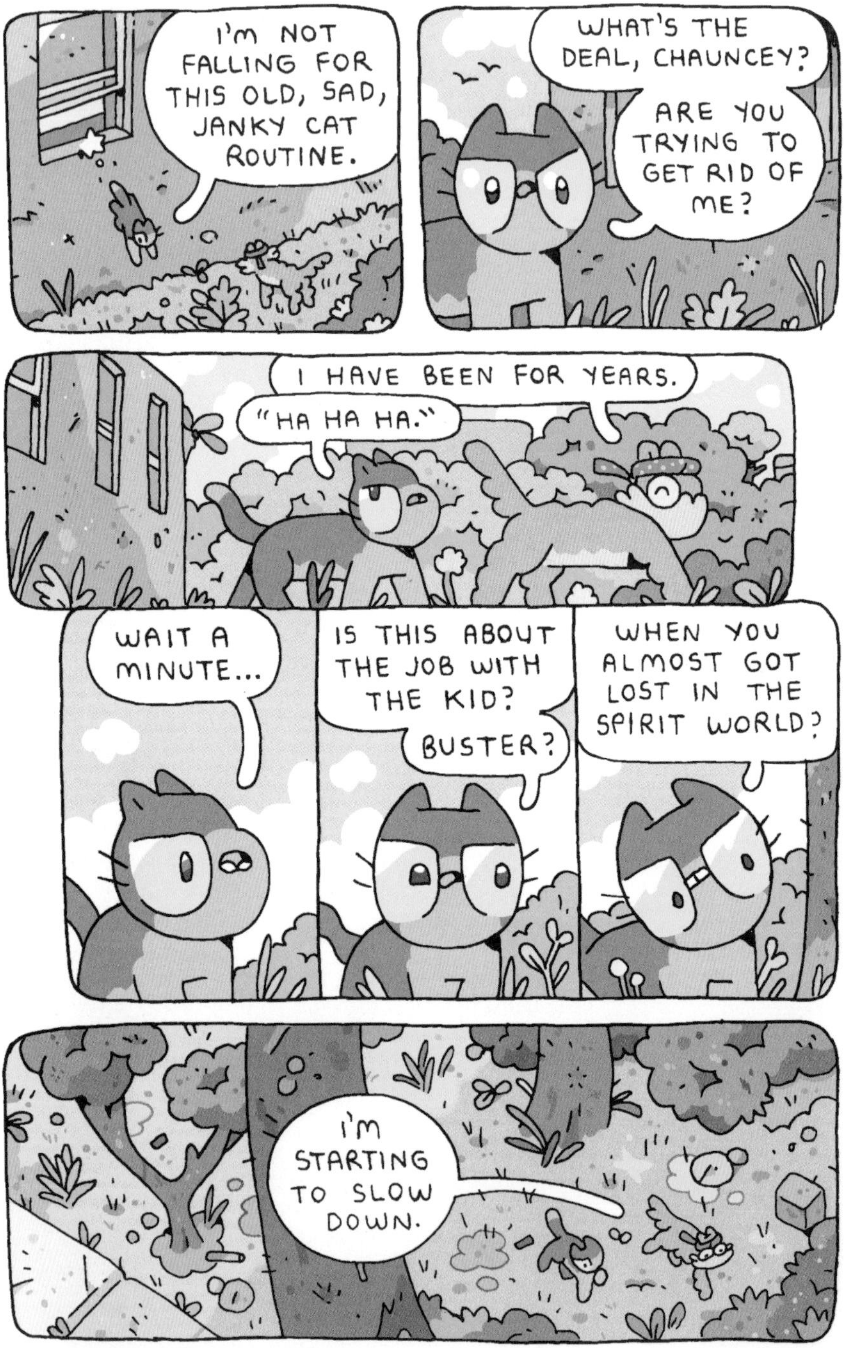
I'M NOT FALLING FOR THIS OLD, SAD, JANKY CAT ROUTINE.
WHAT'S THE DEAL, CHAUNCEY?
ARE YOU TRYING TO GET RID OF ME?
I HAVE BEEN FOR YEARS.
"HA HA HA."
WAIT A MINUTE...
IS THIS ABOUT THE JOB WITH THE KID?
BUSTER?
WHEN YOU ALMOST GOT LOST IN THE SPIRIT WORLD?
I'M STARTING TO SLOW DOWN.

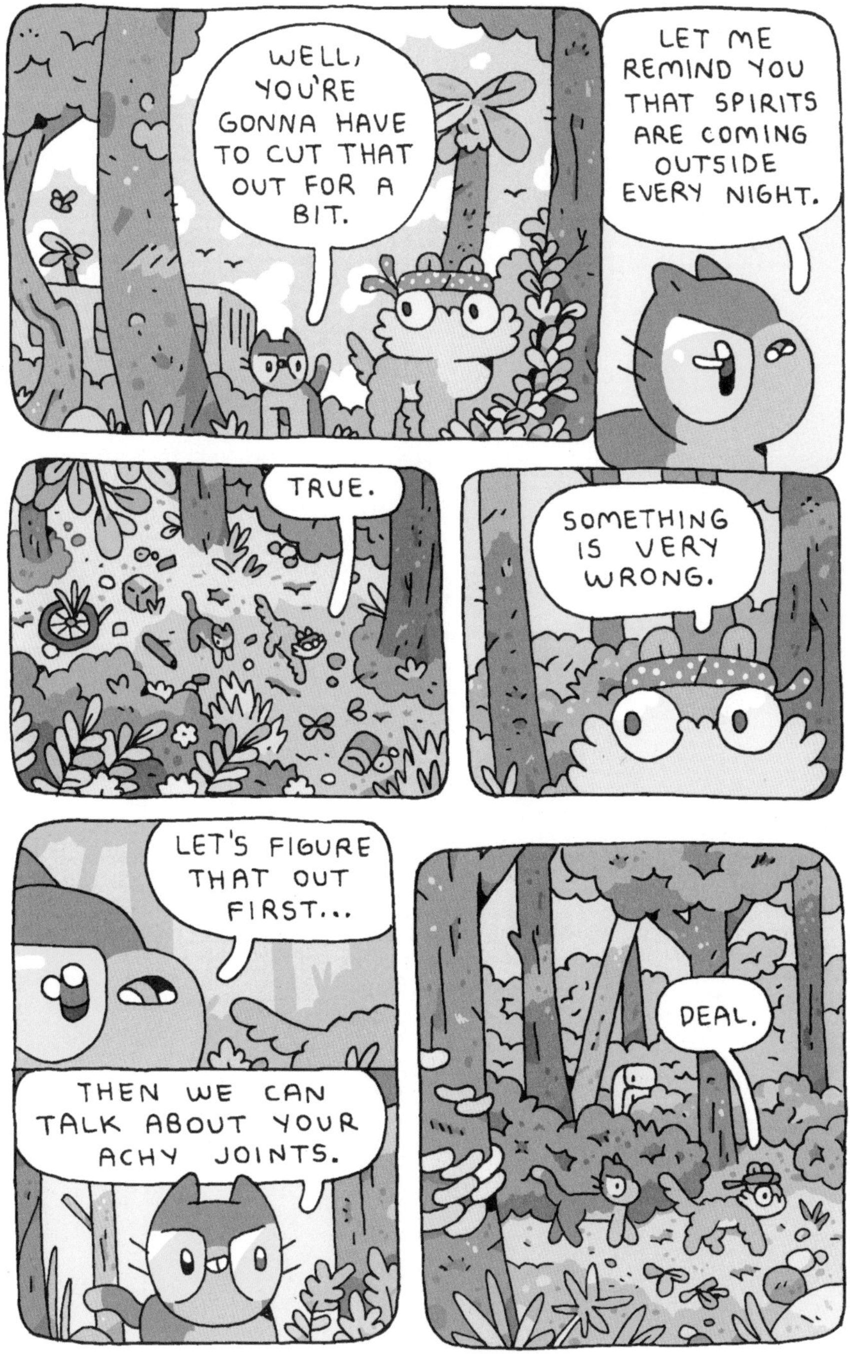
WELL, YOU'RE GONNA HAVE TO CUT THAT OUT FOR A BIT.
LET ME REMIND YOU THAT SPIRITS ARE COMING OUTSIDE EVERY NIGHT.
TRUE.
SOMETHING IS VERY WRONG.
LET'S FIGURE THAT OUT FIRST...
THEN WE CAN TALK ABOUT YOUR ACHY JOINTS.
DEAL.

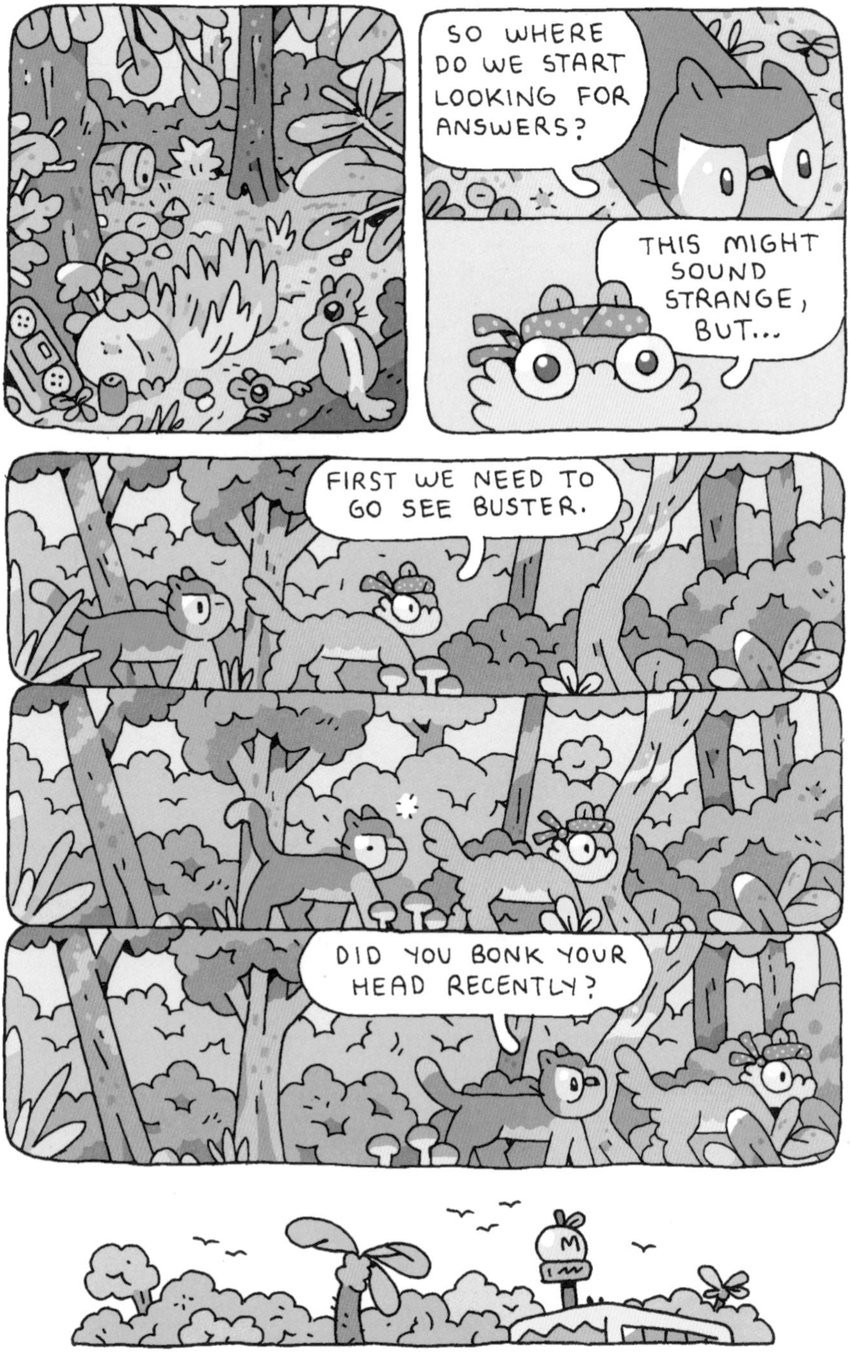
SO WHERE DO WE START LOOKING FOR ANSWERS?
THIS MIGHT SOUND STRANGE, BUT...
FIRST WE NEED TO GO SEE BUSTER.
DID YOU BONK YOUR HEAD RECENTLY?

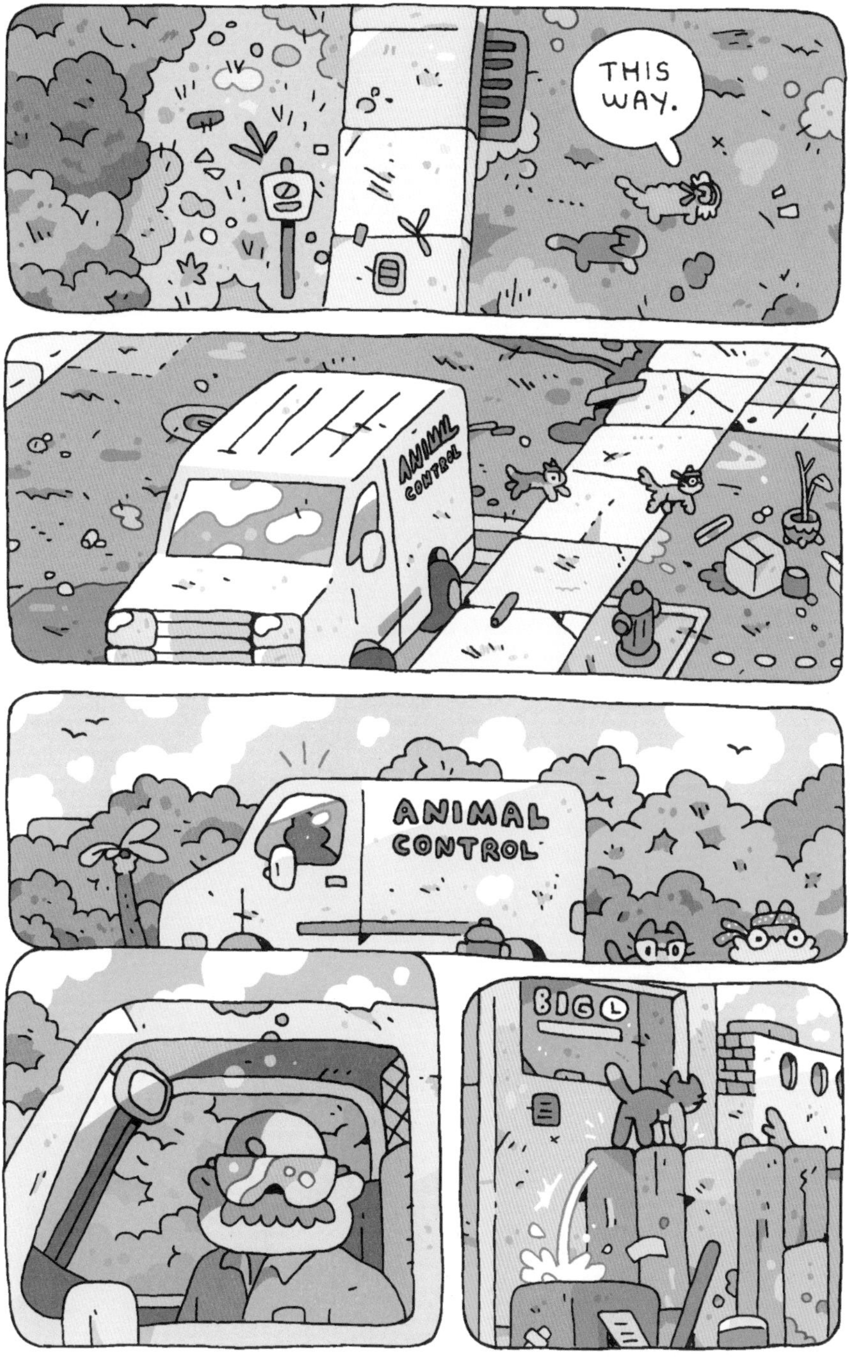
THIS WAY.
ANIMAL CONTROL
ANIMAL CONTROL
BIG L

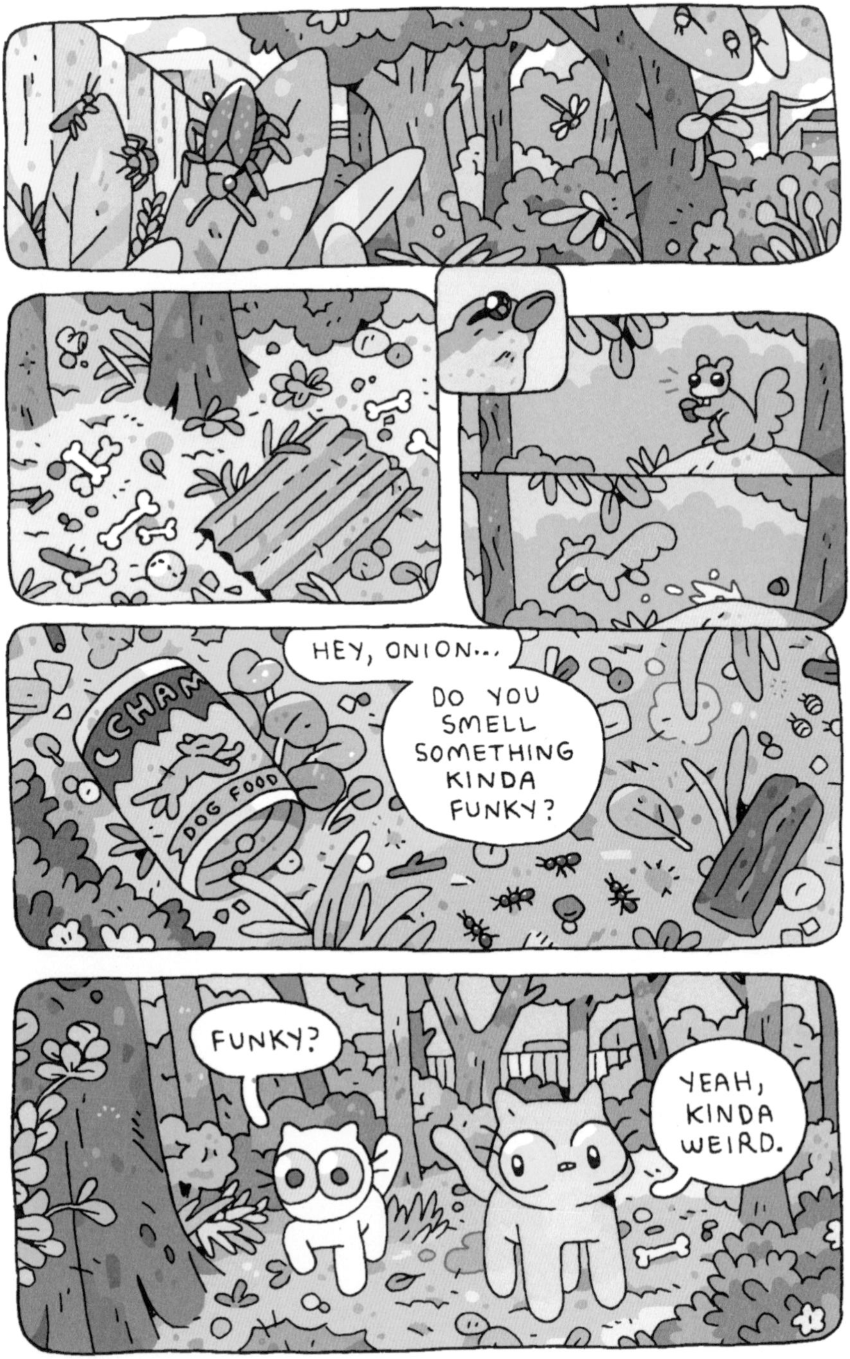
CHAM
DOG FOOD
HEY, ONION...
DO YOU SMELL SOMETHING KINDA FUNKY?
FUNKY?
YEAH, KINDA WEIRD.

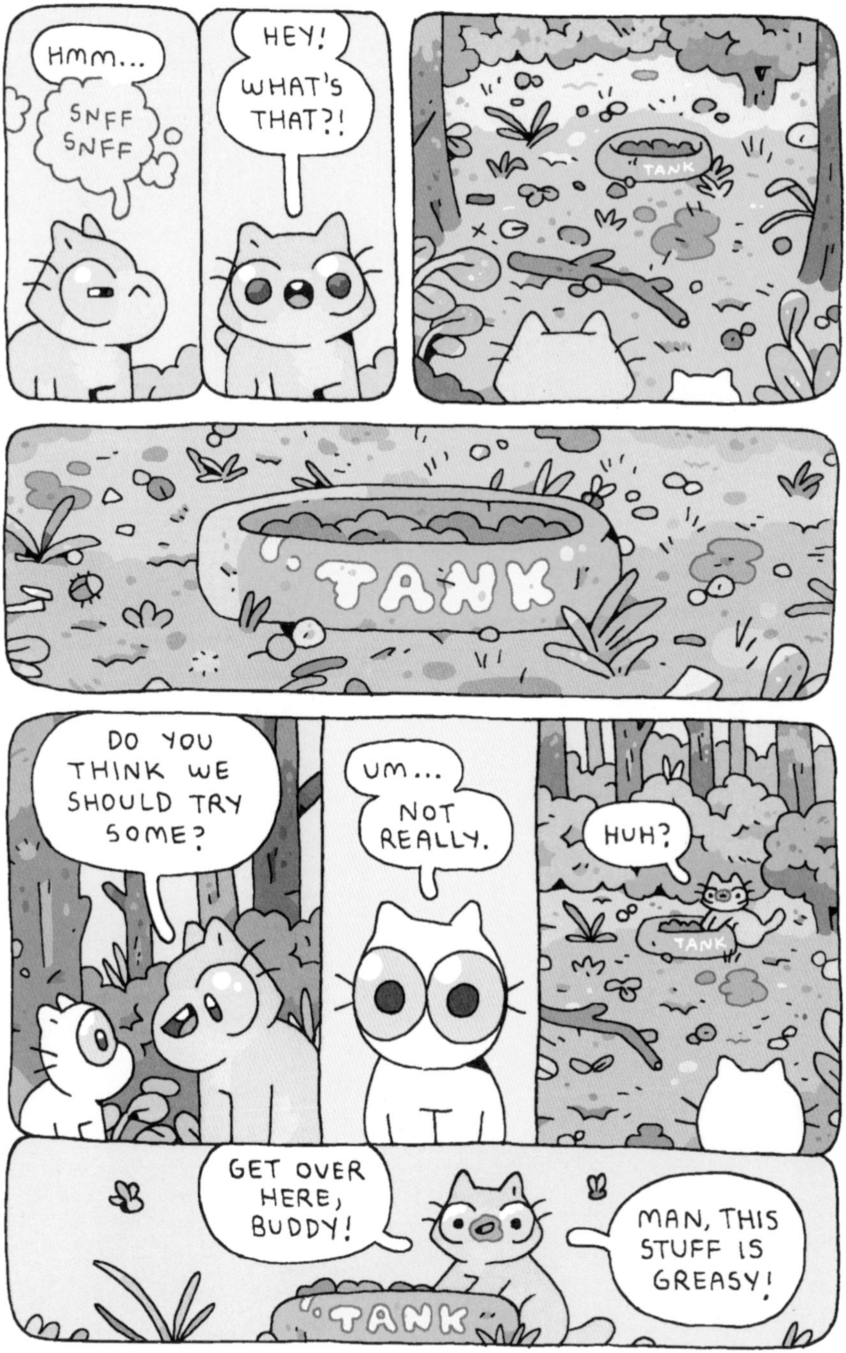
HMM...
SNFF SNFF
HEY!
WHAT'S THAT?!
TANK
TANK
DO YOU THINK WE SHOULD TRY SOME?
UM...
NOT REALLY.
HUH?
TANK
GET OVER HERE, BUDDY!
MAN, THIS STUFF IS GREASY!
TANK

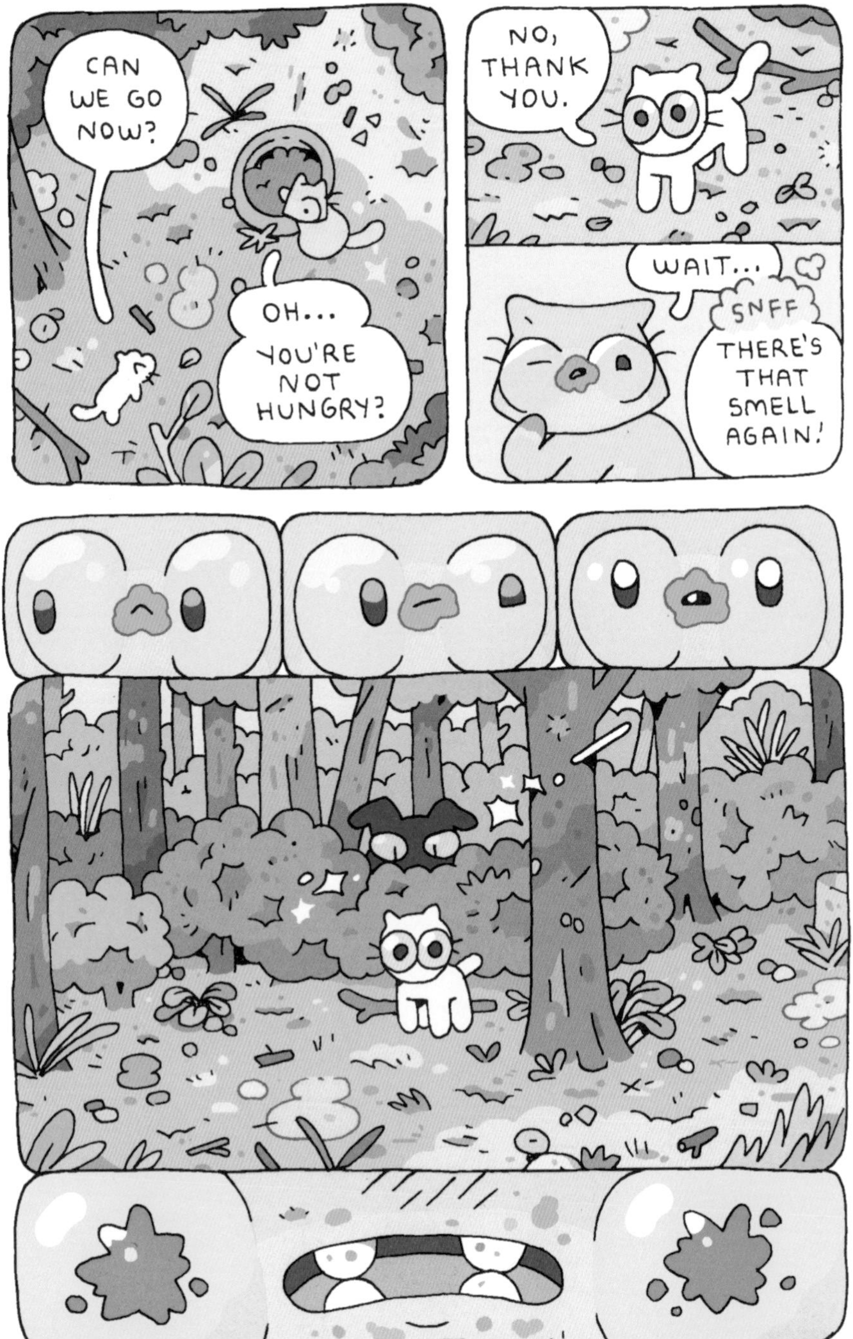
CAN WE GO NOW?
OH... YOU'RE NOT HUNGRY?
NO, THANK YOU.
WAIT...
SNFF
THERE'S THAT SMELL AGAIN!

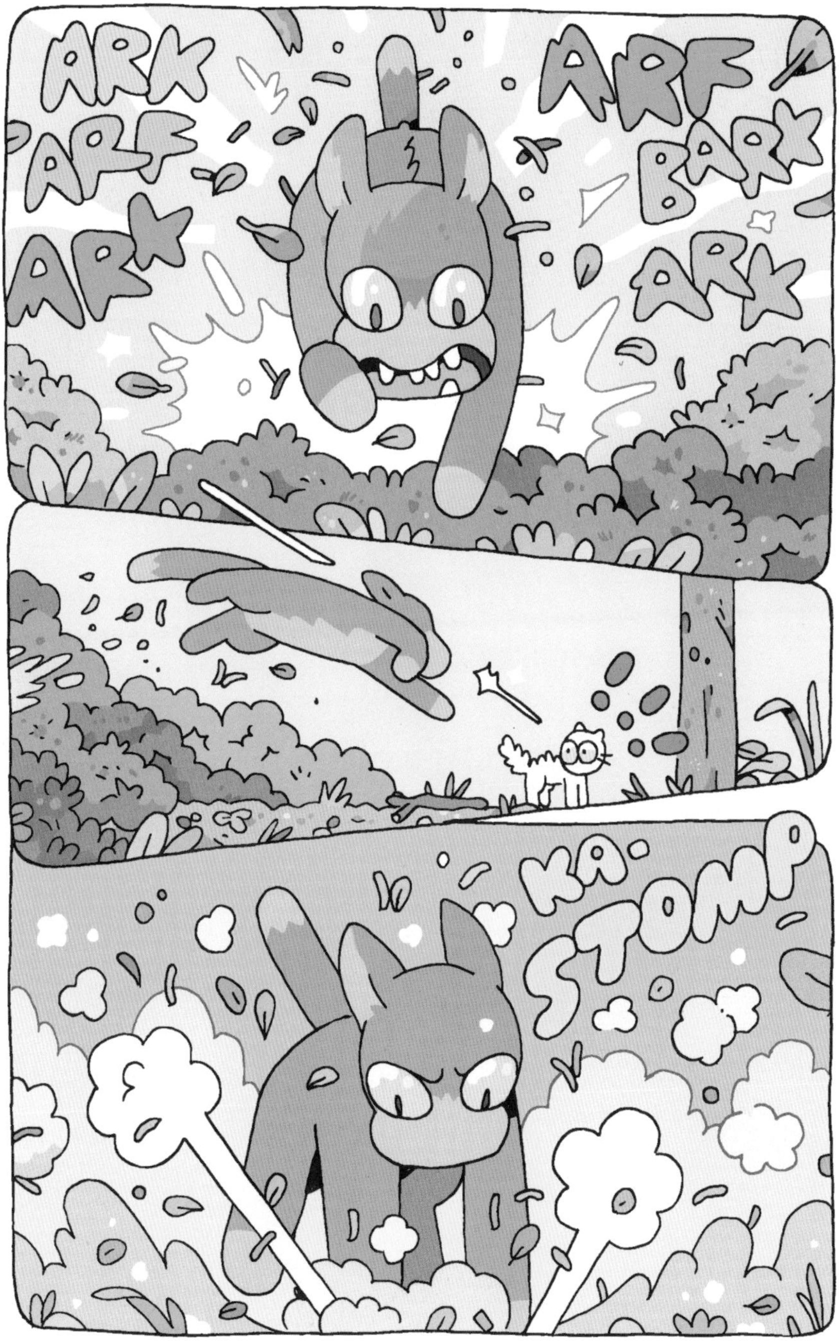
ARK
ARF
ARK
ARF
BARK
ARK
KA-STOMP

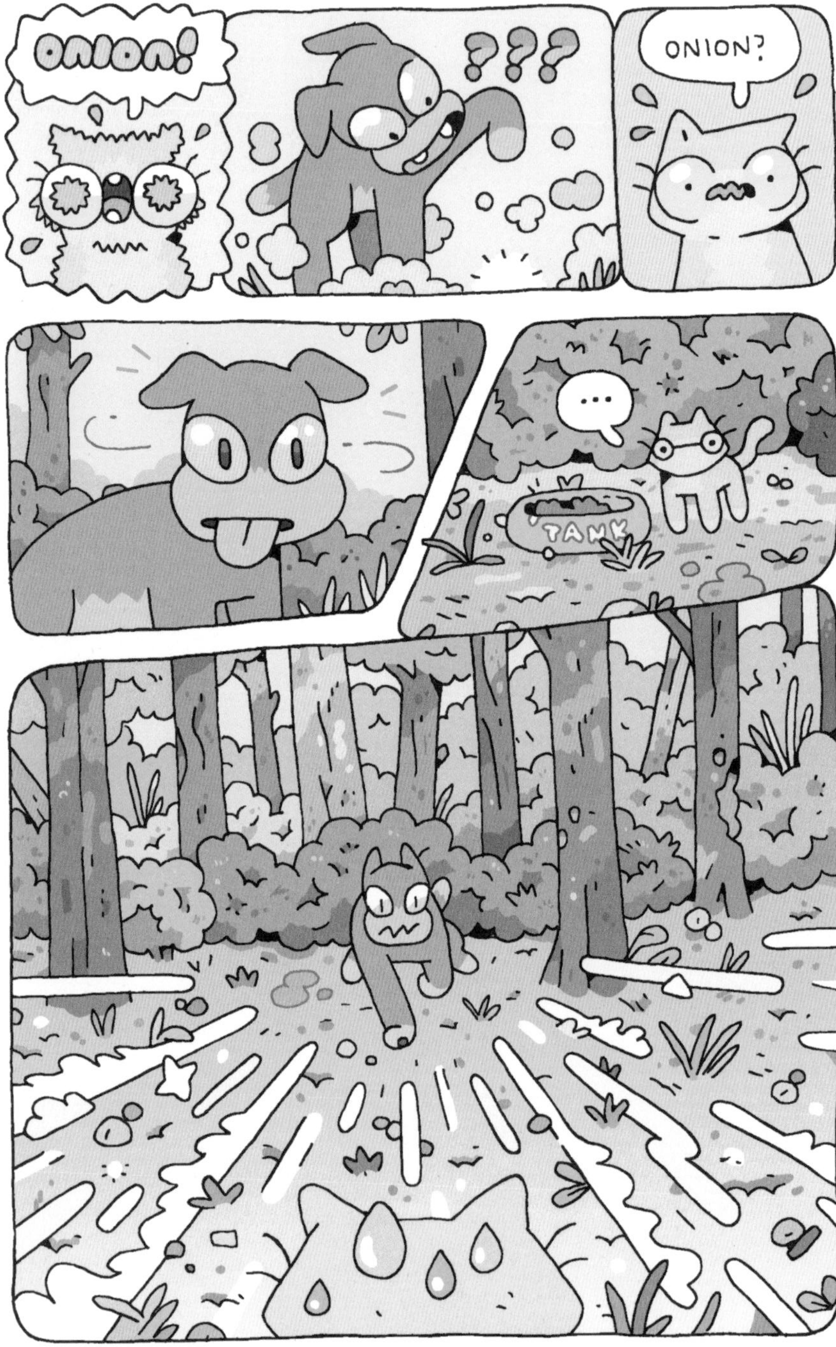
ONION!
???
ONION?
...
TANK

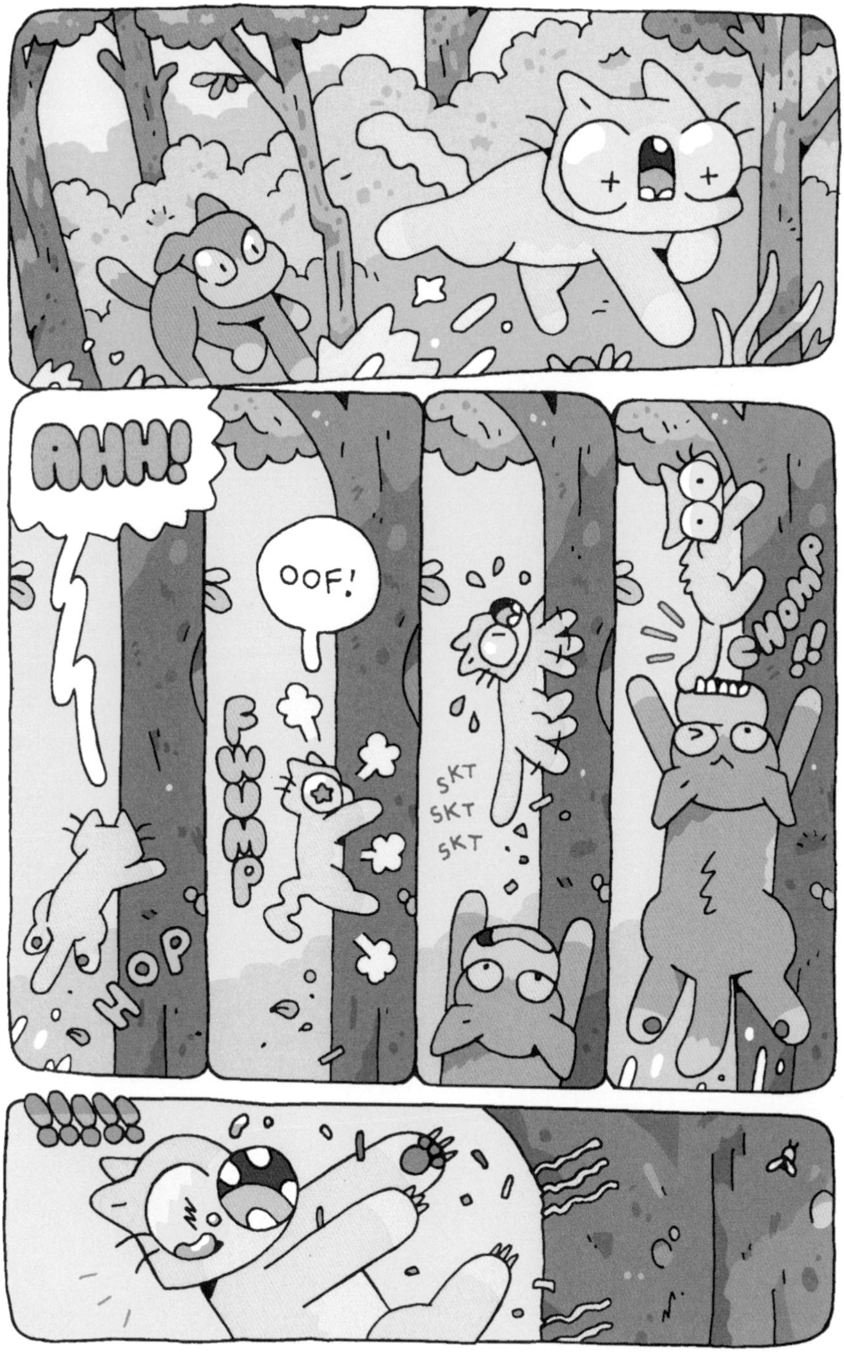
AHH!
HOP
OOF!
FWUMP
SKT
SKT
SKT
CHOMP
!!

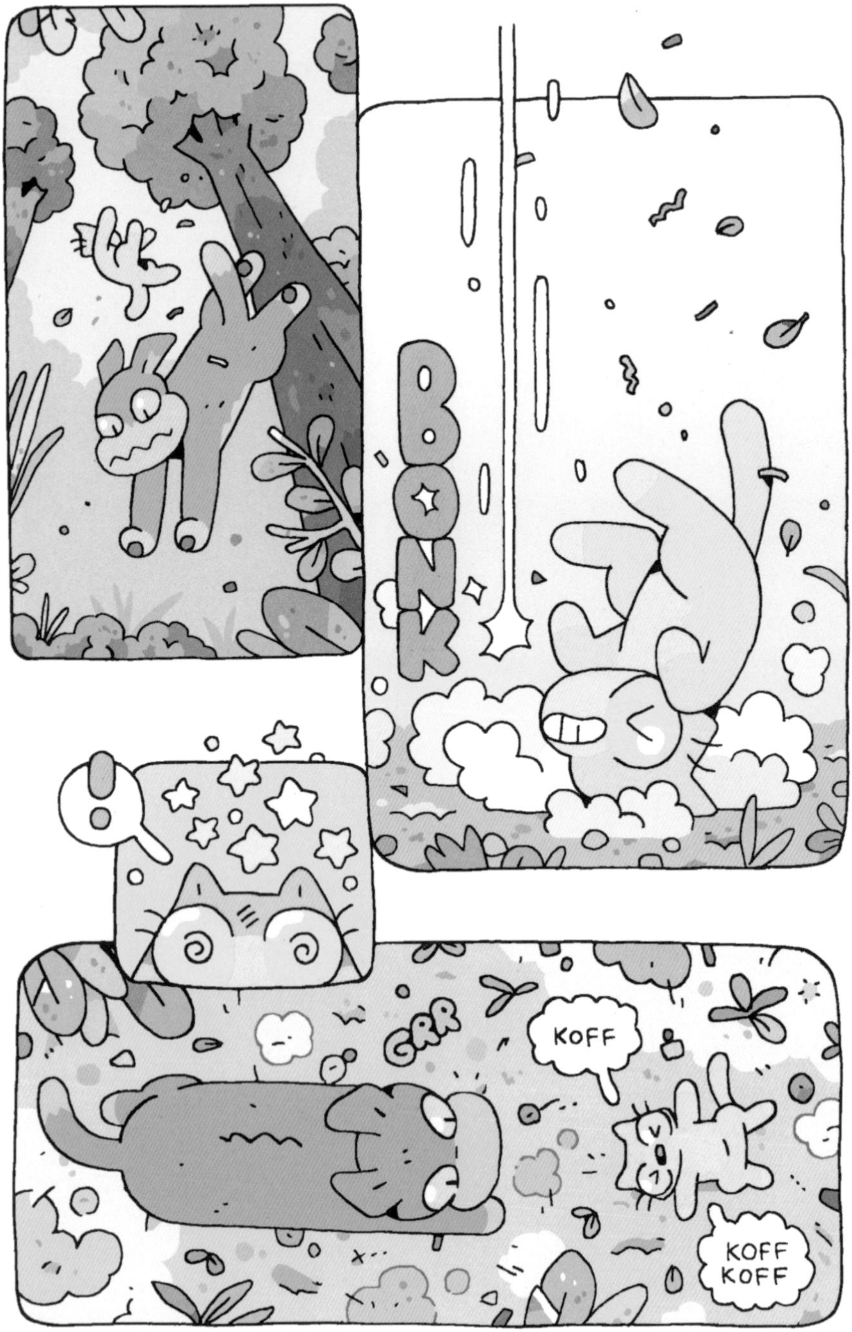
BONK
GRR
KOFF
KOFF KOFF

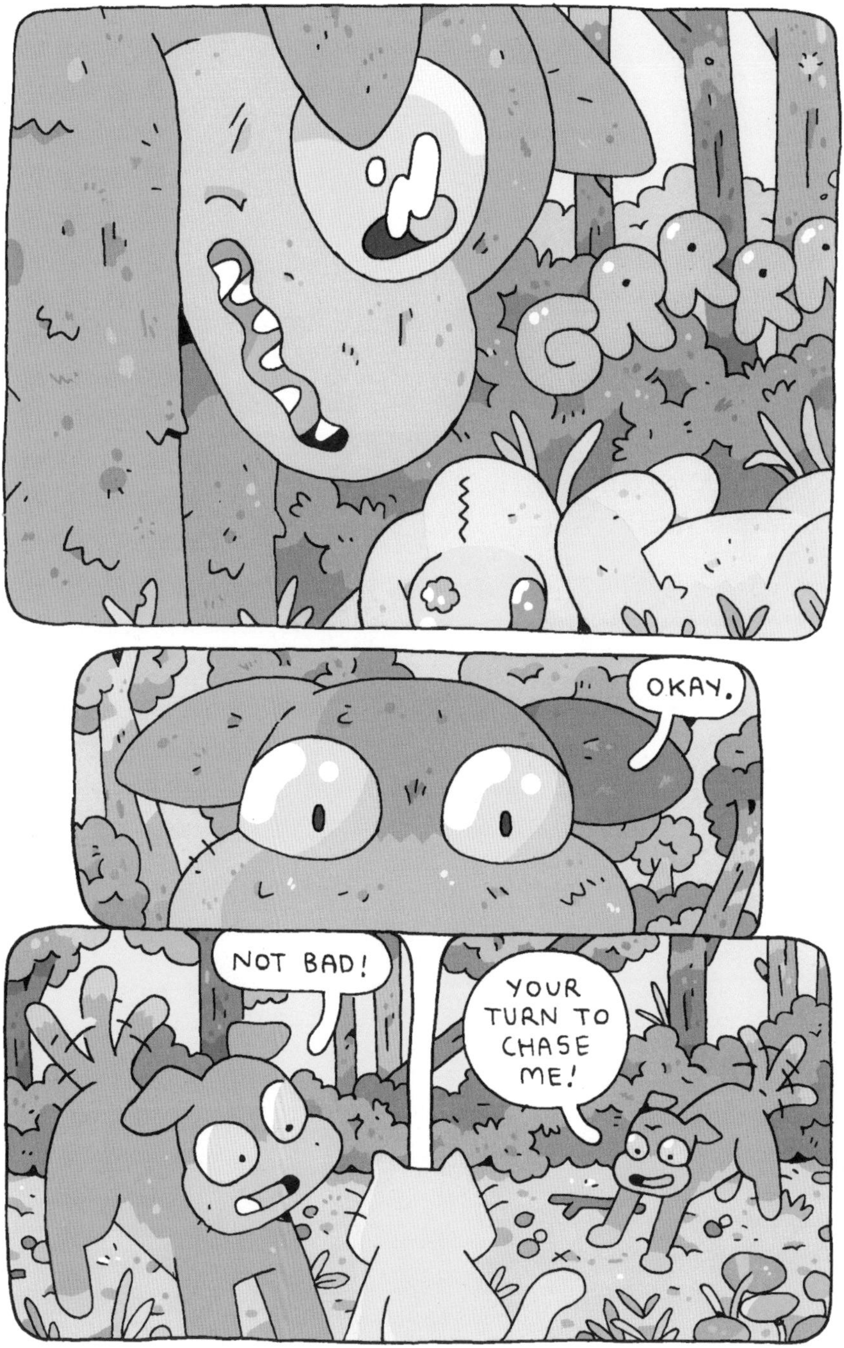
GRRR
OKAY.
NOT BAD!
YOUR TURN TO CHASE ME!

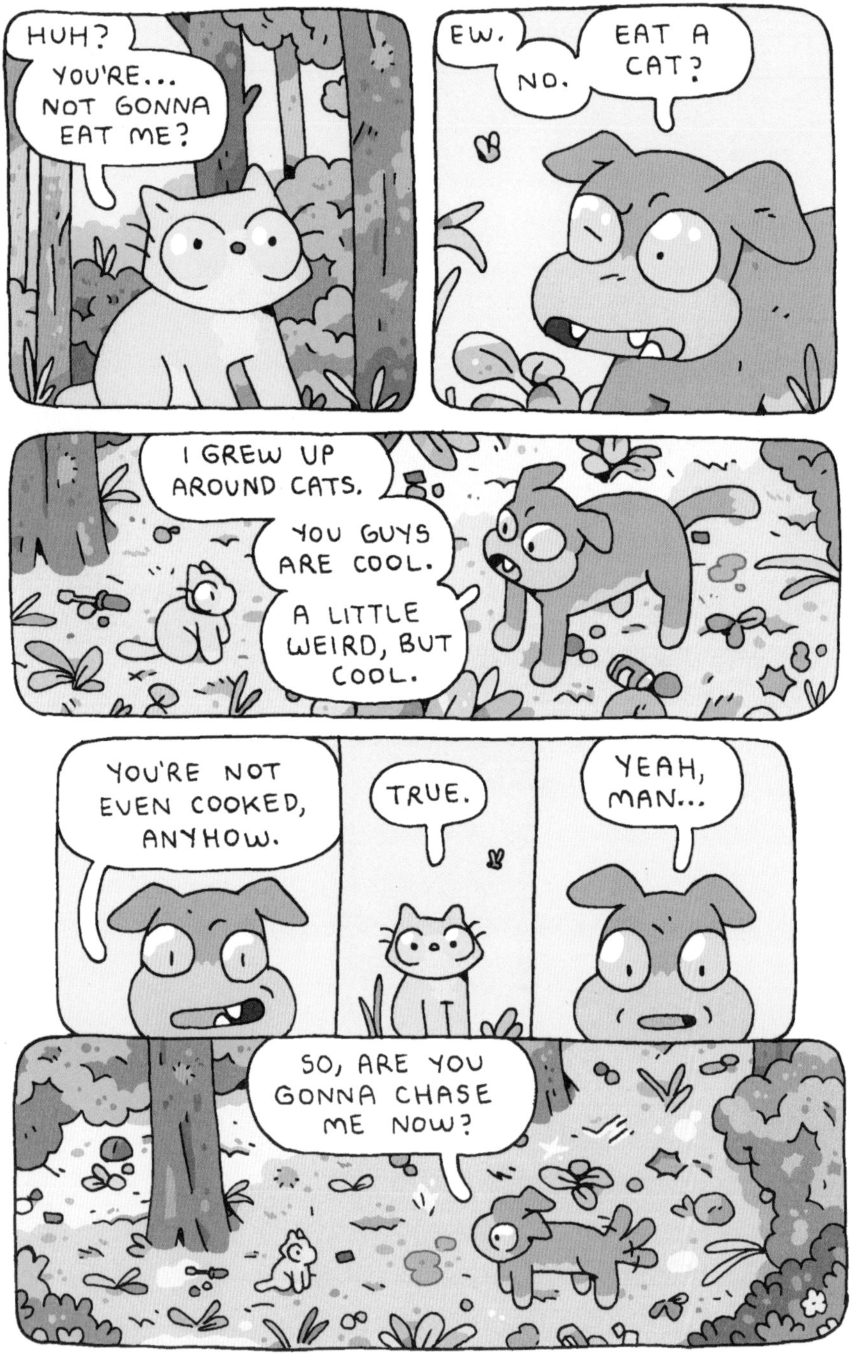
HUH?
YOU'RE... NOT GONNA EAT ME?
EW.
EAT A CAT?
NO.
I GREW UP AROUND CATS.
YOU GUYS ARE COOL.
A LITTLE WEIRD, BUT COOL.
YOU'RE NOT EVEN COOKED, ANYHOW.
TRUE.
YEAH, MAN...
SO, ARE YOU GONNA CHASE ME NOW?

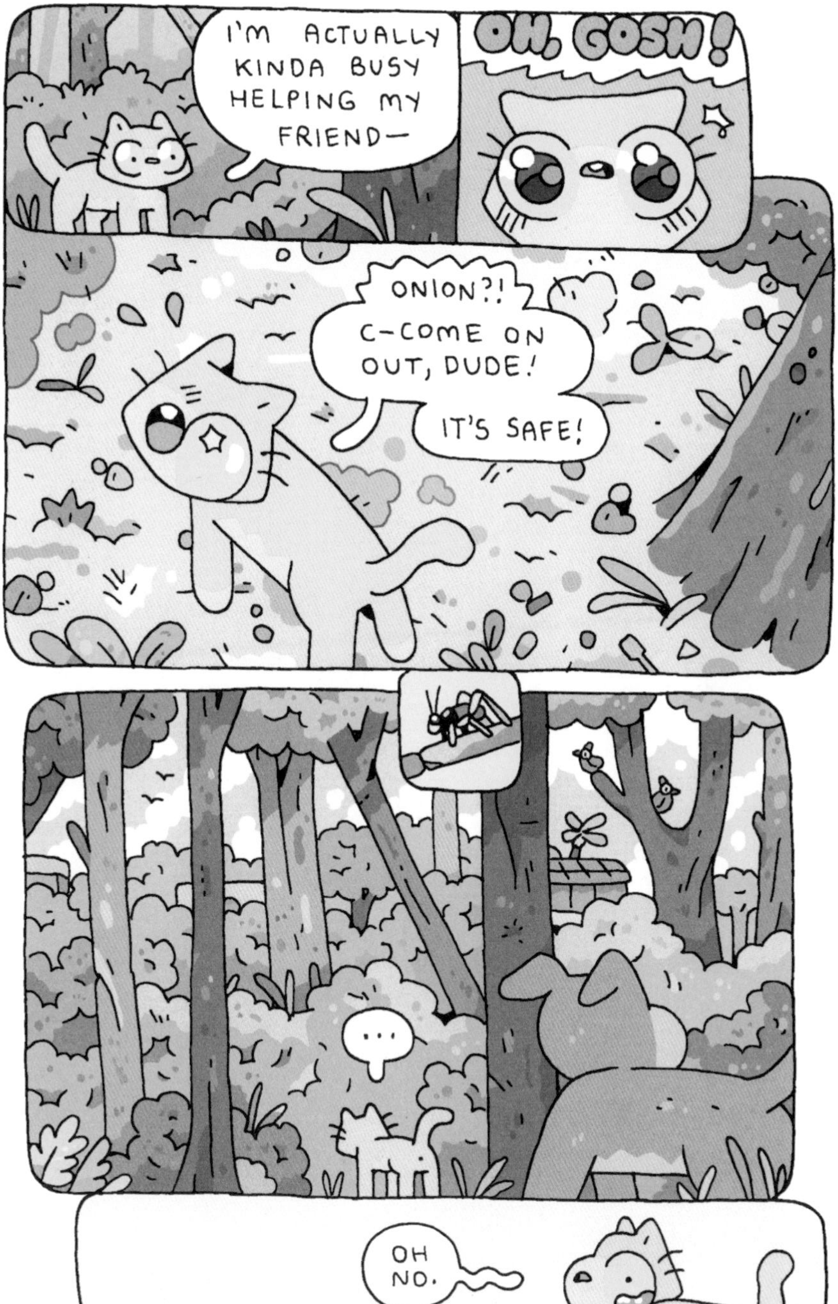
I'M ACTUALLY KINDA BUSY HELPING MY FRIEND—
OH, GOSH!
ONION?!
C-COME ON OUT, DUDE!
IT'S SAFE!
...
OH NO.

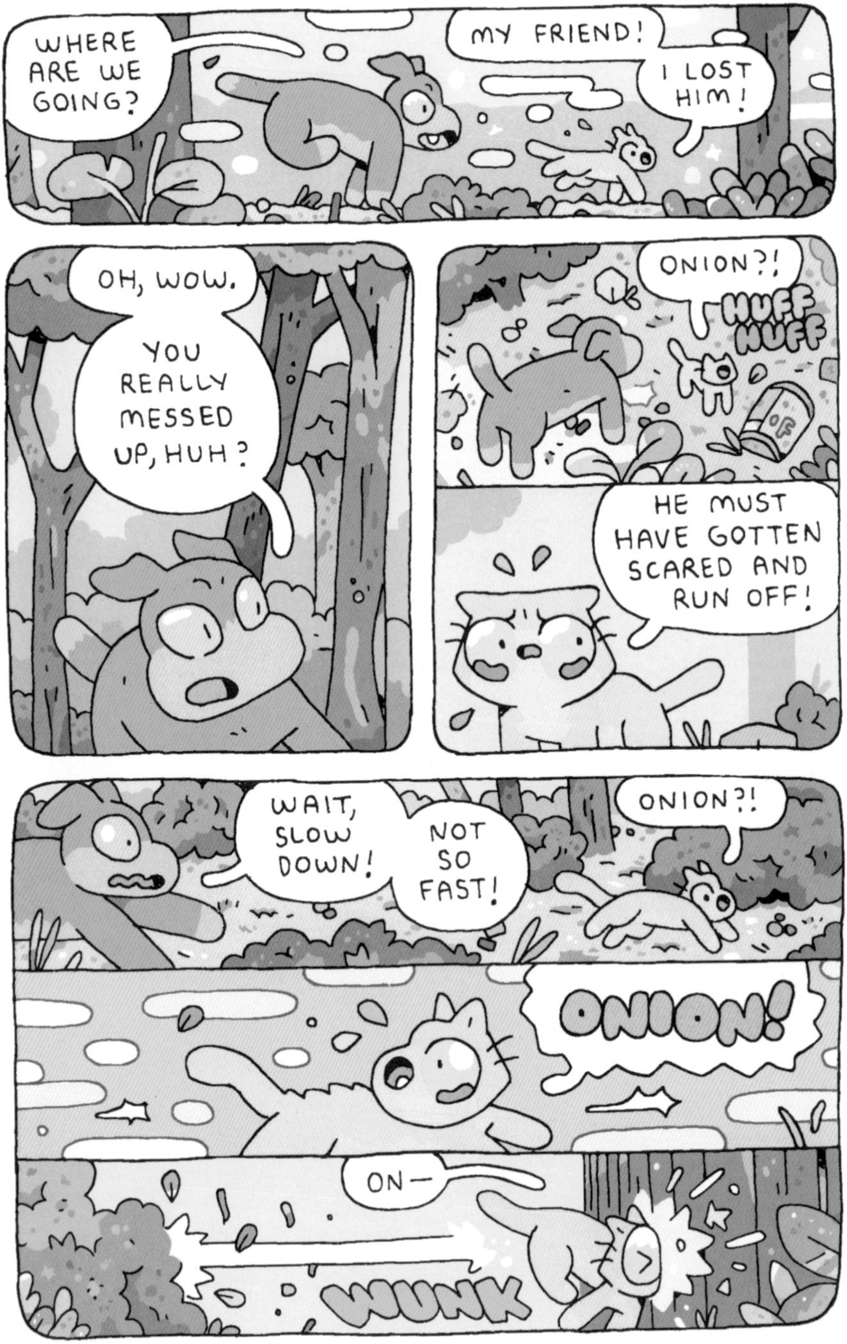
WHERE ARE WE GOING?
MY FRIEND!
I LOST HIM!
OH, WOW.
YOU REALLY MESSED UP, HUH?
ONION?!
HUFF HUFF
HE MUST HAVE GOTTEN SCARED AND RUN OFF!
WAIT, SLOW DOWN!
NOT SO FAST!
ONION?!
ONION!
ON—
WUNK

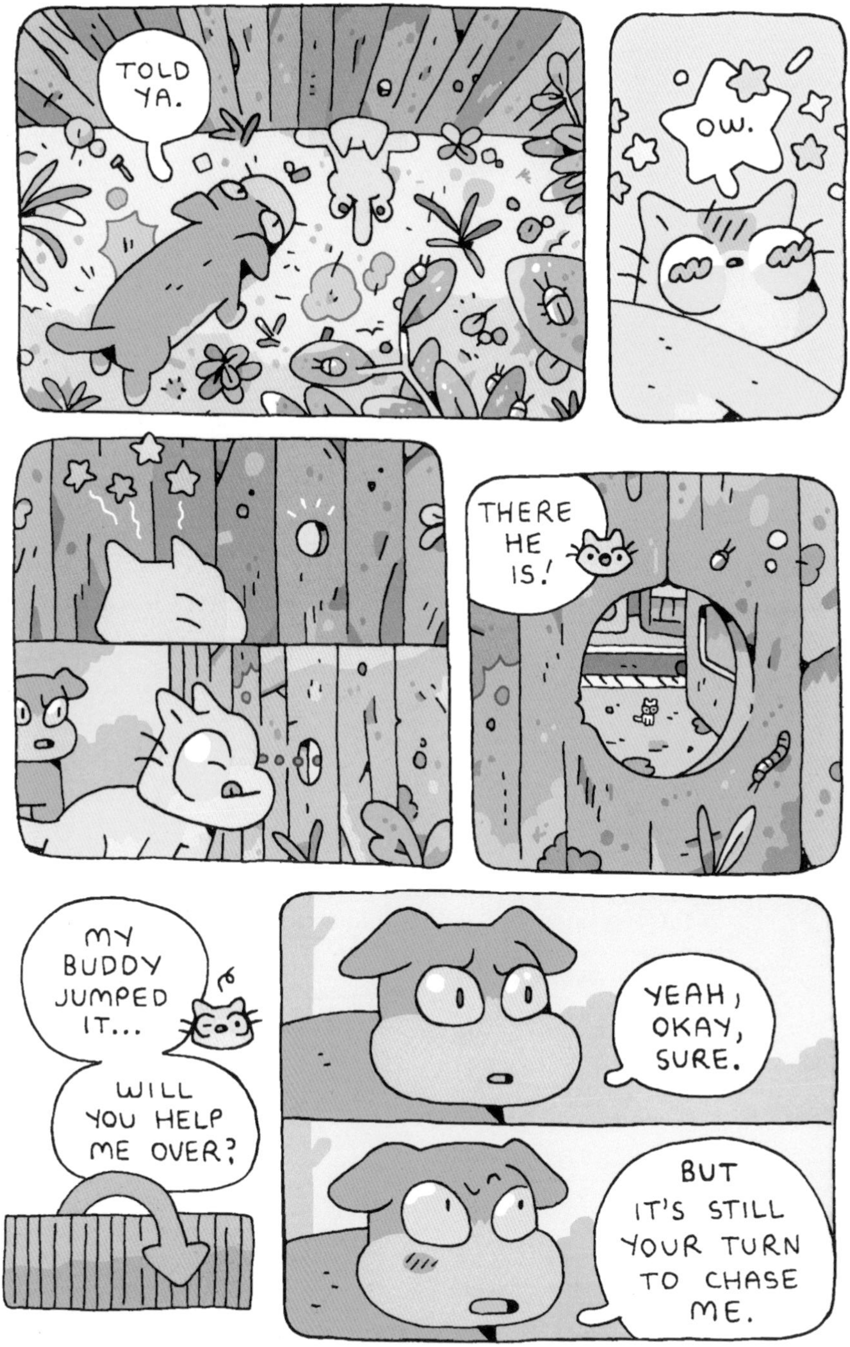
TOLD YA.
OW.
THERE HE IS!
MY BUDDY JUMPED IT...
WILL YOU HELP ME OVER?
YEAH, OKAY, SURE.
BUT IT'S STILL YOUR TURN TO CHASE ME.

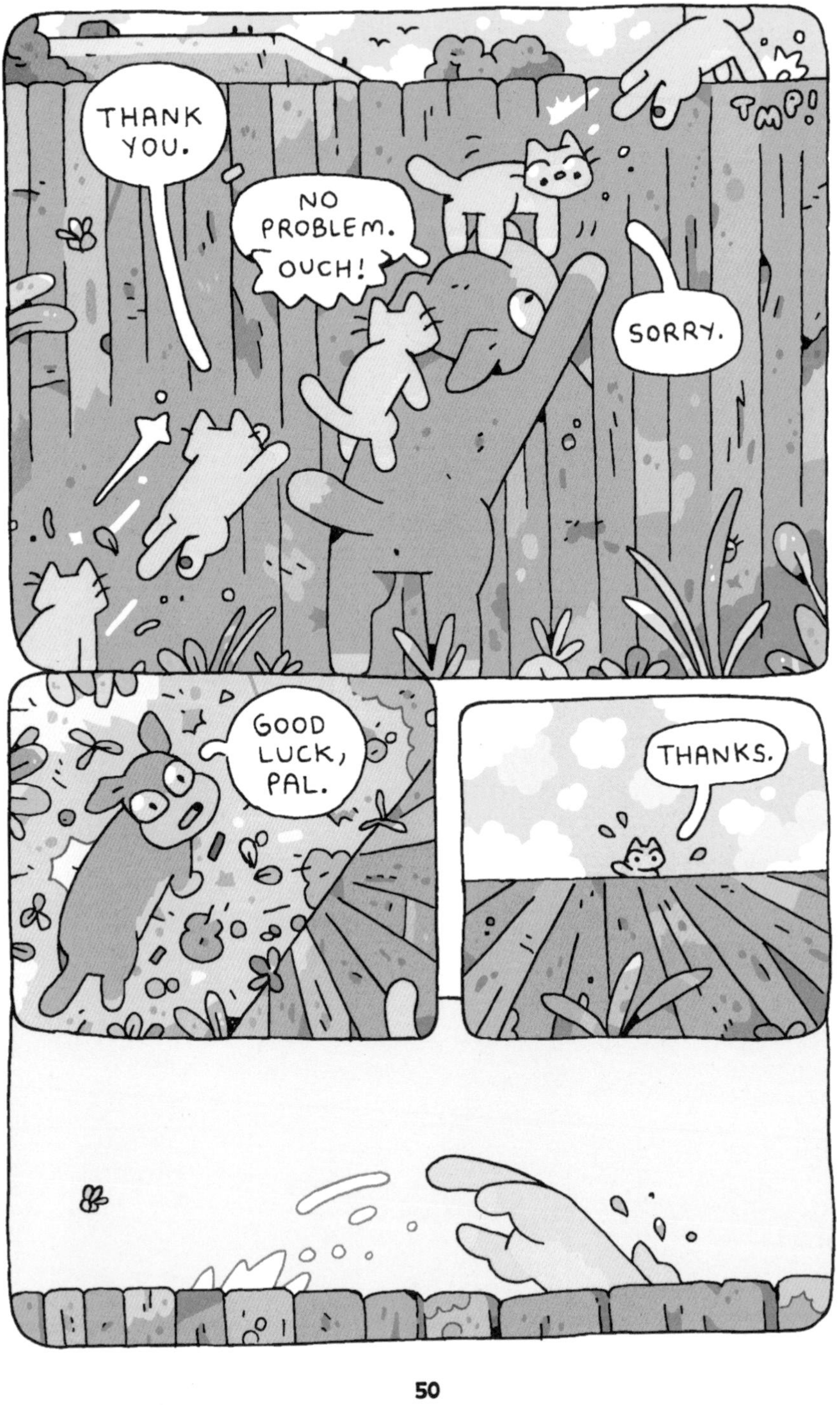
THANK YOU.
NO PROBLEM.
OUCH!
SORRY.
TMP!
GOOD LUCK, PAL.
THANKS.

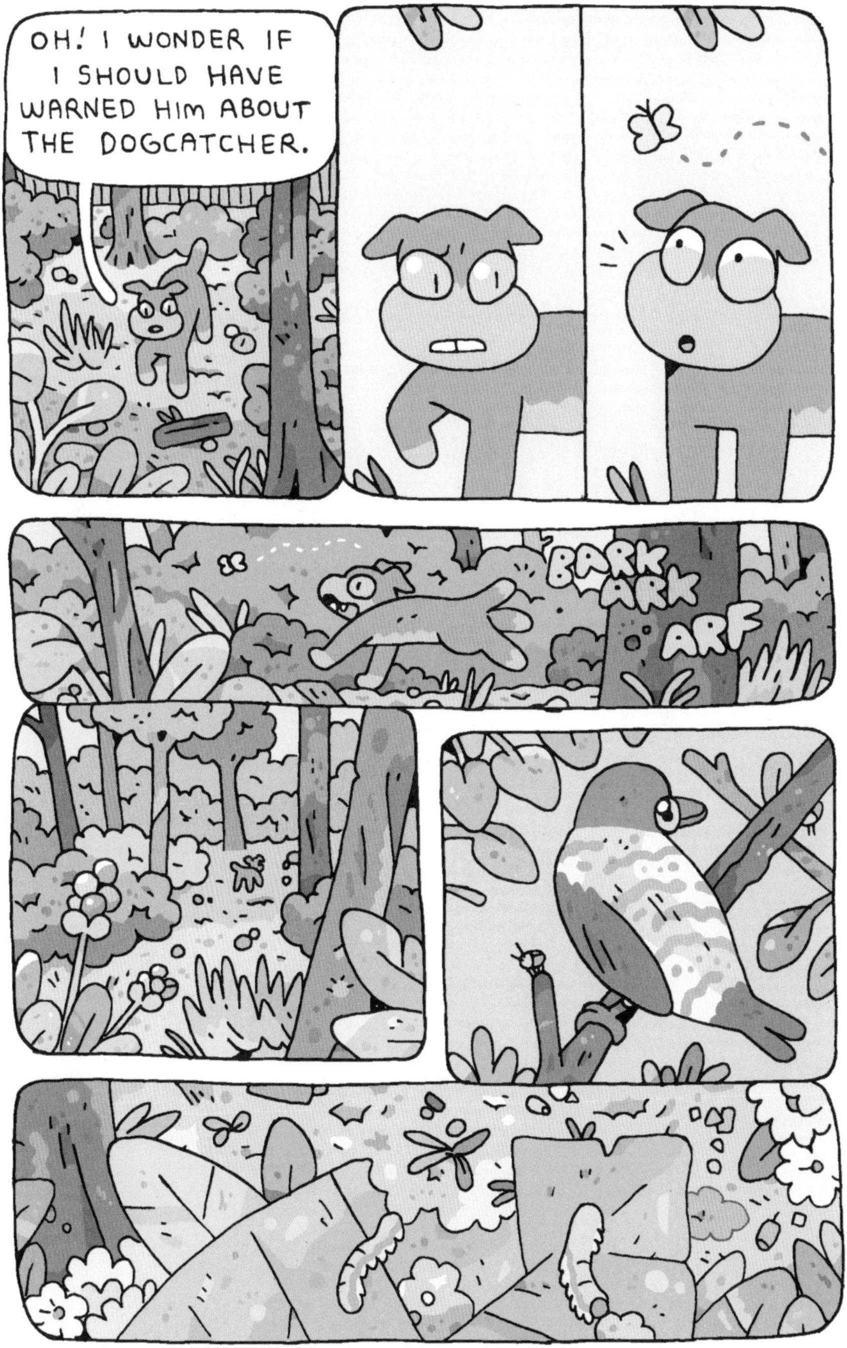
OH! I WONDER IF I SHOULD HAVE WARNED HIM ABOUT THE DOGCATCHER.
BARK
ARK
ARF

CHAPTER 3

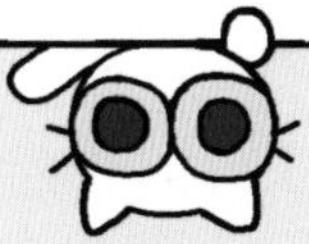

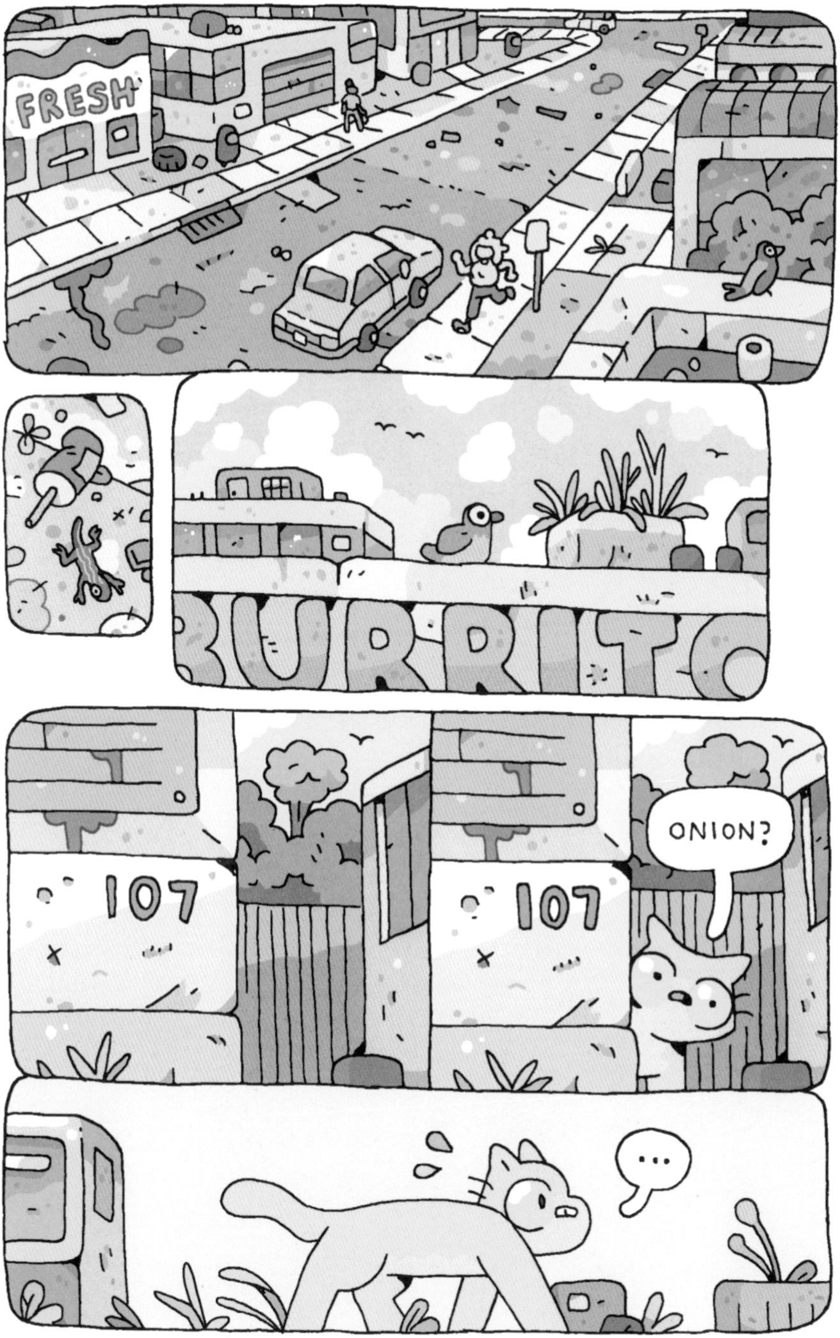
FRESH
BURRITO
107
107
ONION?
...

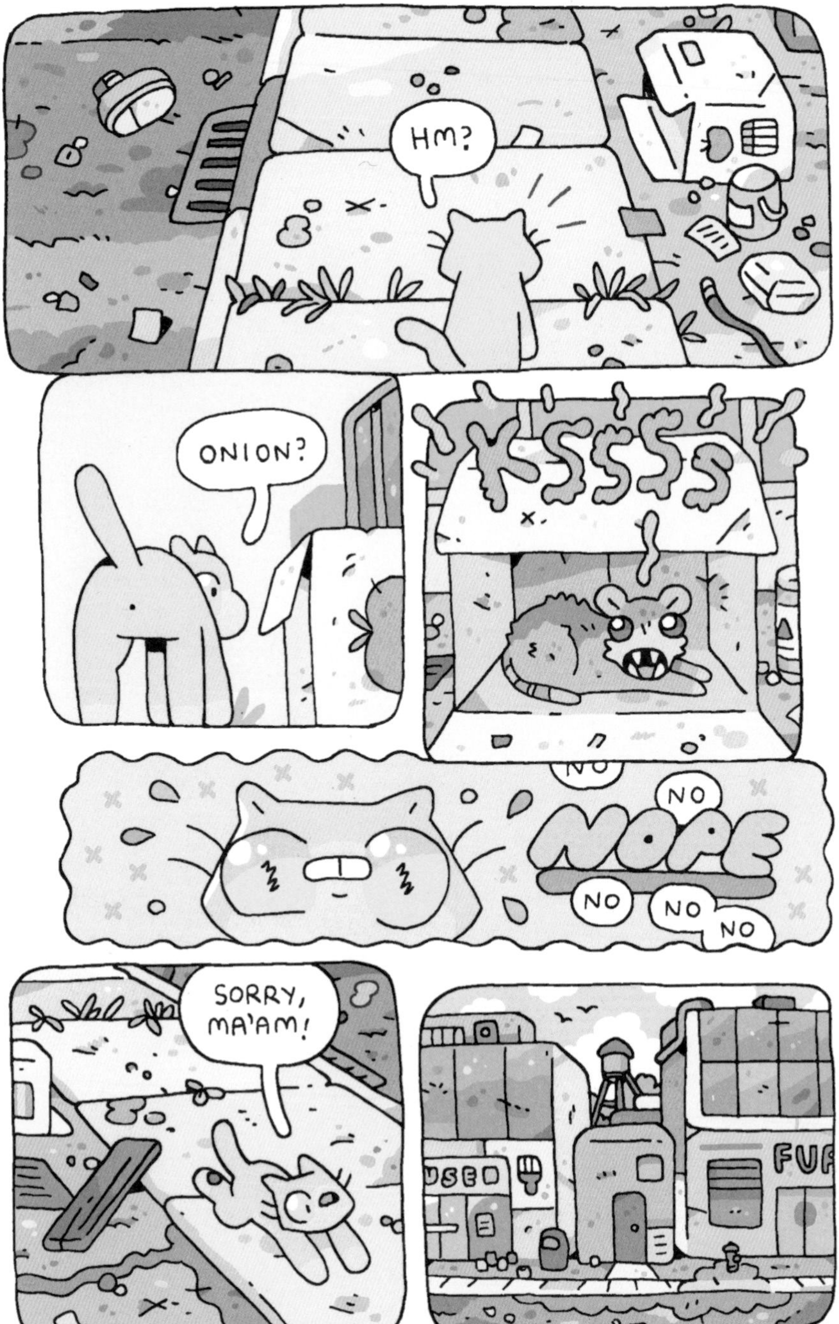
HM?
ONION?
KSSSSS
NO
NO
NOPE
NO
NO
NO
SORRY, MA'AM!
USED
FUR

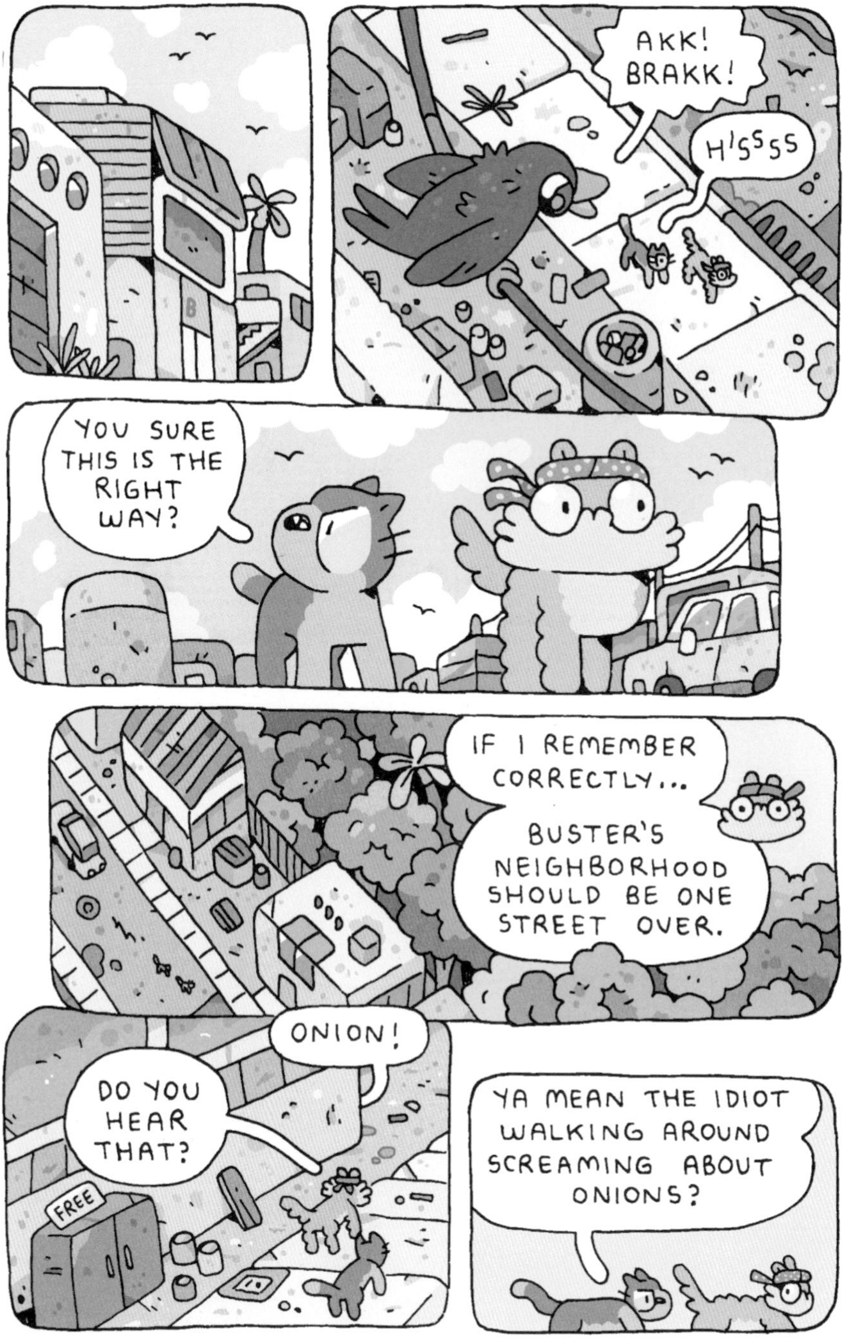
AKK! BRAKK!
HISSSS
YOU SURE THIS IS THE RIGHT WAY?
IF I REMEMBER CORRECTLY...
BUSTER'S NEIGHBORHOOD SHOULD BE ONE STREET OVER.
ONION!
DO YOU HEAR THAT?
FREE
YA MEAN THE IDIOT WALKING AROUND SCREAMING ABOUT ONIONS?

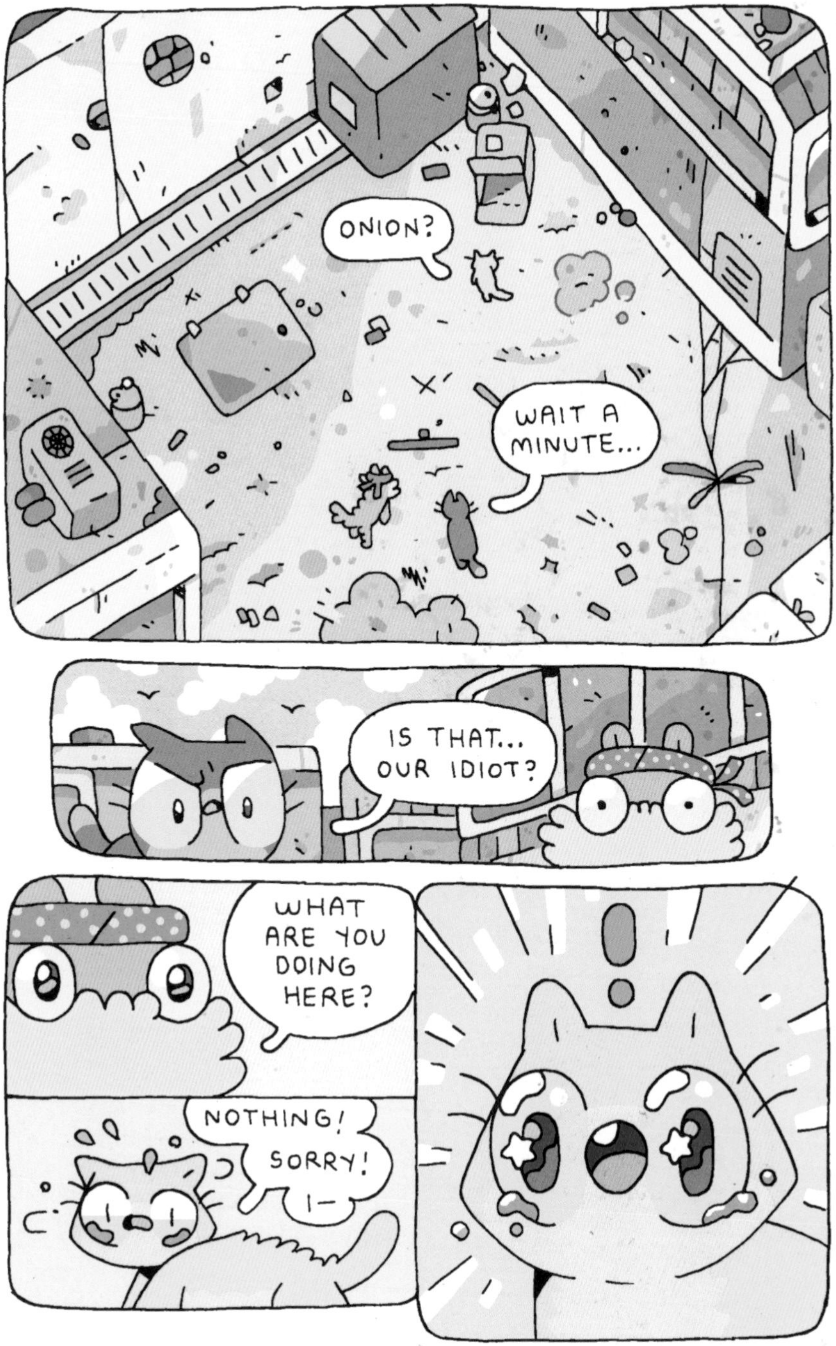
ONION?
WAIT A MINUTE...
IS THAT... OUR IDIOT?
WHAT ARE YOU DOING HERE?
NOTHING! SORRY! I—

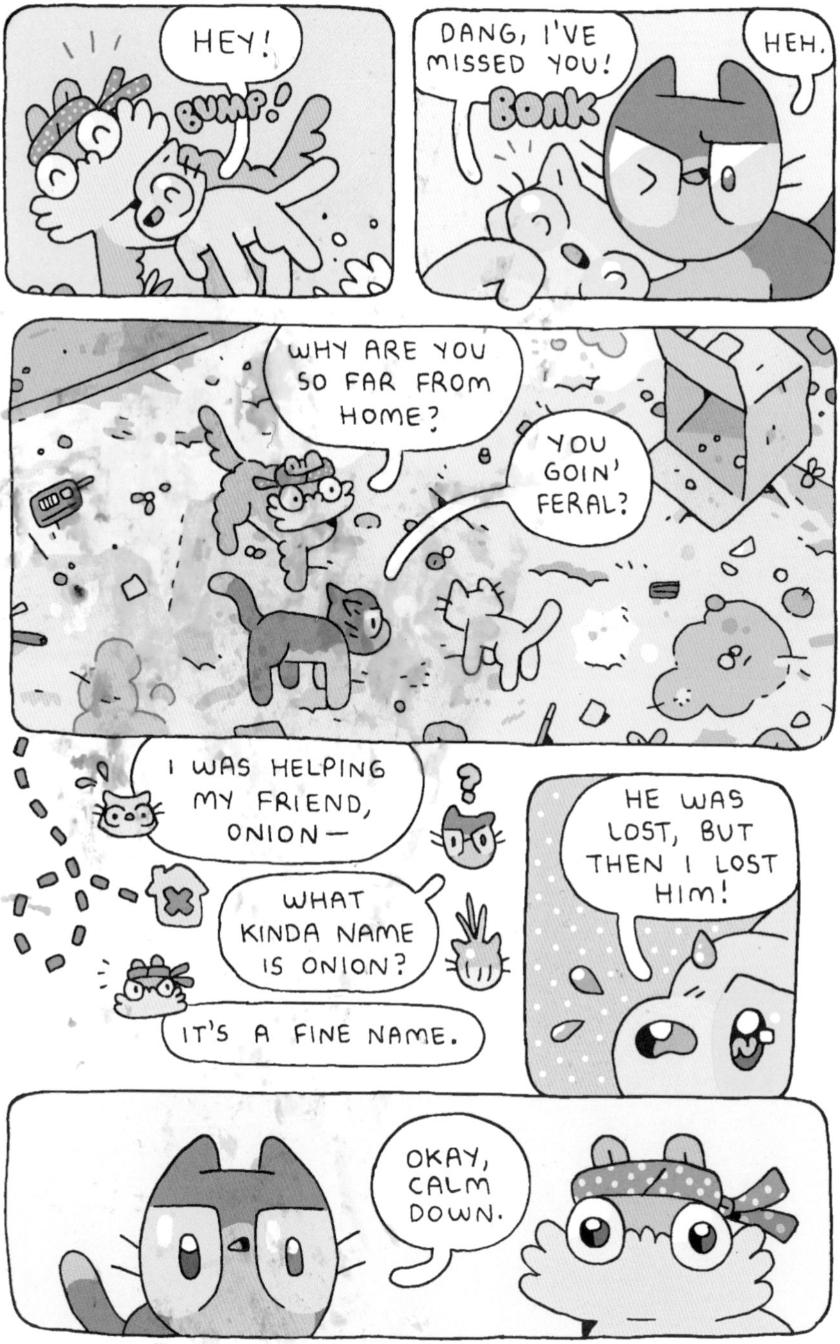
HEY!
BUMP!
DANG, I'VE MISSED YOU!
BONK
HEH.
WHY ARE YOU SO FAR FROM HOME?
YOU GOIN' FERAL?
I WAS HELPING MY FRIEND, ONION—
WHAT KINDA NAME IS ONION?
IT'S A FINE NAME.
HE WAS LOST, BUT THEN I LOST HIM!
OKAY, CALM DOWN.

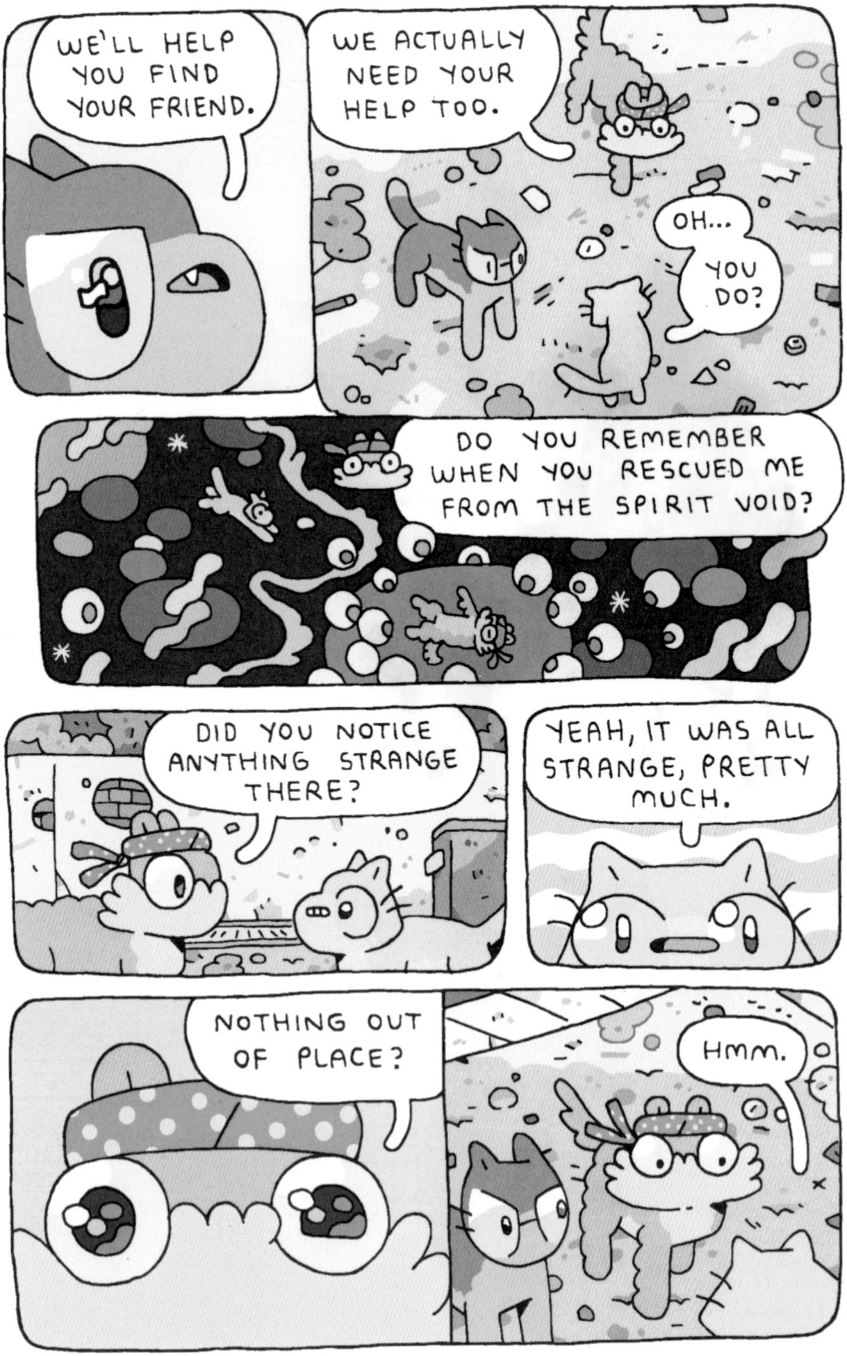
WE'LL HELP YOU FIND YOUR FRIEND.
WE ACTUALLY NEED YOUR HELP TOO.
OH...
YOU DO?
DO YOU REMEMBER WHEN YOU RESCUED ME FROM THE SPIRIT VOID?
DID YOU NOTICE ANYTHING STRANGE THERE?
YEAH, IT WAS ALL STRANGE, PRETTY MUCH.
NOTHING OUT OF PLACE?
HMM.

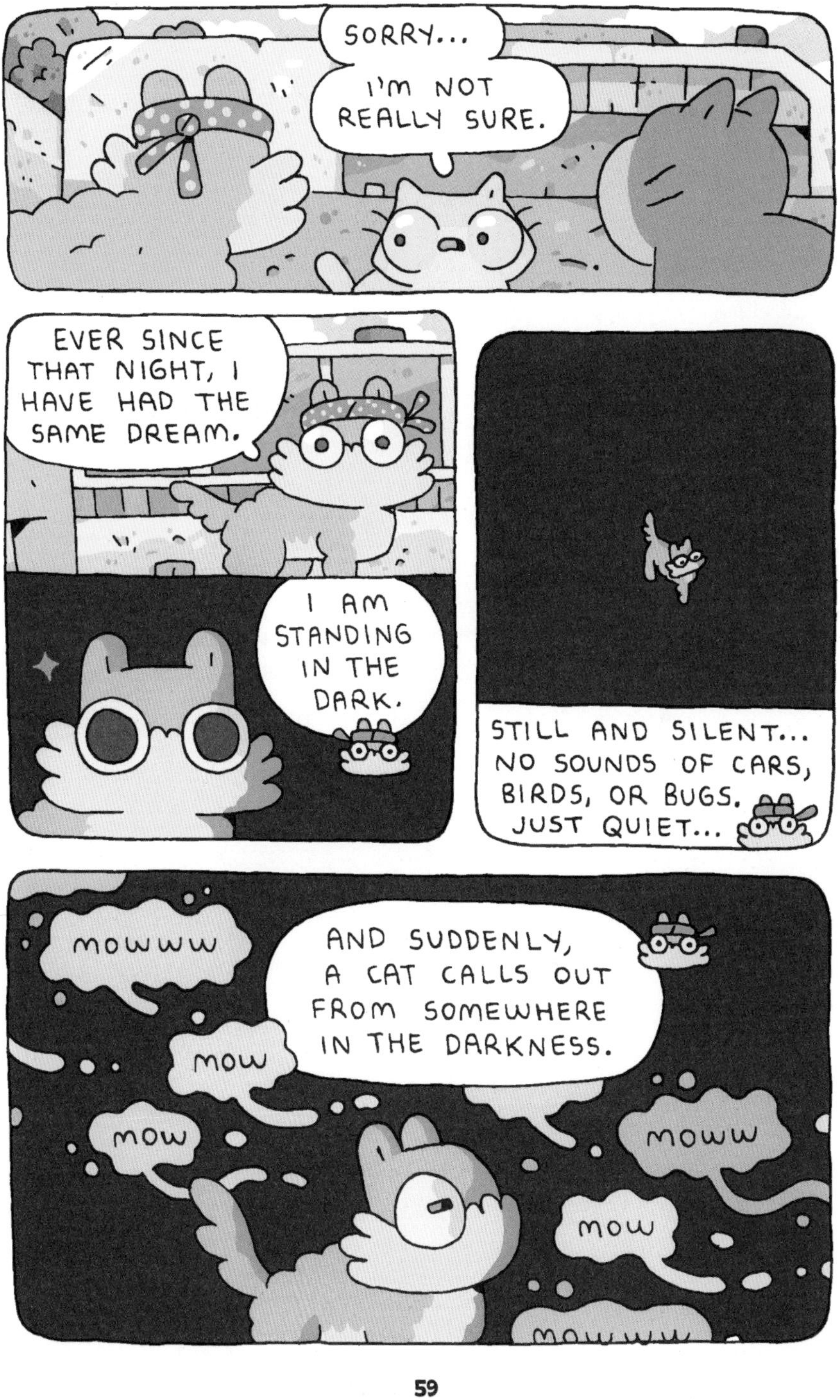
SORRY...
I'M NOT REALLY SURE.
EVER SINCE THAT NIGHT, I HAVE HAD THE SAME DREAM.
I AM STANDING IN THE DARK.
STILL AND SILENT... NO SOUNDS OF CARS, BIRDS, OR BUGS. JUST QUIET...
MOWWW
MOW
AND SUDDENLY, A CAT CALLS OUT FROM SOMEWHERE IN THE DARKNESS.
MOW
MOWW
MOW

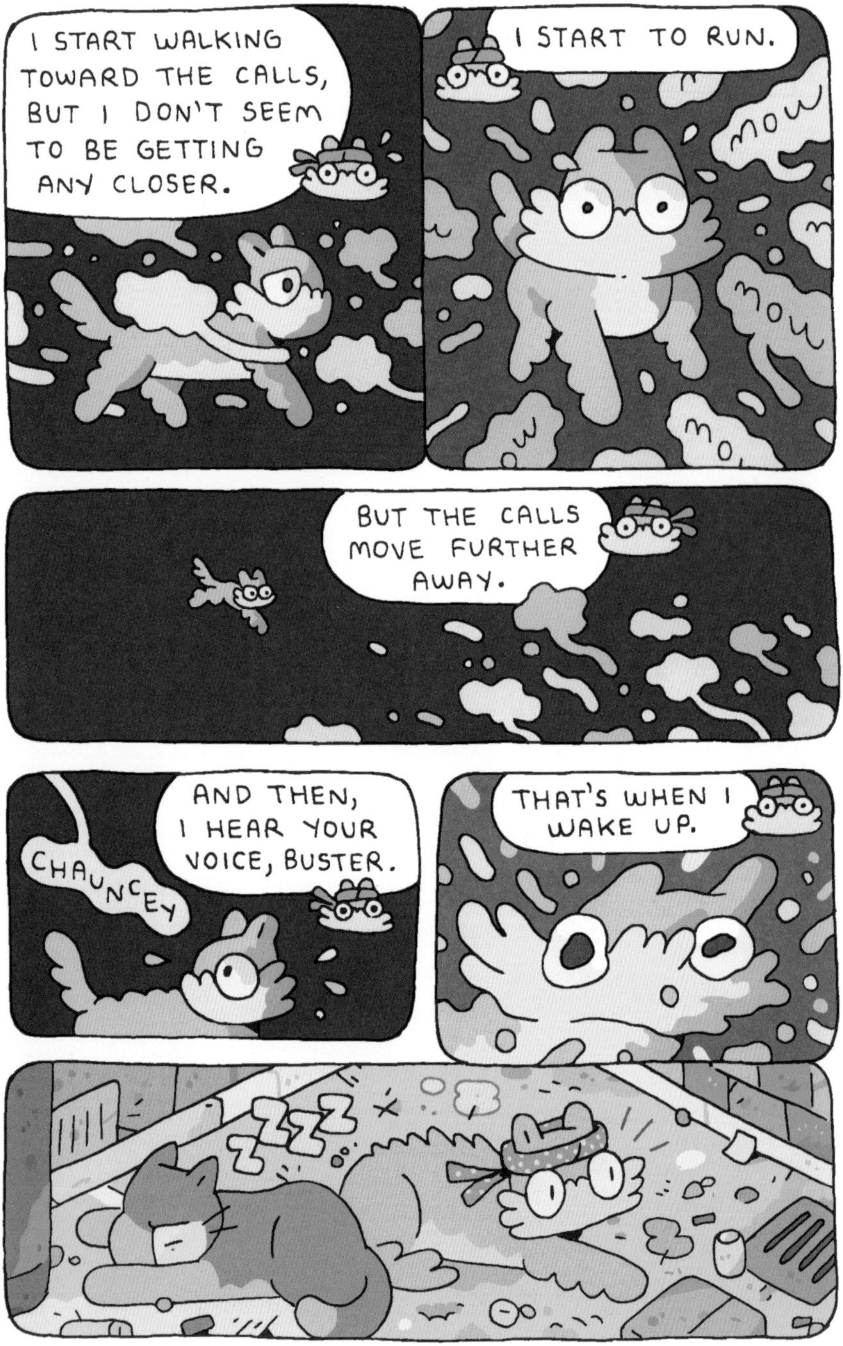
I START WALKING TOWARD THE CALLS, BUT I DON'T SEEM TO BE GETTING ANY CLOSER.
I START TO RUN.
MOW
MOW
MO
BUT THE CALLS MOVE FURTHER AWAY.
AND THEN, I HEAR YOUR VOICE, BUSTER.
CHAUNCEY
THAT'S WHEN I WAKE UP.
ZZZ

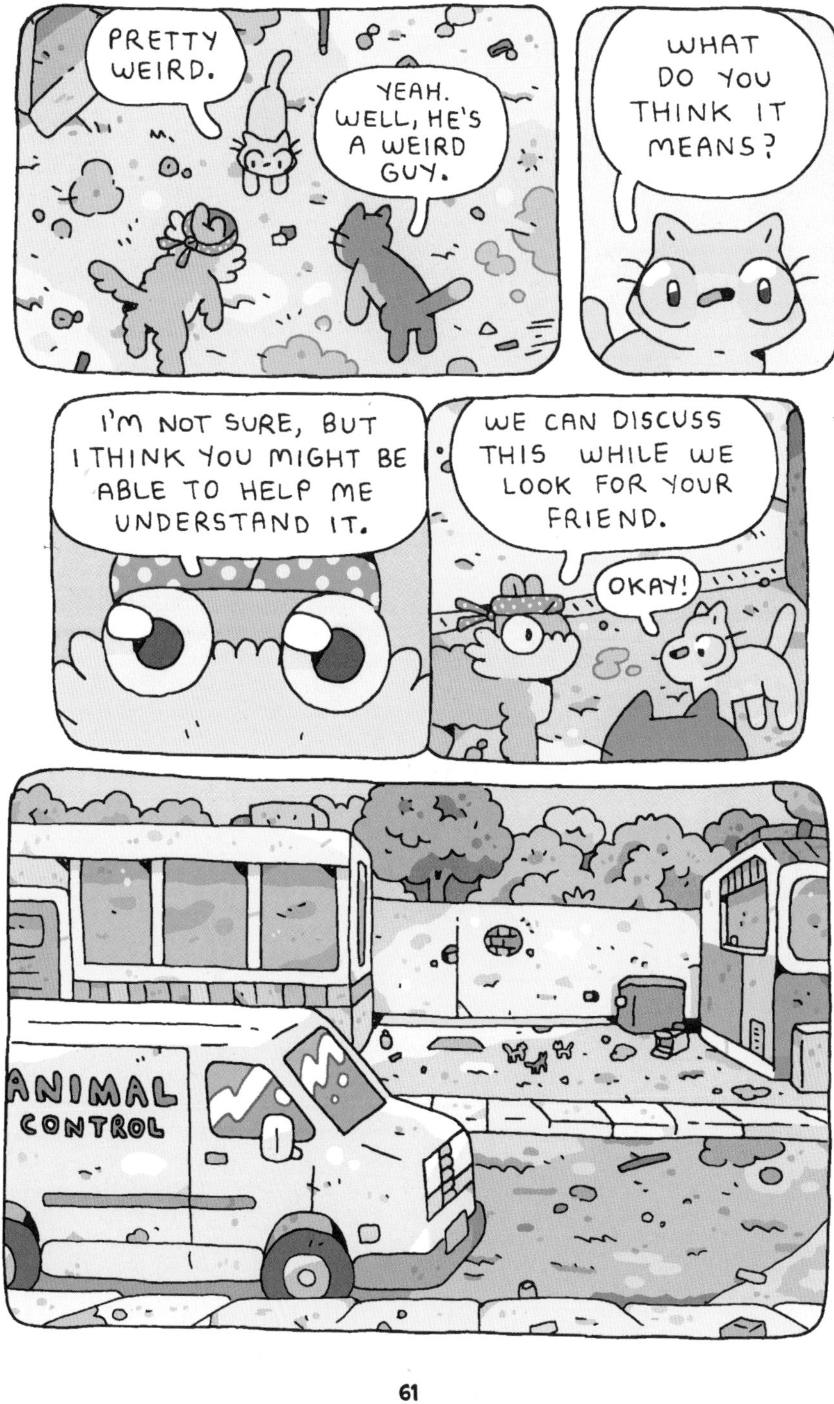
PRETTY WEIRD.
YEAH. WELL, HE'S A WEIRD GUY.
WHAT DO YOU THINK IT MEANS?
I'M NOT SURE, BUT I THINK YOU MIGHT BE ABLE TO HELP ME UNDERSTAND IT.
WE CAN DISCUSS THIS WHILE WE LOOK FOR YOUR FRIEND.
OKAY!
ANIMAL CONTROL

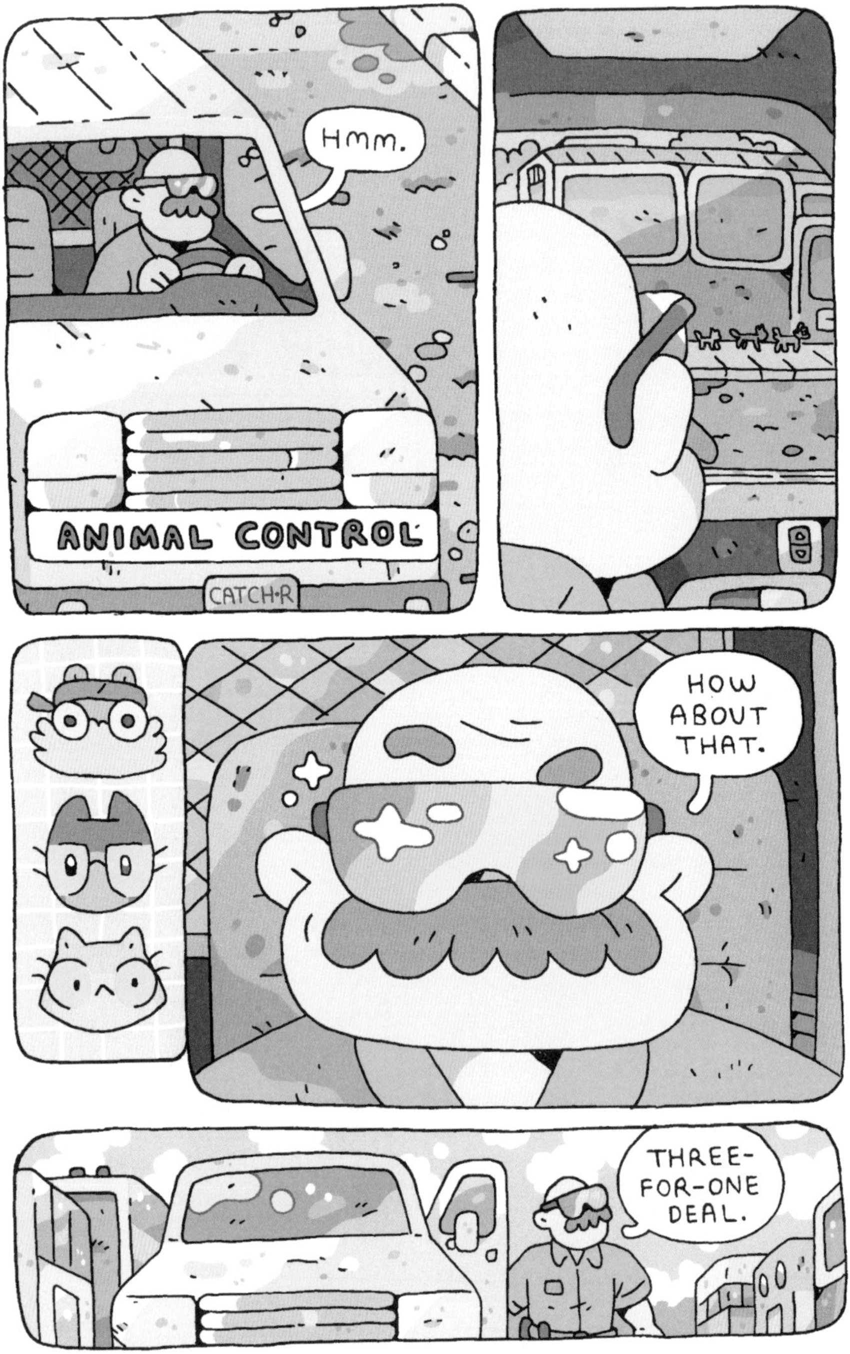
HMM.
ANIMAL CONTROL
CATCH-R
HOW ABOUT THAT.
THREE-FOR-ONE DEAL.

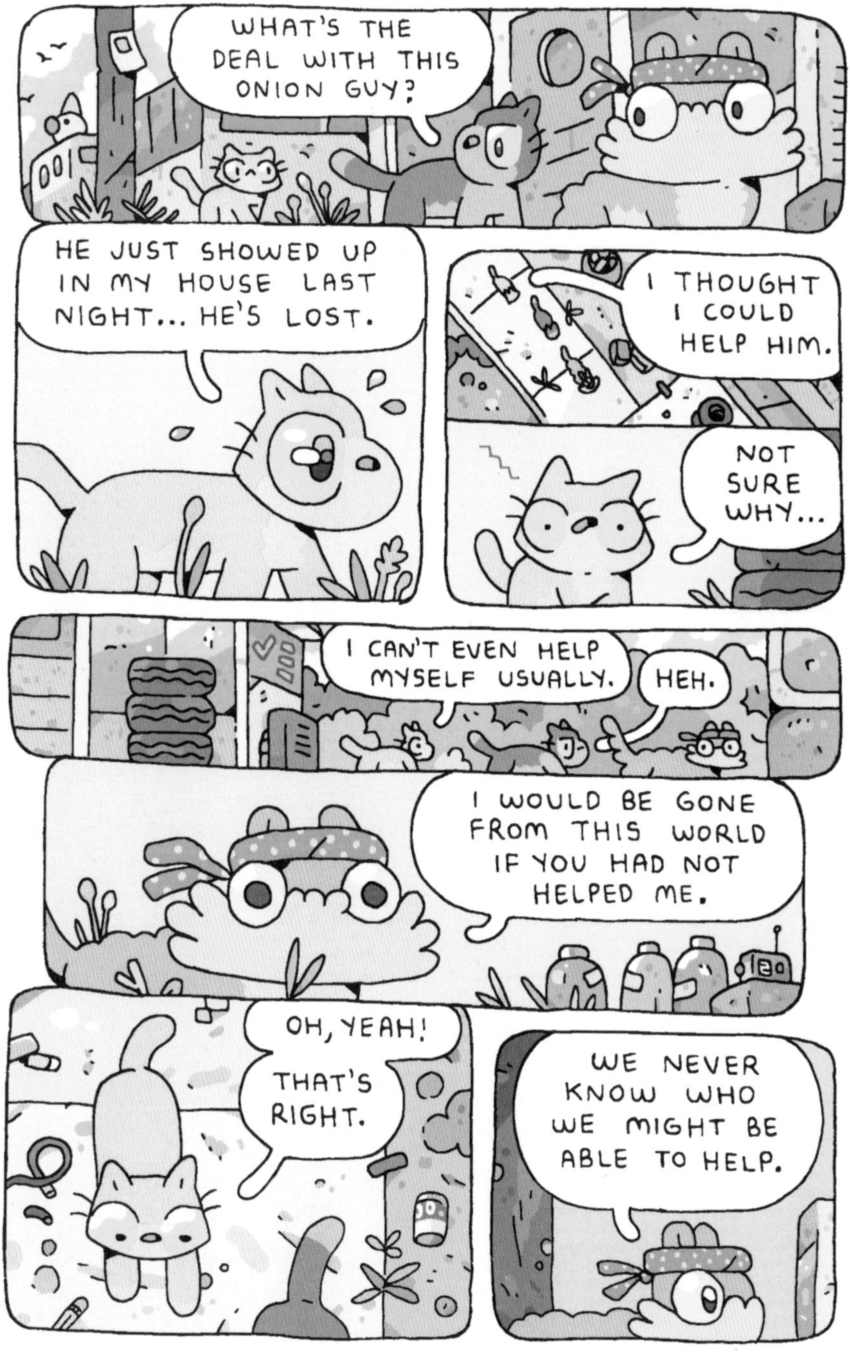
WHAT'S THE DEAL WITH THIS ONION GUY?
HE JUST SHOWED UP IN MY HOUSE LAST NIGHT... HE'S LOST.
I THOUGHT I COULD HELP HIM.
NOT SURE WHY...
I CAN'T EVEN HELP MYSELF USUALLY.
HEH.
I WOULD BE GONE FROM THIS WORLD IF YOU HAD NOT HELPED ME.
OH, YEAH!
THAT'S RIGHT.
WE NEVER KNOW WHO WE MIGHT BE ABLE TO HELP.

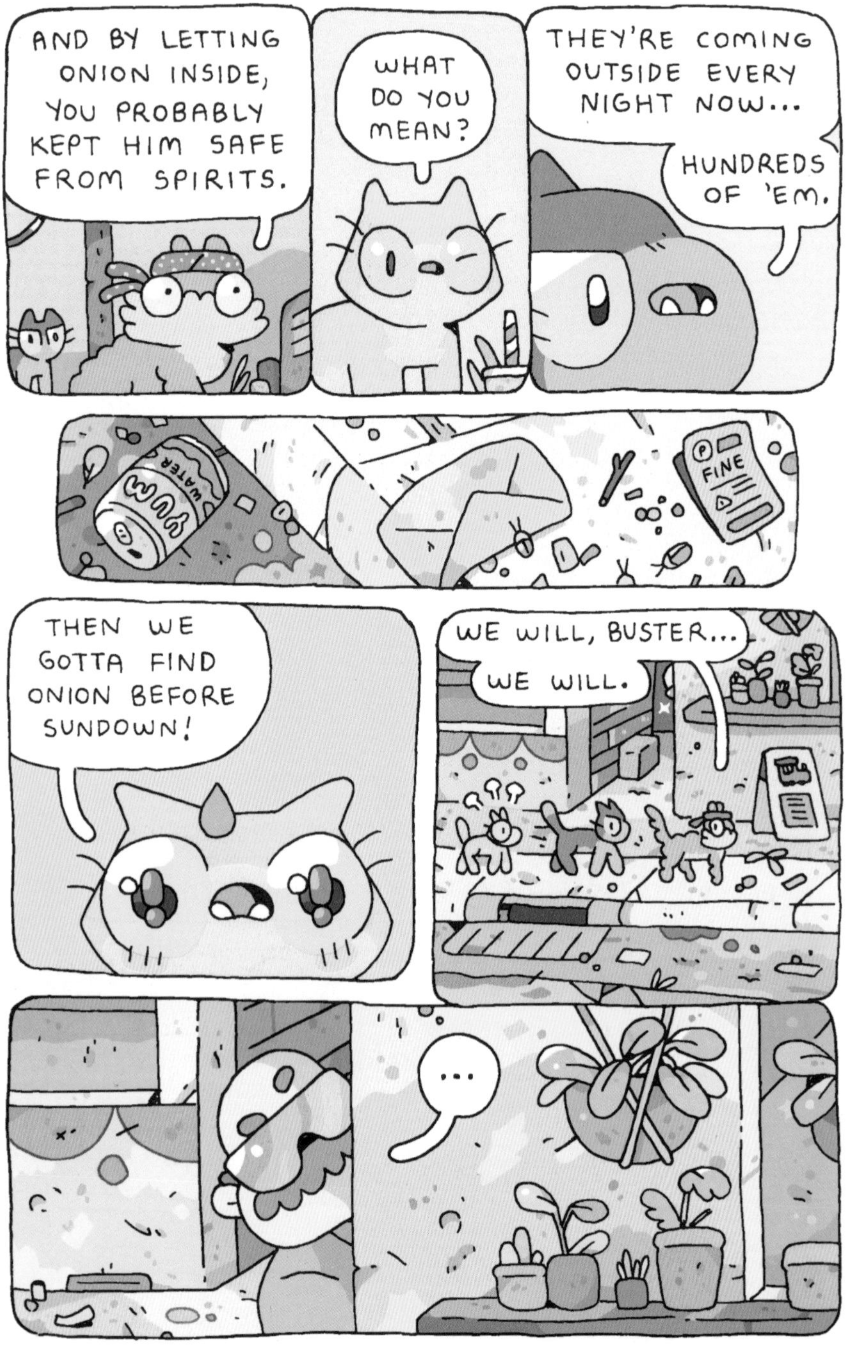
AND BY LETTING ONION INSIDE, YOU PROBABLY KEPT HIM SAFE FROM SPIRITS.
WHAT DO YOU MEAN?
THEY'RE COMING OUTSIDE EVERY NIGHT NOW...
HUNDREDS OF 'EM.
WATER
YUM
FINE
THEN WE GOTTA FIND ONION BEFORE SUNDOWN!
WE WILL, BUSTER...
WE WILL.
...

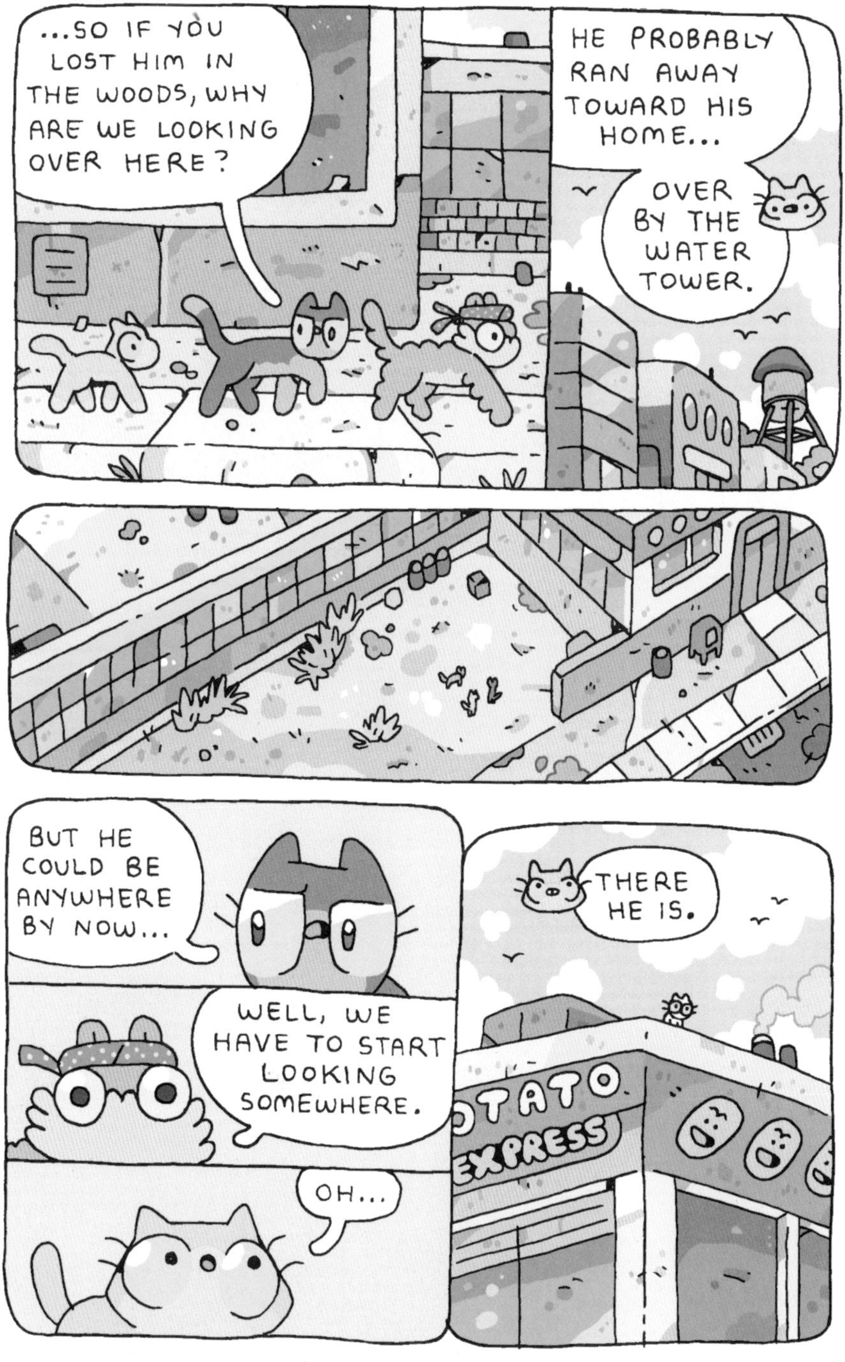
...SO IF YOU LOST HIM IN THE WOODS, WHY ARE WE LOOKING OVER HERE?
HE PROBABLY RAN AWAY TOWARD HIS HOME...
OVER BY THE WATER TOWER.
BUT HE COULD BE ANYWHERE BY NOW...
WELL, WE HAVE TO START LOOKING SOMEWHERE.
OH...
THERE HE IS.
OTATO
EXPRESS

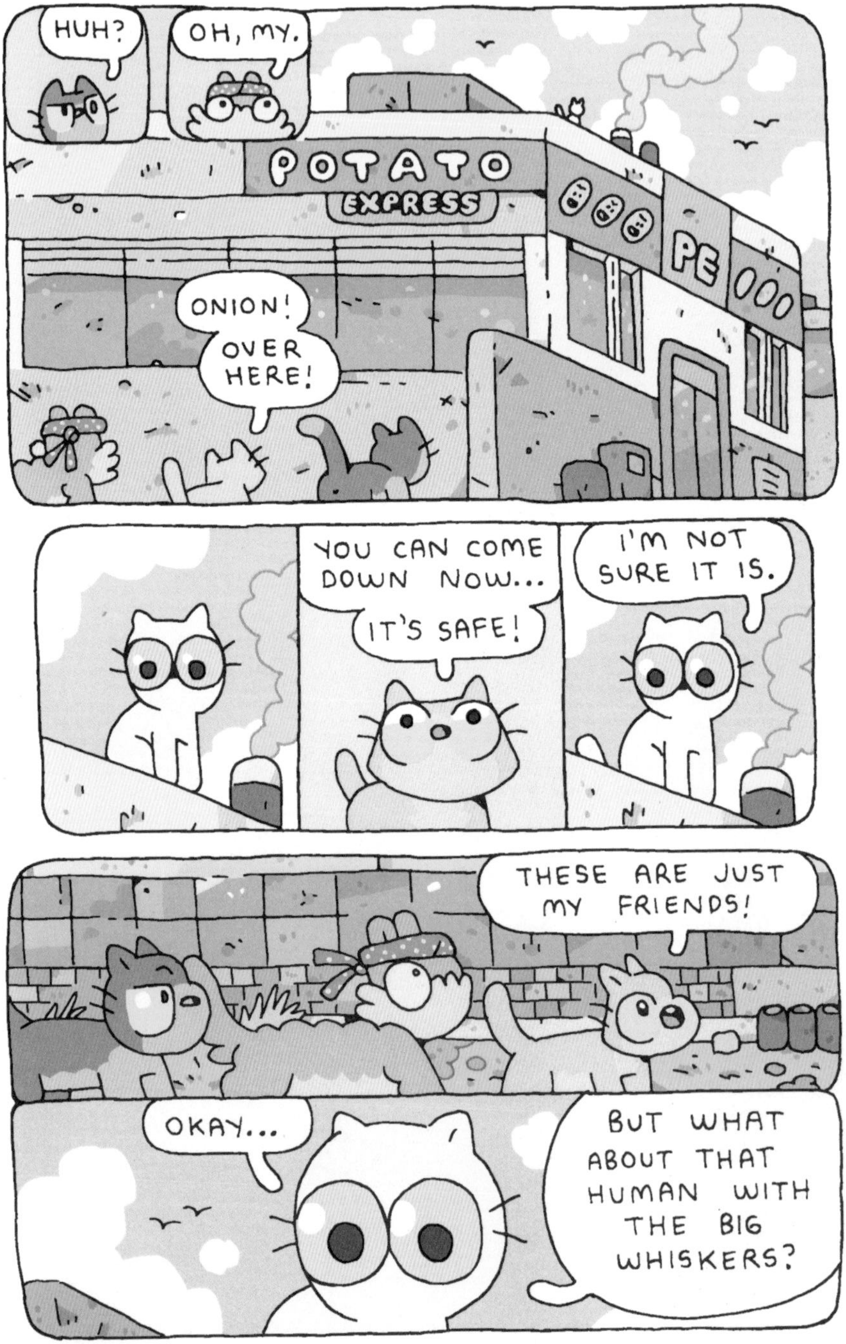
HUH?
OH, MY.
POTATO EXPRESS
PE
ONION! OVER HERE!
YOU CAN COME DOWN NOW...
IT'S SAFE!
I'M NOT SURE IT IS.
THESE ARE JUST MY FRIENDS!
OKAY...
BUT WHAT ABOUT THAT HUMAN WITH THE BIG WHISKERS?

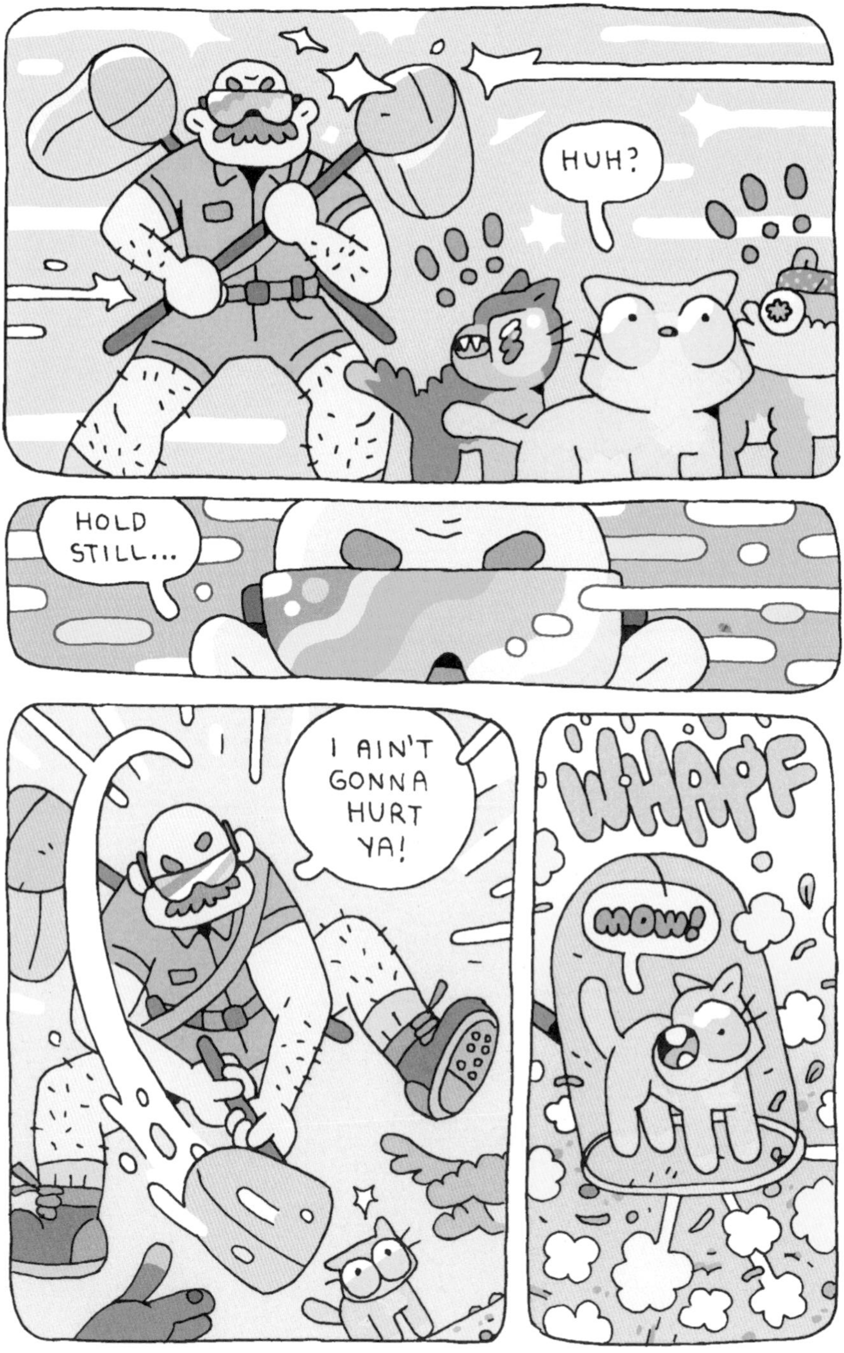
HUH?
HOLD STILL...
I AIN'T GONNA HURT YA!
WHAPF
MOW!

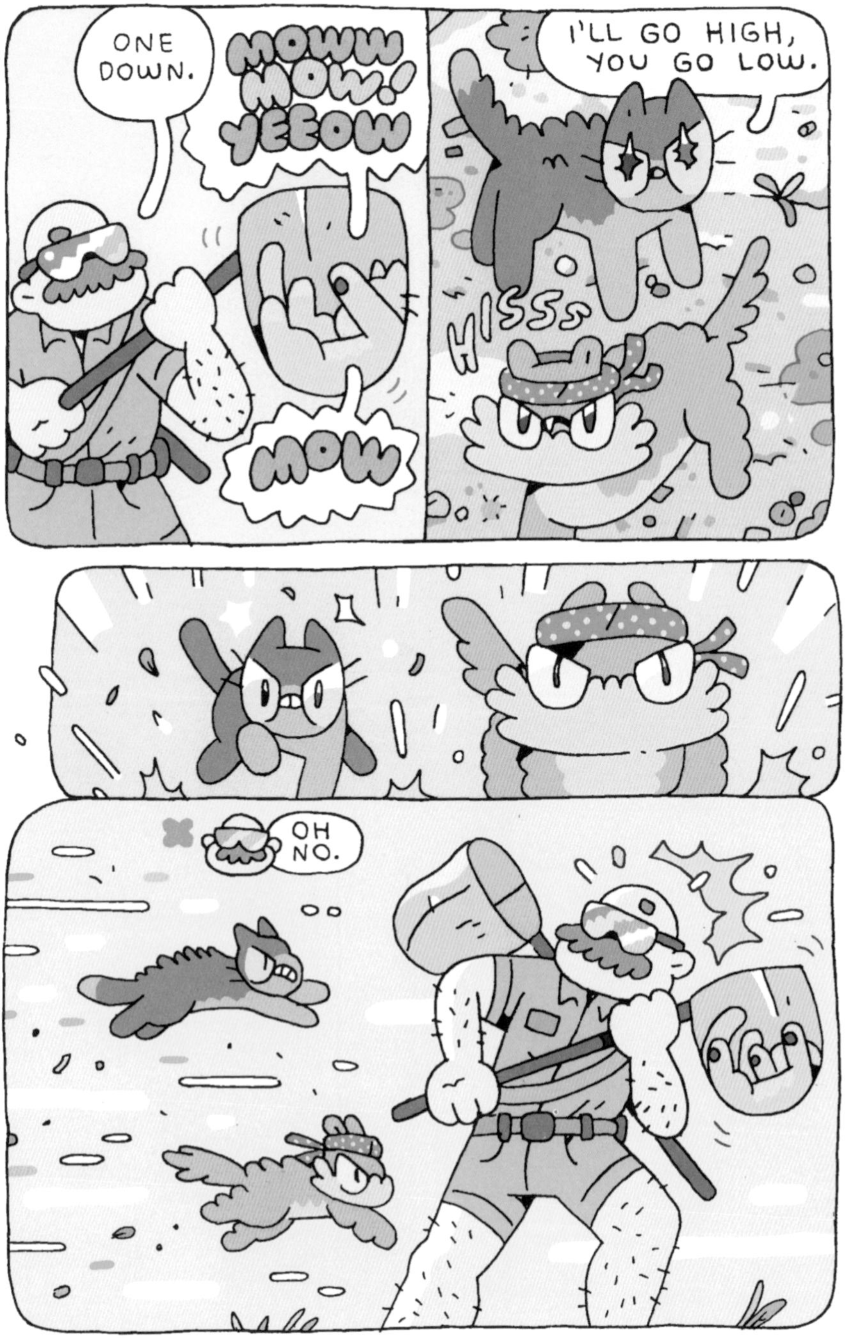

ONE DOWN.
MOWW MOW! YEEOW
MOW
I'LL GO HIGH, YOU GO LOW.
HISSS
OH NO.

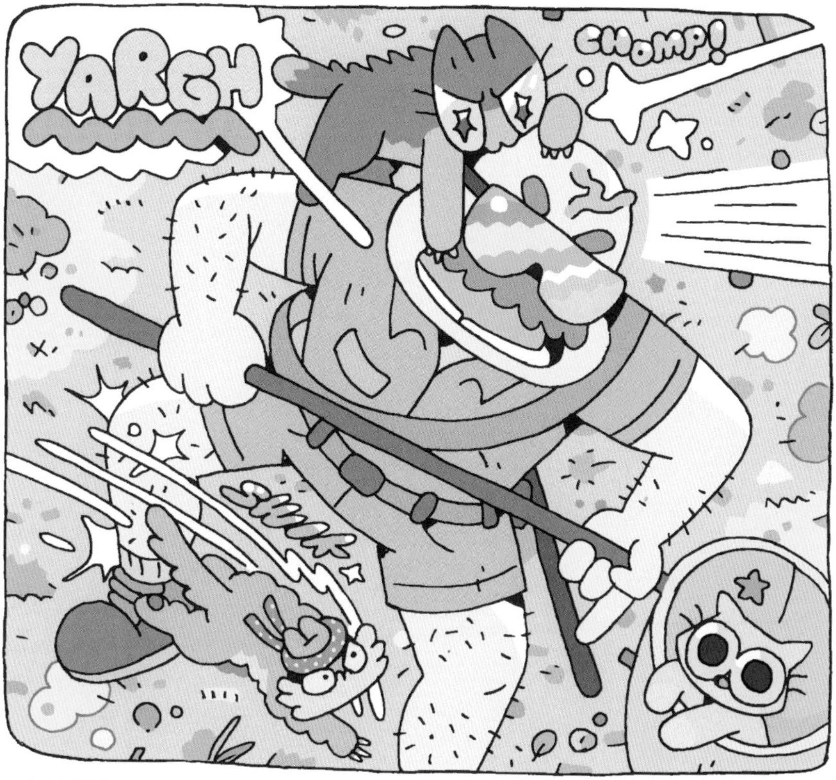
YARGH
CHOMP!
SWIK

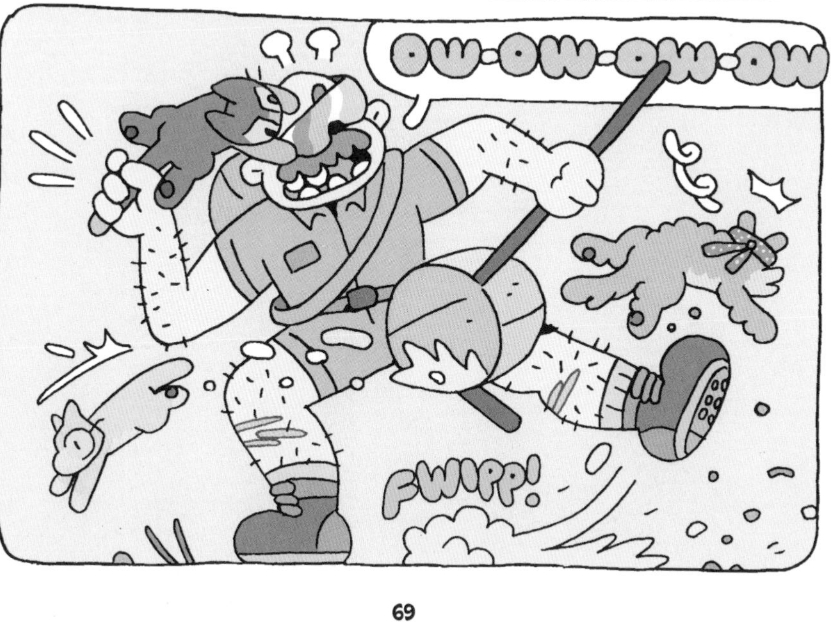
OW-OW-OW-OW
FWIPP!

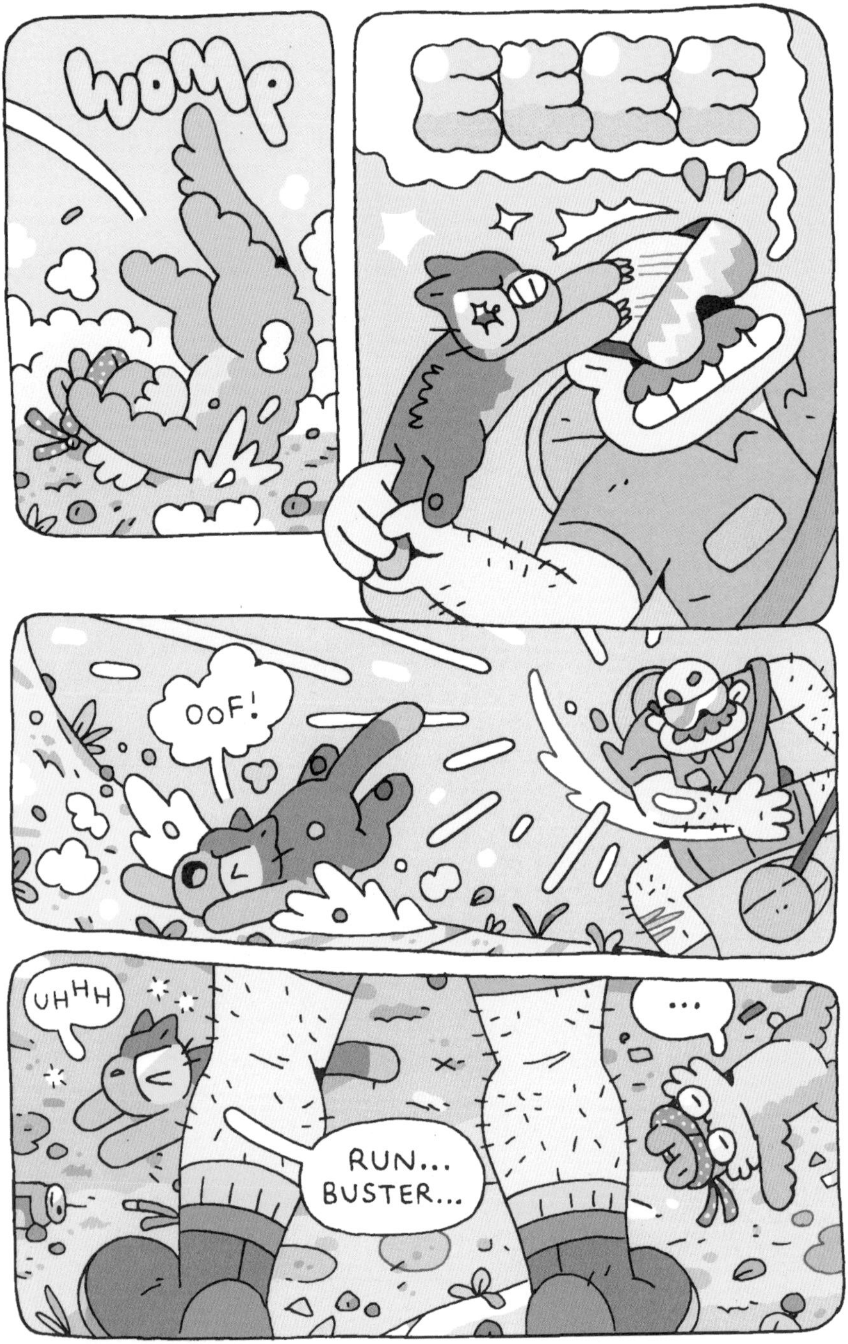
WOMP
EEEE
OOF!
UHHH
...
RUN... BUSTER...

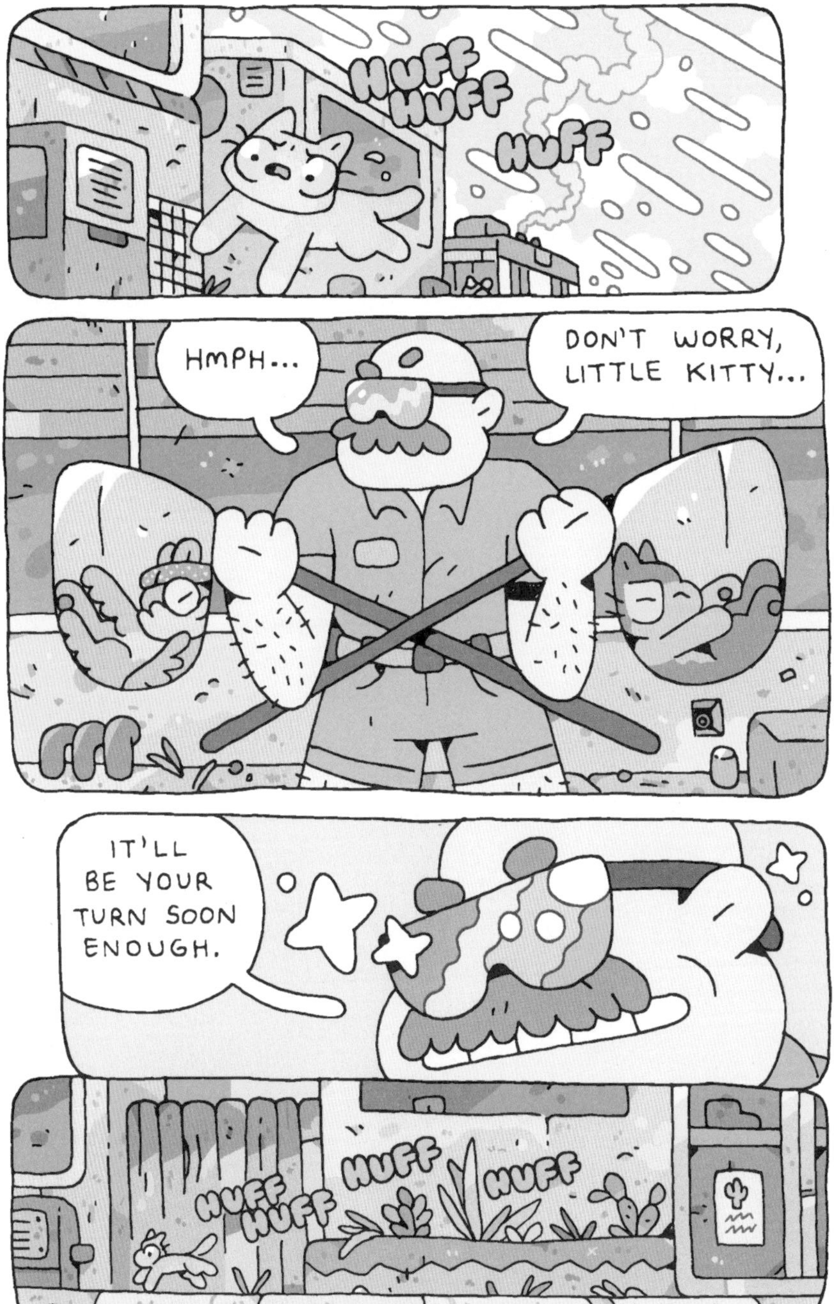
HUFF
HUFF
HUFF
HMPH...
DON'T WORRY, LITTLE KITTY...
IT'LL BE YOUR TURN SOON ENOUGH.
HUFF
HUFF
HUFF
HUFF

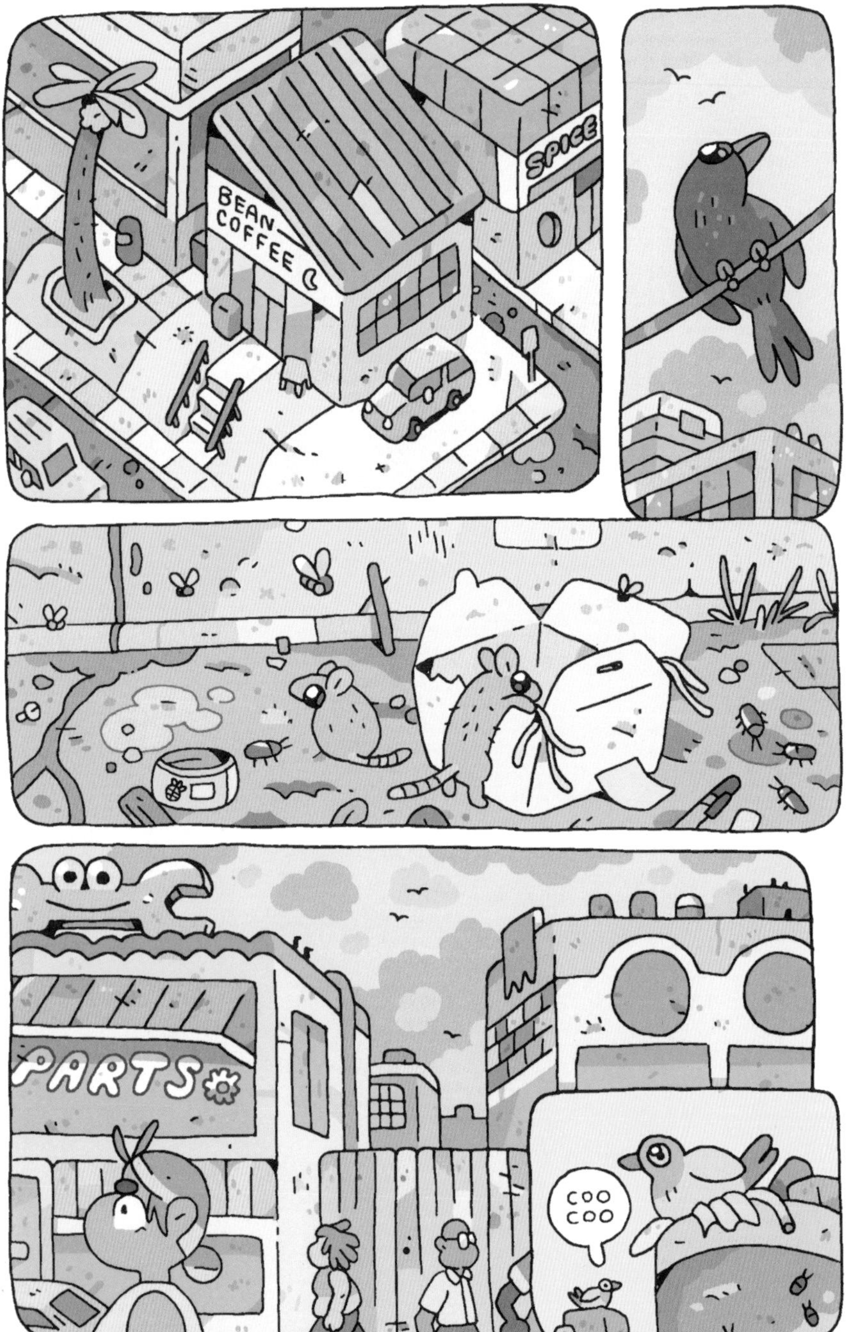
BEAN COFFEE
SPICE
PARTS
COO COO

CHAPTER 4

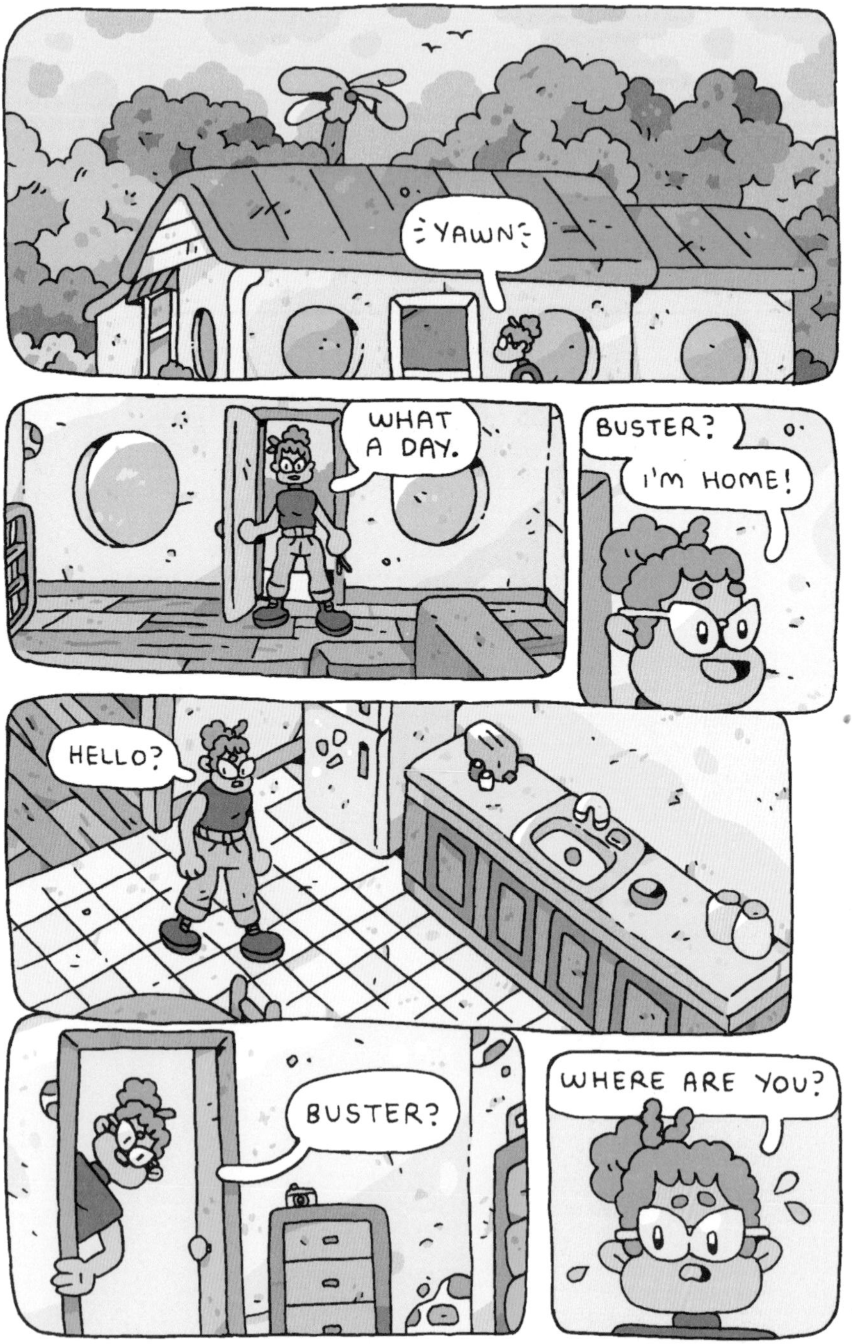
YAWN
WHAT A DAY.
BUSTER?
I'M HOME!
HELLO?
BUSTER?
WHERE ARE YOU?

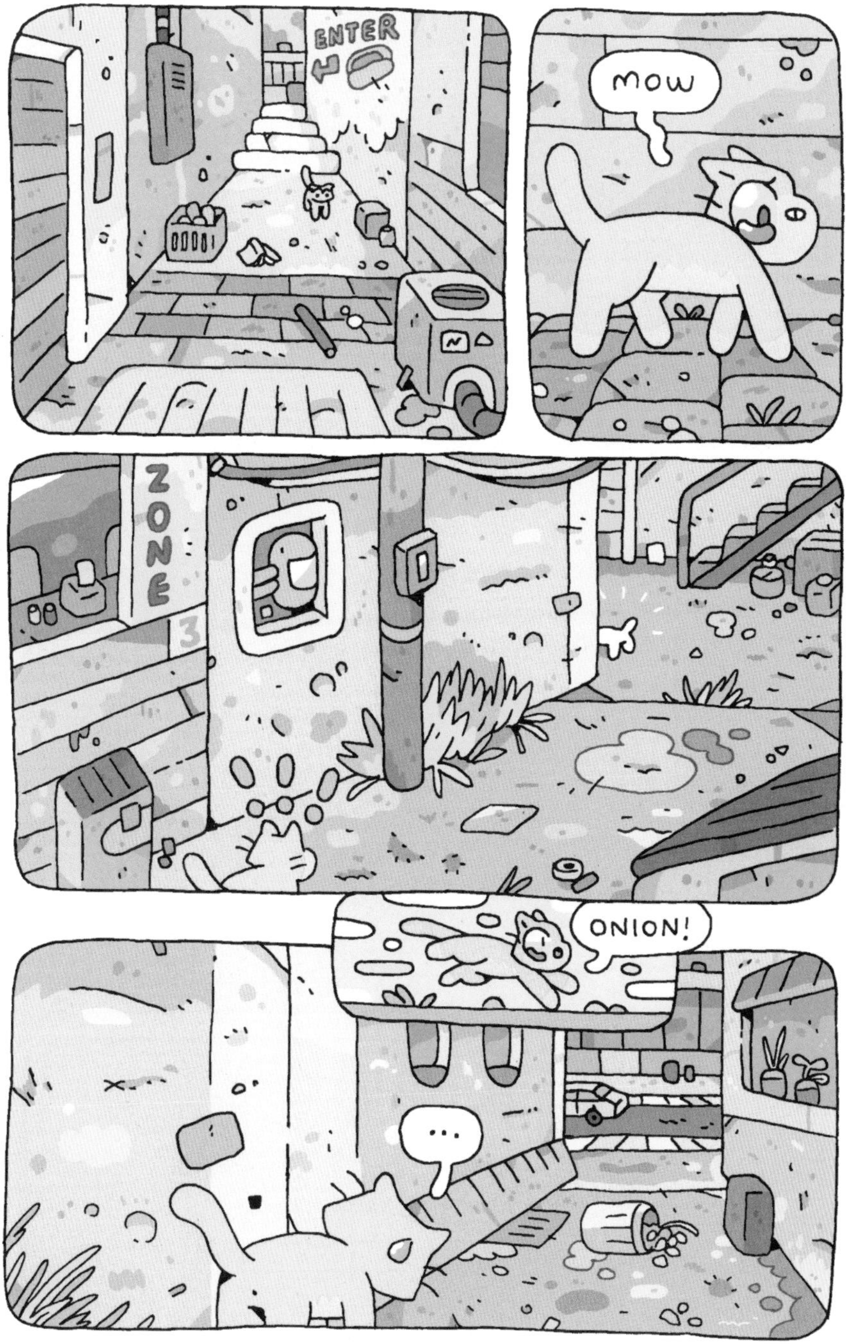
ENTER
MOW
ZONE
3
ONION!
...

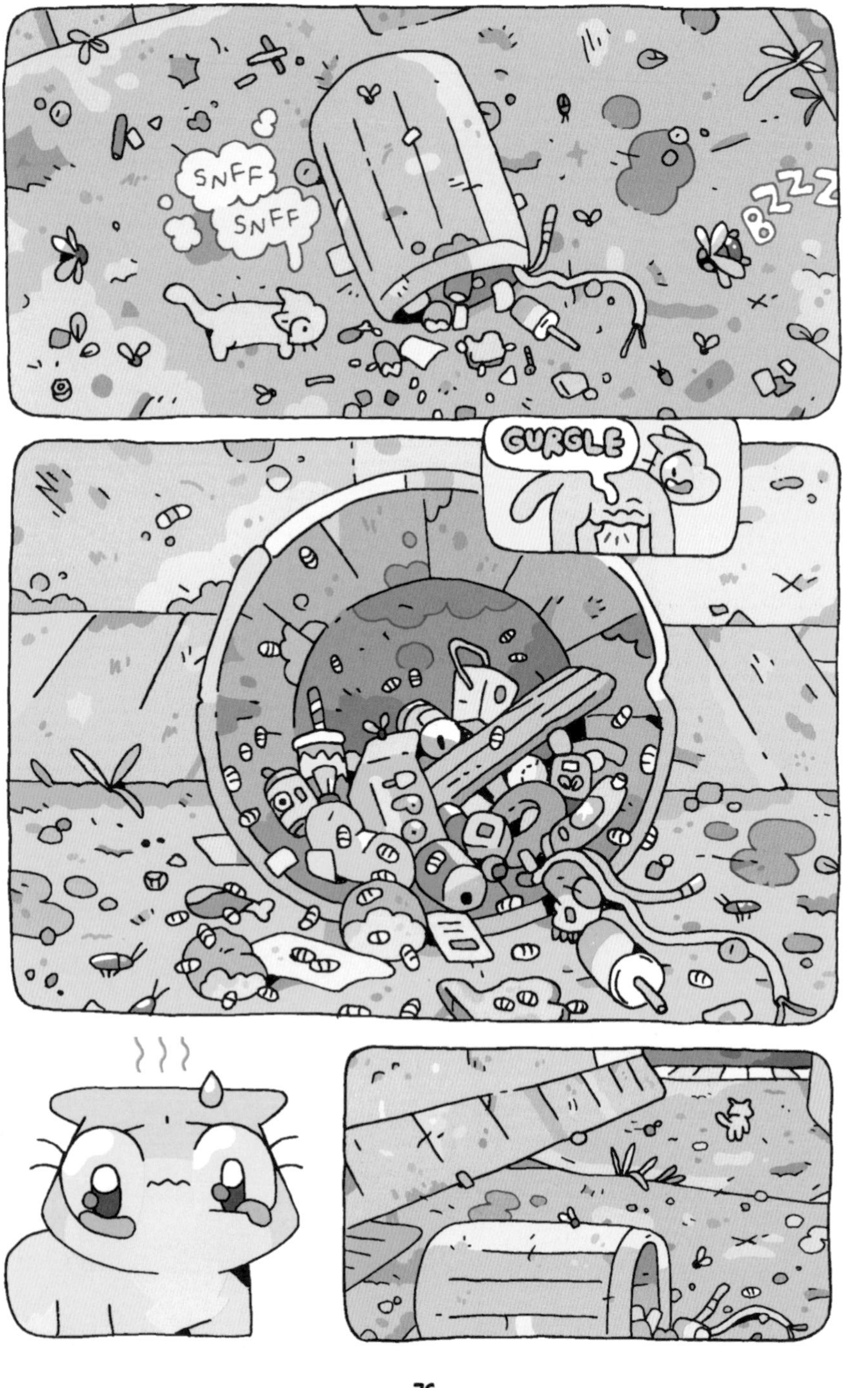
SNFF
SNFF
BZZZ
GURGLE

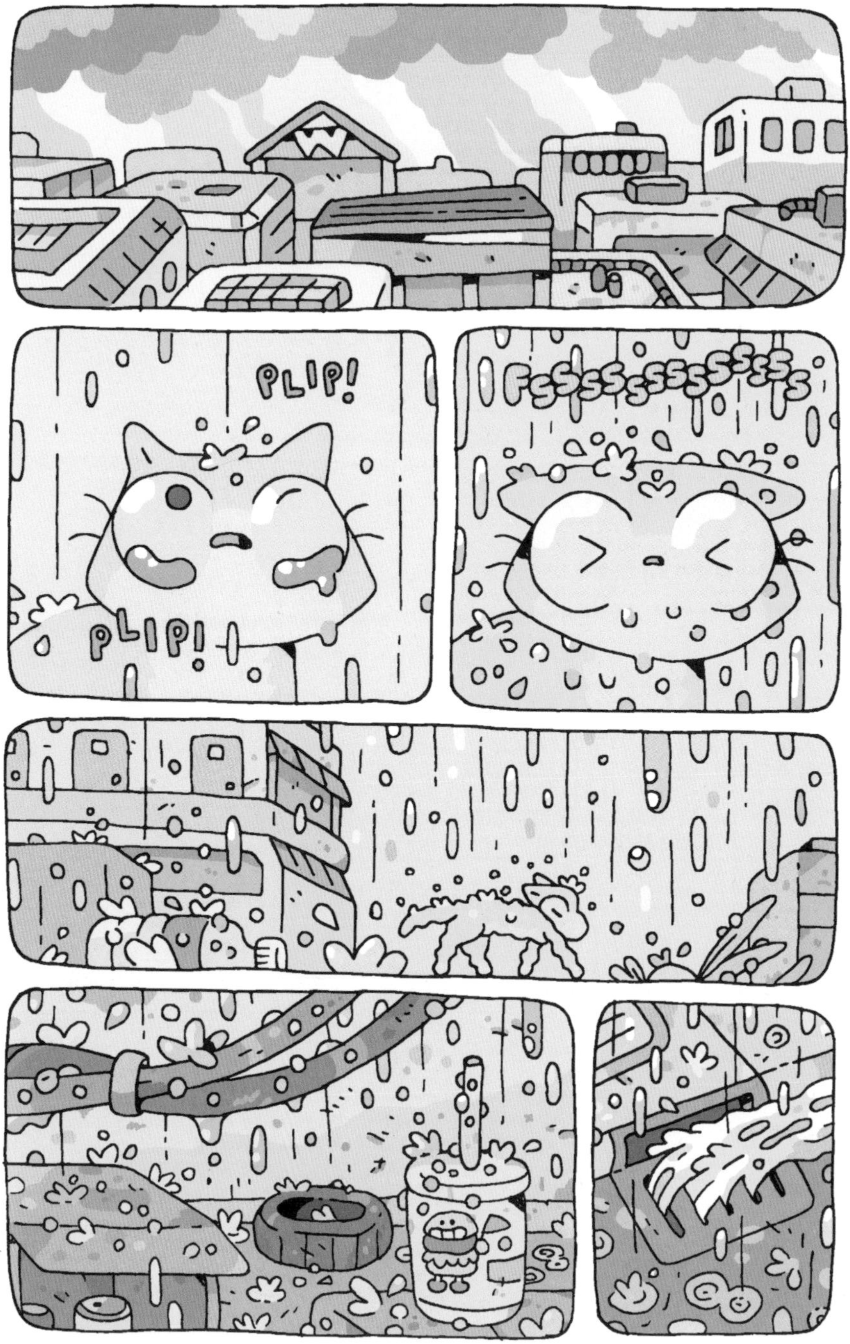
PLIP!
PLIP!
FSSSSSSSSSSSSS

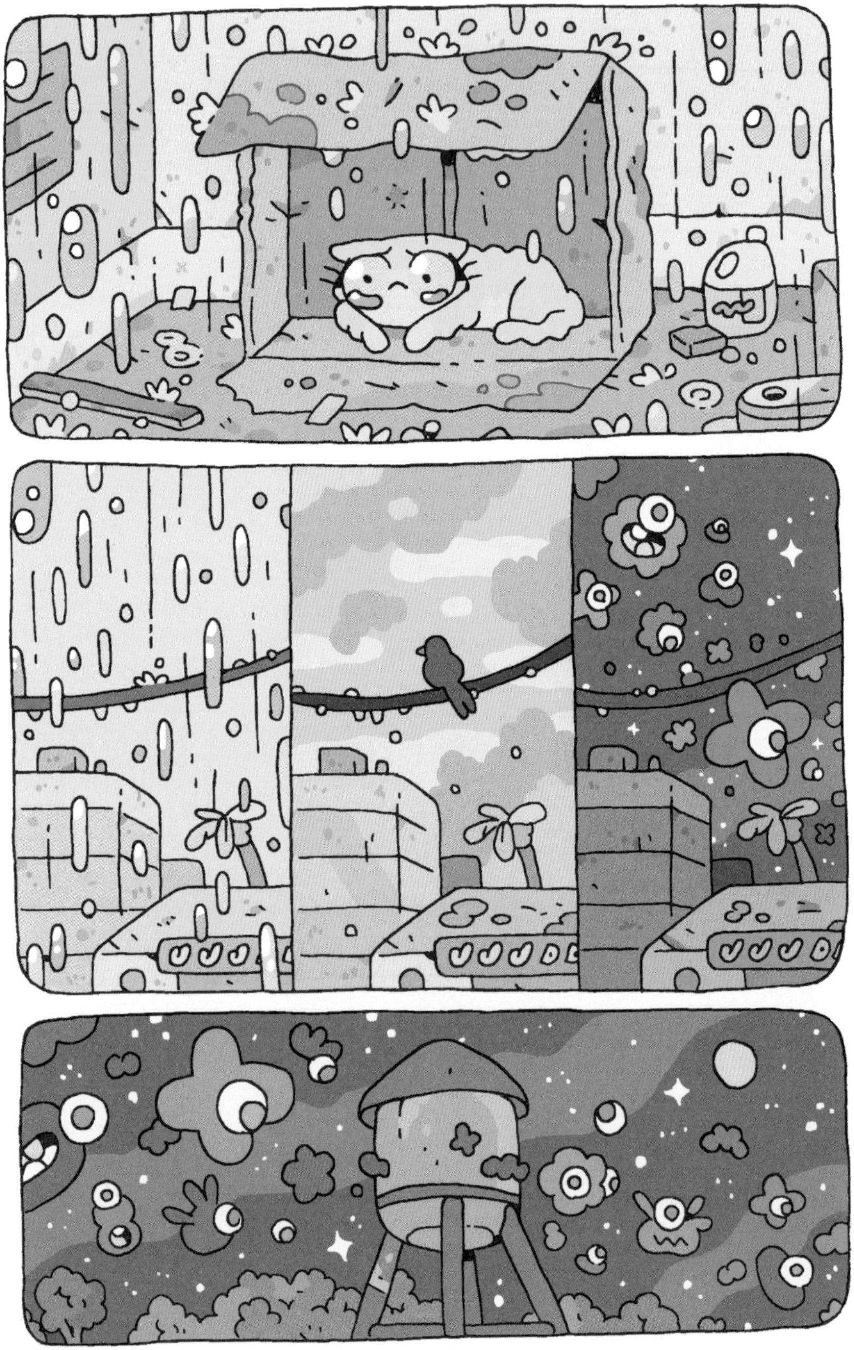

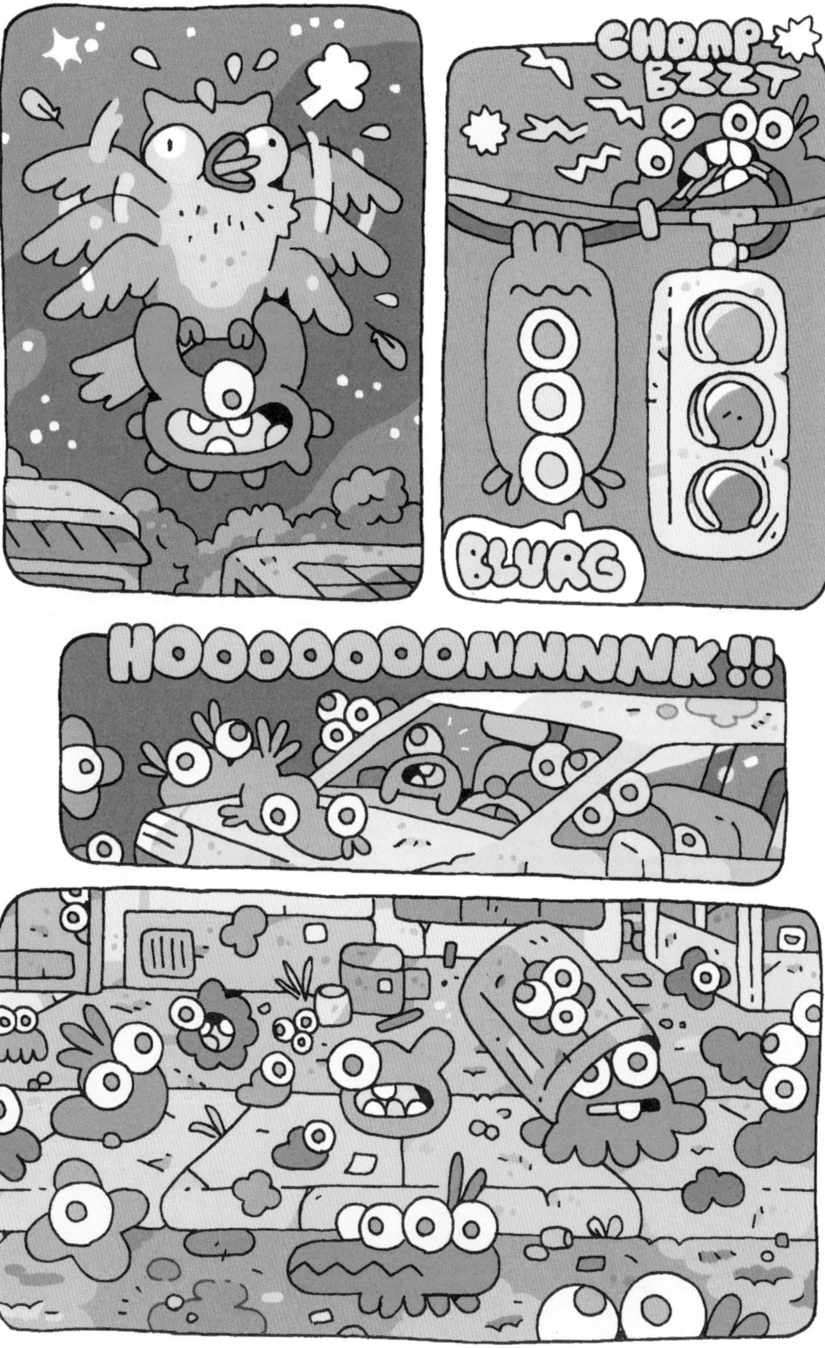
CHOMP
BZZT
BLURG
HOOOOOOONNNNNK!!

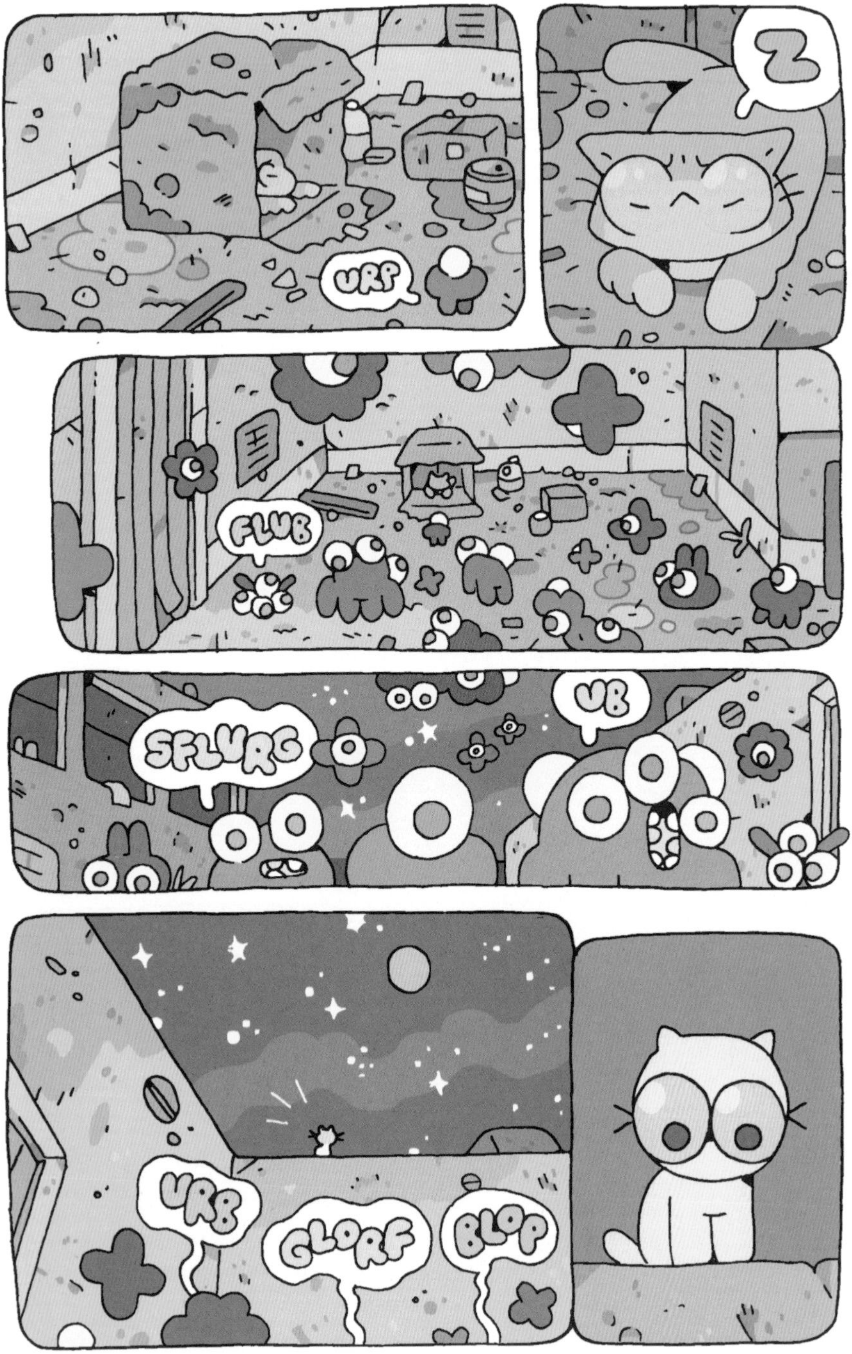
URP
Z
FLUB
SFLURG
UB
URB
GLORF
BLOP

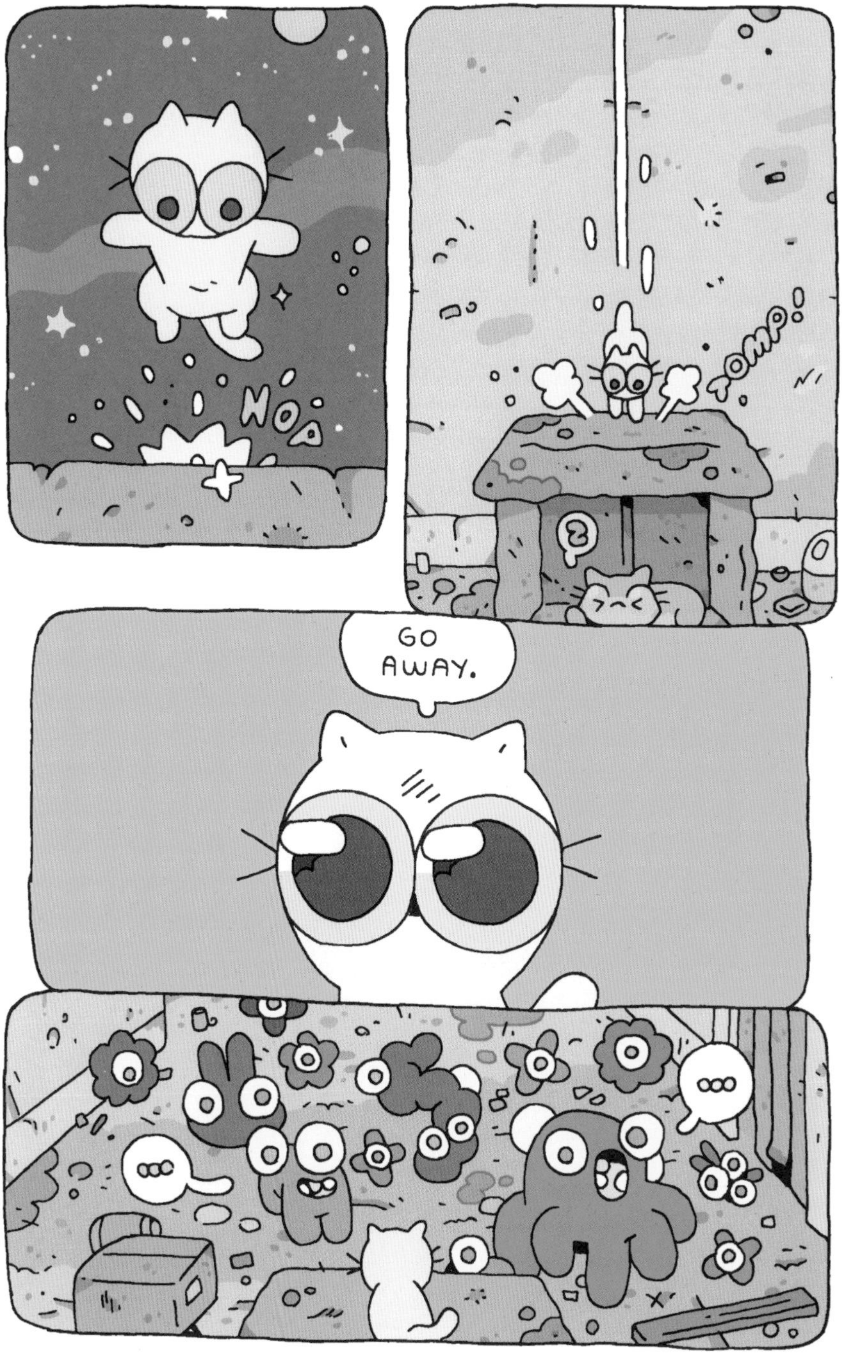
HOP
TOMP!
GO AWAY.

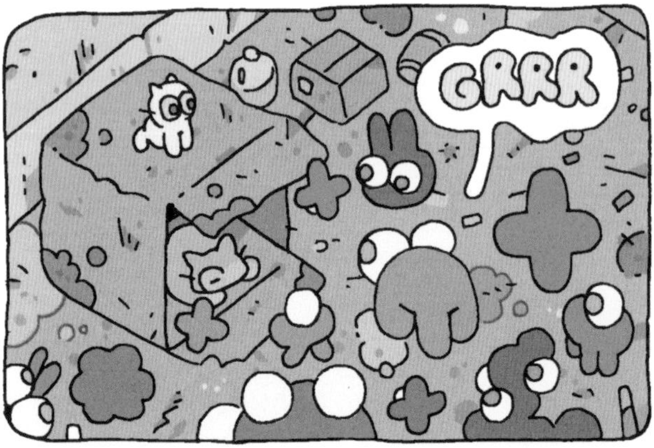
GRRR
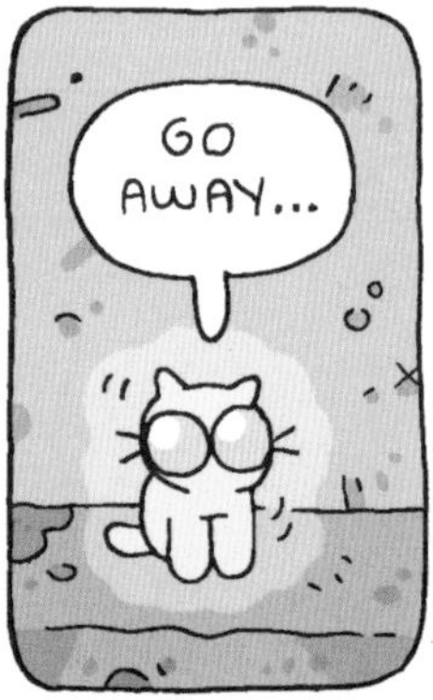
GO AWAY...
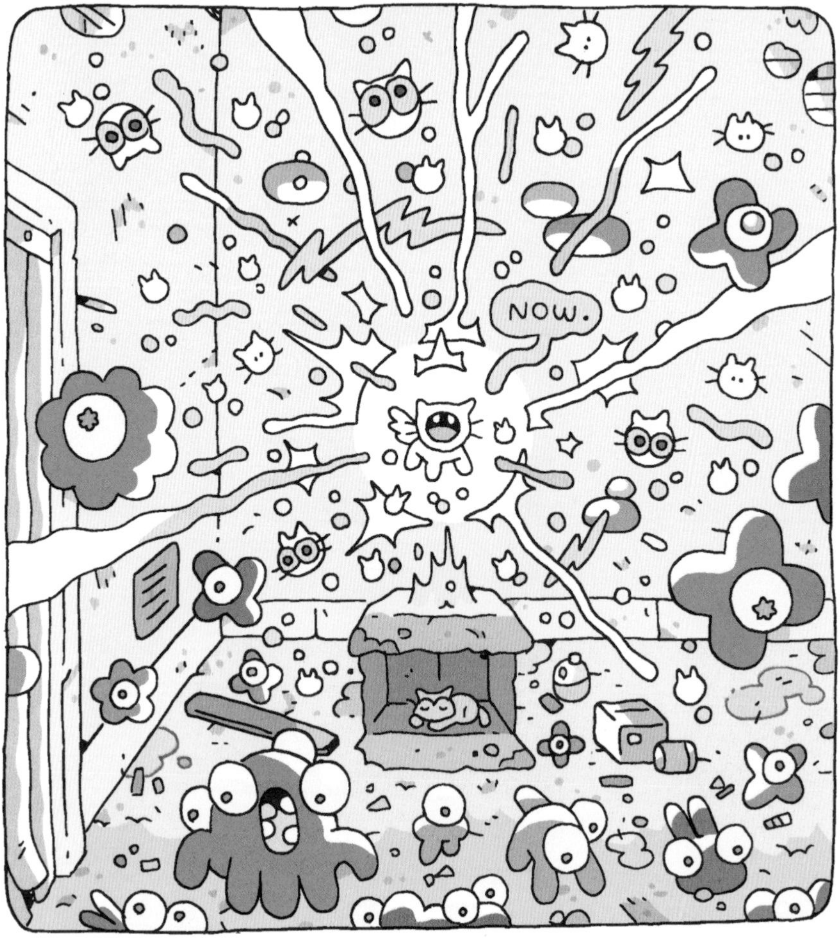
NOW.

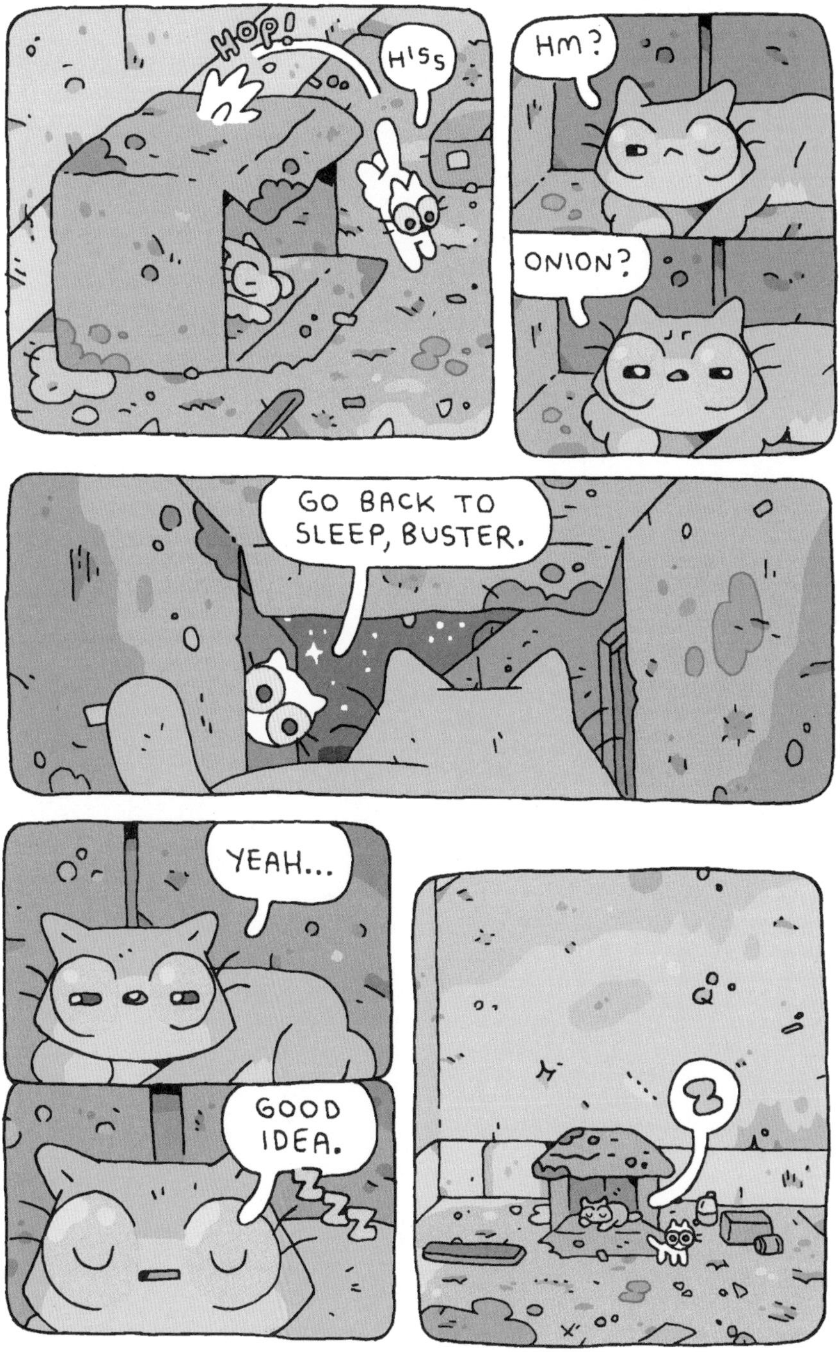
HOP!
HISS
HM?
ONION?
GO BACK TO SLEEP, BUSTER.
YEAH...
GOOD IDEA.
ZZZ

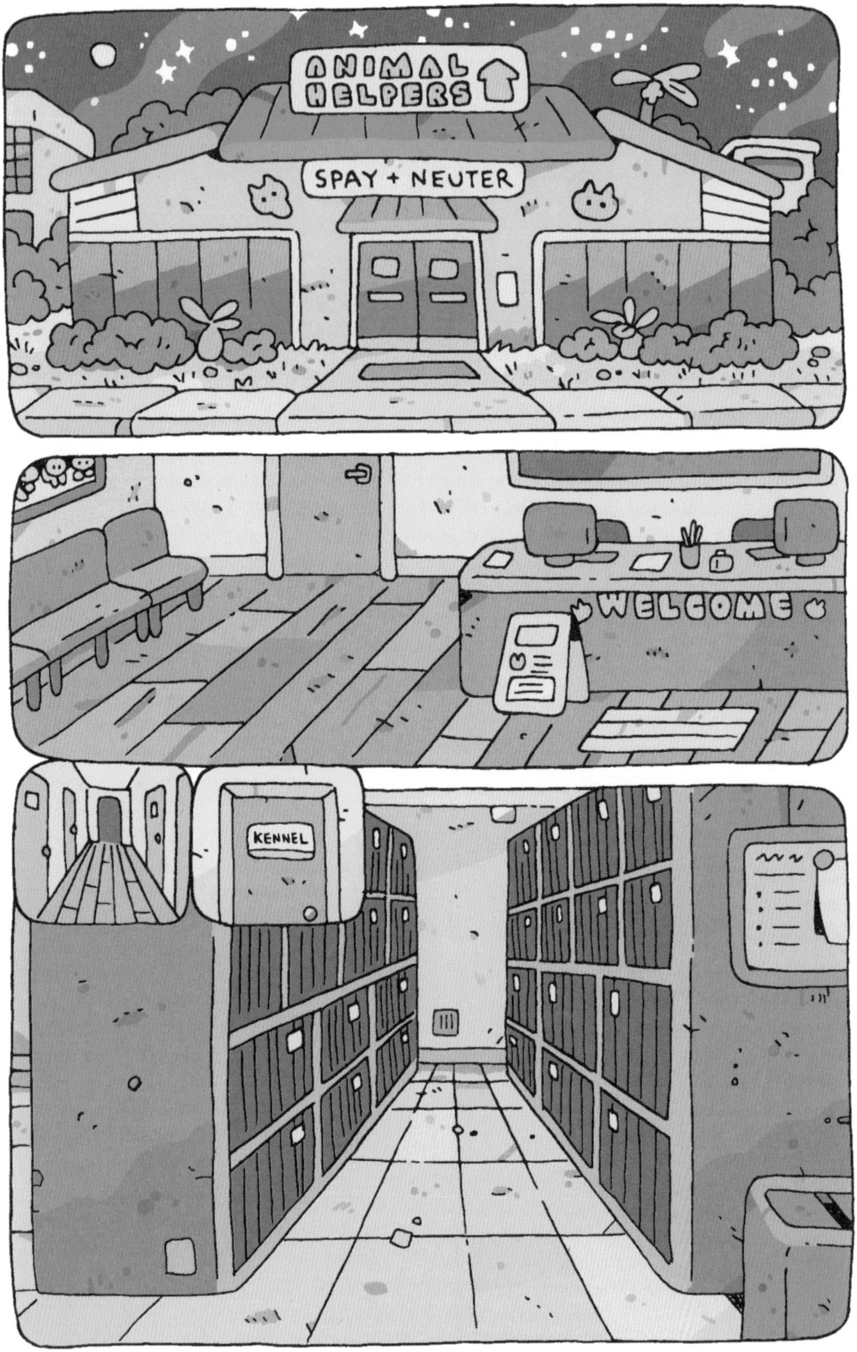
ANIMAL HELPERS
SPAY + NEUTER
WELCOME
KENNEL

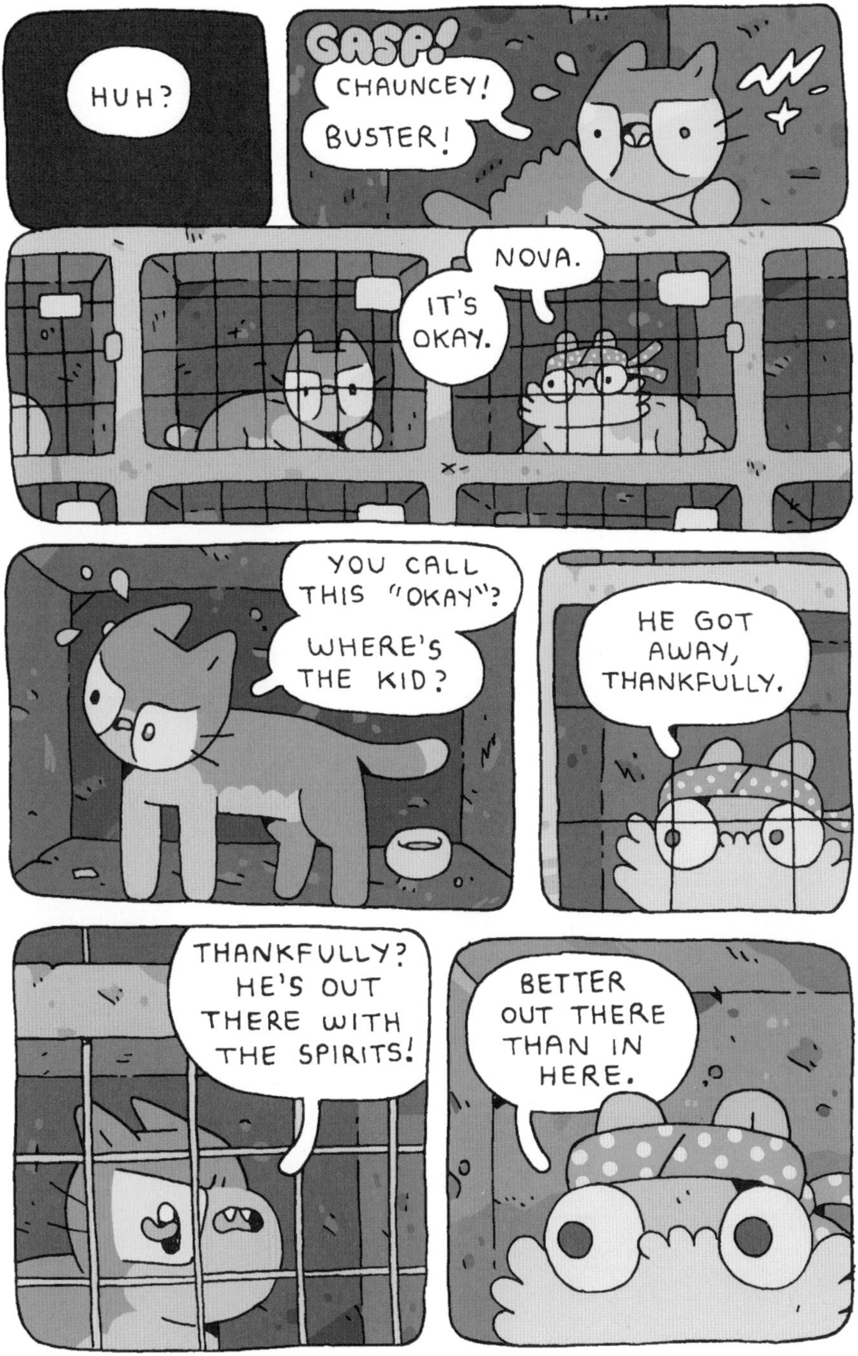
HUH?
GASP!
CHAUNCEY!
BUSTER!
NOVA.
IT'S OKAY.
YOU CALL THIS "OKAY"?
WHERE'S THE KID?
HE GOT AWAY, THANKFULLY.
THANKFULLY? HE'S OUT THERE WITH THE SPIRITS!
BETTER OUT THERE THAN IN HERE.

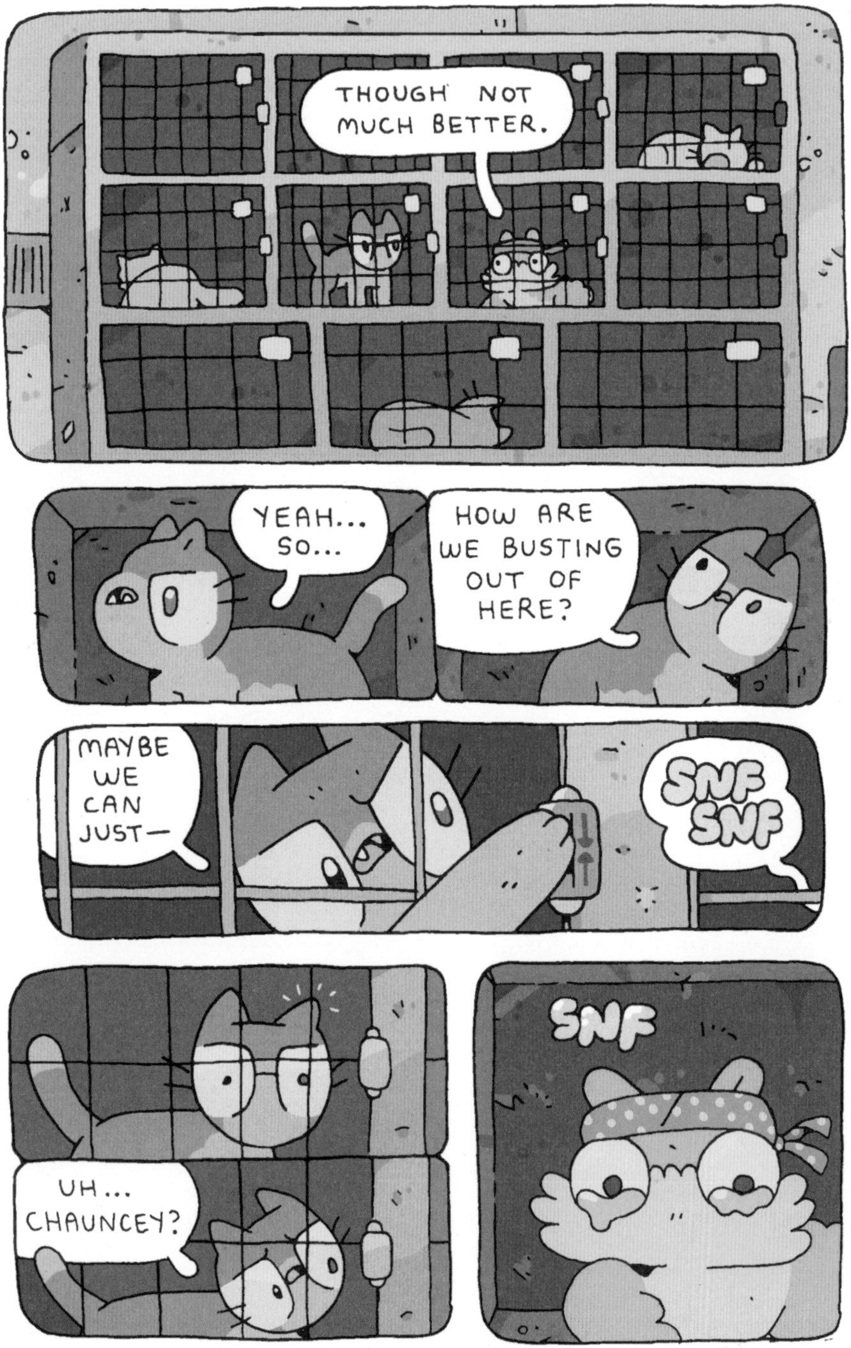
THOUGH NOT MUCH BETTER.
YEAH... SO...
HOW ARE WE BUSTING OUT OF HERE?
MAYBE WE CAN JUST—
SNF SNF
UH... CHAUNCEY?
SNF

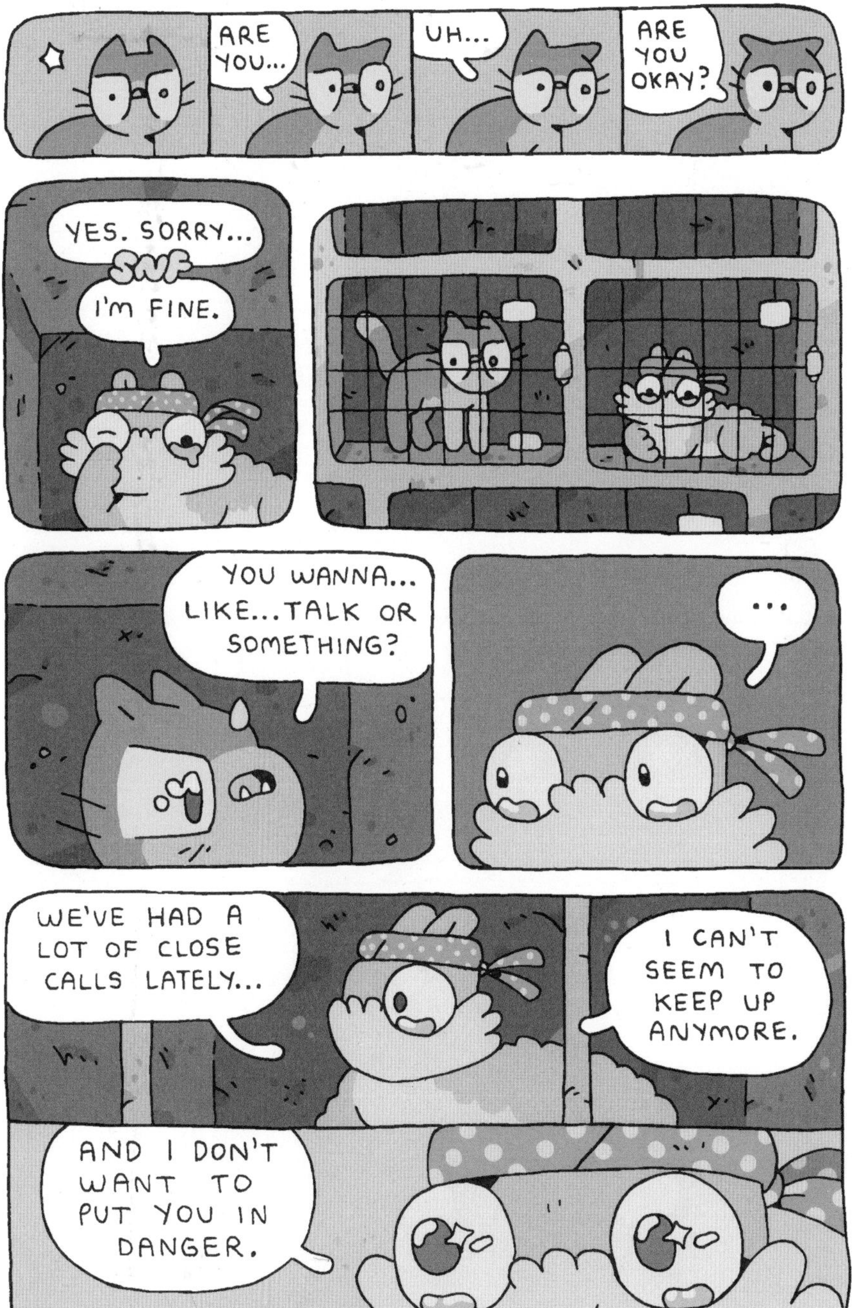
ARE YOU...
UH...
ARE YOU OKAY?
YES. SORRY...
SNF
I'M FINE.
YOU WANNA... LIKE...TALK OR SOMETHING?
...
WE'VE HAD A LOT OF CLOSE CALLS LATELY...
I CAN'T SEEM TO KEEP UP ANYMORE.
AND I DON'T WANT TO PUT YOU IN DANGER.

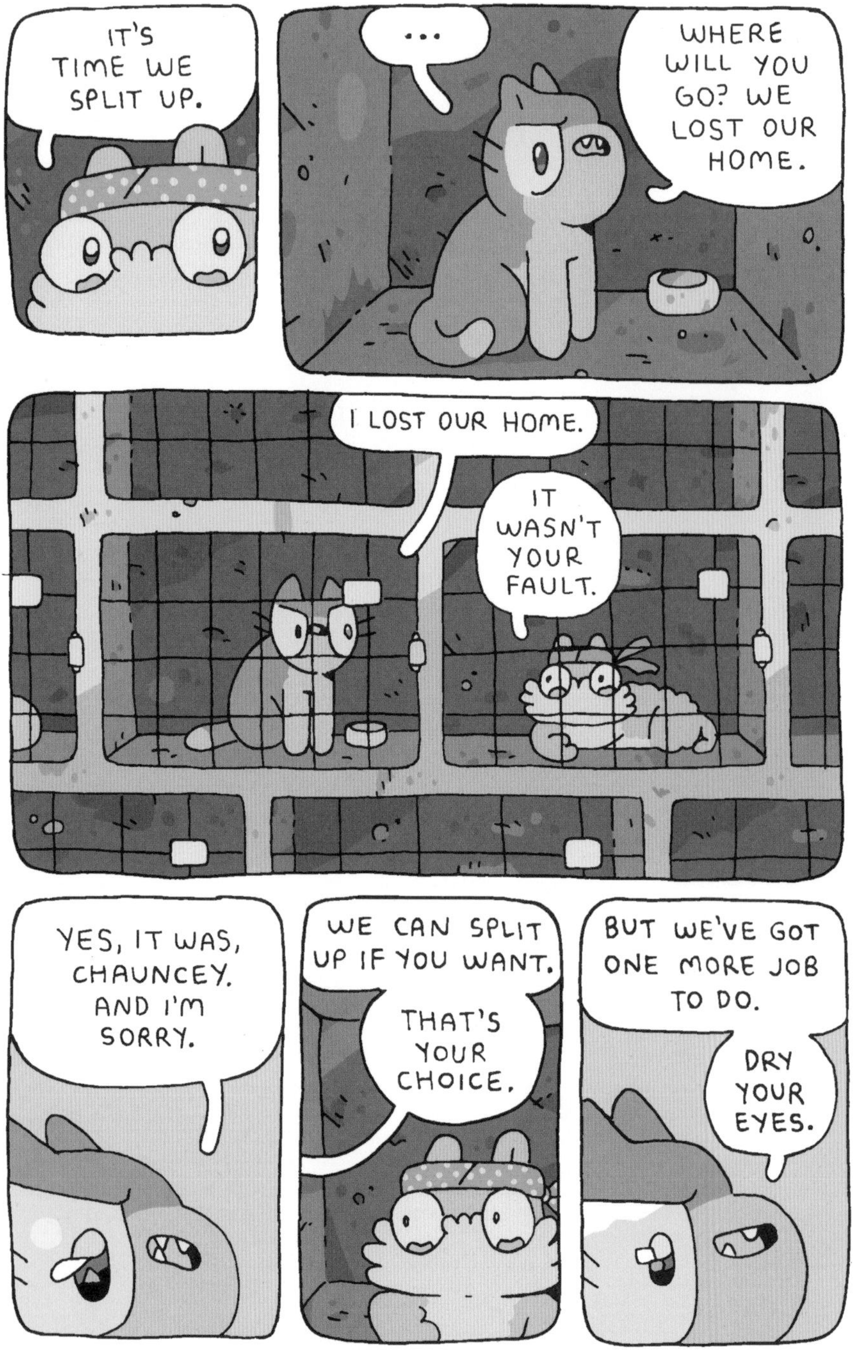
IT'S TIME WE SPLIT UP.
...
WHERE WILL YOU GO? WE LOST OUR HOME.
I LOST OUR HOME.
IT WASN'T YOUR FAULT.
YES, IT WAS, CHAUNCEY. AND I'M SORRY.
WE CAN SPLIT UP IF YOU WANT.
THAT'S YOUR CHOICE.
BUT WE'VE GOT ONE MORE JOB TO DO.
DRY YOUR EYES.

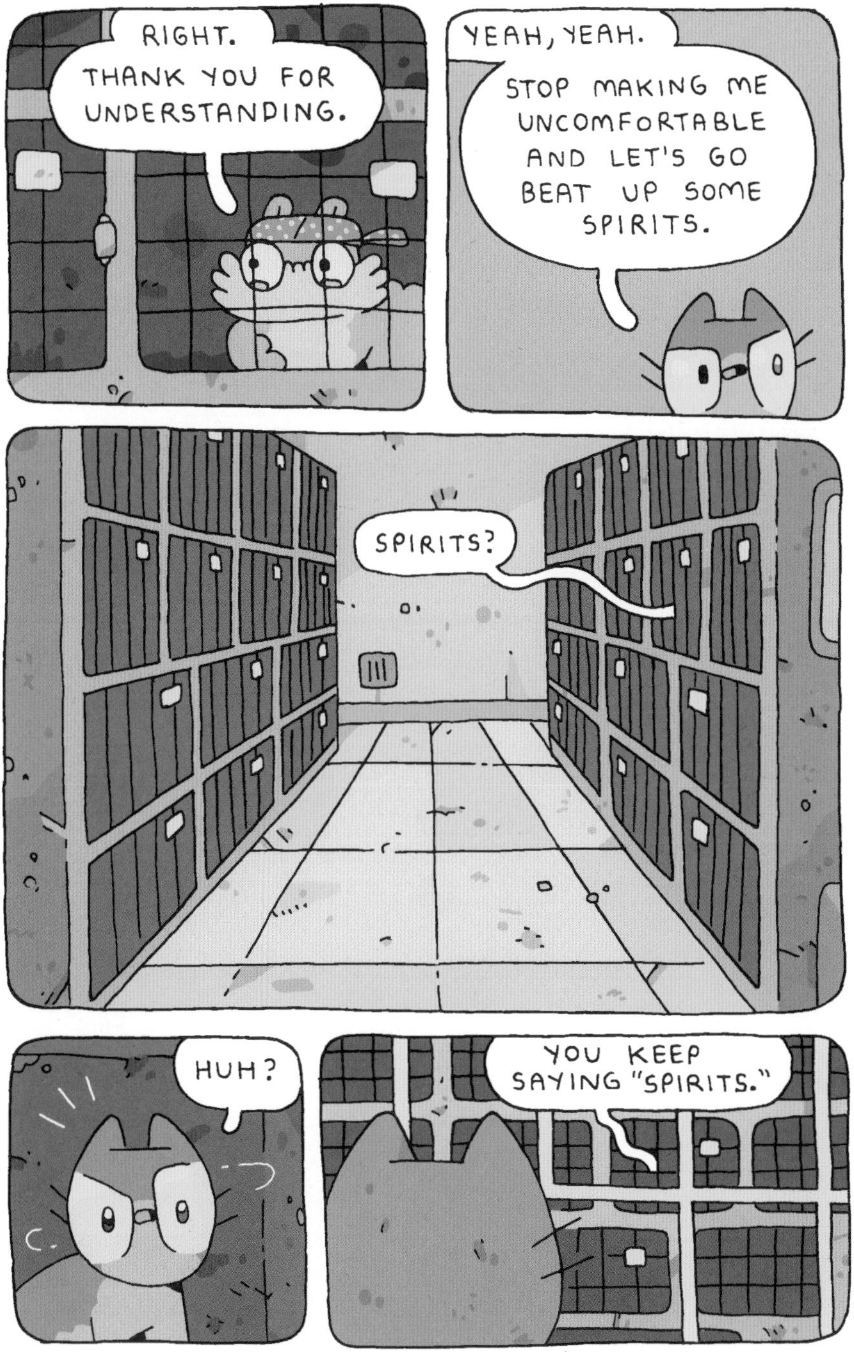
RIGHT.
THANK YOU FOR UNDERSTANDING.
YEAH, YEAH.
STOP MAKING ME UNCOMFORTABLE AND LET'S GO BEAT UP SOME SPIRITS.
SPIRITS?
HUH?
YOU KEEP SAYING "SPIRITS."

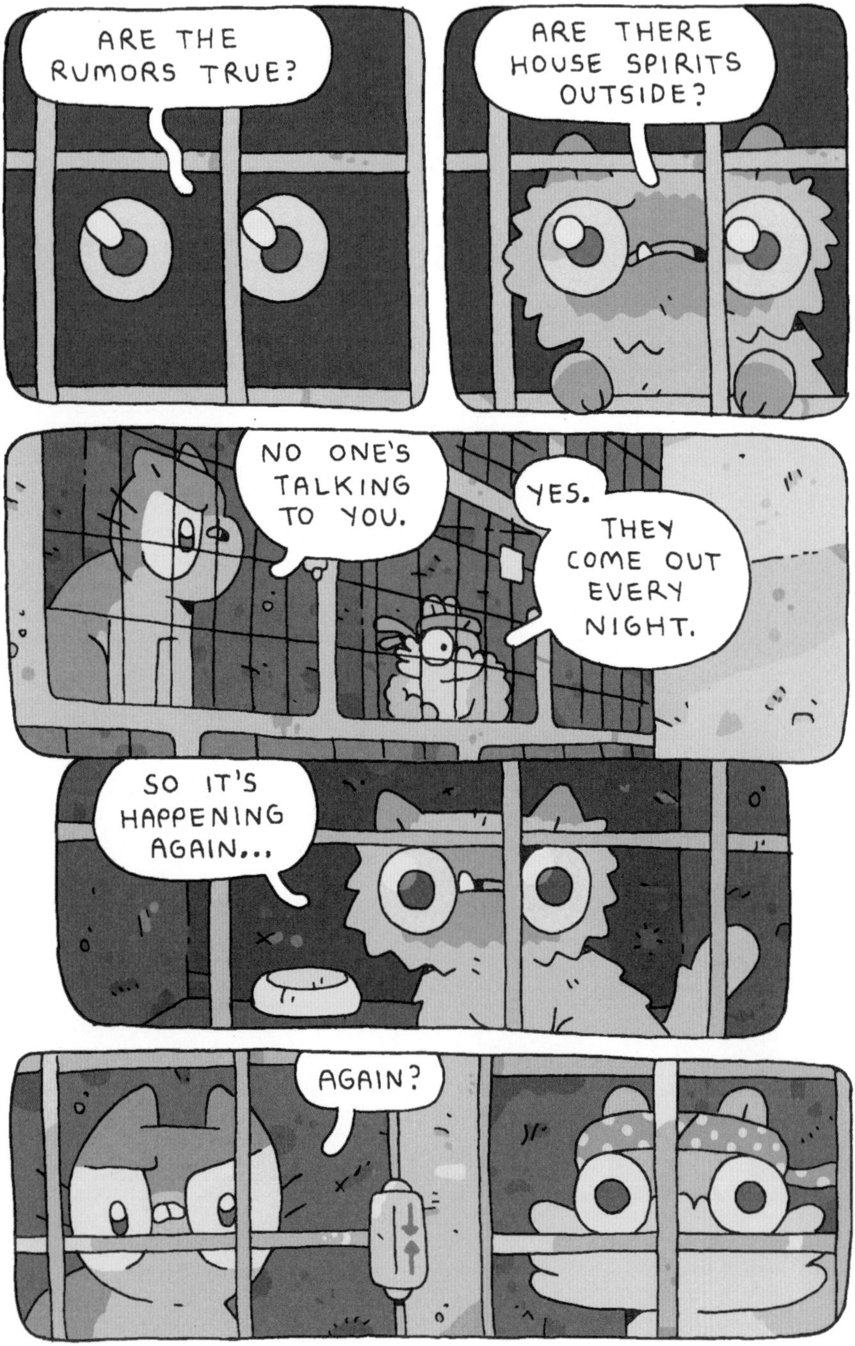
ARE THE RUMORS TRUE?
ARE THERE HOUSE SPIRITS OUTSIDE?
NO ONE'S TALKING TO YOU.
YES.
THEY COME OUT EVERY NIGHT.
SO IT'S HAPPENING AGAIN...
AGAIN?

CHAPTER 5

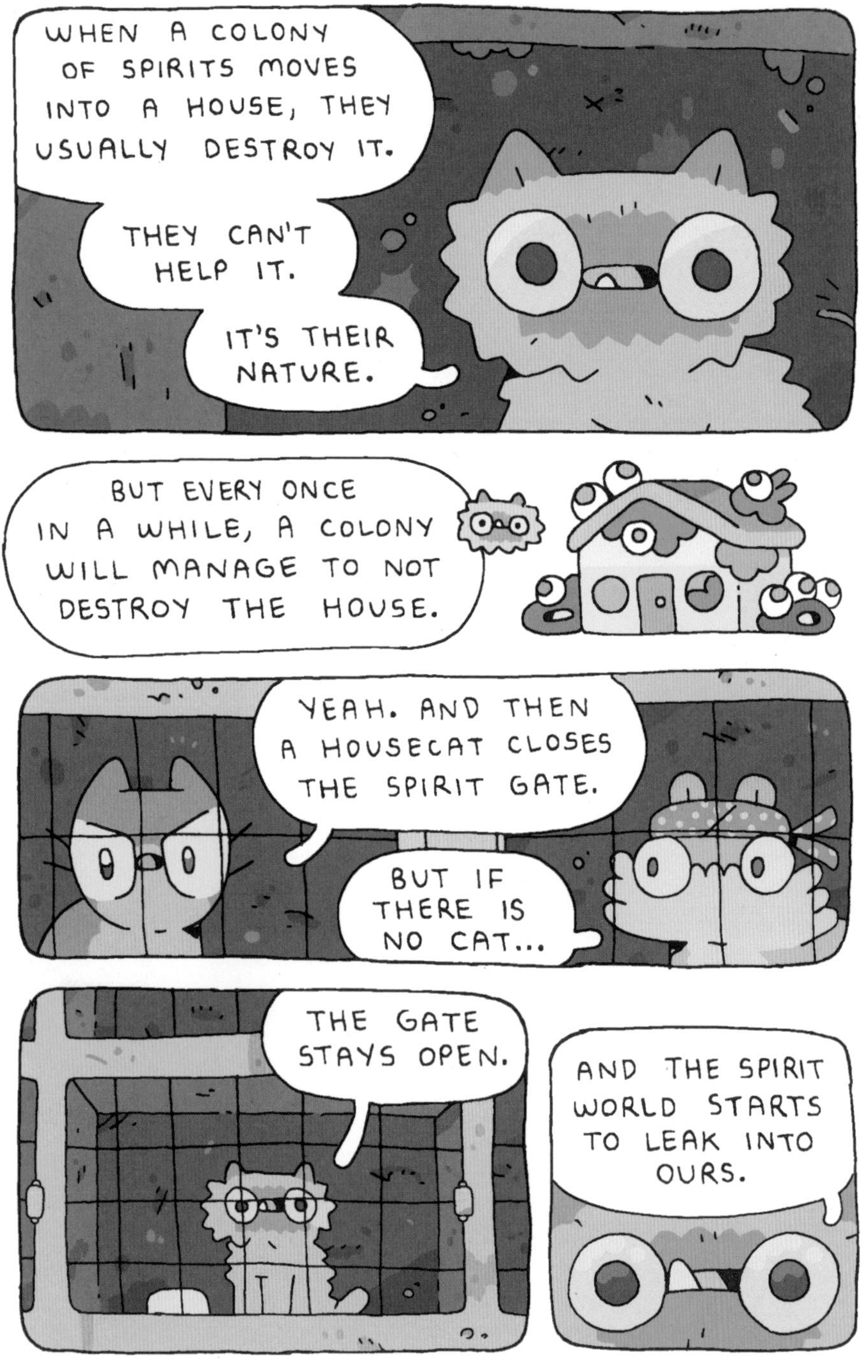
WHEN A COLONY OF SPIRITS MOVES INTO A HOUSE, THEY USUALLY DESTROY IT.
THEY CAN'T HELP IT.
IT'S THEIR NATURE.
BUT EVERY ONCE IN A WHILE, A COLONY WILL MANAGE TO NOT DESTROY THE HOUSE.
YEAH. AND THEN A HOUSECAT CLOSES THE SPIRIT GATE.
BUT IF THERE IS NO CAT...
THE GATE STAYS OPEN.
AND THE SPIRIT WORLD STARTS TO LEAK INTO OURS.

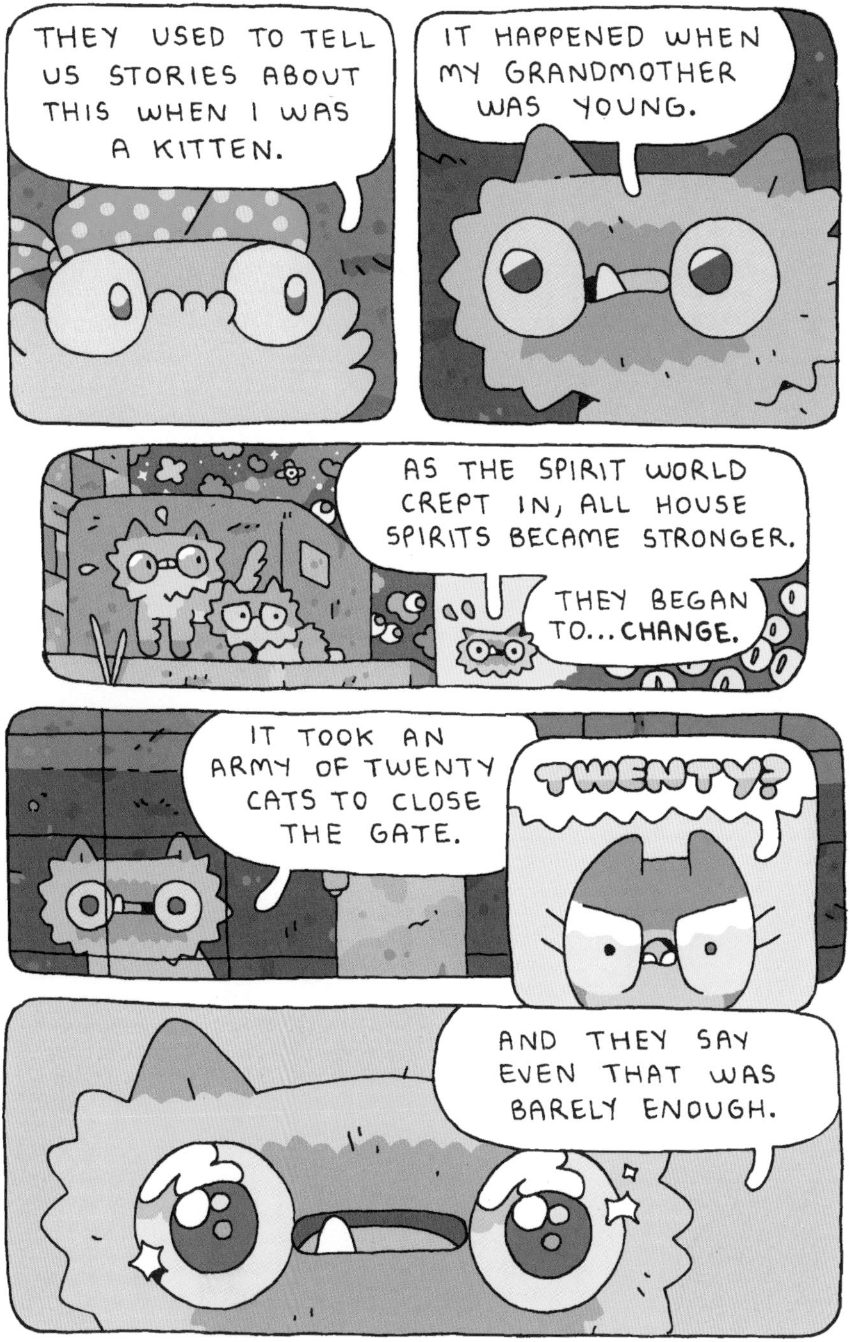
THEY USED TO TELL US STORIES ABOUT THIS WHEN I WAS A KITTEN.
IT HAPPENED WHEN MY GRANDMOTHER WAS YOUNG.
AS THE SPIRIT WORLD CREPT IN, ALL HOUSE SPIRITS BECAME STRONGER.
THEY BEGAN TO... CHANGE.
IT TOOK AN ARMY OF TWENTY CATS TO CLOSE THE GATE.
TWENTY?
AND THEY SAY EVEN THAT WAS BARELY ENOUGH.

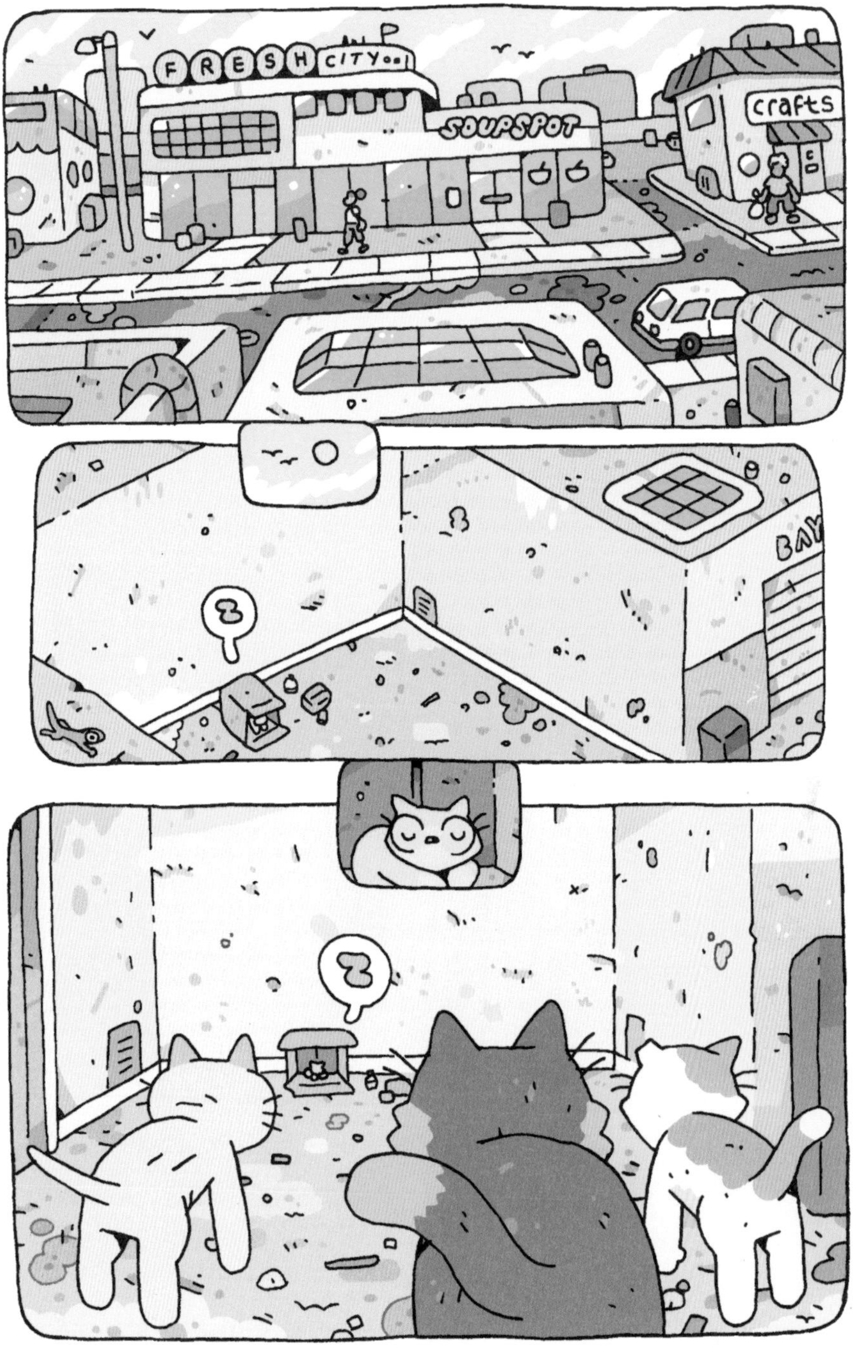
FRESH
CITY
SOUPSPOT
crafts
BAY
Z
Z

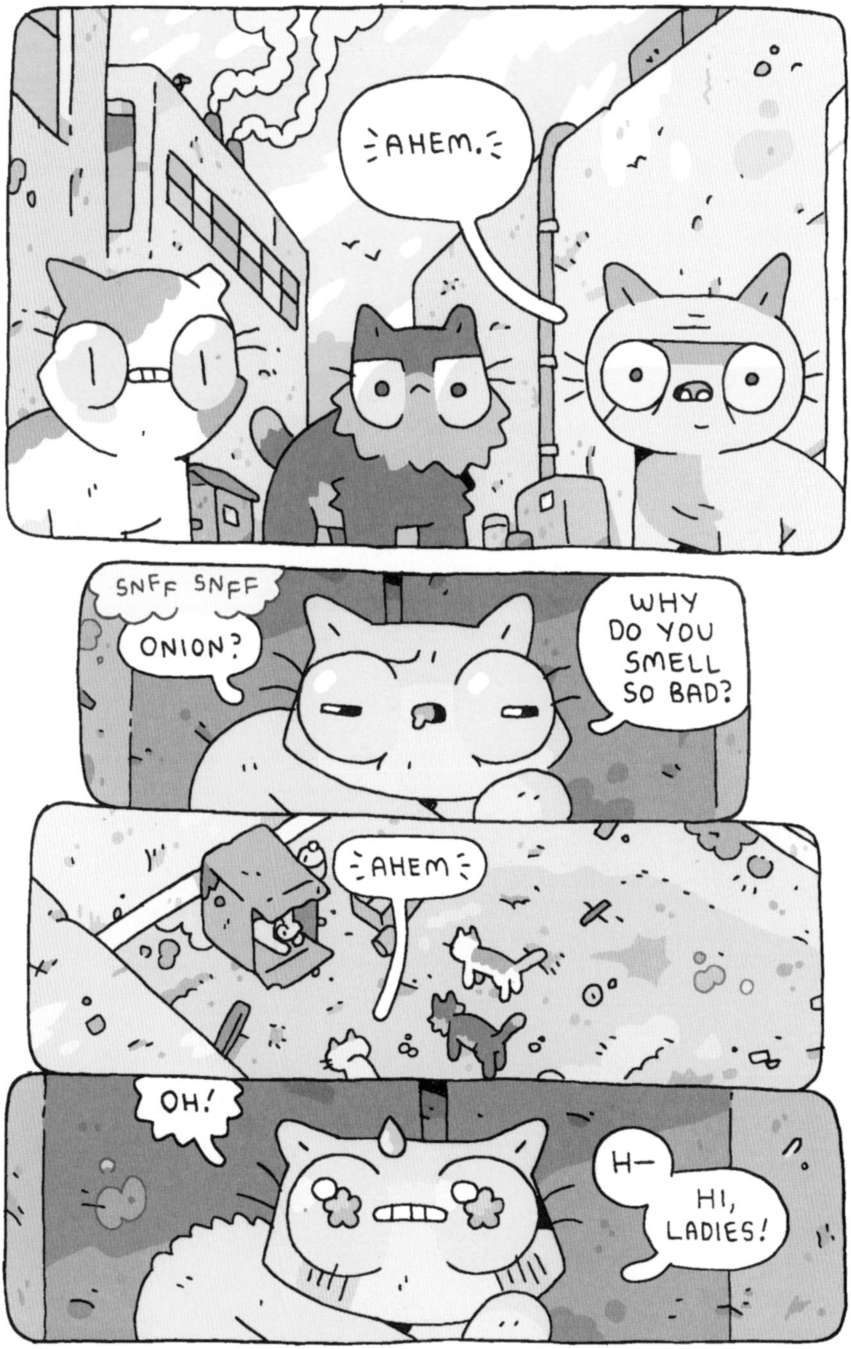
AHEM.
SNFF SNFF
ONION?
WHY DO YOU SMELL SO BAD?
AHEM
OH!
H—
HI, LADIES!

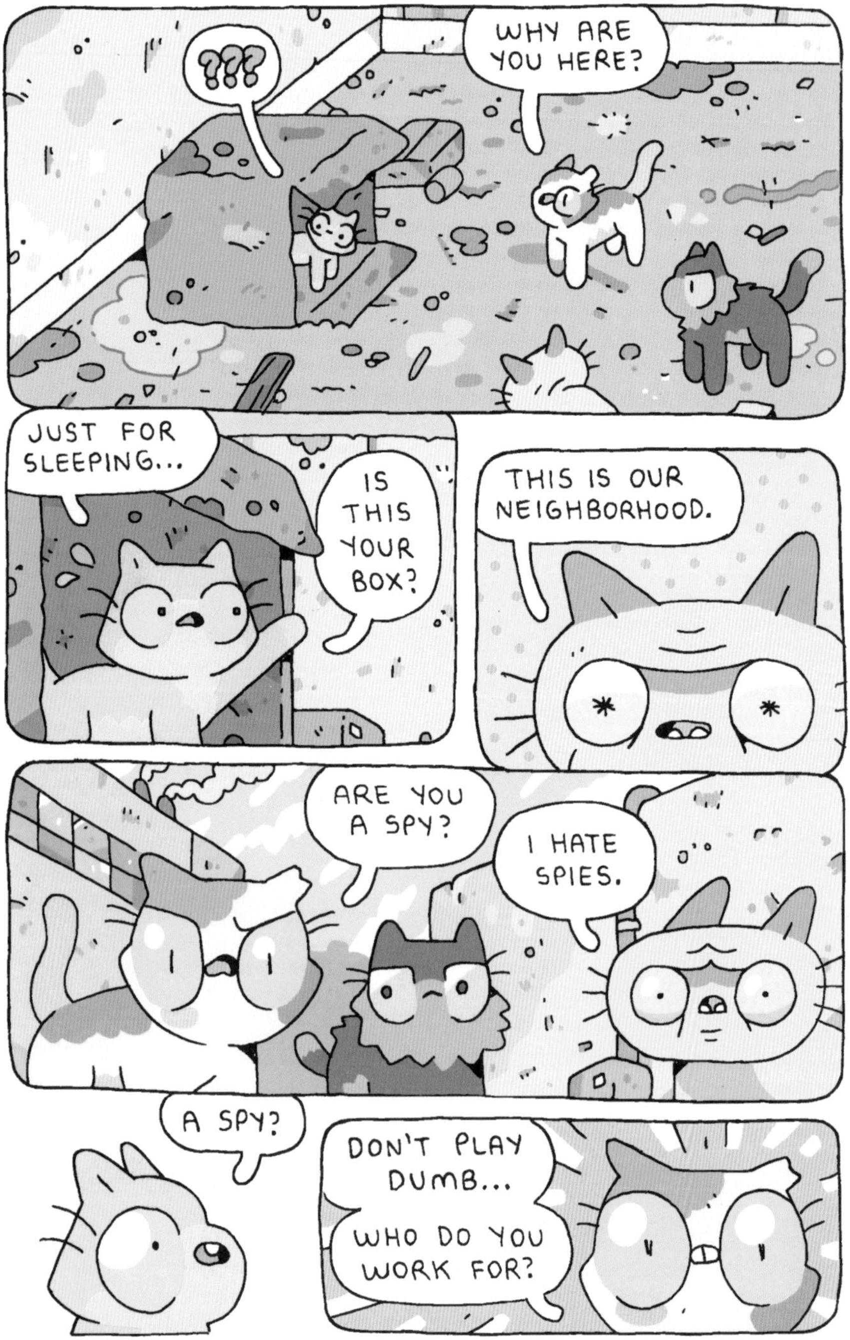
???
WHY ARE YOU HERE?
JUST FOR SLEEPING...
IS THIS YOUR BOX?
THIS IS OUR NEIGHBORHOOD.
ARE YOU A SPY?
I HATE SPIES.
A SPY?
DON'T PLAY DUMB...
WHO DO YOU WORK FOR?

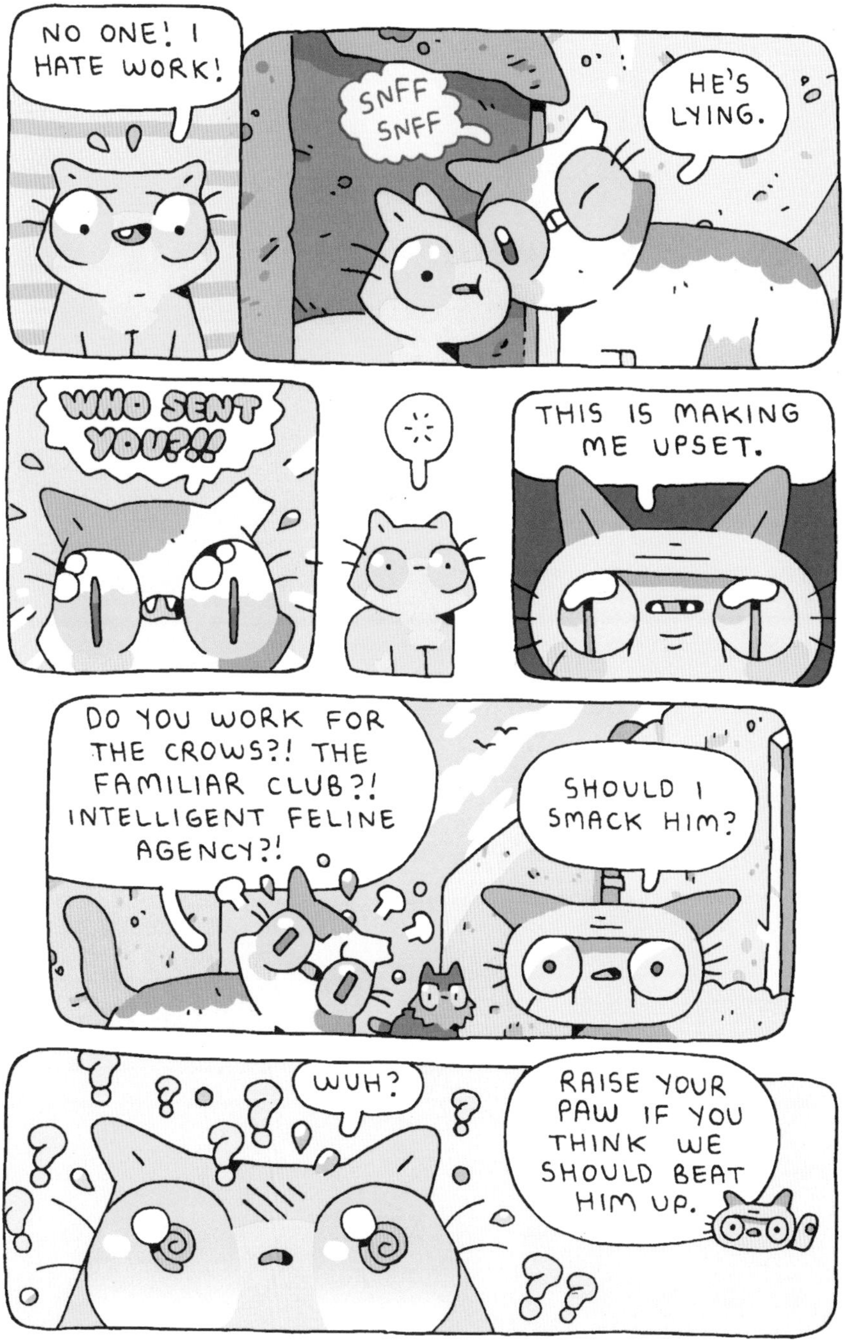
NO ONE! I HATE WORK!
SNFF SNFF
HE'S LYING.
WHO SENT YOU?!!
THIS IS MAKING ME UPSET.
DO YOU WORK FOR THE CROWS?! THE FAMILIAR CLUB?! INTELLIGENT FELINE AGENCY?!
SHOULD I SMACK HIM?
WUH?
RAISE YOUR PAW IF YOU THINK WE SHOULD BEAT HIM UP.

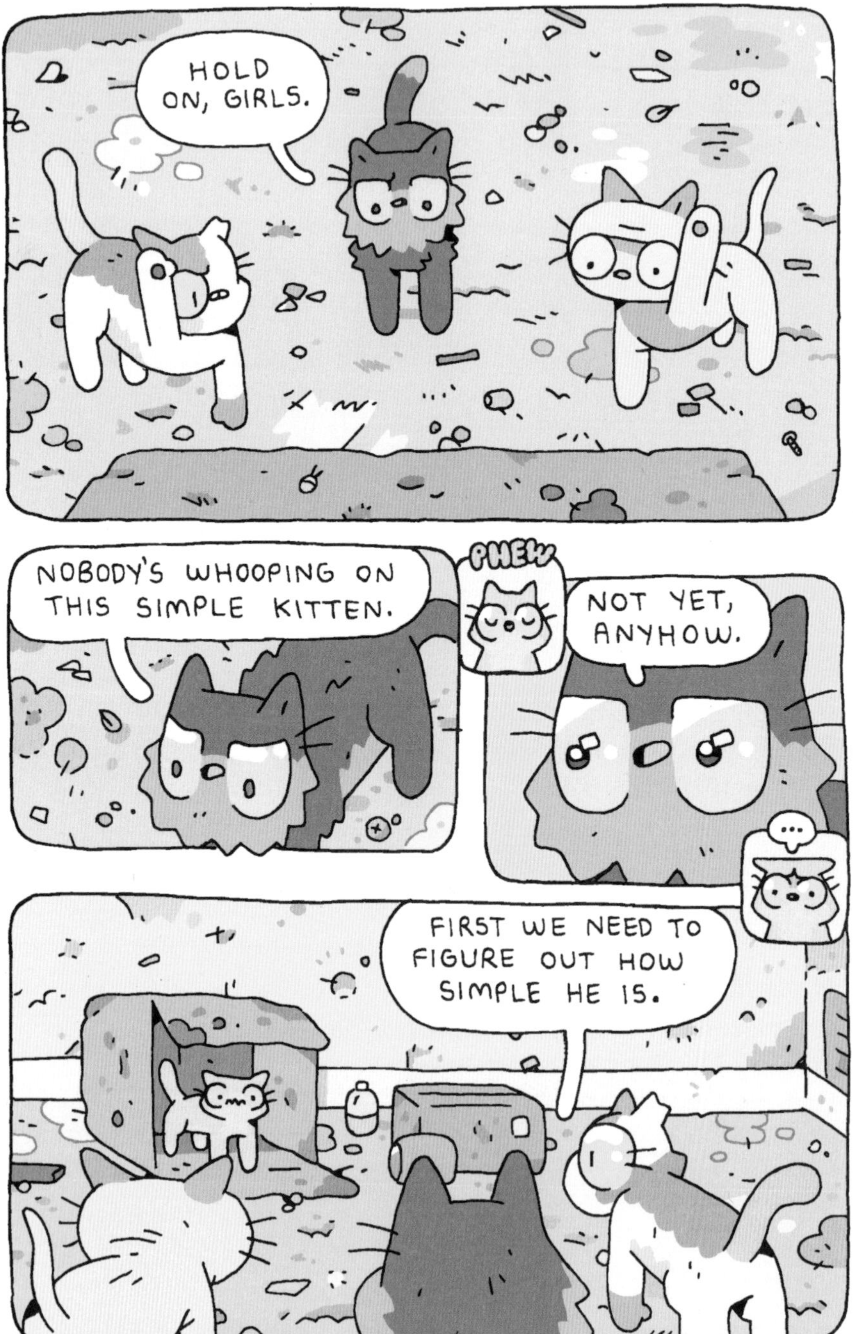
HOLD ON, GIRLS.
NOBODY'S WHOOPING ON THIS SIMPLE KITTEN.
PHEW
NOT YET, ANYHOW.
...
FIRST WE NEED TO FIGURE OUT HOW SIMPLE HE IS.

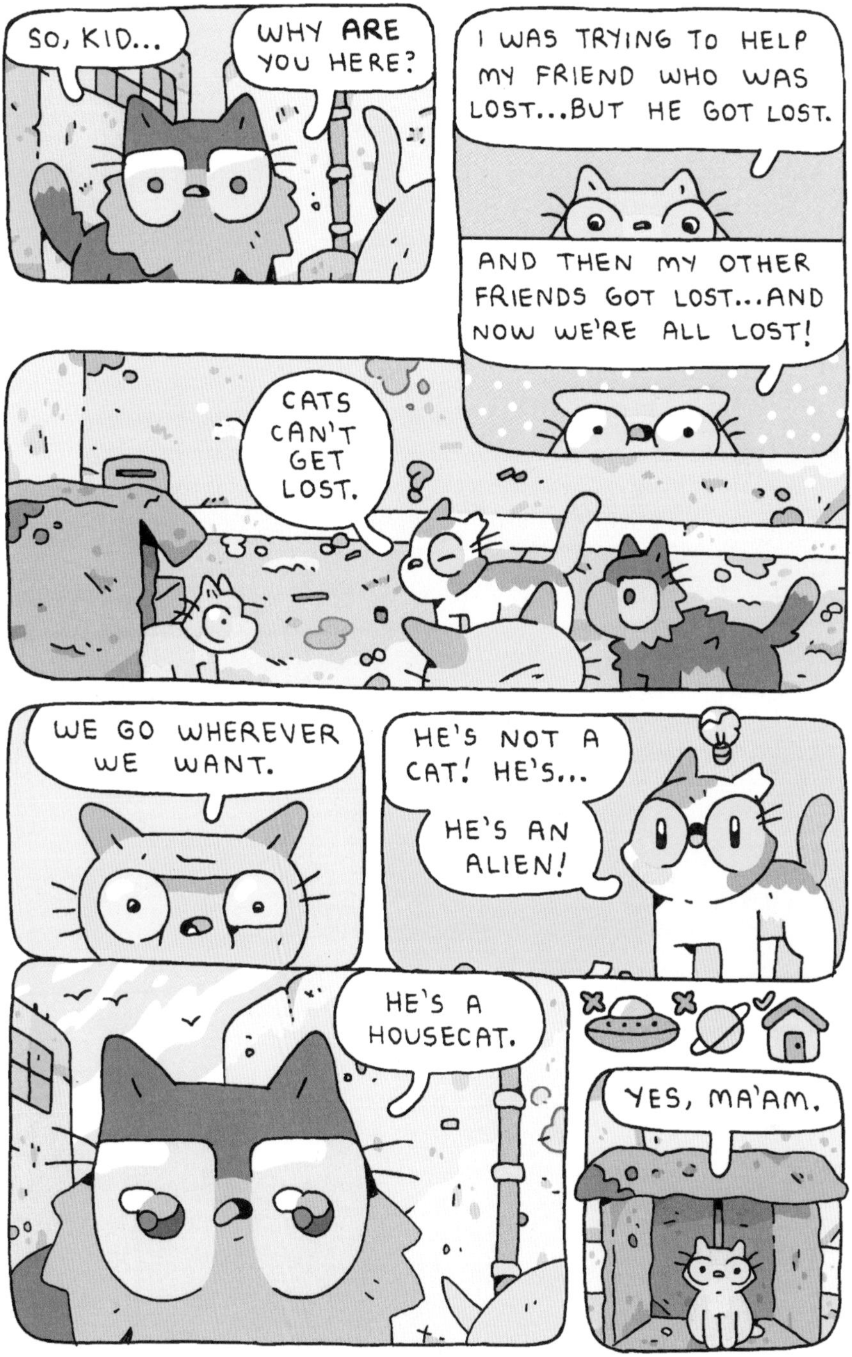
SO, KID...
WHY ARE YOU HERE?
I WAS TRYING TO HELP MY FRIEND WHO WAS LOST...BUT HE GOT LOST.
AND THEN MY OTHER FRIENDS GOT LOST...AND NOW WE'RE ALL LOST!
CATS CAN'T GET LOST.
WE GO WHEREVER WE WANT.
HE'S NOT A CAT! HE'S...
HE'S AN ALIEN!
HE'S A HOUSECAT.
YES, MA'AM.

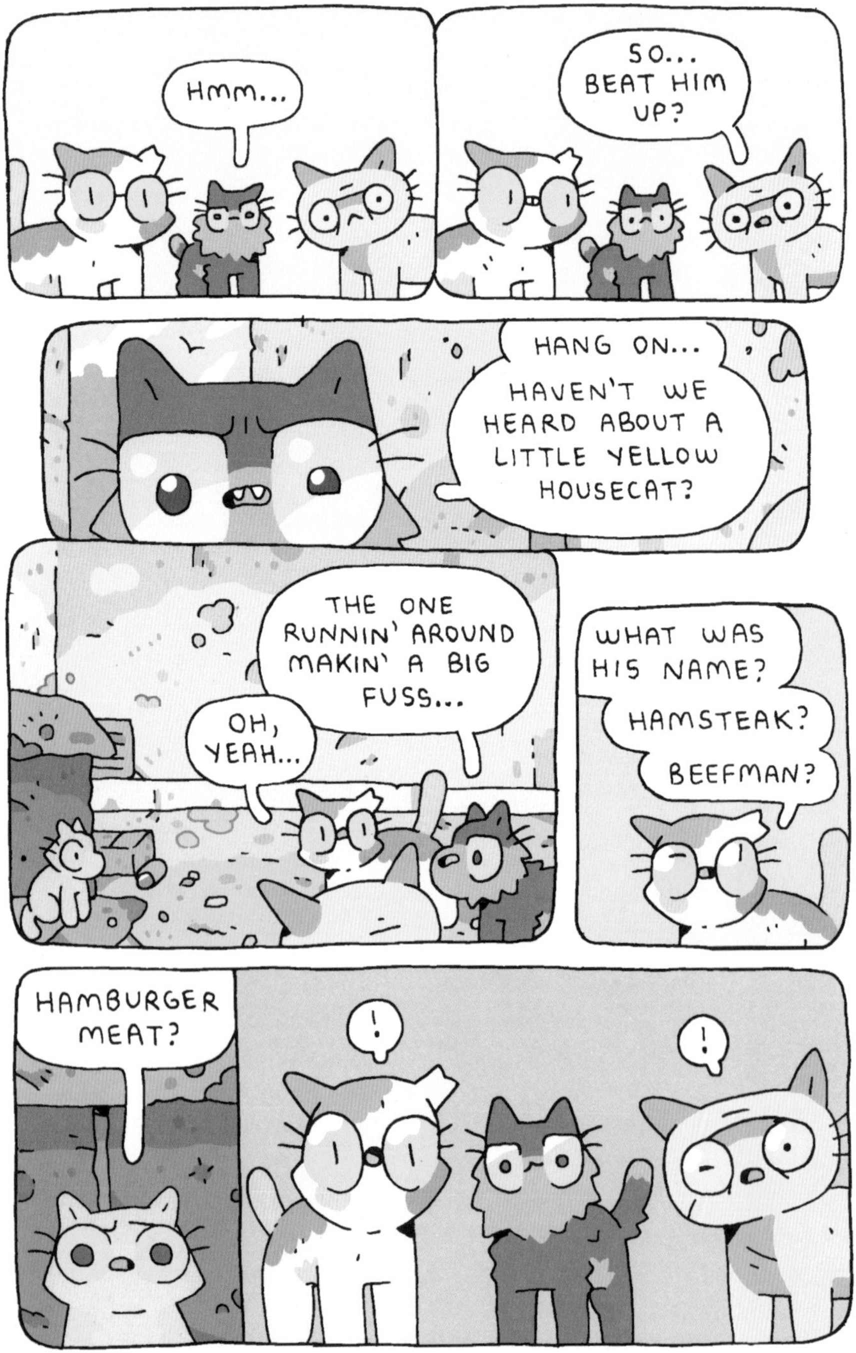
Hmm...
SO... BEAT HIM UP?
HANG ON...
HAVEN'T WE HEARD ABOUT A LITTLE YELLOW HOUSECAT?
THE ONE RUNNIN' AROUND MAKIN' A BIG FUSS...
OH, YEAH...
WHAT WAS HIS NAME?
HAMSTEAK?
BEEFMAN?
HAMBURGER MEAT?
!
!

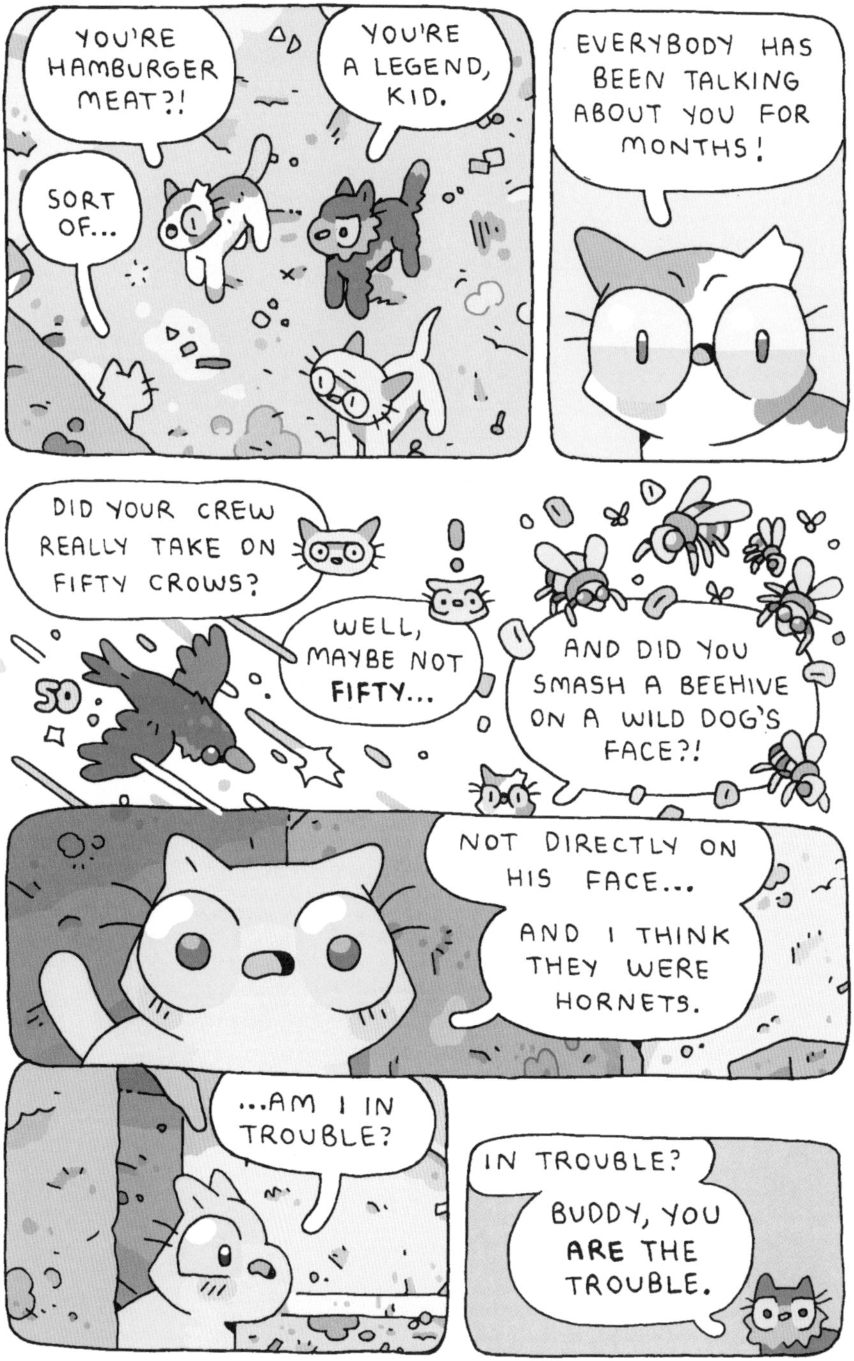

YOU'RE HAMBURGER MEAT?!
YOU'RE A LEGEND, KID.
SORT OF...
EVERYBODY HAS BEEN TALKING ABOUT YOU FOR MONTHS!
DID YOUR CREW REALLY TAKE ON FIFTY CROWS?
50
WELL, MAYBE NOT **FIFTY**...
AND DID YOU SMASH A BEEHIVE ON A WILD DOG'S FACE?!
NOT DIRECTLY ON HIS FACE...
AND I THINK THEY WERE HORNETS.
...AM I IN TROUBLE?
IN TROUBLE?
BUDDY, YOU **ARE** THE TROUBLE.

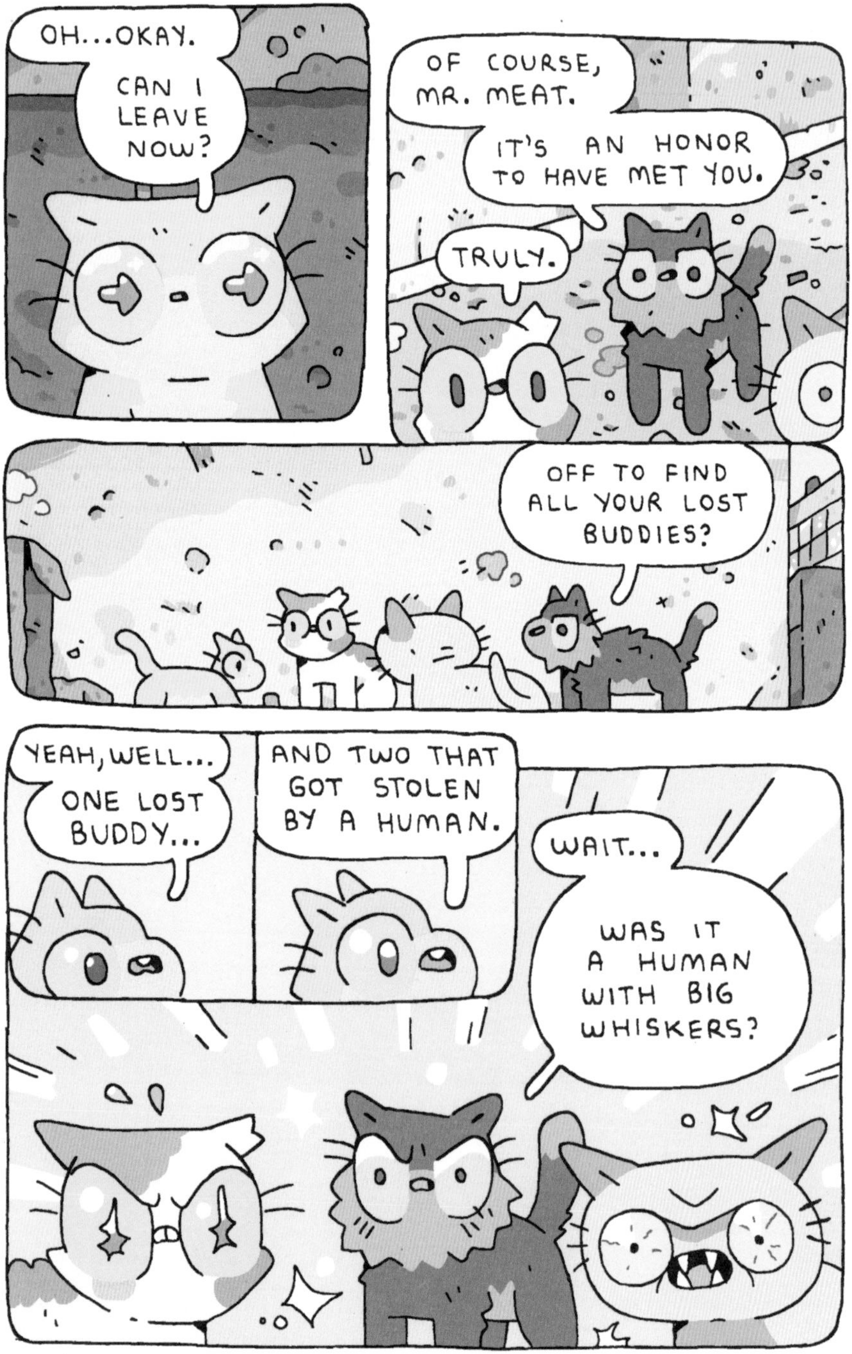
OH...OKAY.
CAN I LEAVE NOW?
OF COURSE, MR. MEAT.
IT'S AN HONOR TO HAVE MET YOU.
TRULY.
OFF TO FIND ALL YOUR LOST BUDDIES?
YEAH, WELL...
ONE LOST BUDDY...
AND TWO THAT GOT STOLEN BY A HUMAN.
WAIT...
WAS IT A HUMAN WITH BIG WHISKERS?

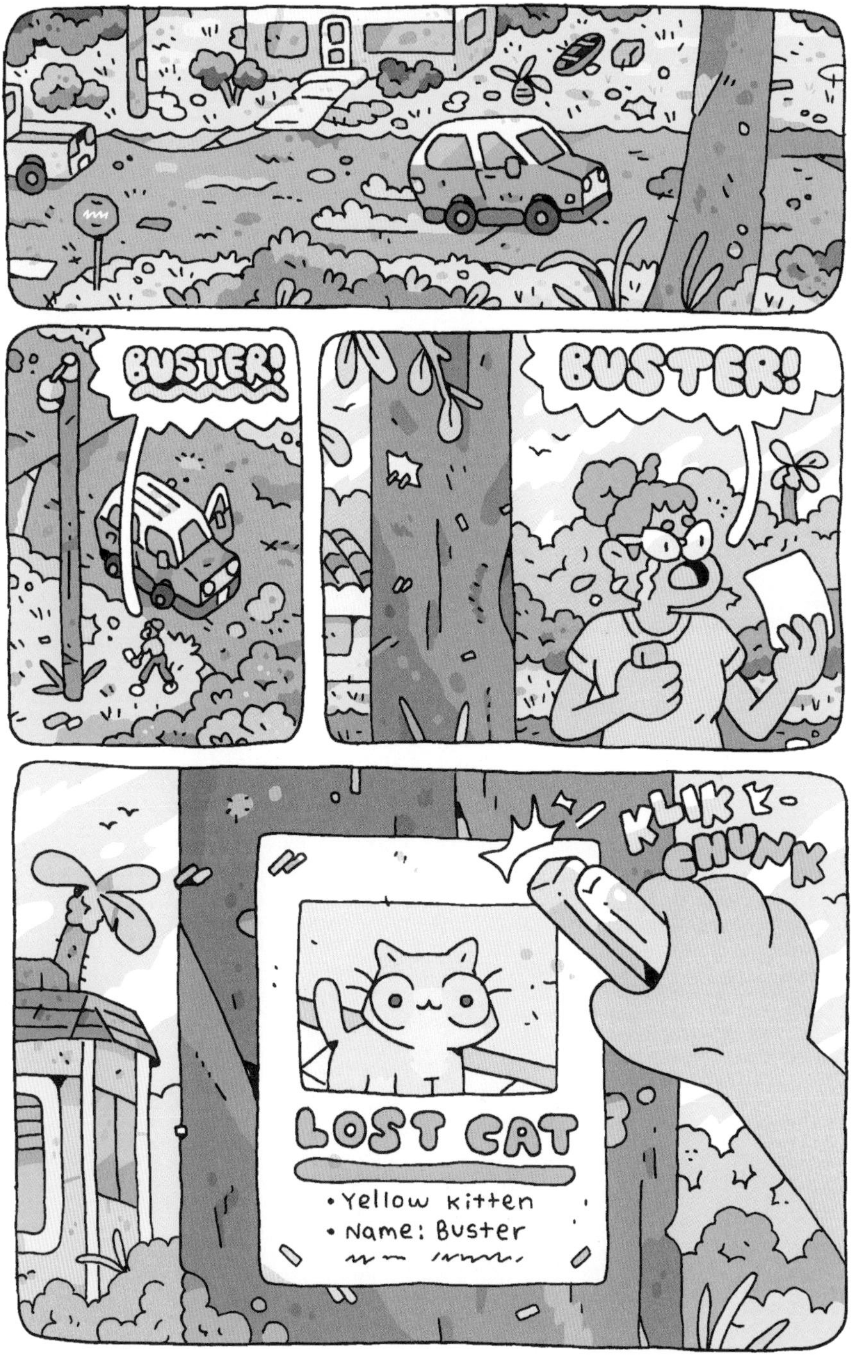
BUSTER!
BUSTER!
KLIK
CHUNK
LOST CAT
• Yellow kitten
• Name: Buster

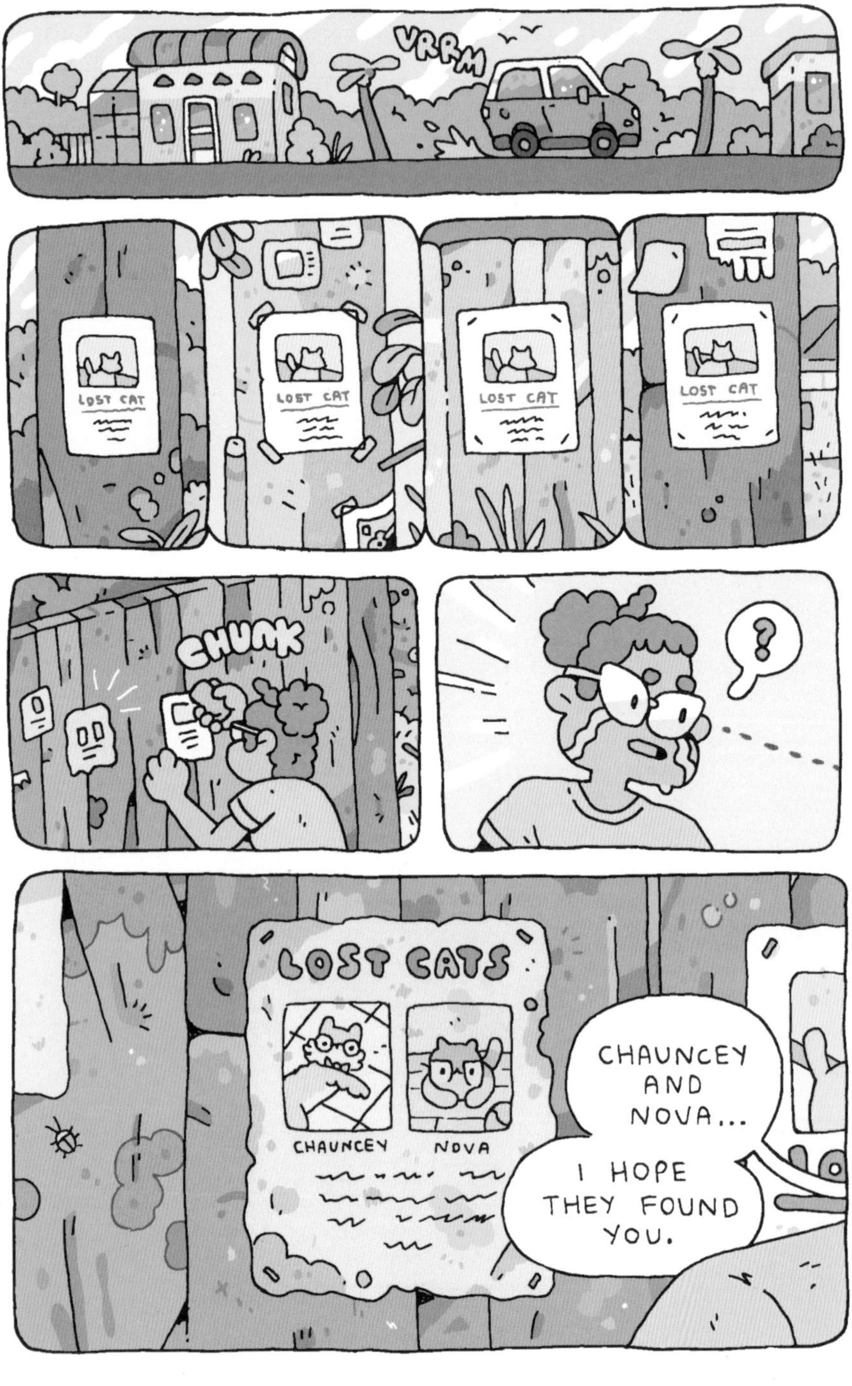
VRRM
LOST CAT
LOST CAT
LOST CAT
LOST CAT
CHUNK
?
LOST CATS
CHAUNCEY
NOVA
CHAUNCEY AND NOVA...
I HOPE THEY FOUND YOU.

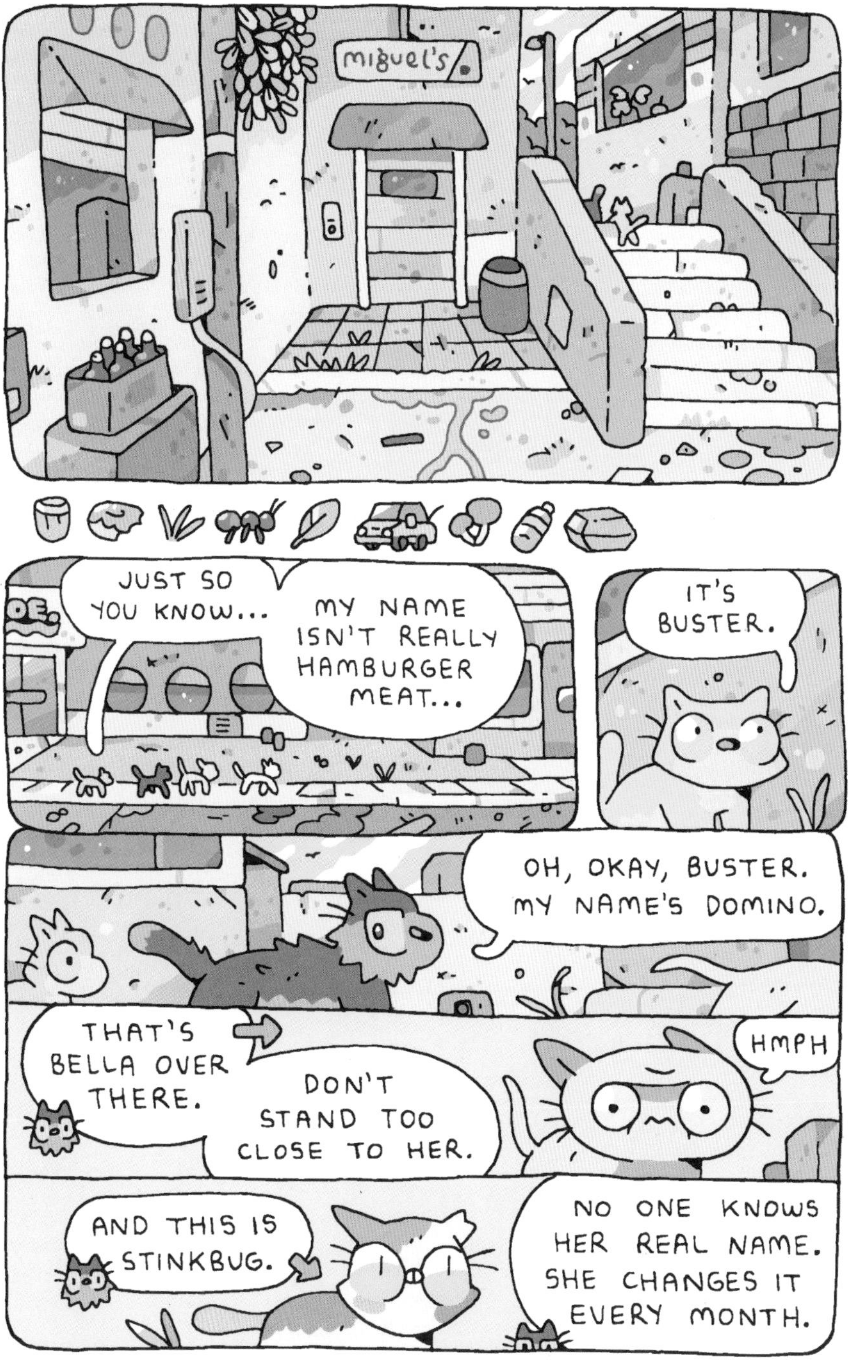
miguel's
JUST SO YOU KNOW...
MY NAME ISN'T REALLY HAMBURGER MEAT...
IT'S BUSTER.
OH, OKAY, BUSTER. MY NAME'S DOMINO.
THAT'S BELLA OVER THERE.
DON'T STAND TOO CLOSE TO HER.
HMPH
AND THIS IS STINKBUG.
NO ONE KNOWS HER REAL NAME. SHE CHANGES IT EVERY MONTH.

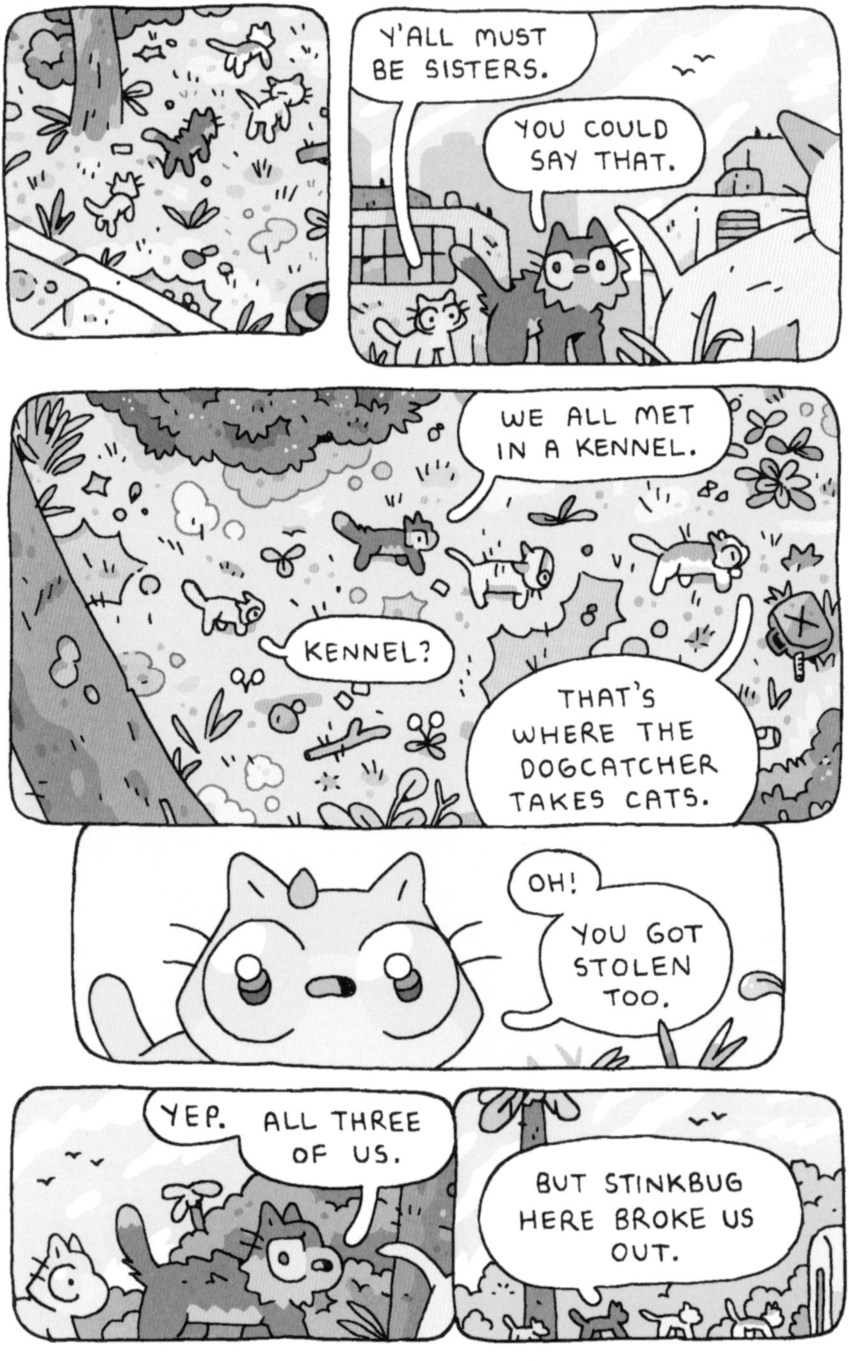
Y'ALL MUST BE SISTERS.
YOU COULD SAY THAT.
WE ALL MET IN A KENNEL.
KENNEL?
THAT'S WHERE THE DOGCATCHER TAKES CATS.
OH!
YOU GOT STOLEN TOO.
YEP.
ALL THREE OF US.
BUT STINKBUG HERE BROKE US OUT.

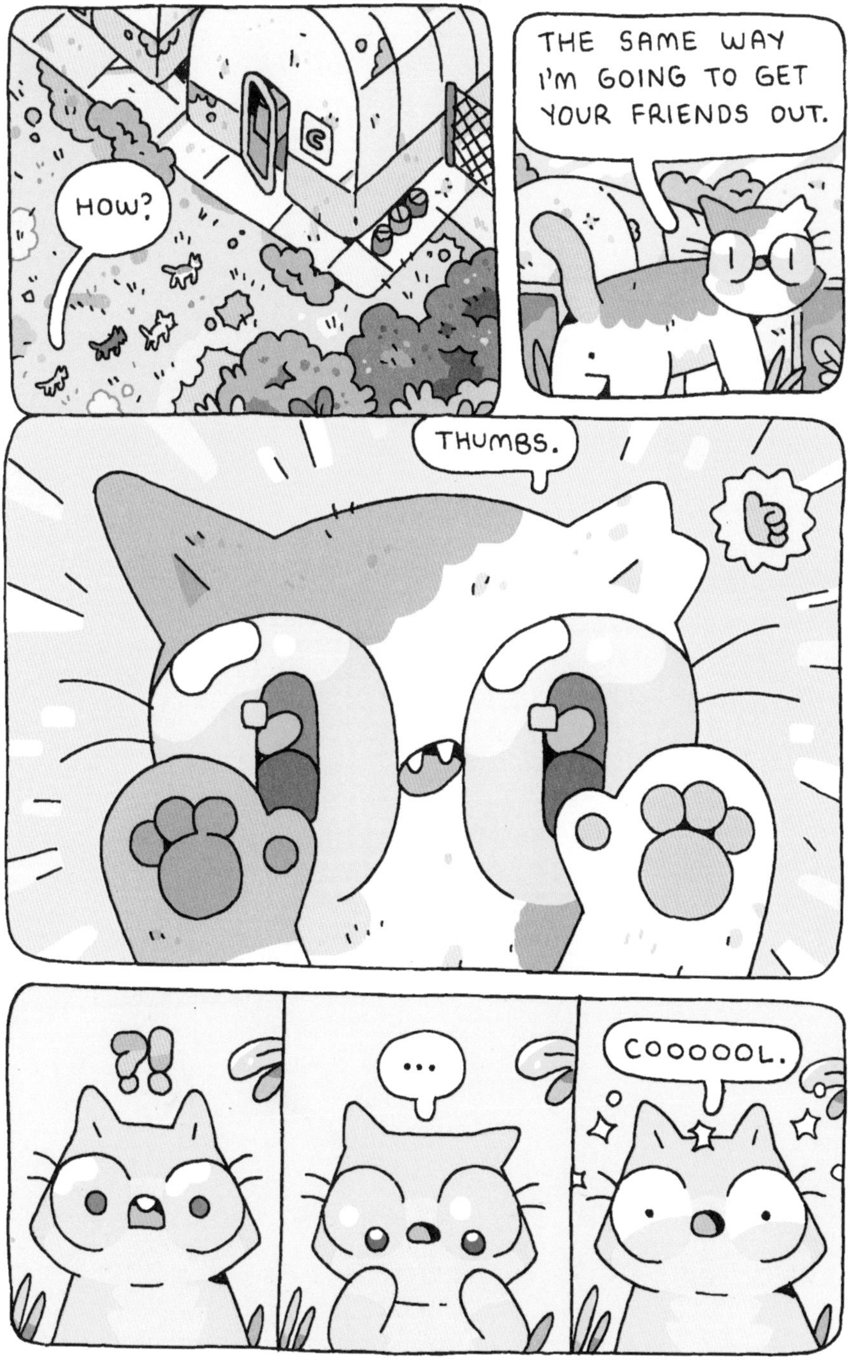
HOW?
THE SAME WAY I'M GOING TO GET YOUR FRIENDS OUT.
THUMBS.
?!
...
COOOOOL.

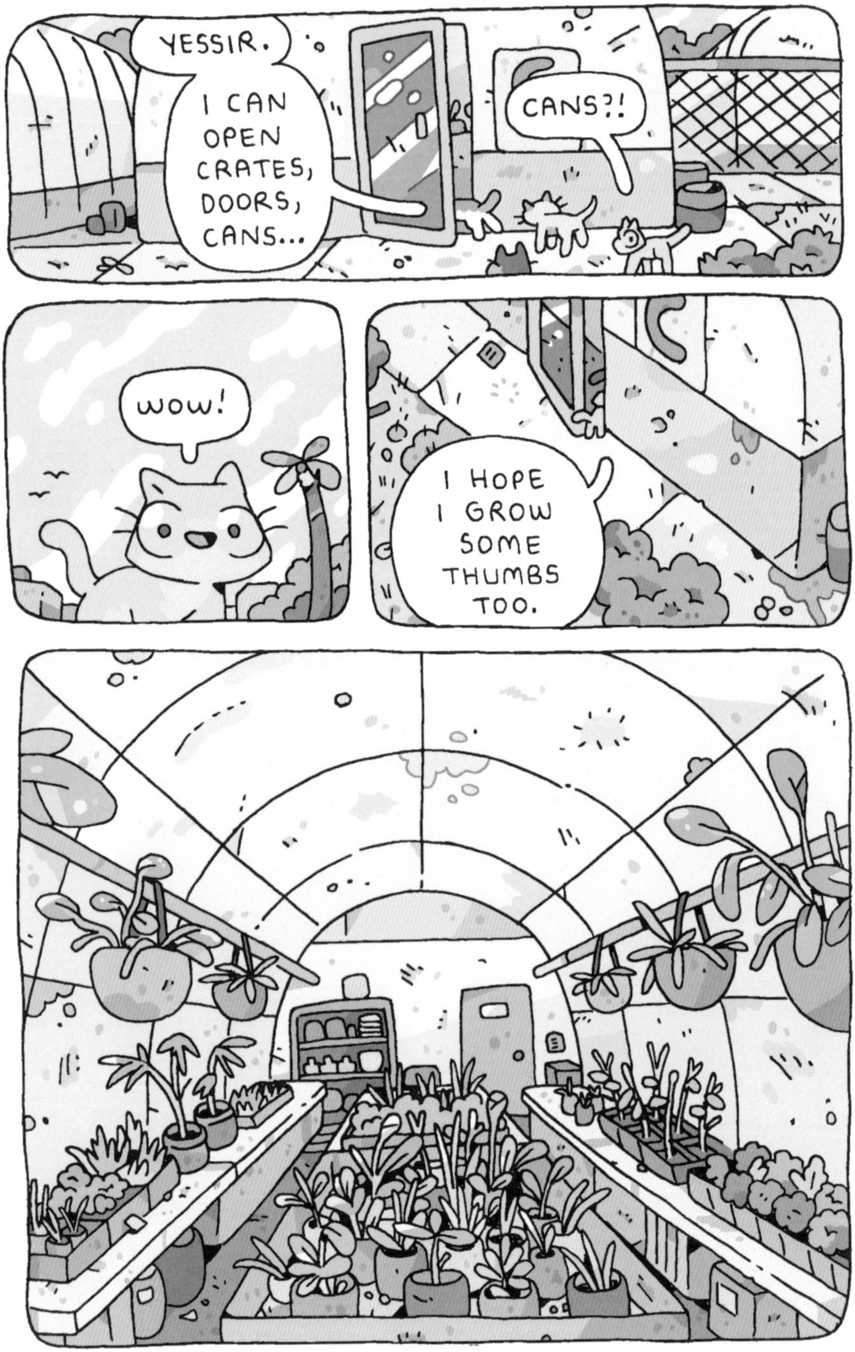
YESSIR.
I CAN OPEN CRATES, DOORS, CANS...
CANS?!
WOW!
I HOPE I GROW SOME THUMBS TOO.

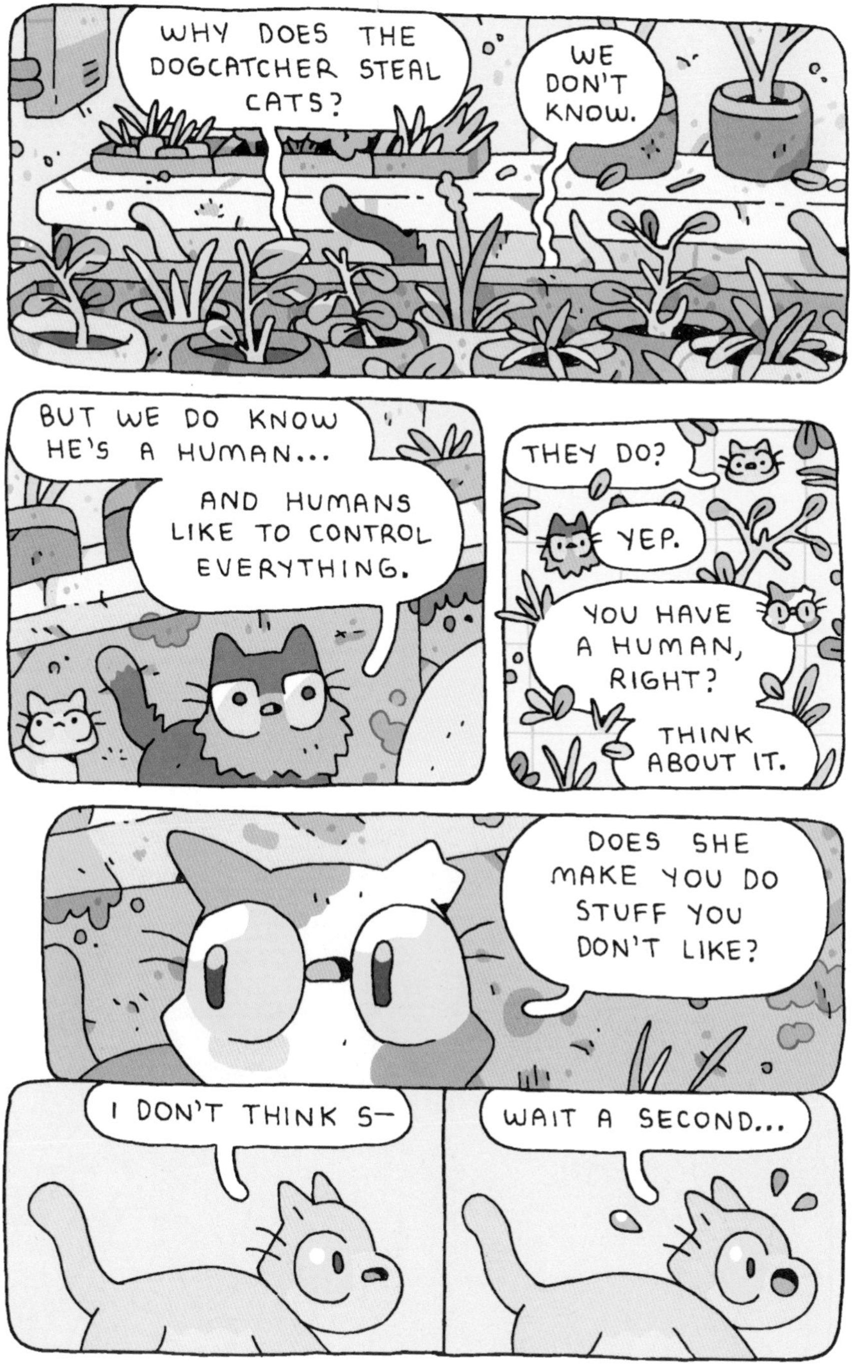
WHY DOES THE DOGCATCHER STEAL CATS?
WE DON'T KNOW.
BUT WE DO KNOW HE'S A HUMAN...
AND HUMANS LIKE TO CONTROL EVERYTHING.
THEY DO?
YEP.
YOU HAVE A HUMAN, RIGHT?
THINK ABOUT IT.
DOES SHE MAKE YOU DO STUFF YOU DON'T LIKE?
I DON'T THINK S—
WAIT A SECOND...

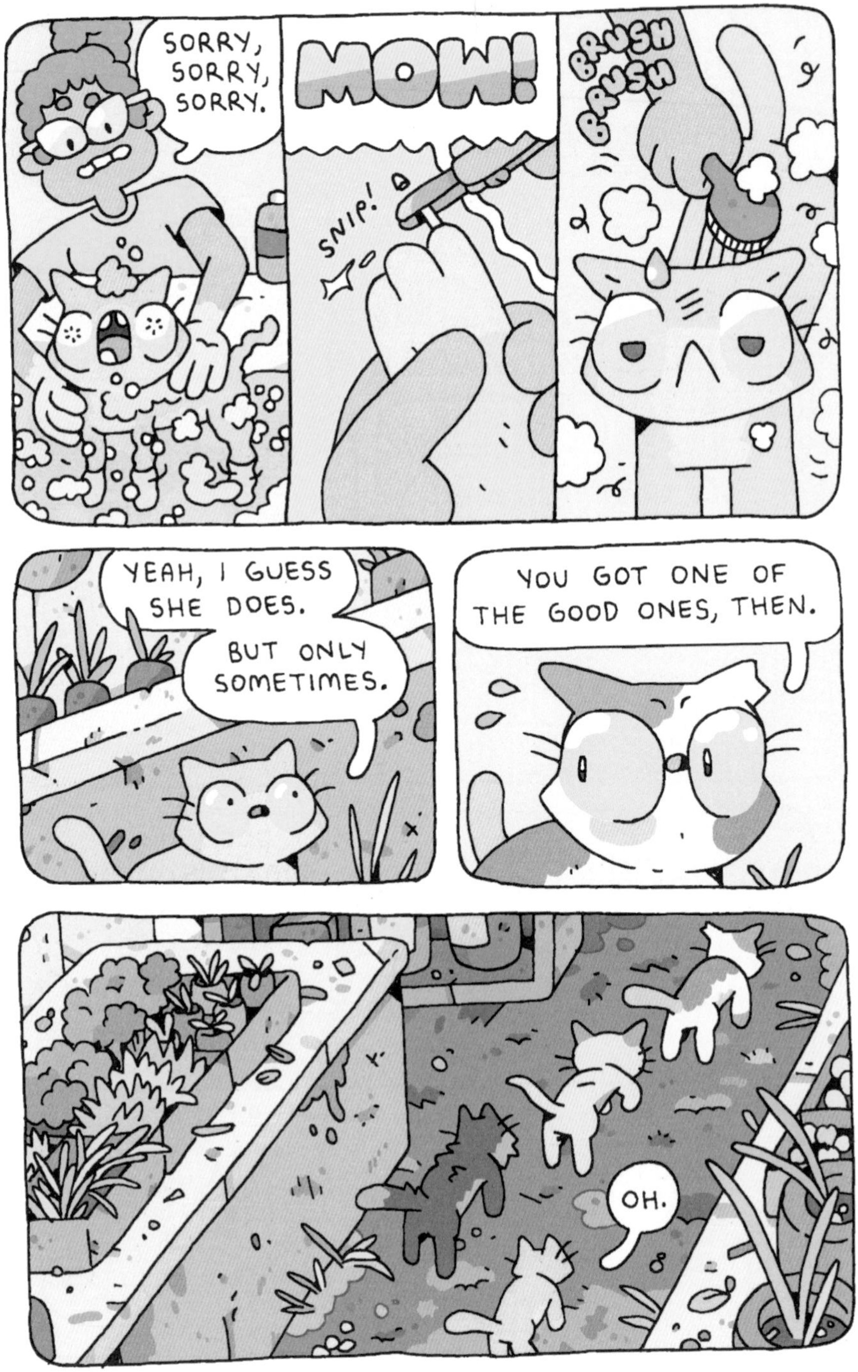
SORRY, SORRY, SORRY.
MOW!
SNIP!
BRUSH BRUSH
YEAH, I GUESS SHE DOES.
BUT ONLY SOMETIMES.
YOU GOT ONE OF THE GOOD ONES, THEN.
OH.

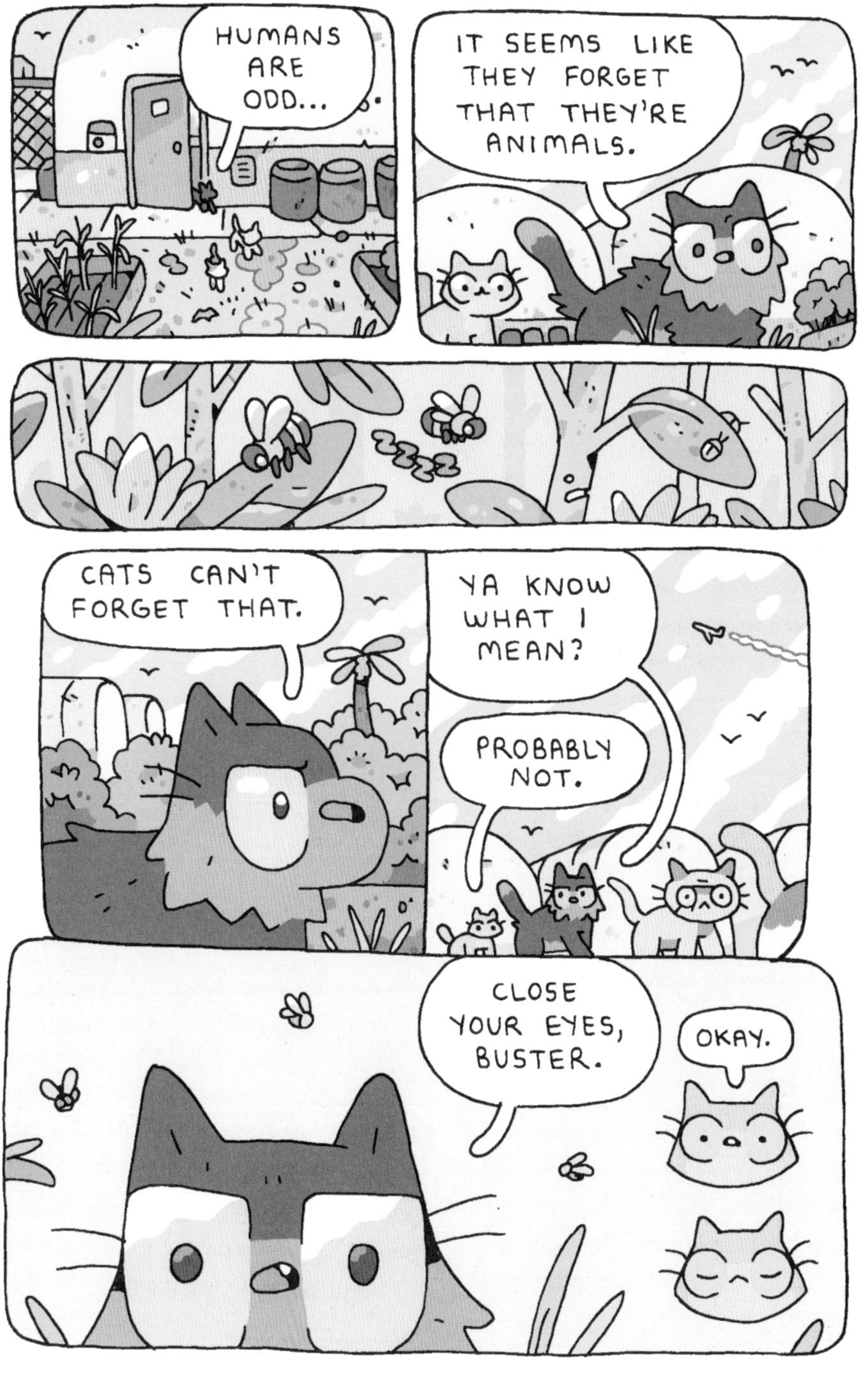
HUMANS ARE ODD...
IT SEEMS LIKE THEY FORGET THAT THEY'RE ANIMALS.
ZZZZ
CATS CAN'T FORGET THAT.
YA KNOW WHAT I MEAN?
PROBABLY NOT.
CLOSE YOUR EYES, BUSTER.
OKAY.

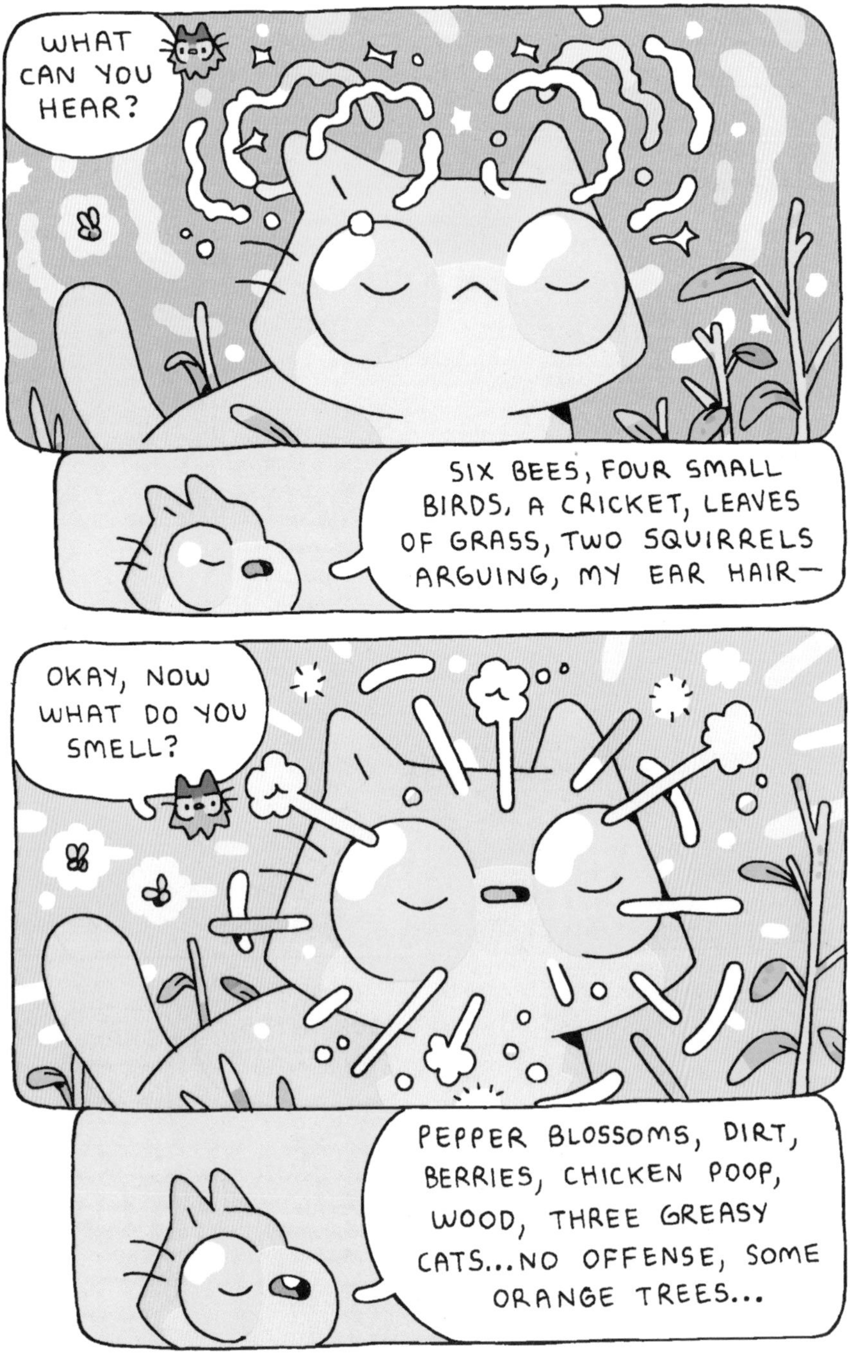
WHAT CAN YOU HEAR?
SIX BEES, FOUR SMALL BIRDS, A CRICKET, LEAVES OF GRASS, TWO SQUIRRELS ARGUING, MY EAR HAIR—
OKAY, NOW WHAT DO YOU SMELL?
PEPPER BLOSSOMS, DIRT, BERRIES, CHICKEN POOP, WOOD, THREE GREASY CATS...NO OFFENSE, SOME ORANGE TREES...

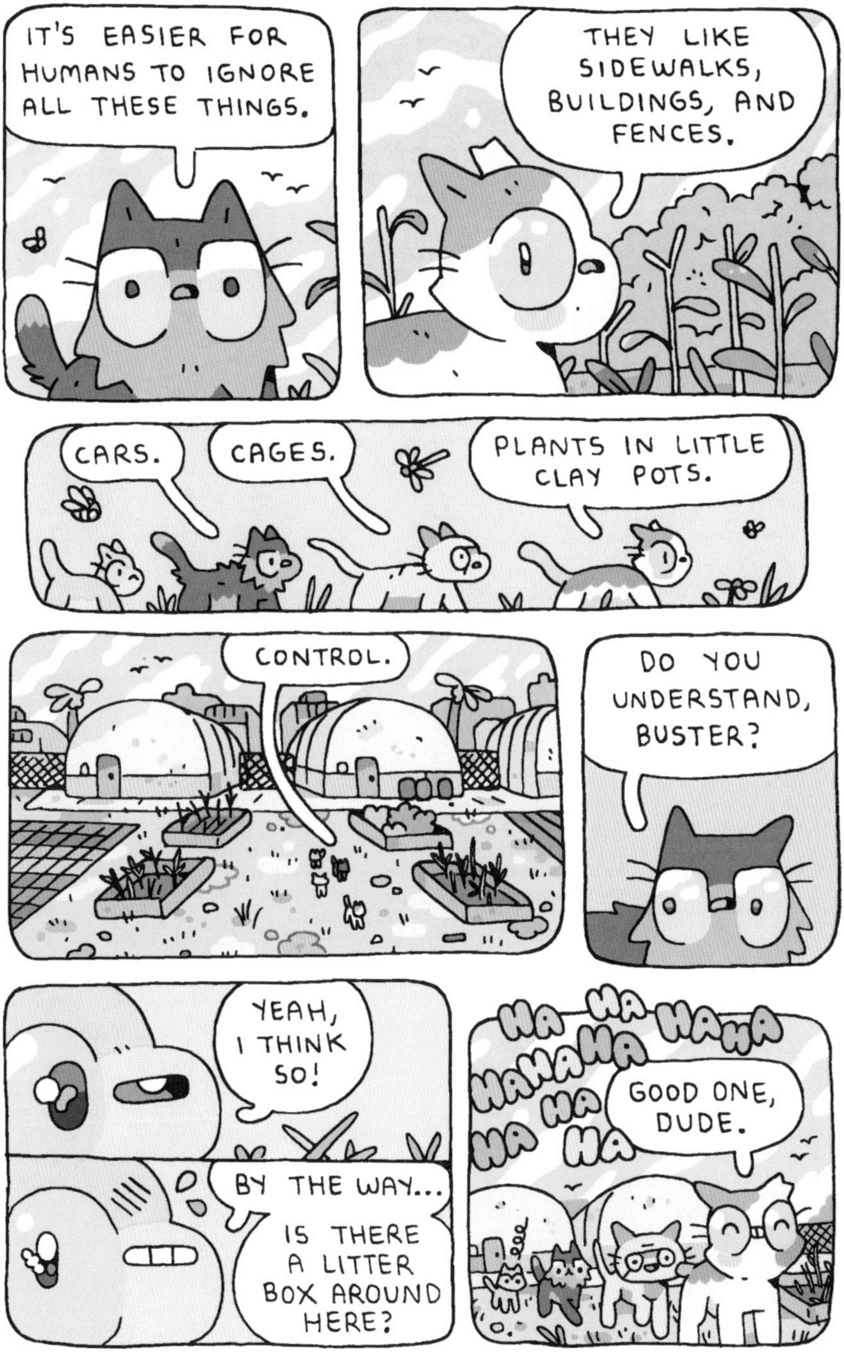
IT'S EASIER FOR HUMANS TO IGNORE ALL THESE THINGS.
THEY LIKE SIDEWALKS, BUILDINGS, AND FENCES.
CARS.
CAGES.
PLANTS IN LITTLE CLAY POTS.
CONTROL.
DO YOU UNDERSTAND, BUSTER?
YEAH, I THINK SO!
BY THE WAY...
IS THERE A LITTER BOX AROUND HERE?
HA HA HA HAHA HAHAHA HA HA HA HA
GOOD ONE, DUDE.

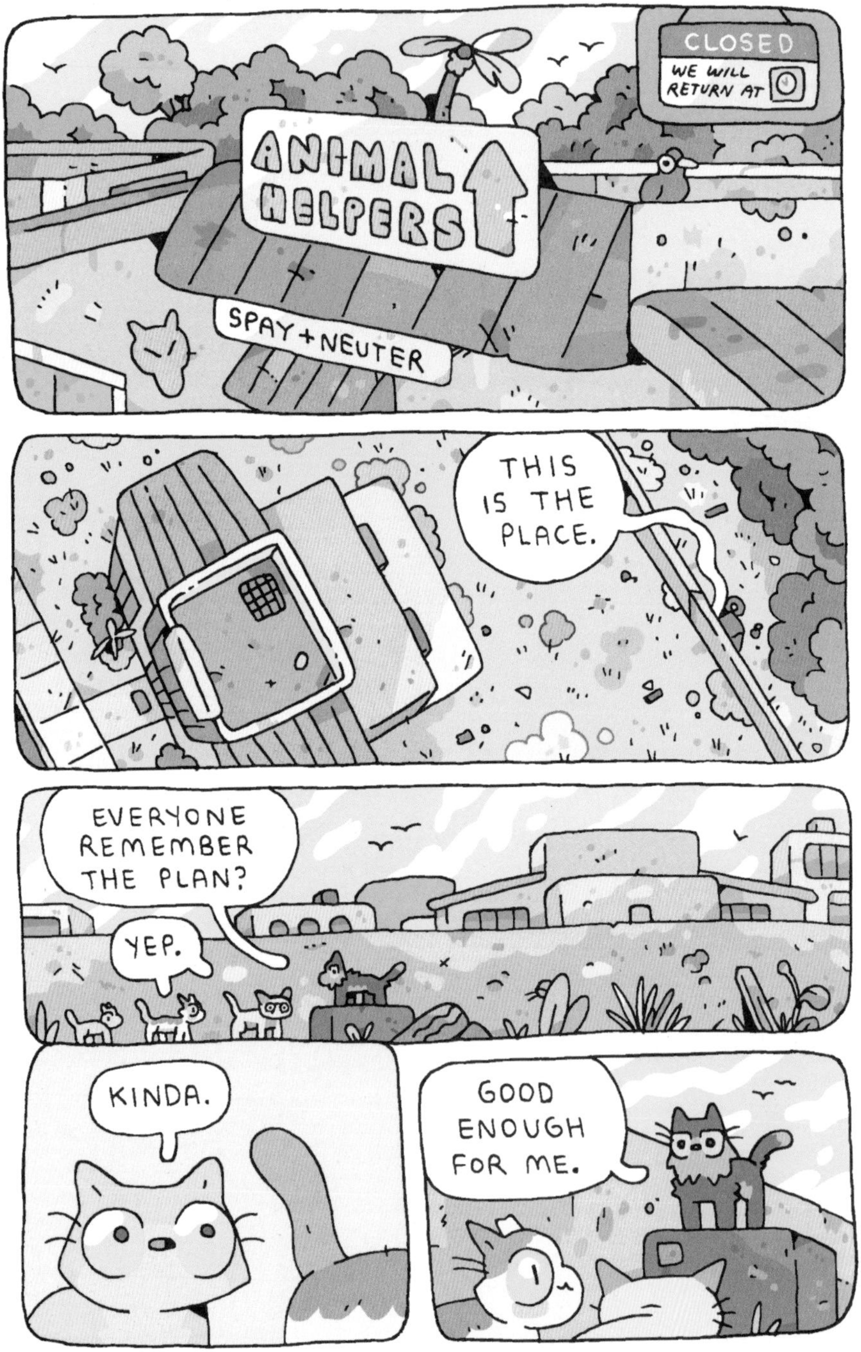
CLOSED
WE WILL RETURN AT
ANIMAL HELPERS
SPAY + NEUTER
THIS IS THE PLACE.
EVERYONE REMEMBER THE PLAN?
YEP.
KINDA.
GOOD ENOUGH FOR ME.

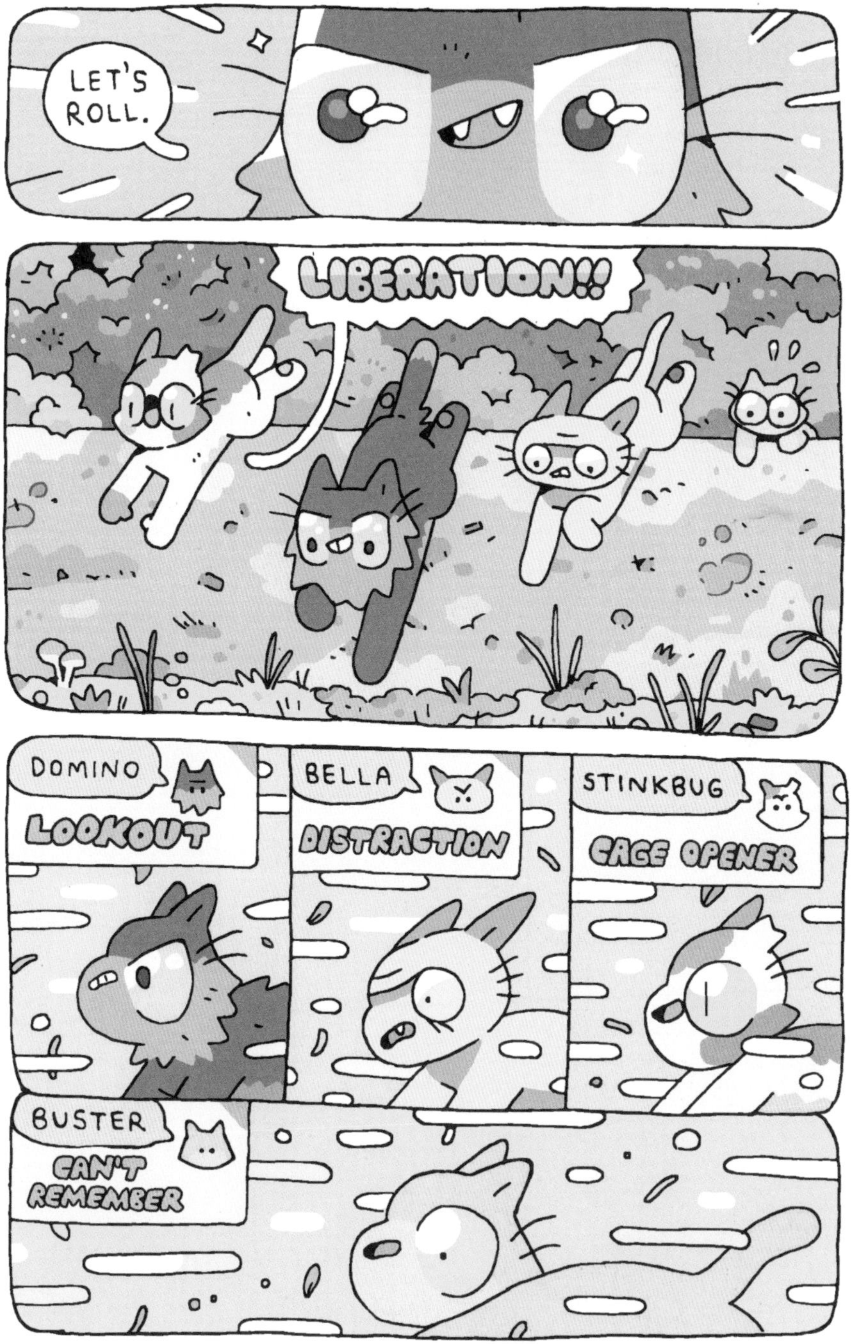
LET'S ROLL.
LIBERATION!!
DOMINO
LOOKOUT
BELLA
DISTRACTION
STINKBUG
CAGE OPENER
BUSTER
CAN'T REMEMBER

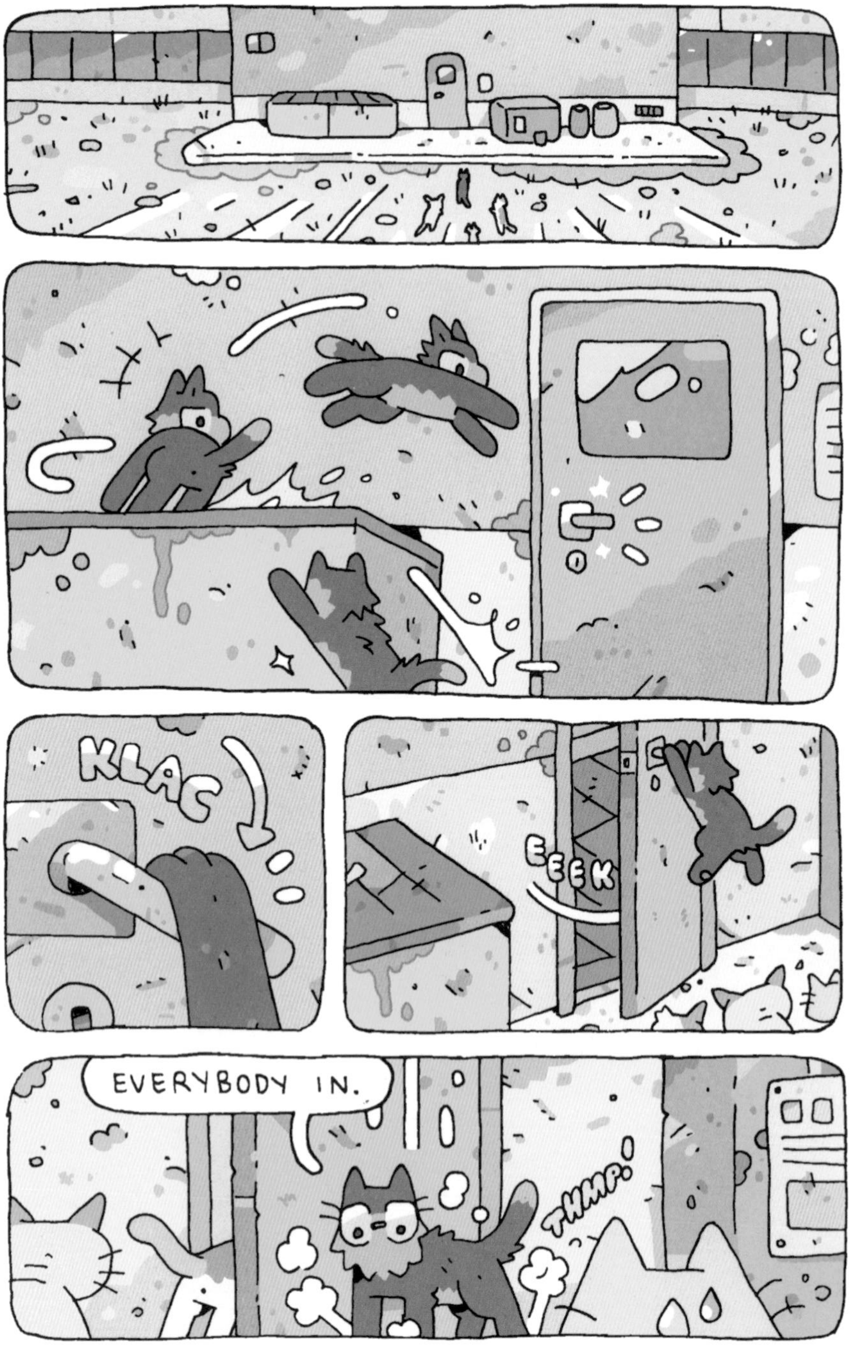
KLAC
EEEK
EVERYBODY IN.
THMP!

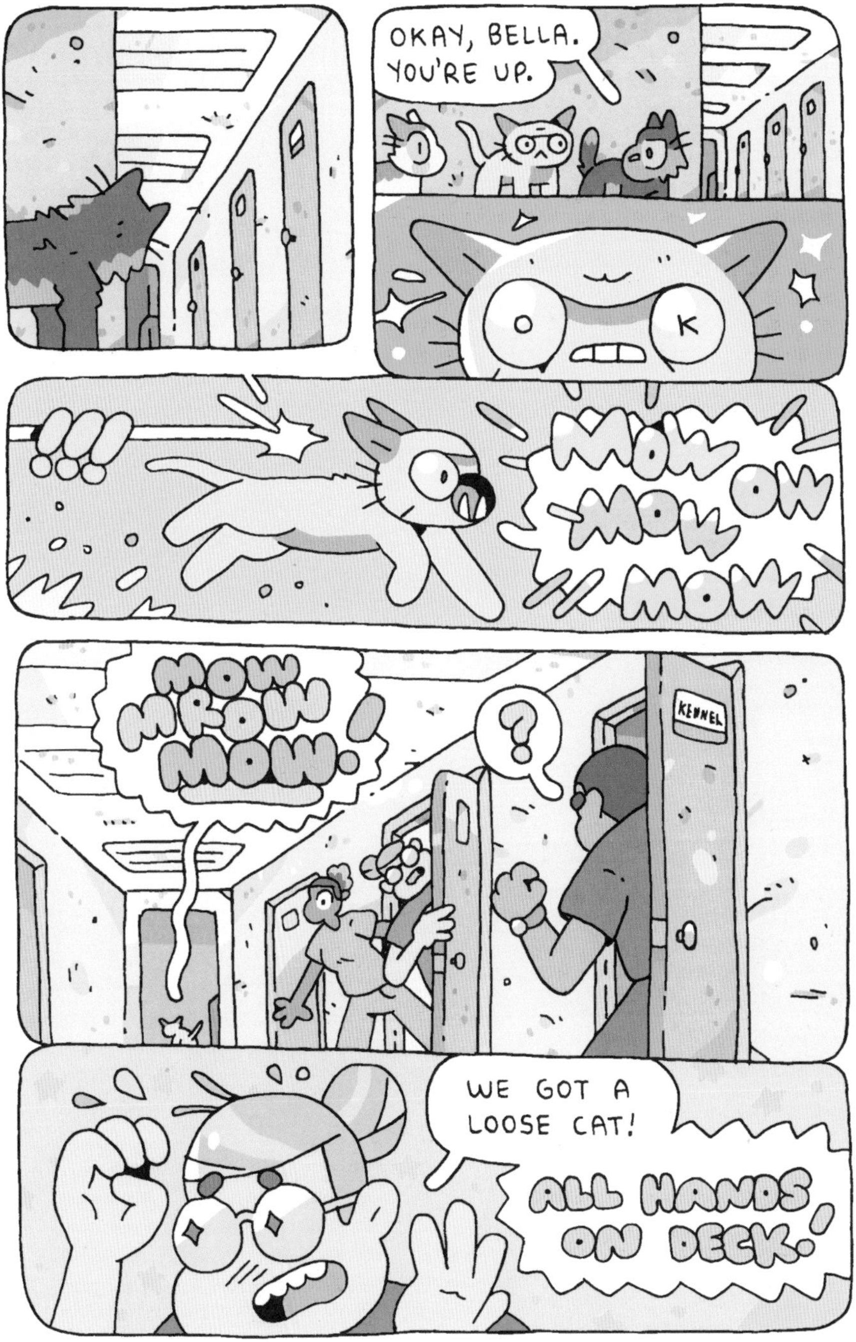
OKAY, BELLA. YOU'RE UP.
MOW MOW OW MOW MOW
MOW MROW MOW!
?
KENNEL
WE GOT A LOOSE CAT!
ALL HANDS ON DECK!

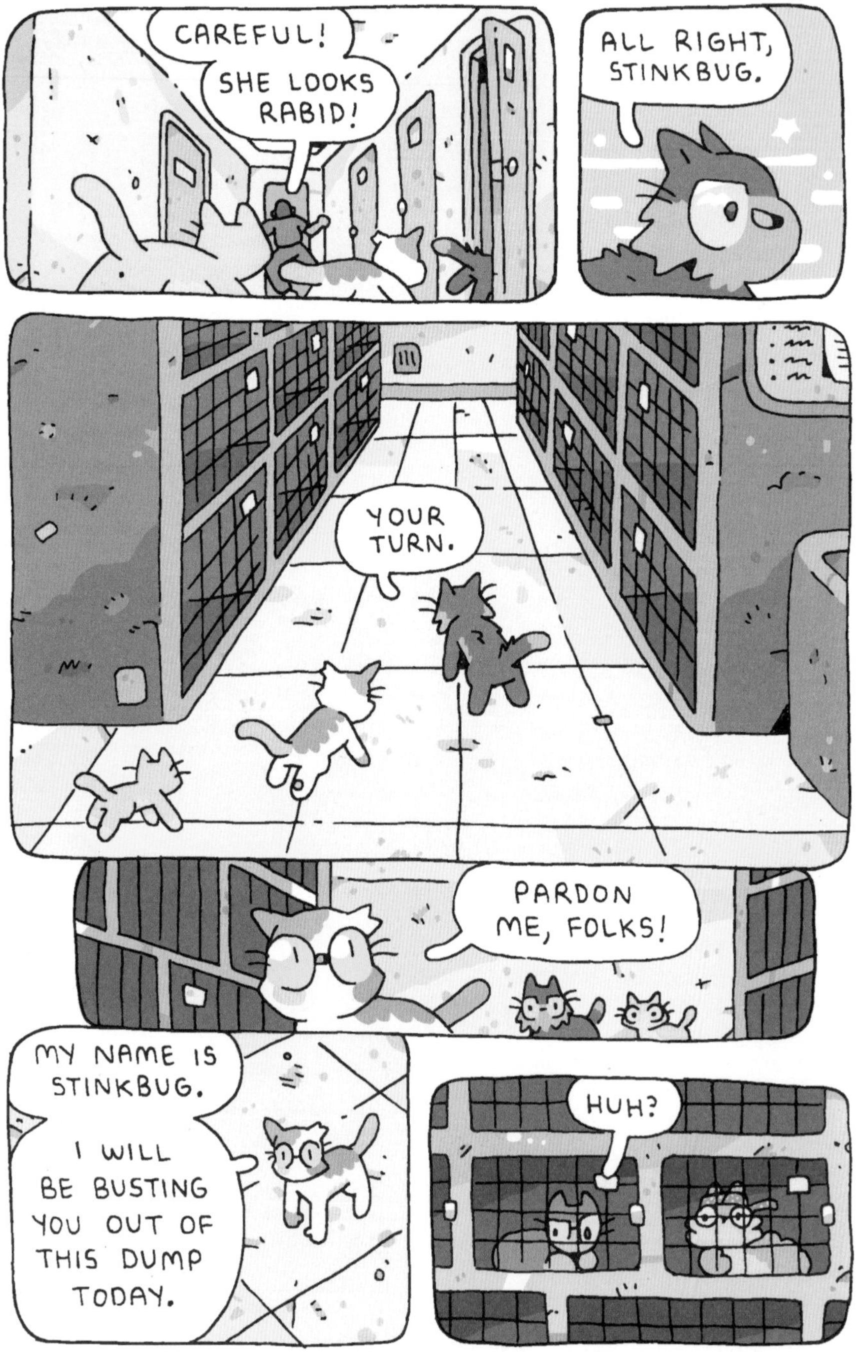
CAREFUL!
SHE LOOKS RABID!
ALL RIGHT, STINKBUG.
YOUR TURN.
PARDON ME, FOLKS!
MY NAME IS STINKBUG.
I WILL BE BUSTING YOU OUT OF THIS DUMP TODAY.
HUH?

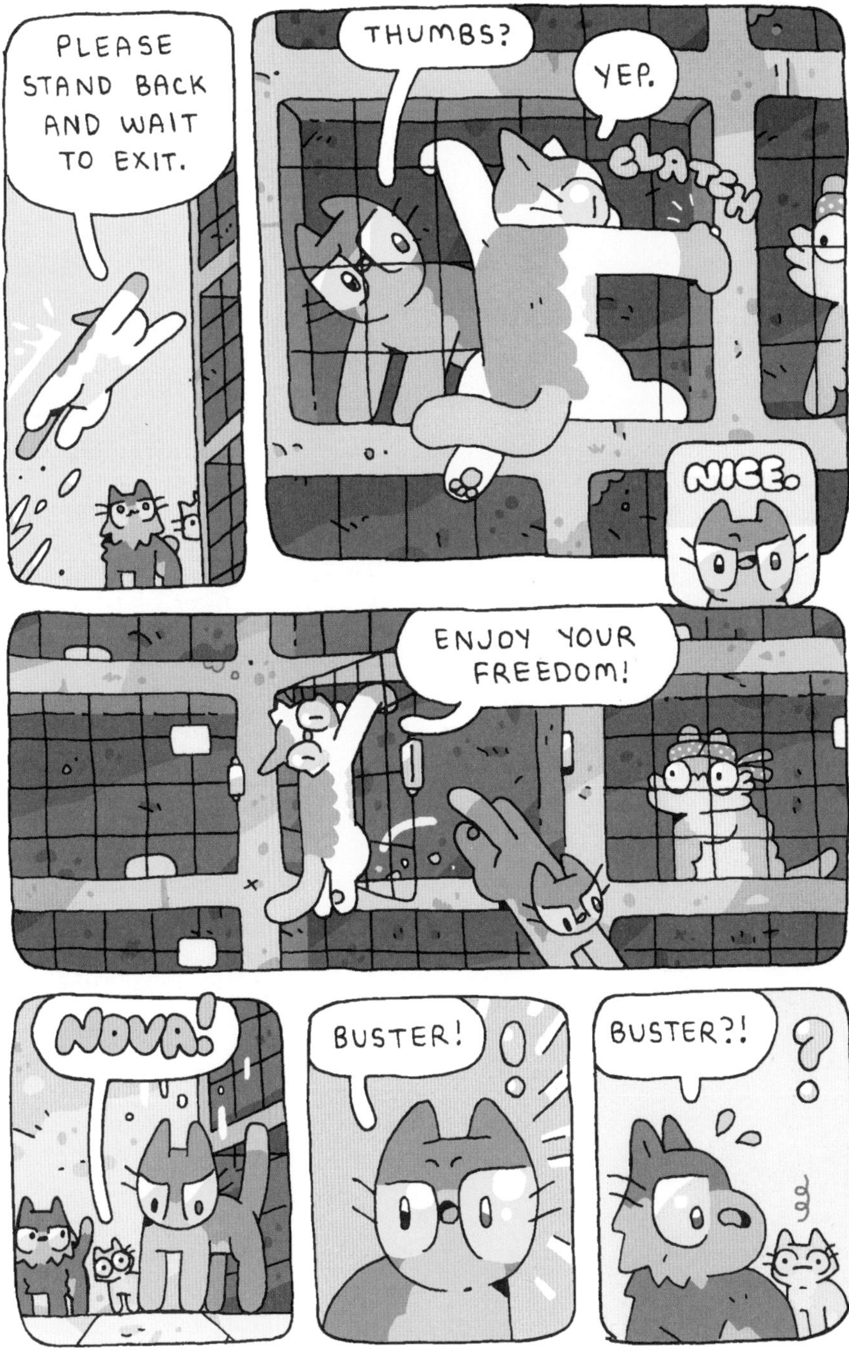
PLEASE STAND BACK AND WAIT TO EXIT.
THUMBS?
YEP.
CLATCH
NICE.
ENJOY YOUR FREEDOM!
NOVA!
BUSTER!
BUSTER?!

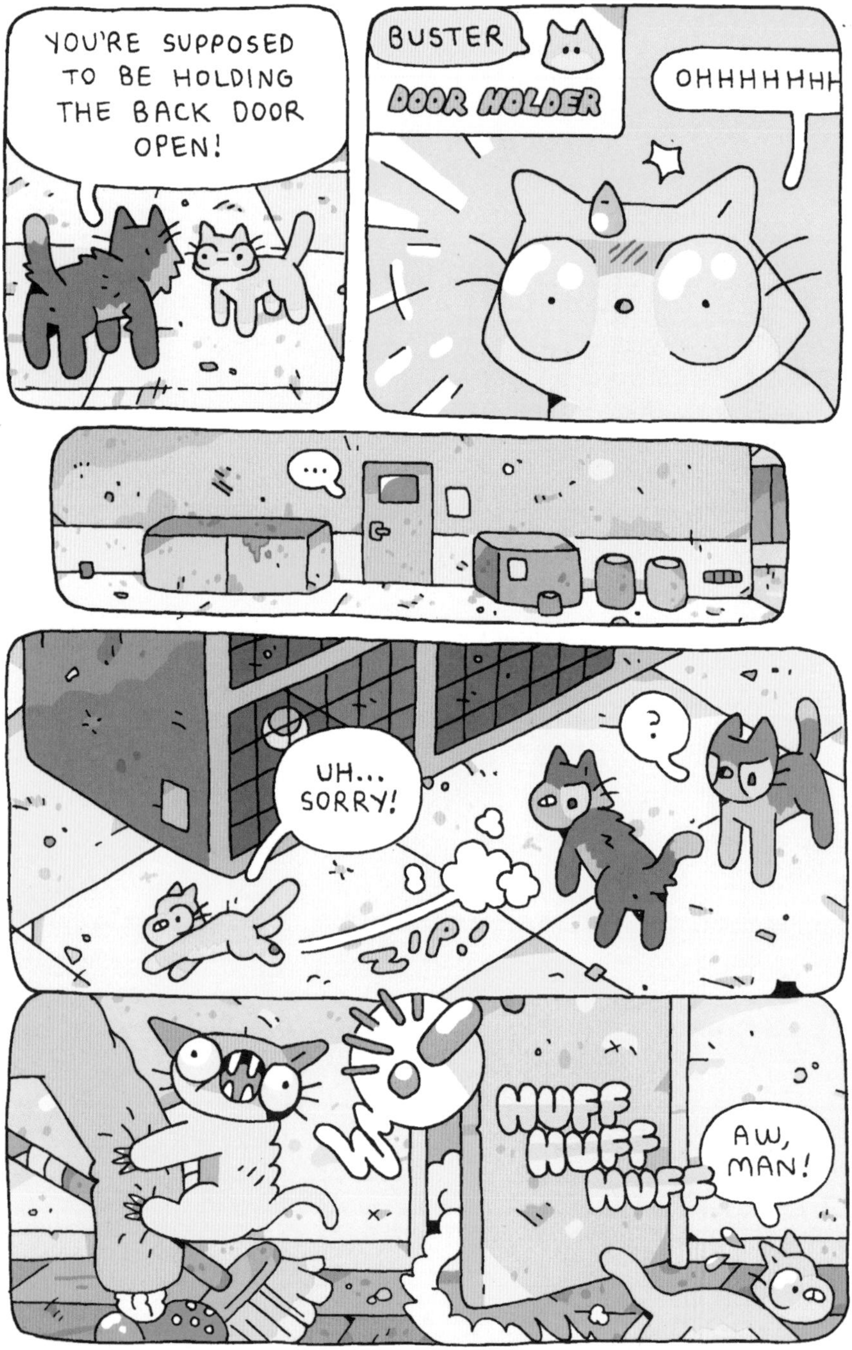

YOU'RE SUPPOSED TO BE HOLDING THE BACK DOOR OPEN!
BUSTER
DOOR HOLDER
OHHHHHHH
...
?
UH... SORRY!
ZIP
W
HUFF HUFF HUFF
AW, MAN!

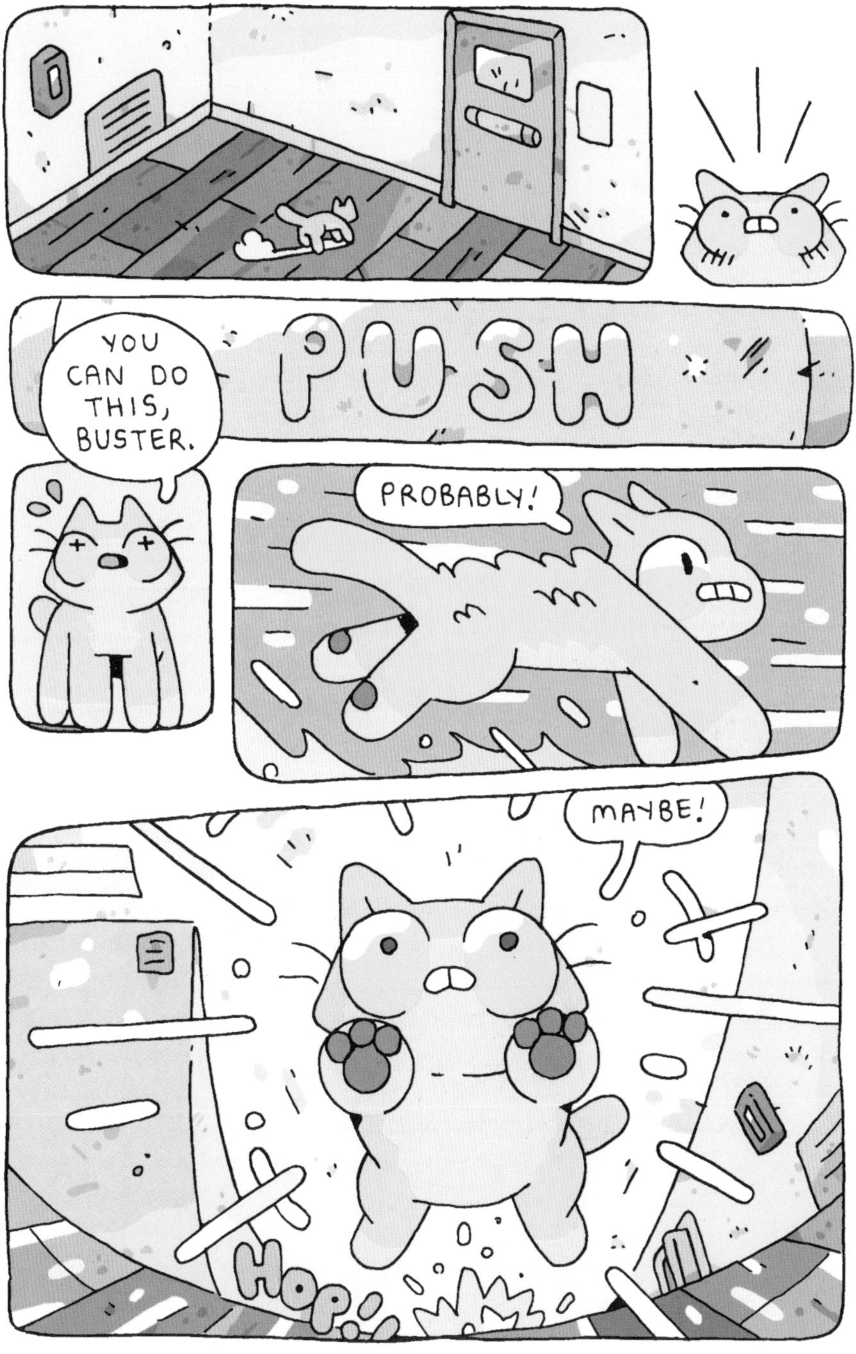
PUSH
YOU CAN DO THIS, BUSTER.
PROBABLY!
MAYBE!
HOP!

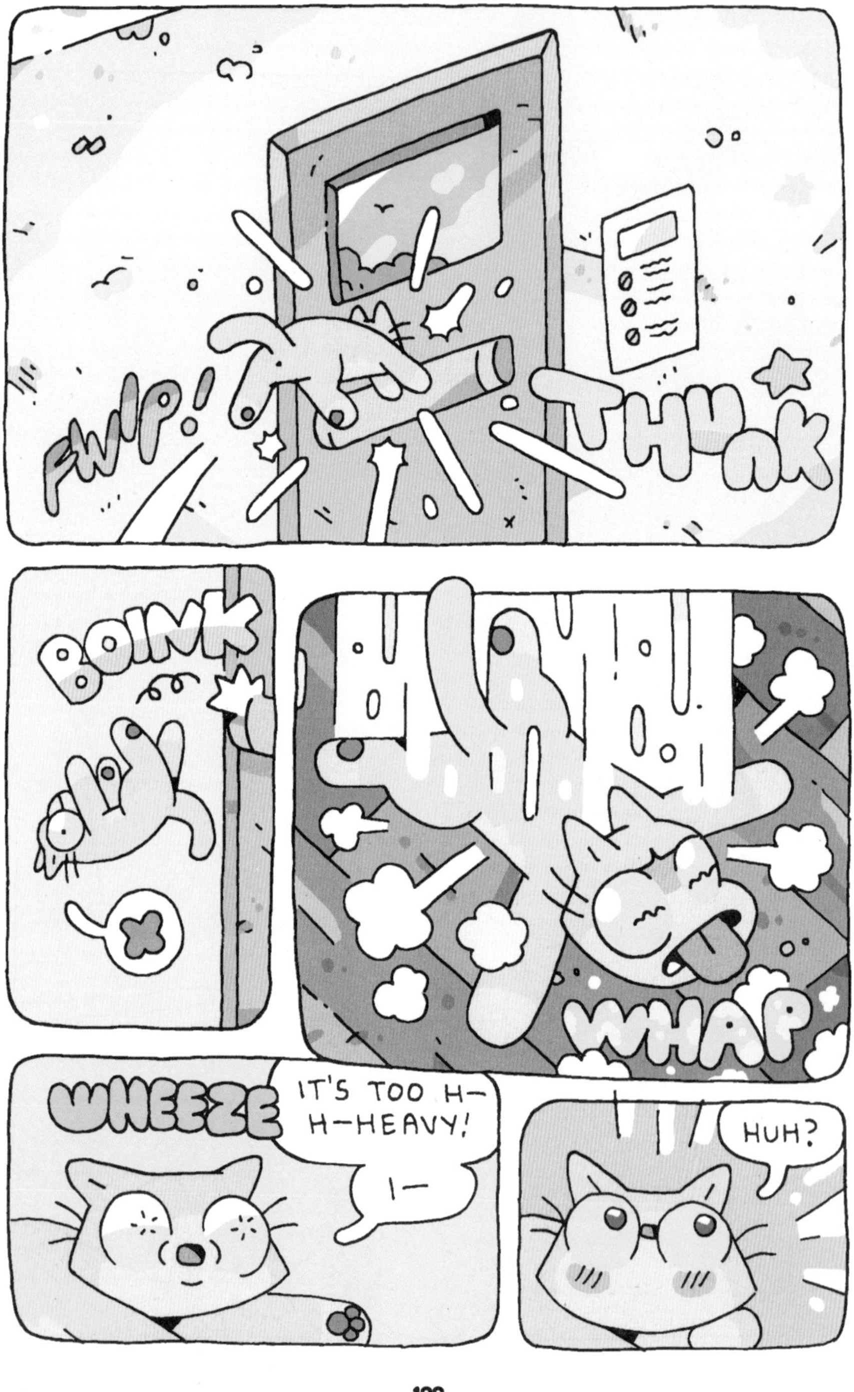
FWIP!
THUNK
BOINK
WHAP
WHEEZE
IT'S TOO H—
H—HEAVY!
I—
HUH?

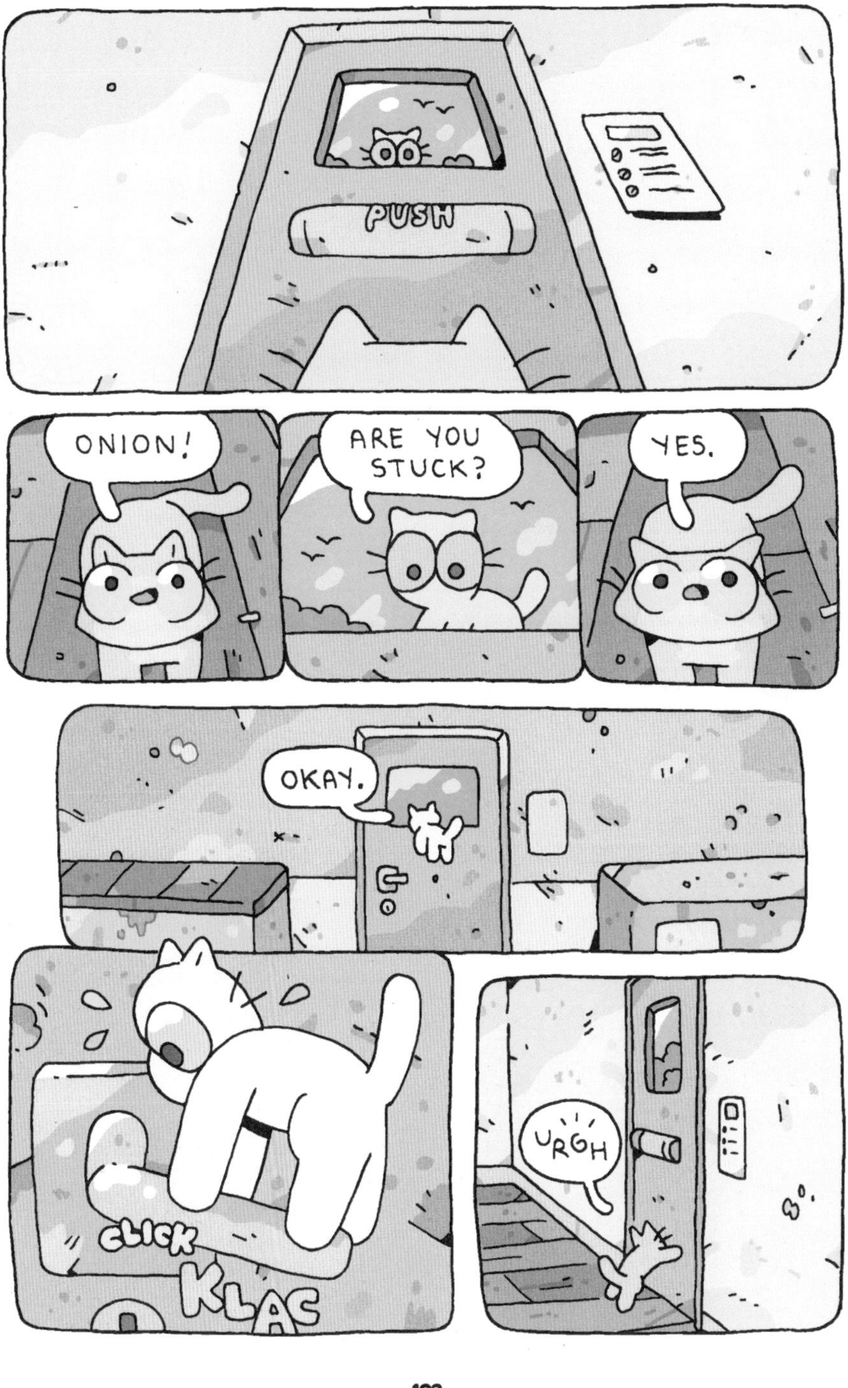
PUSH
ONION!
ARE YOU STUCK?
YES.
OKAY.
CLICK
KLAC
URGH

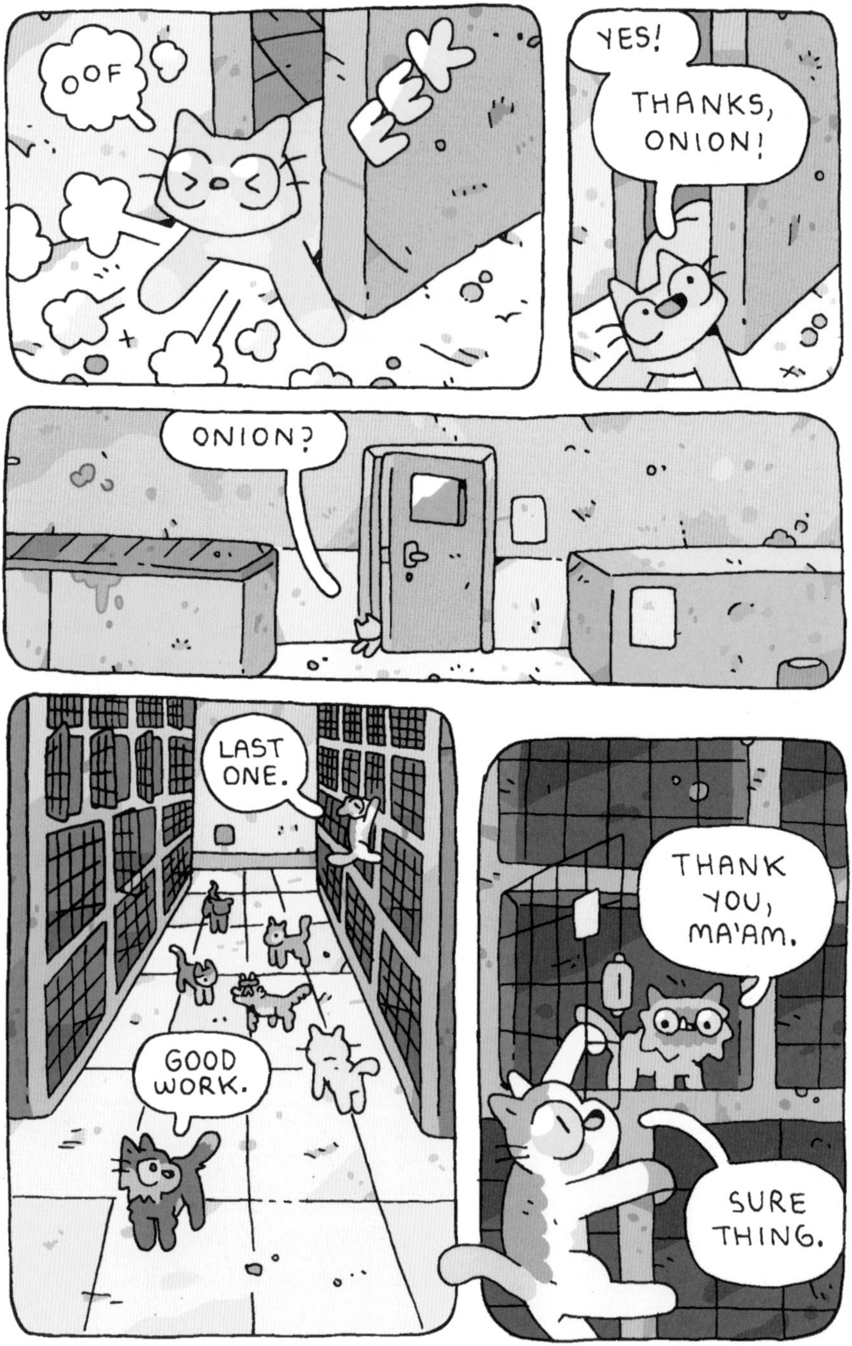
OOF
EEK
YES!
THANKS, ONION!
ONION?
LAST ONE.
GOOD WORK.
THANK YOU, MA'AM.
SURE THING.

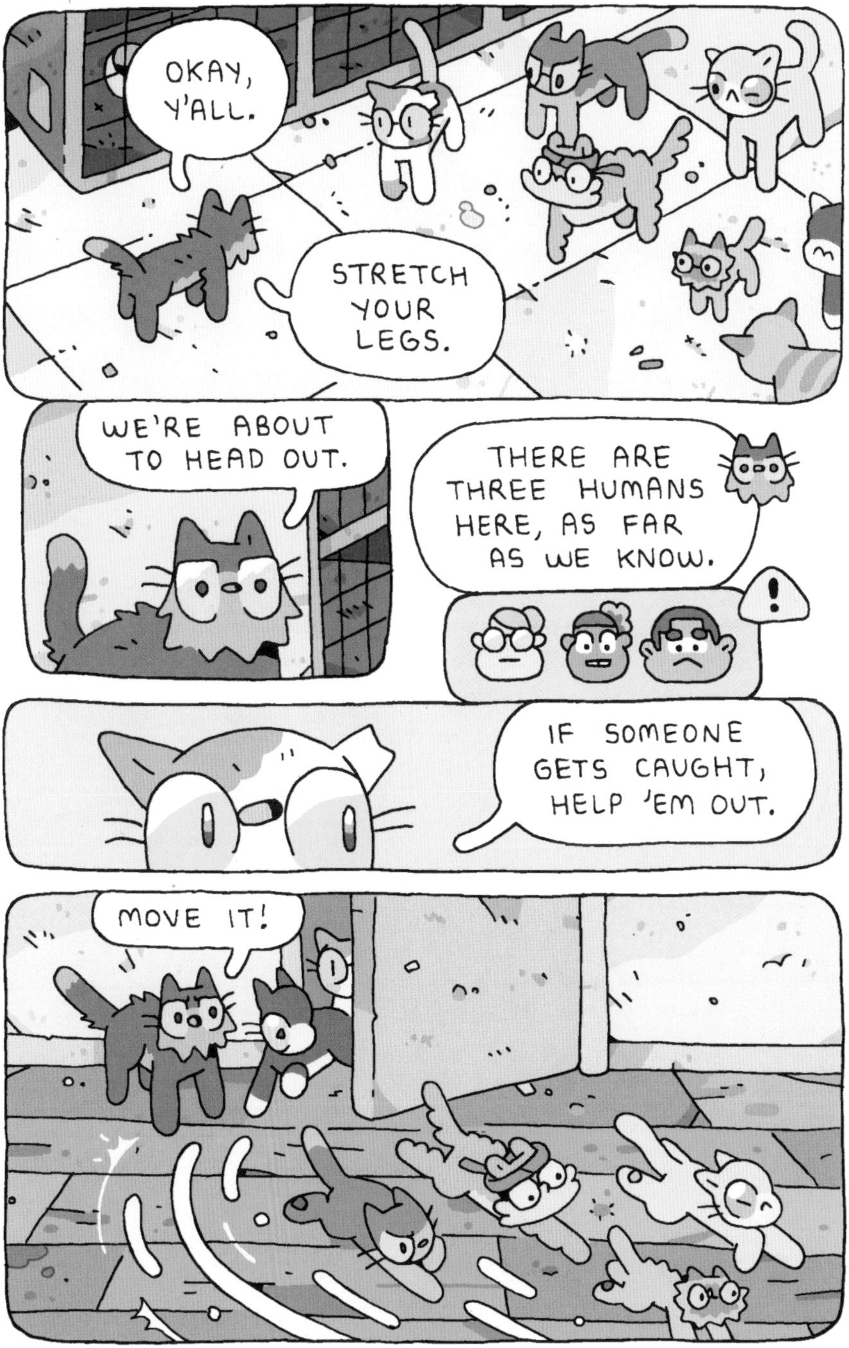
OKAY, Y'ALL.
STRETCH YOUR LEGS.
WE'RE ABOUT TO HEAD OUT.
THERE ARE THREE HUMANS HERE, AS FAR AS WE KNOW.
!
IF SOMEONE GETS CAUGHT, HELP 'EM OUT.
MOVE IT!

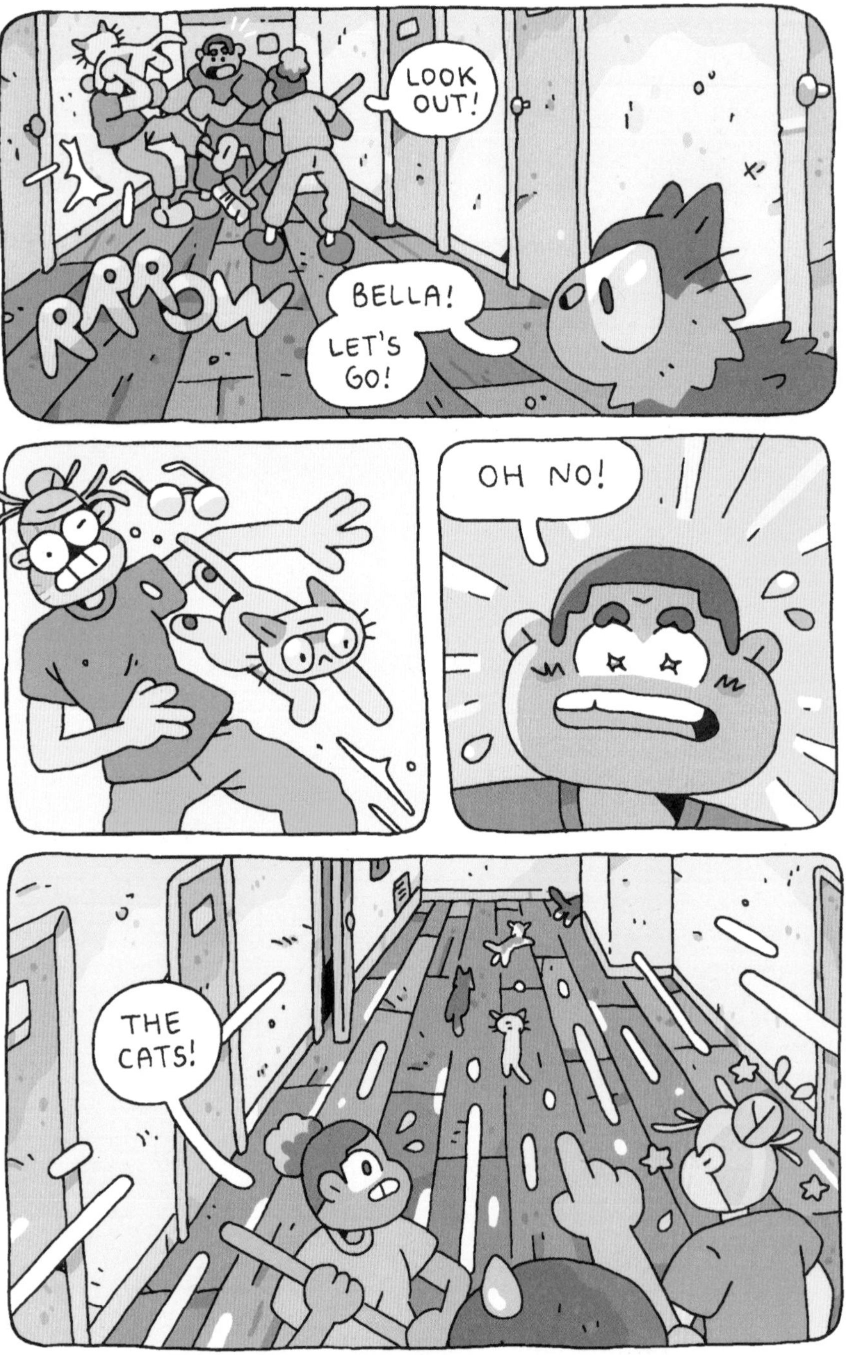
LOOK OUT!
RRROW
BELLA!
LET'S GO!
OH NO!
THE CATS!

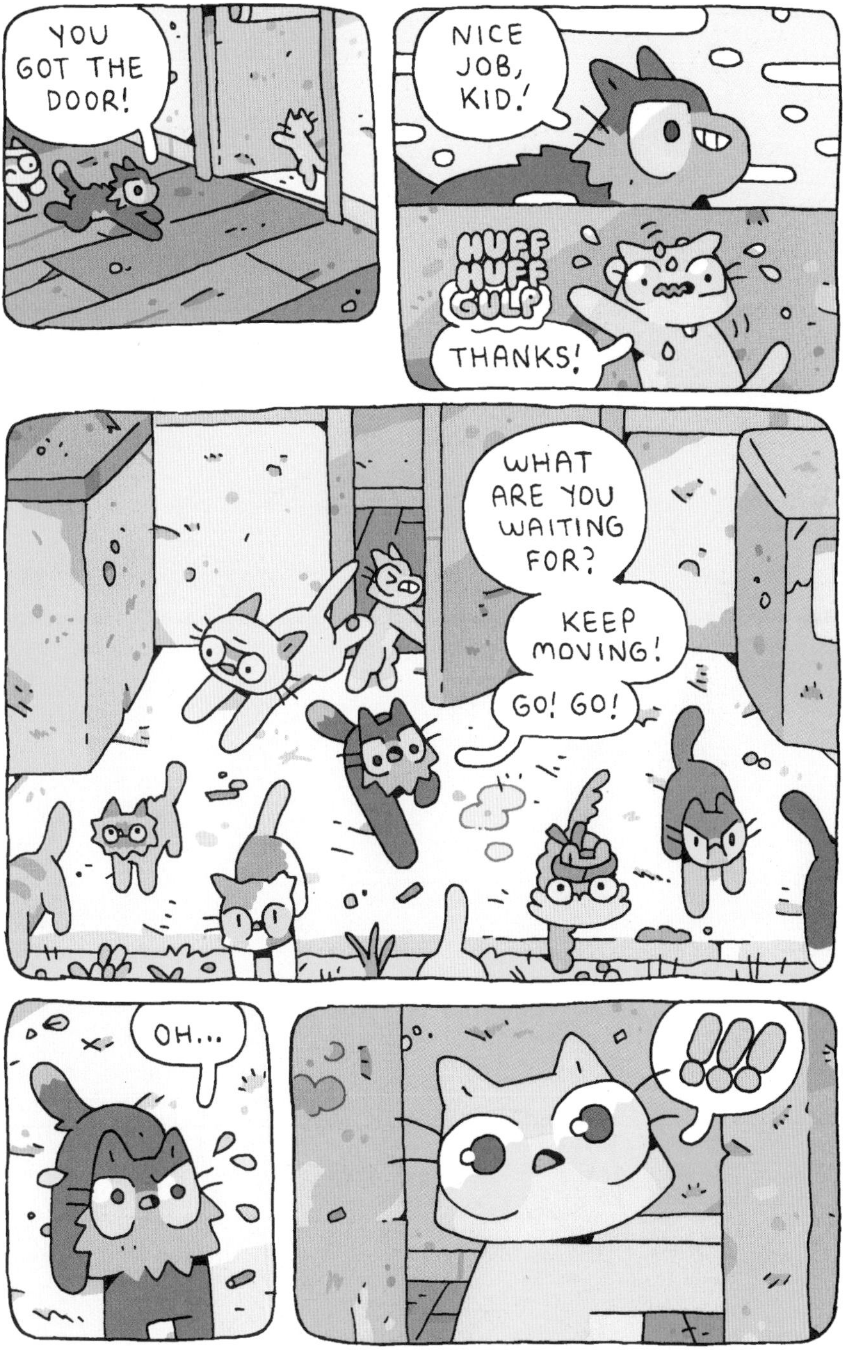
YOU GOT THE DOOR!
NICE JOB, KID!
HUFF HUFF GULP
THANKS!
WHAT ARE YOU WAITING FOR?
KEEP MOVING!
GO! GO!
OH...

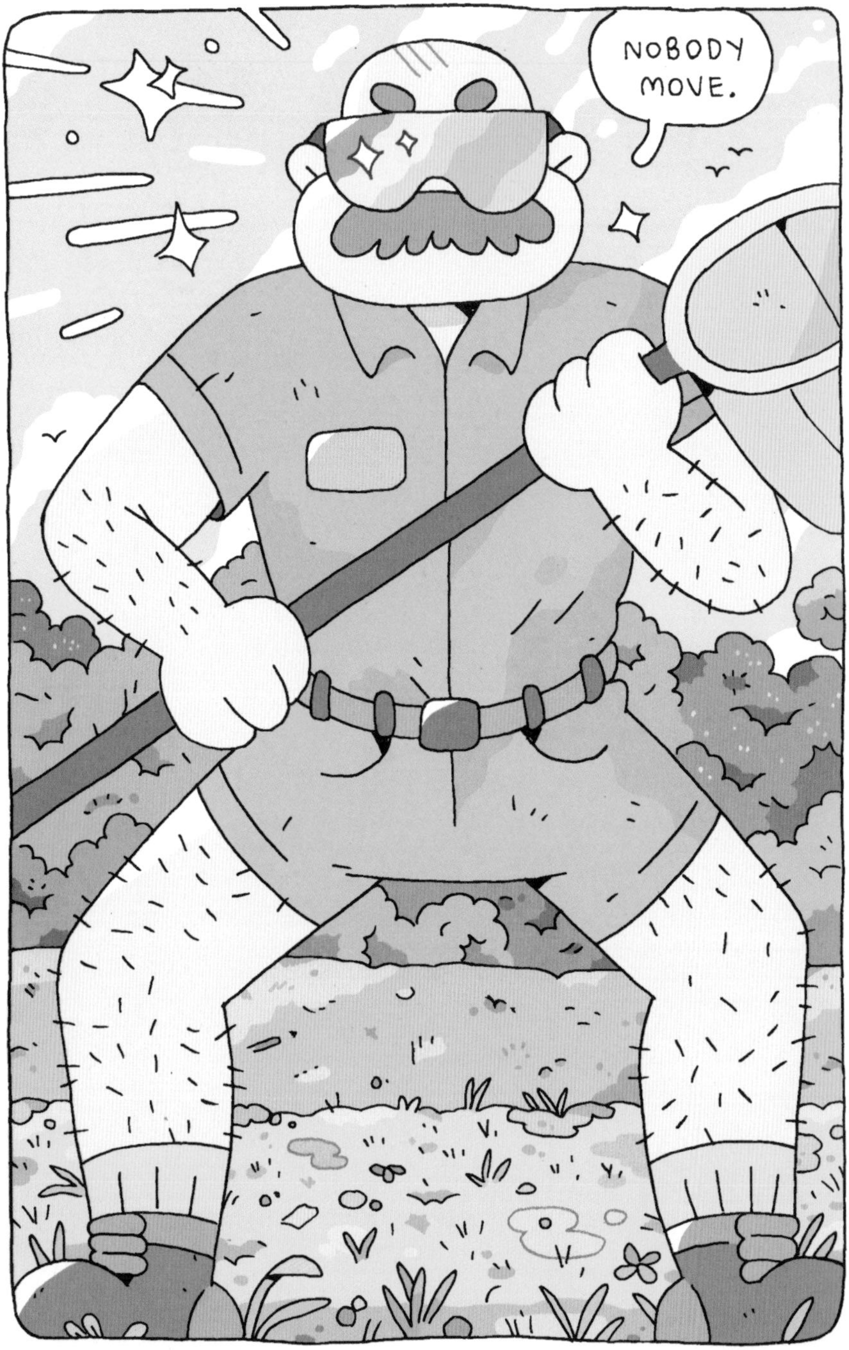
NOBODY MOVE.

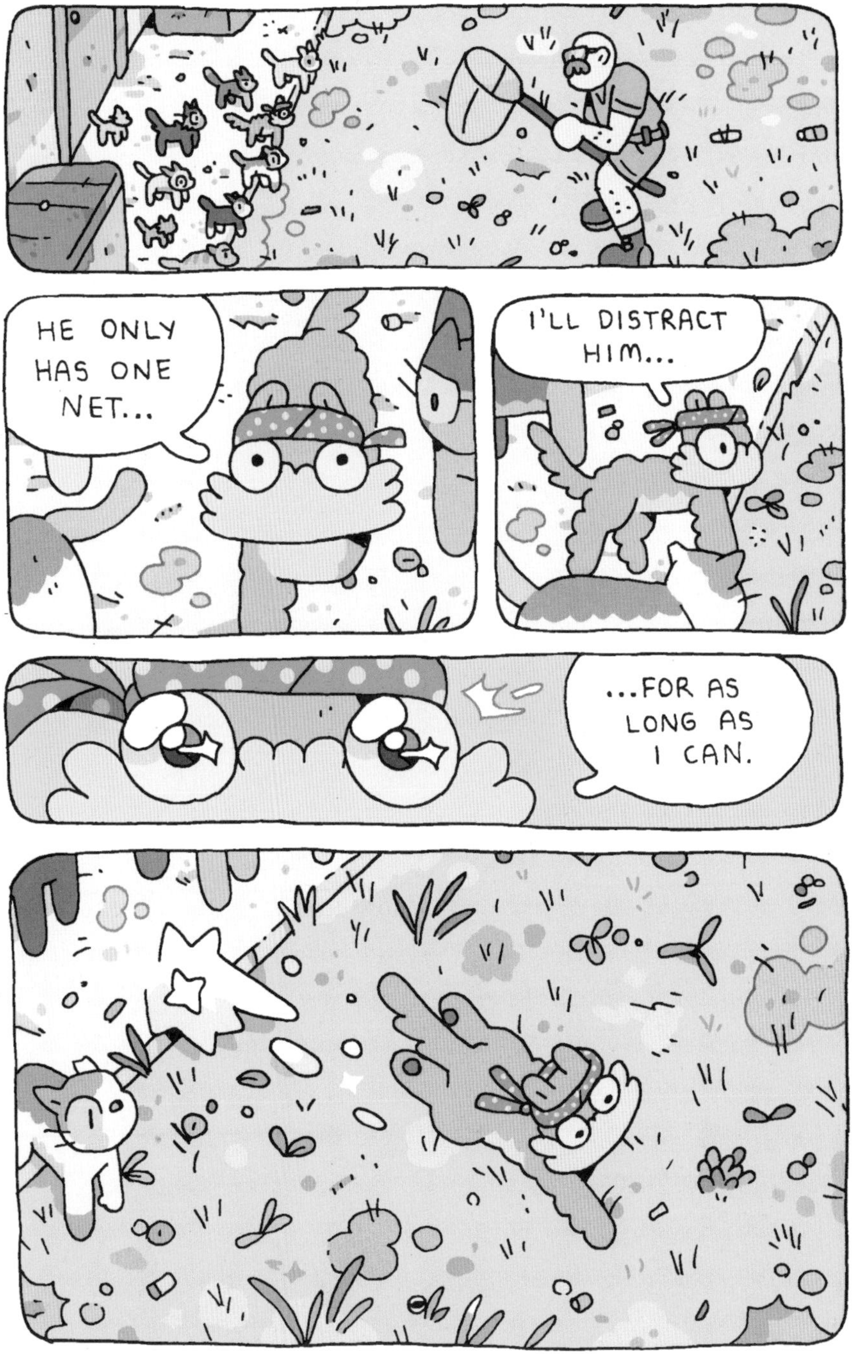
HE ONLY HAS ONE NET...
I'LL DISTRACT HIM...
...FOR AS LONG AS I CAN.

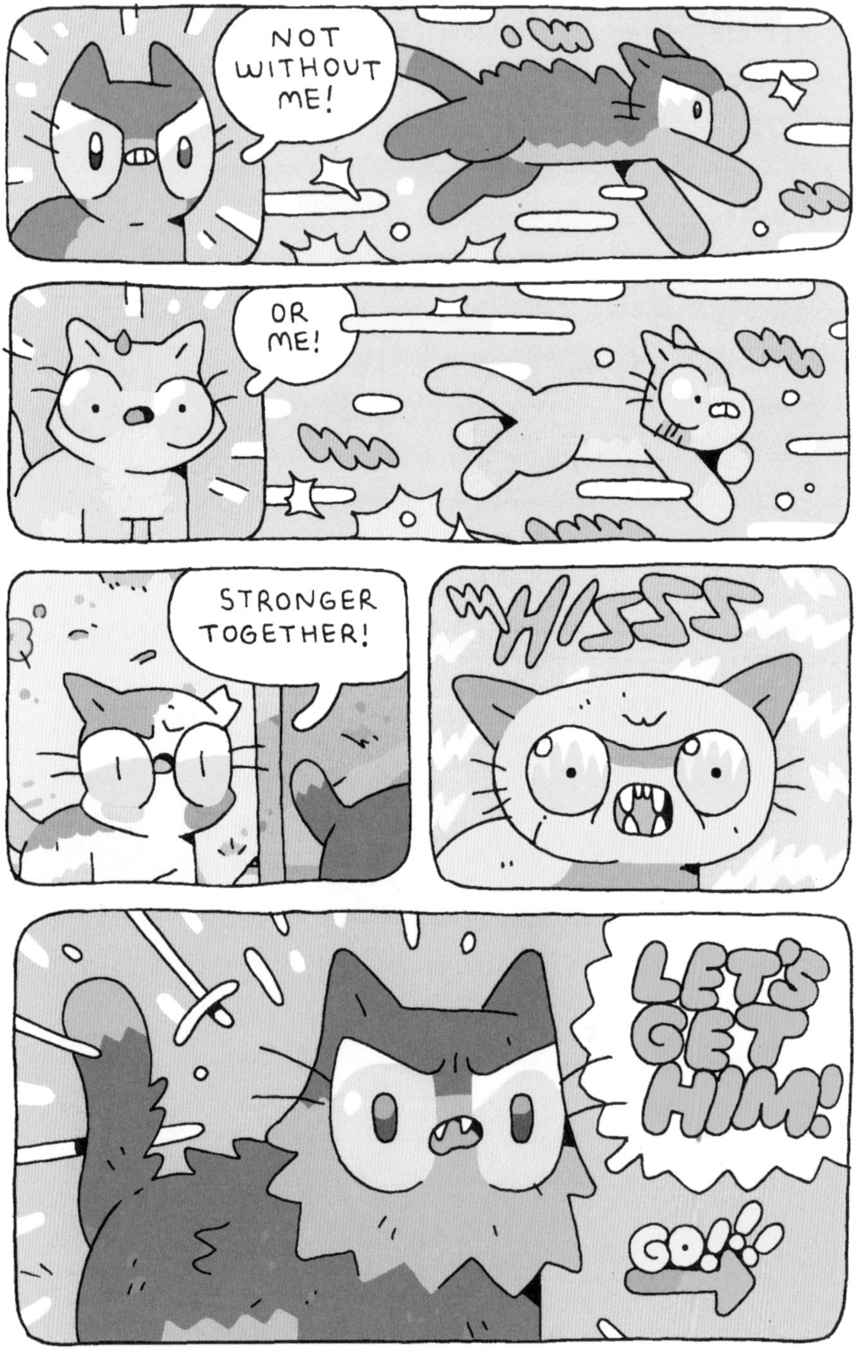
NOT WITHOUT ME!
OR ME!
STRONGER TOGETHER!
HISSS
LET'S GET HIM!
GO!!!

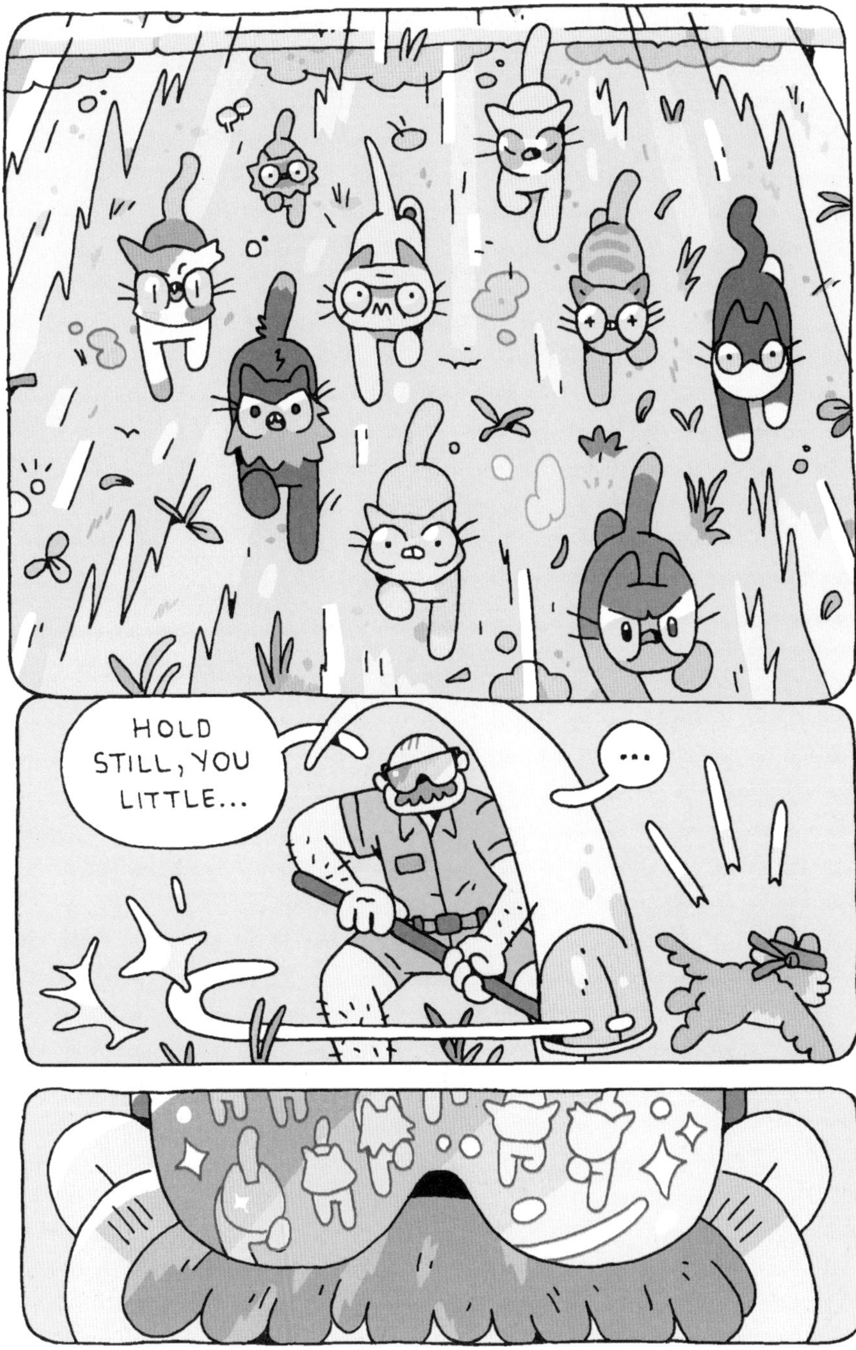
HOLD STILL, YOU LITTLE...
...

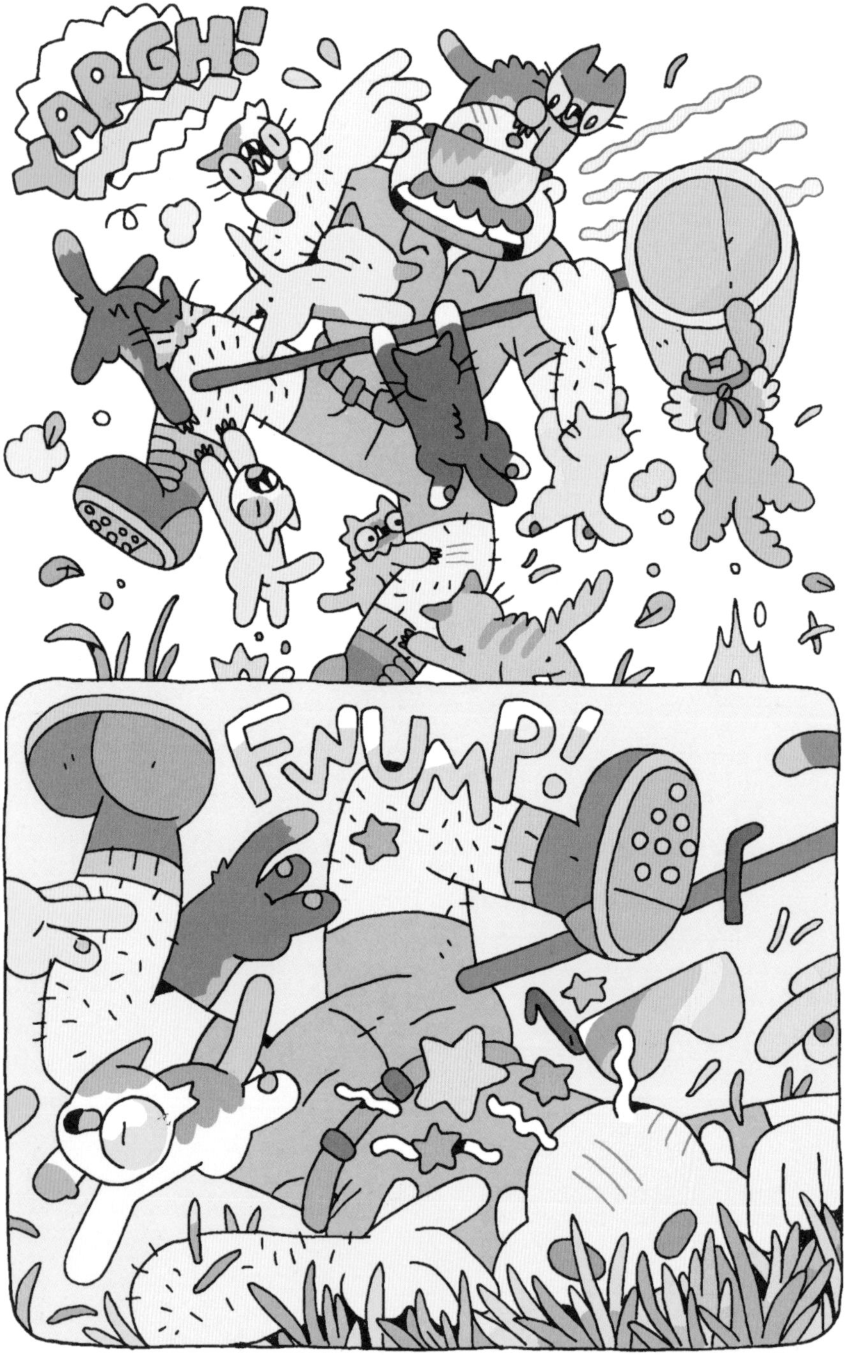
YARGH!
FWUMP!

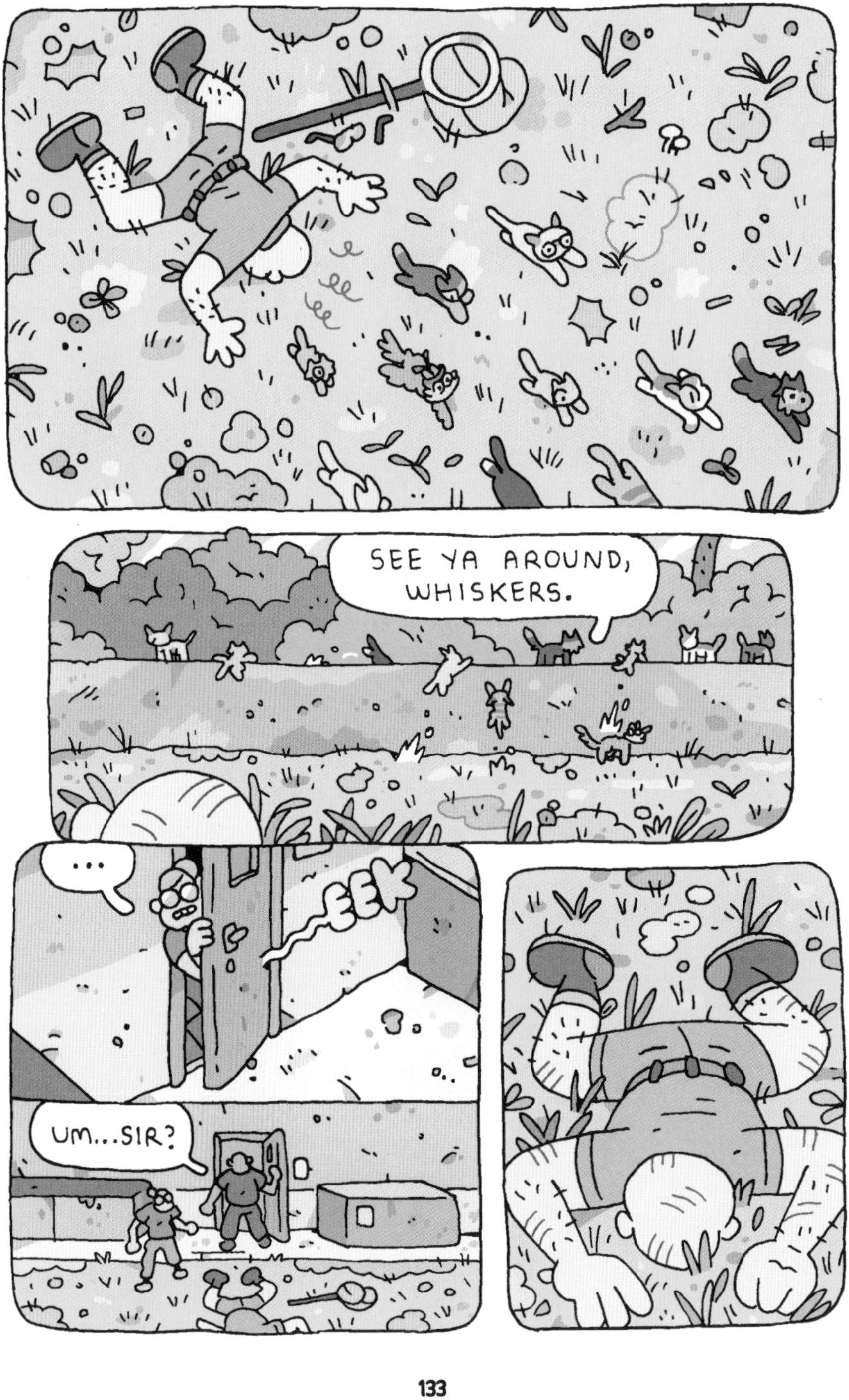
SEE YA AROUND, WHISKERS.
...
EEK
UM...SIR?

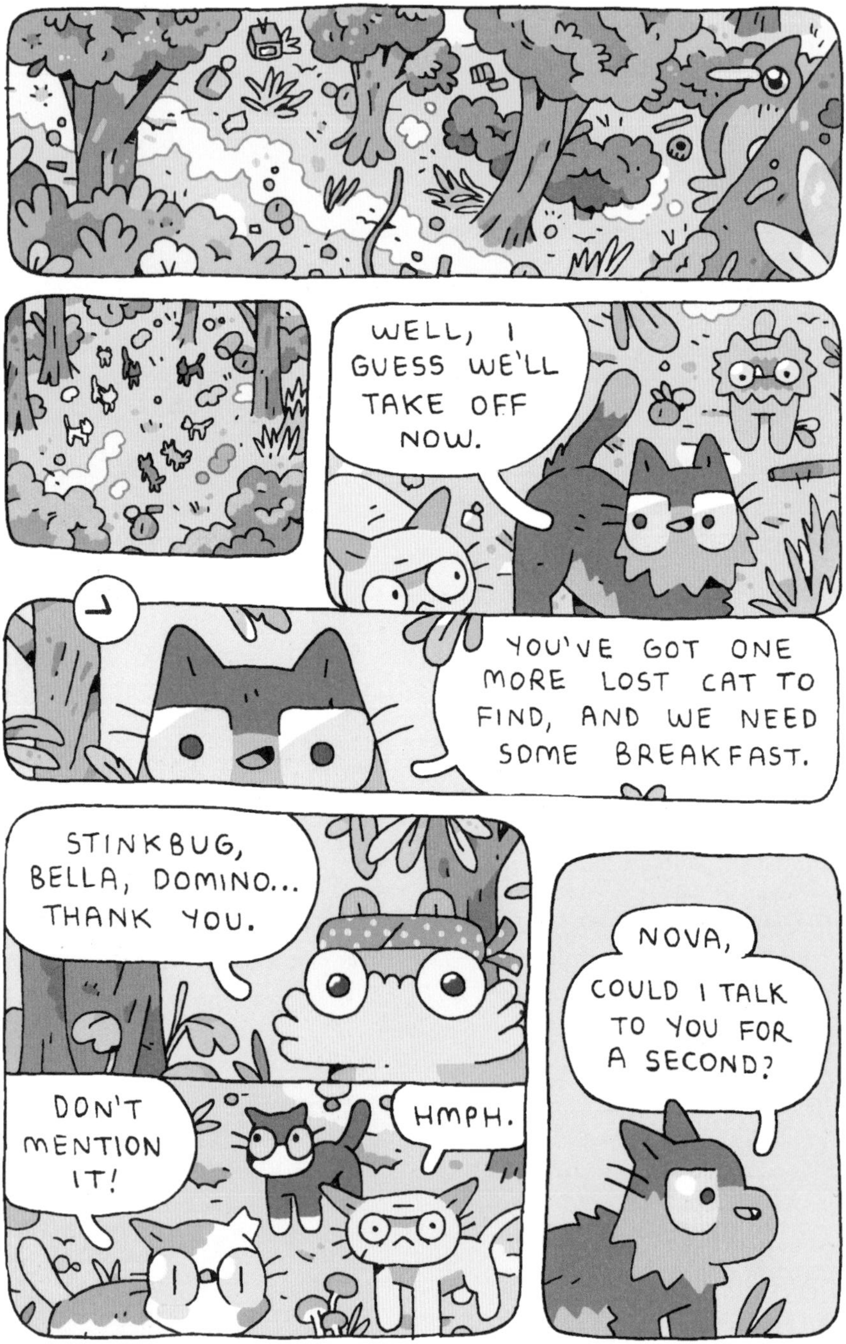
WELL, I GUESS WE'LL TAKE OFF NOW.
YOU'VE GOT ONE MORE LOST CAT TO FIND, AND WE NEED SOME BREAKFAST.
STINKBUG, BELLA, DOMINO... THANK YOU.
DON'T MENTION IT!
HMPH.
NOVA,
COULD I TALK TO YOU FOR A SECOND?

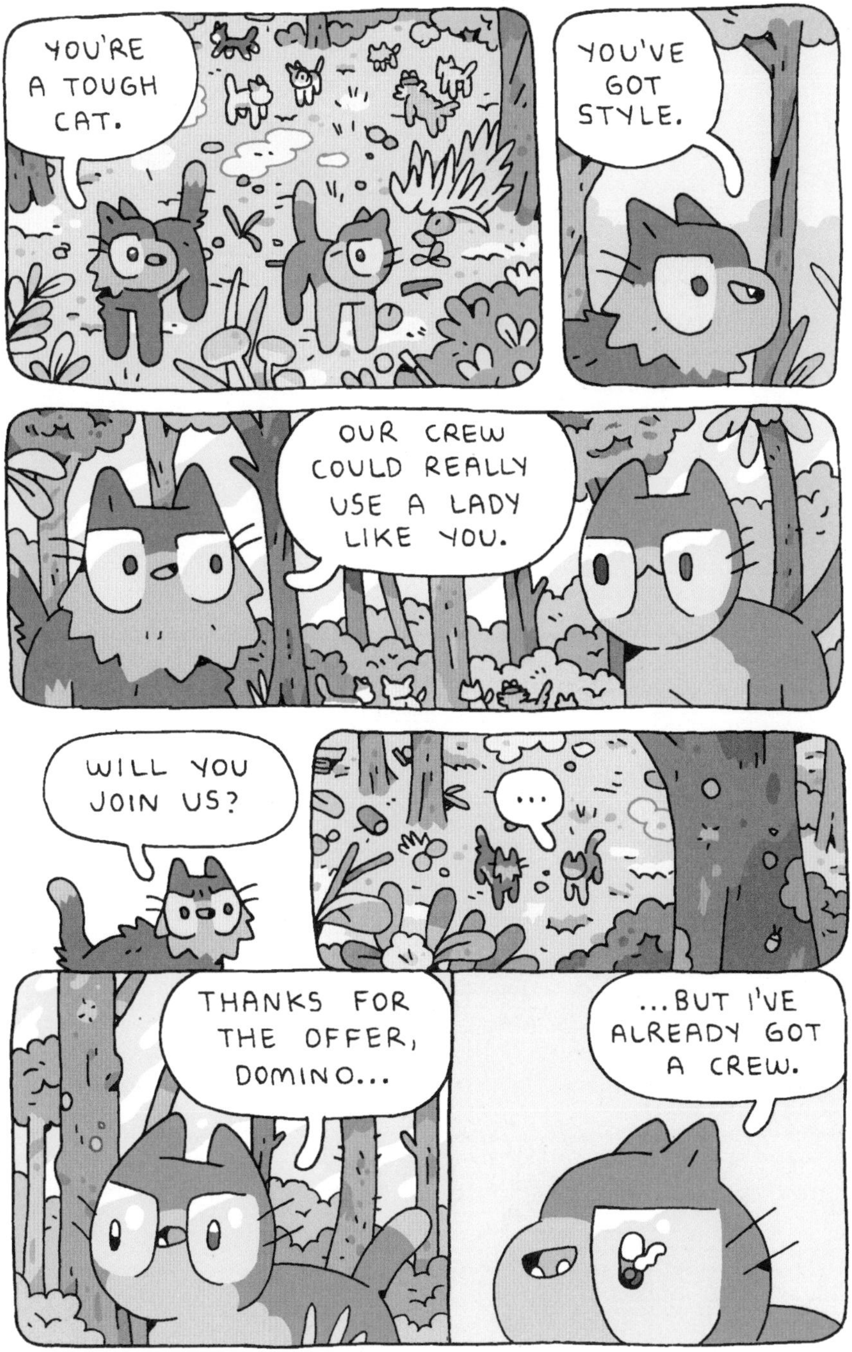
YOU'RE A TOUGH CAT.
YOU'VE GOT STYLE.
OUR CREW COULD REALLY USE A LADY LIKE YOU.
WILL YOU JOIN US?
...
THANKS FOR THE OFFER, DOMINO...
...BUT I'VE ALREADY GOT A CREW.

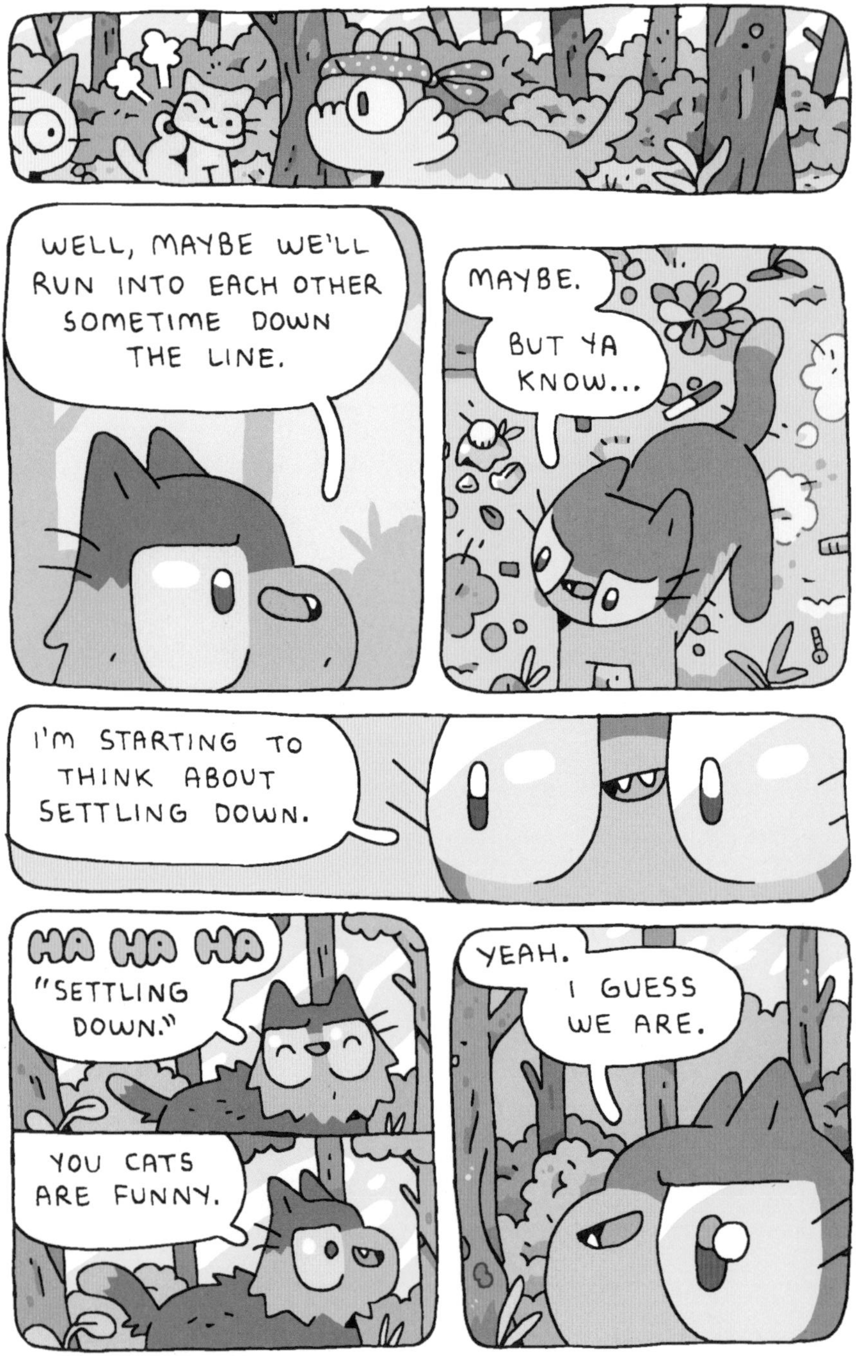
WELL, MAYBE WE'LL RUN INTO EACH OTHER SOMETIME DOWN THE LINE.
MAYBE.
BUT YA KNOW...
I'M STARTING TO THINK ABOUT SETTLING DOWN.
HA HA HA
"SETTLING DOWN."
YOU CATS ARE FUNNY.
YEAH.
I GUESS WE ARE.

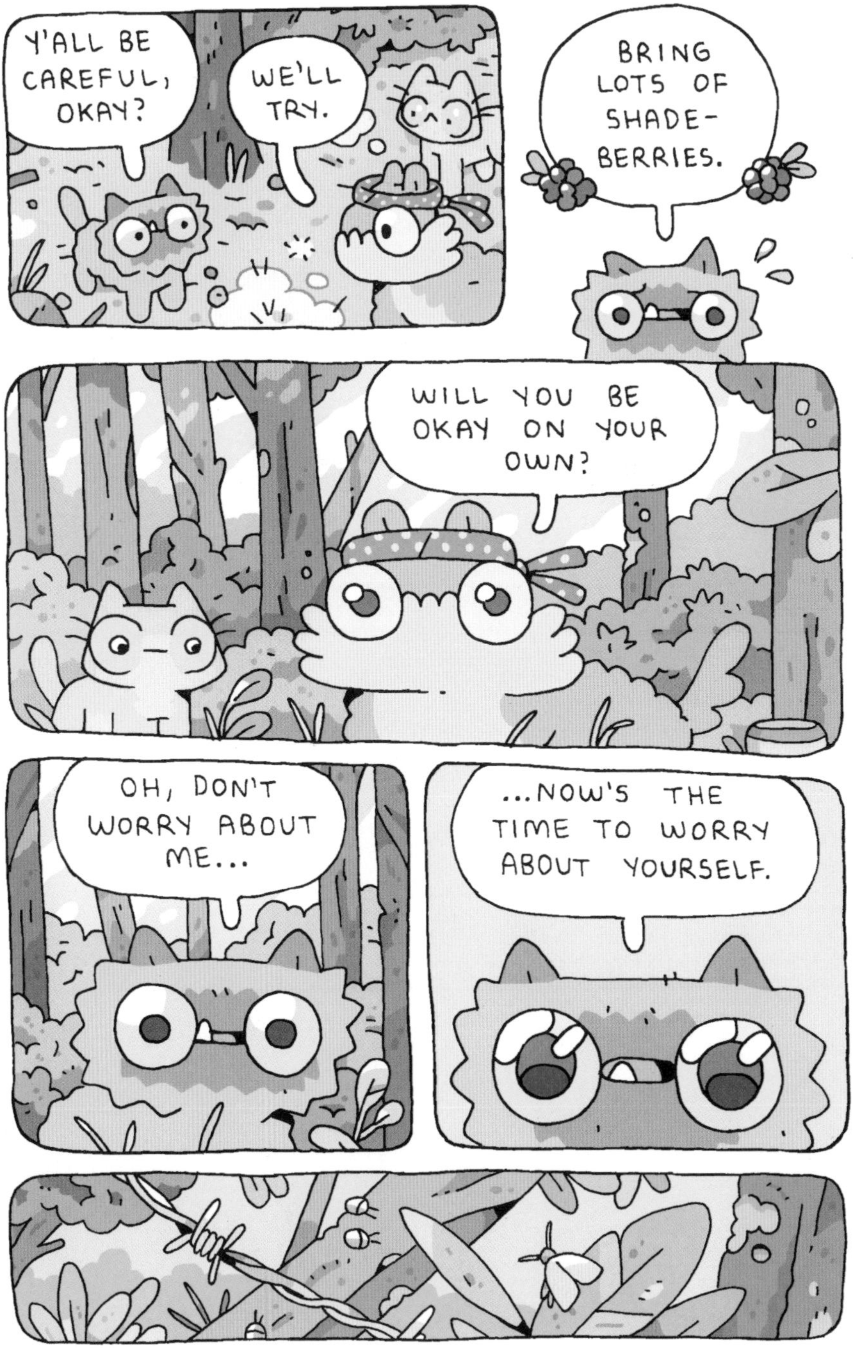
Y'ALL BE CAREFUL, OKAY?
WE'LL TRY.
BRING LOTS OF SHADE-BERRIES.
WILL YOU BE OKAY ON YOUR OWN?
OH, DON'T WORRY ABOUT ME...
...NOW'S THE TIME TO WORRY ABOUT YOURSELF.

CHAPTER 6

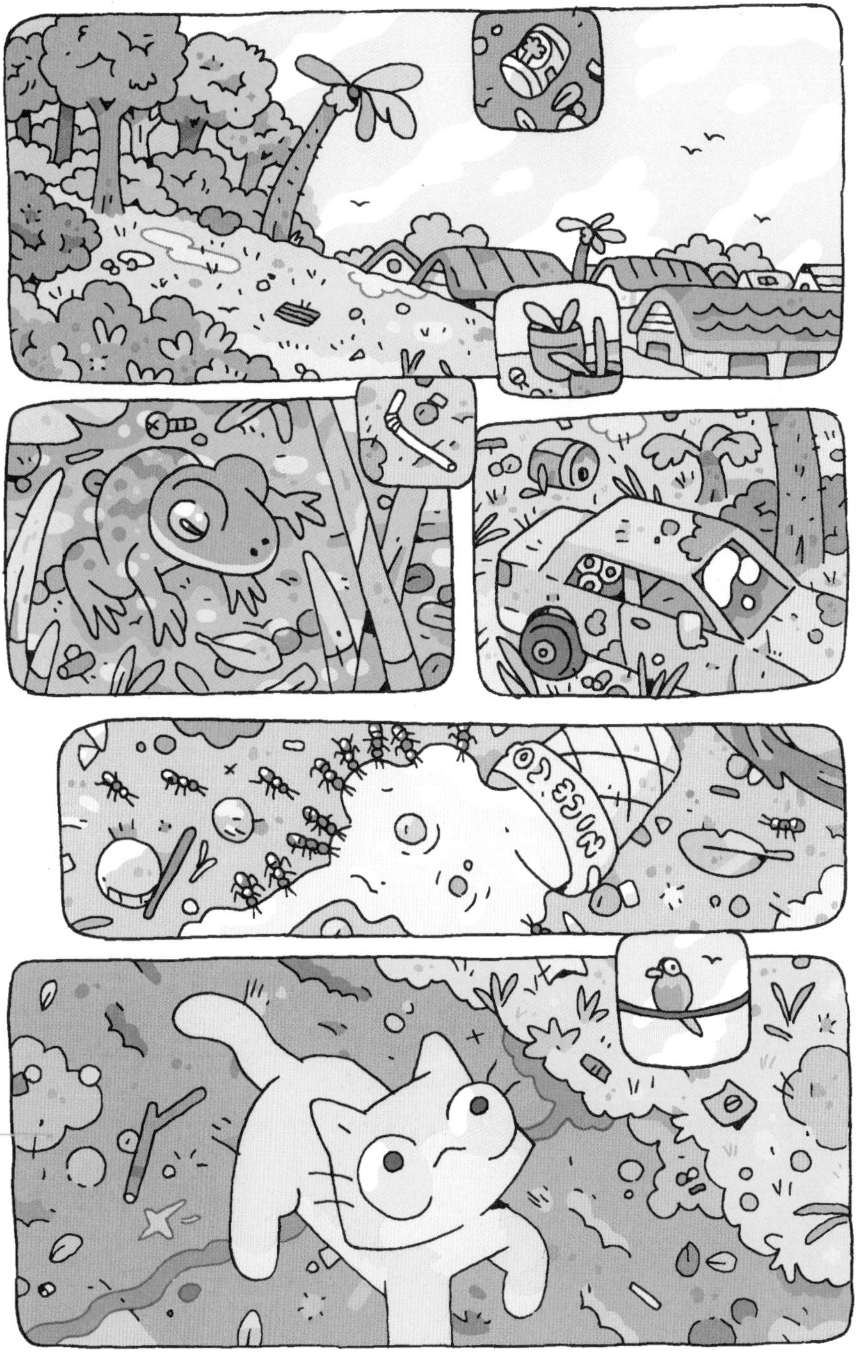

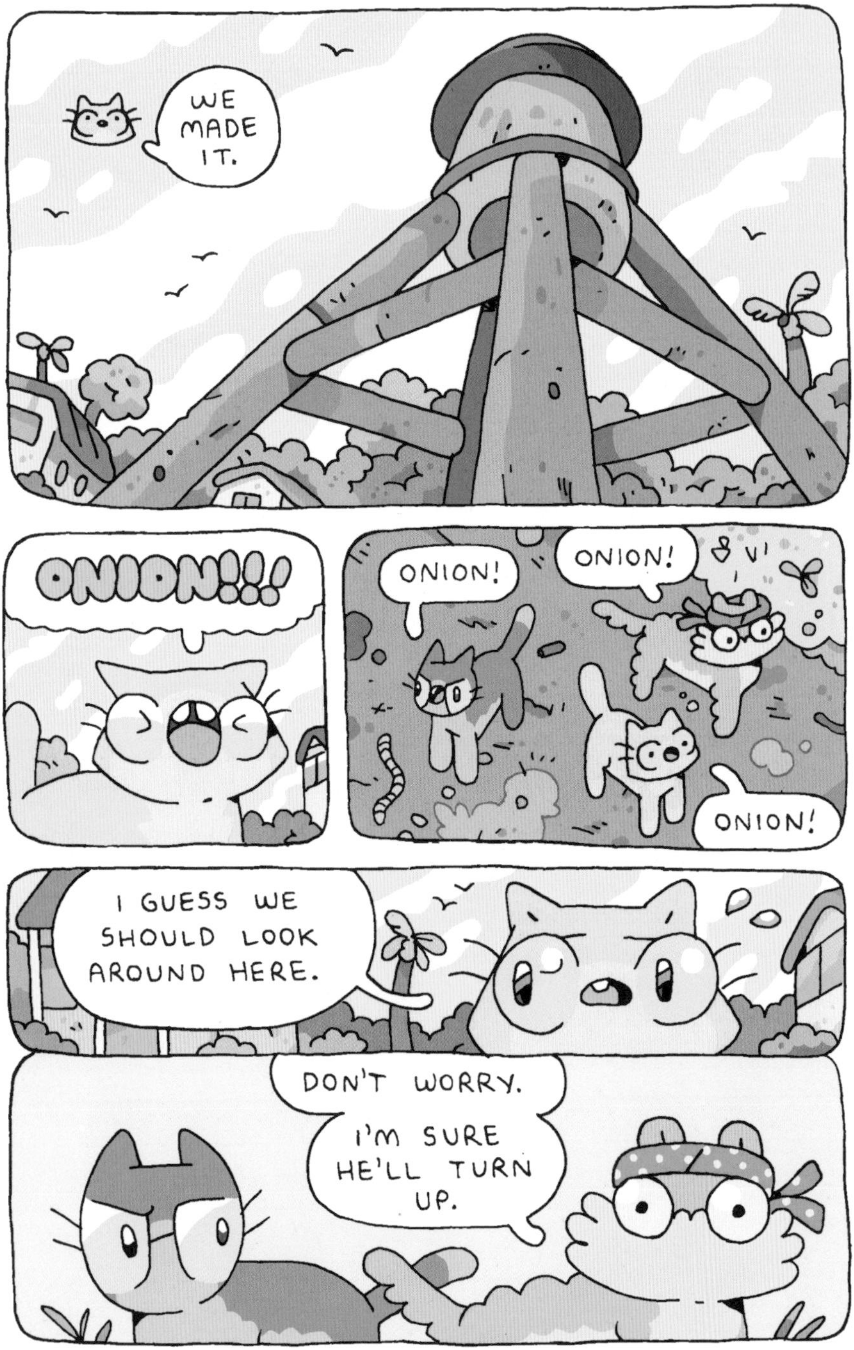
WE MADE IT.
ONION!!!
ONION!
ONION!
ONION!
I GUESS WE SHOULD LOOK AROUND HERE.
DON'T WORRY.
I'M SURE HE'LL TURN UP.

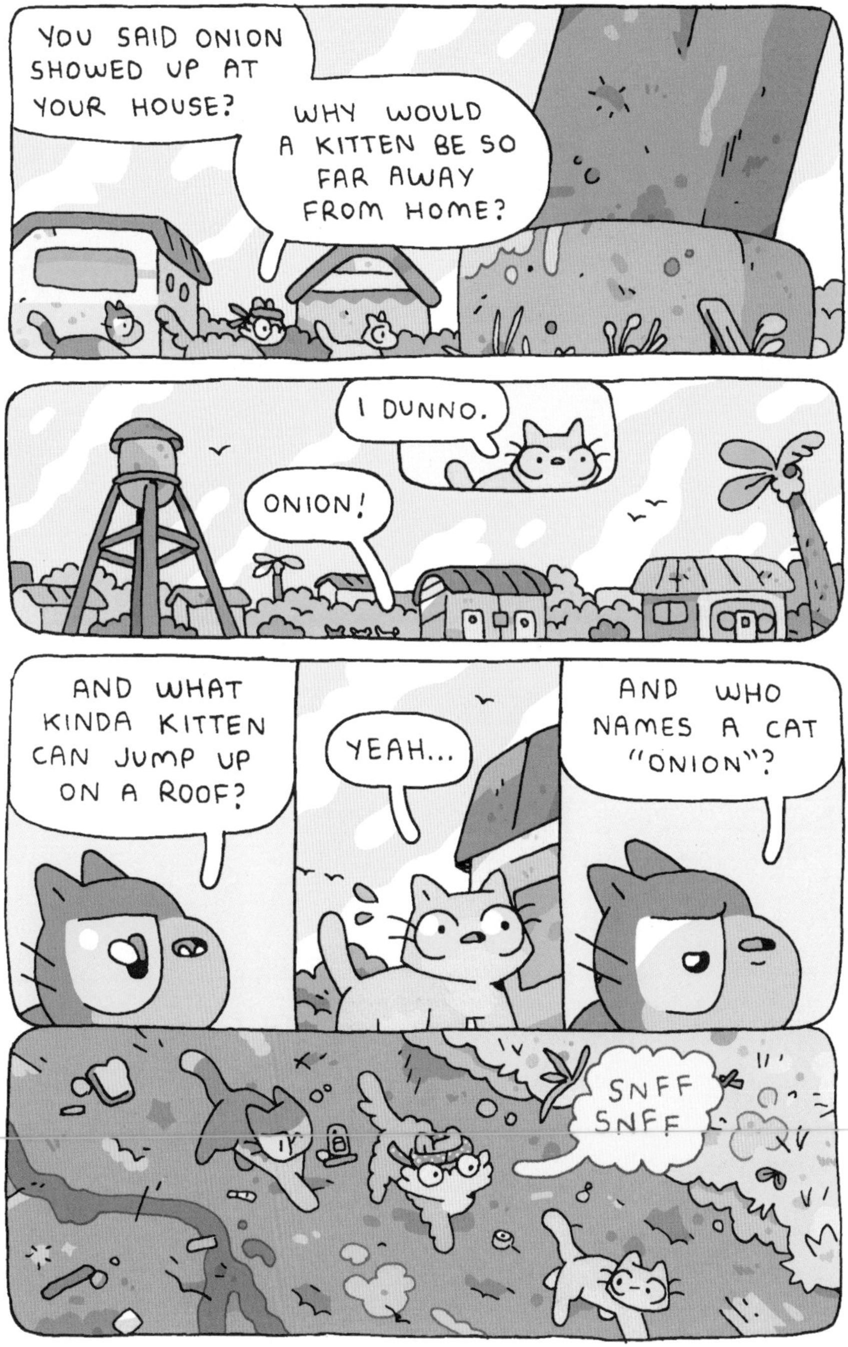
YOU SAID ONION SHOWED UP AT YOUR HOUSE?
WHY WOULD A KITTEN BE SO FAR AWAY FROM HOME?
ONION!
I DUNNO.
AND WHAT KINDA KITTEN CAN JUMP UP ON A ROOF?
YEAH...
AND WHO NAMES A CAT "ONION"?
SNFF SNFF

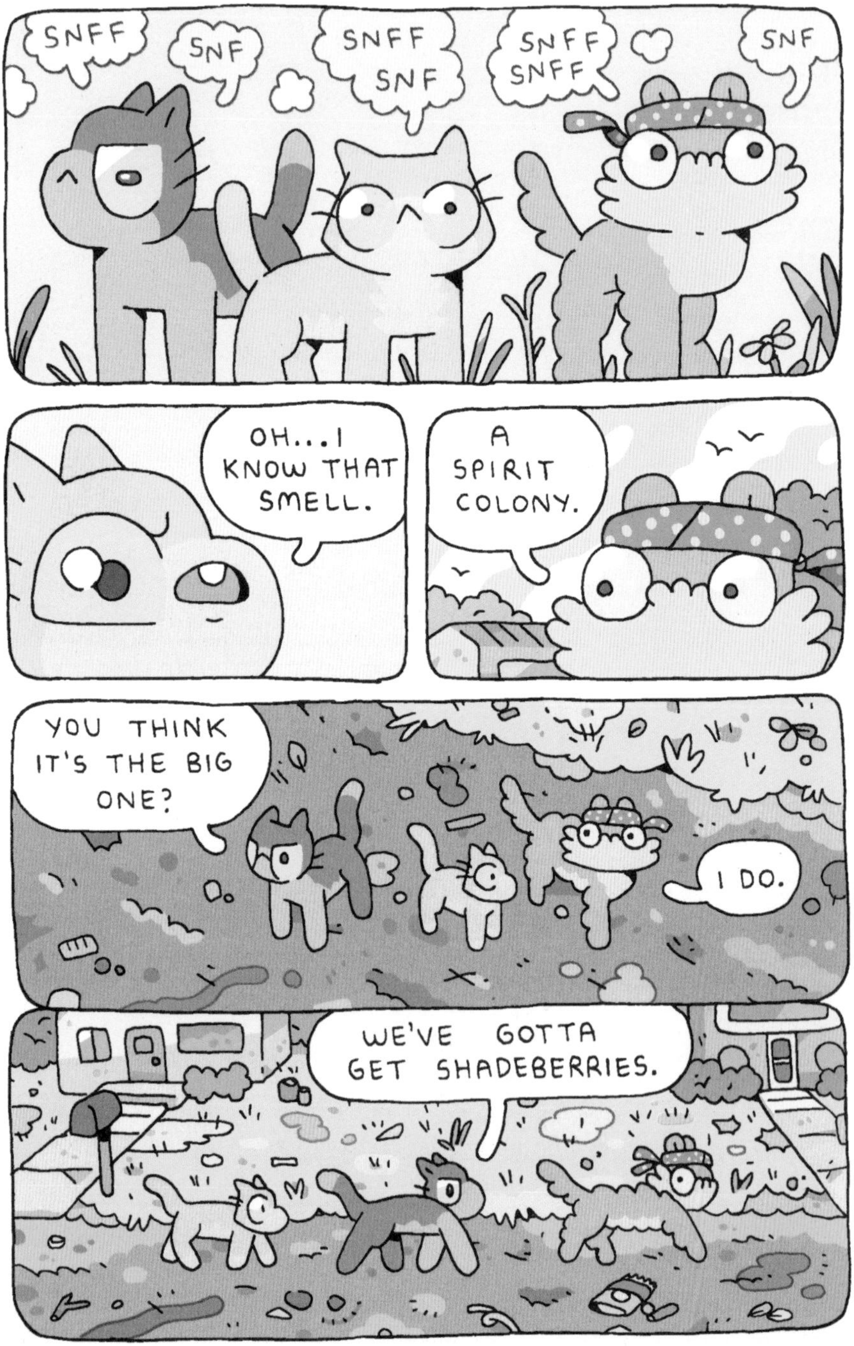
SNFF
SNF
SNFF SNF
SNFF SNFF
SNF
OH...I KNOW THAT SMELL.
A SPIRIT COLONY.
YOU THINK IT'S THE BIG ONE?
I DO.
WE'VE GOTTA GET SHADEBERRIES.

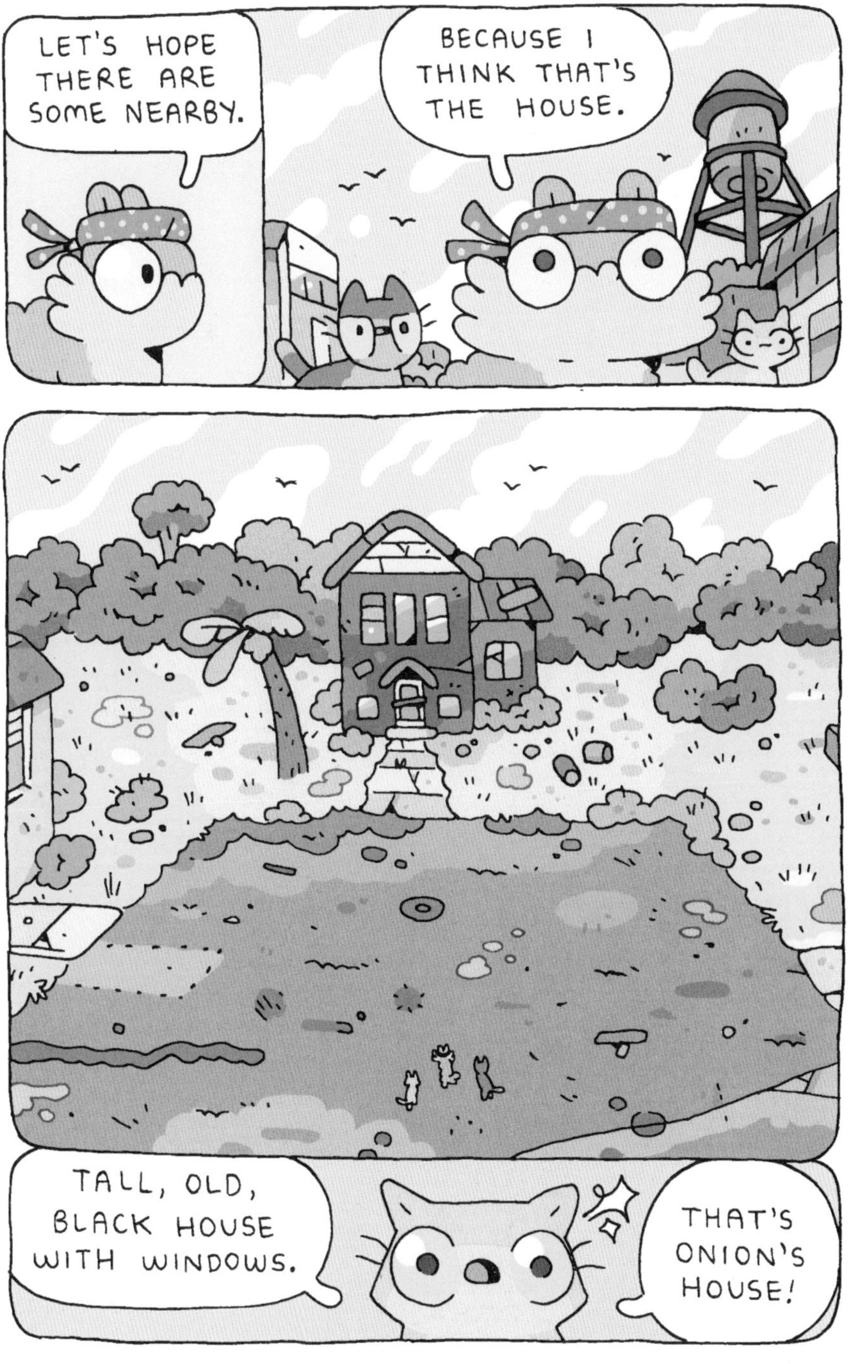
LET'S HOPE THERE ARE SOME NEARBY.
BECAUSE I THINK THAT'S THE HOUSE.
TALL, OLD, BLACK HOUSE WITH WINDOWS.
THAT'S ONION'S HOUSE!

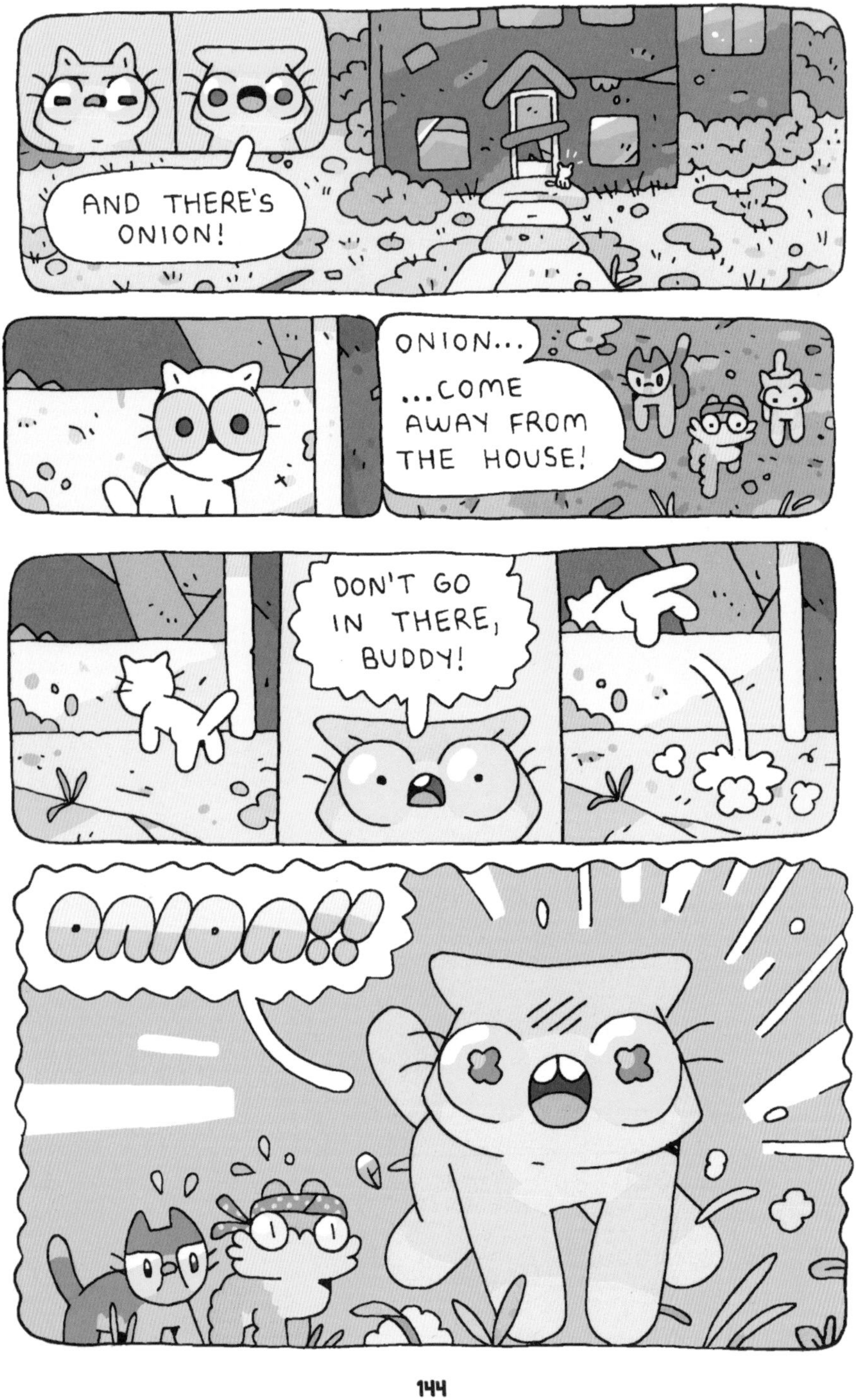
AND THERE'S ONION!
ONION...
...COME AWAY FROM THE HOUSE!
DON'T GO IN THERE, BUDDY!
ONION!!

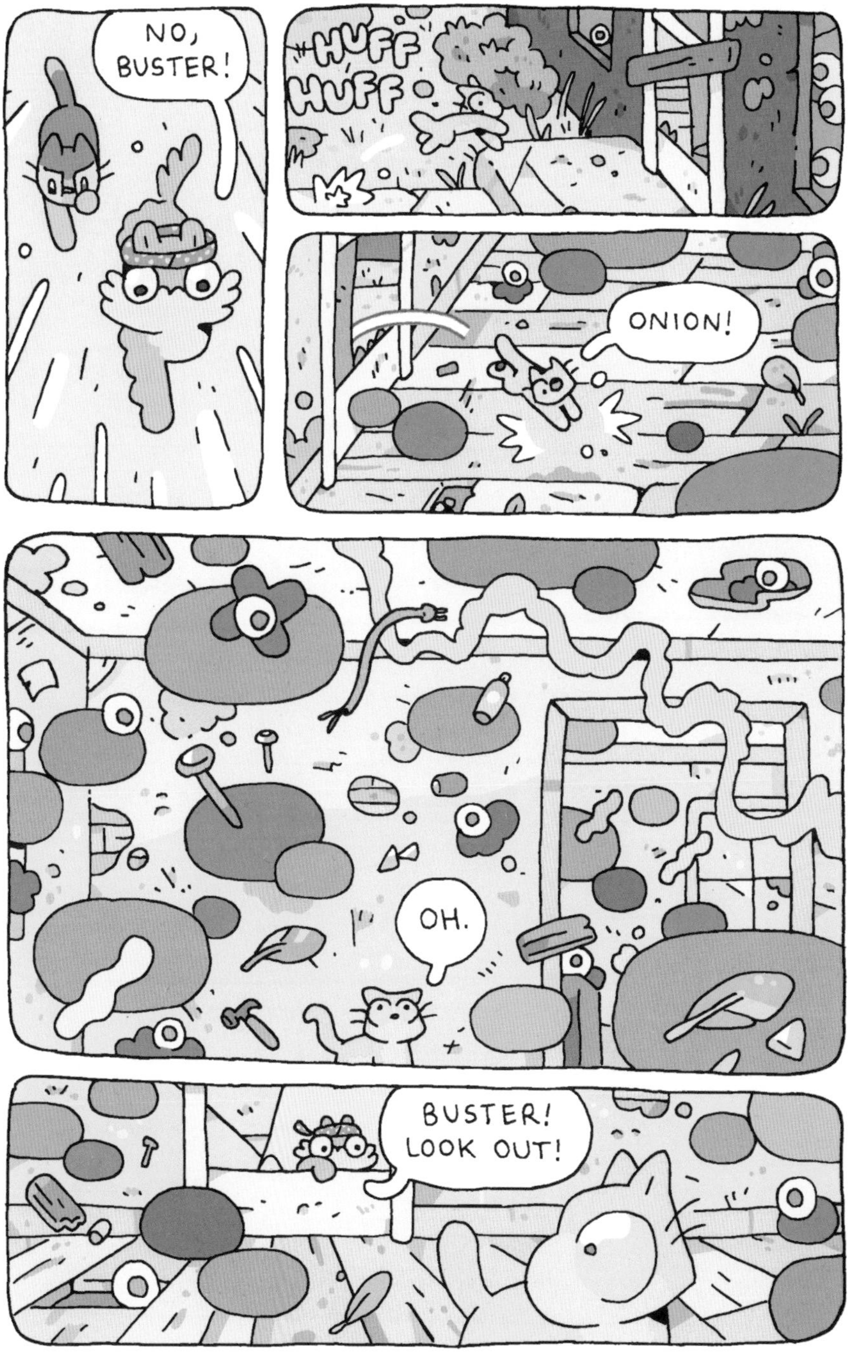
NO, BUSTER!
HUFF
HUFF
ONION!
OH.
BUSTER! LOOK OUT!

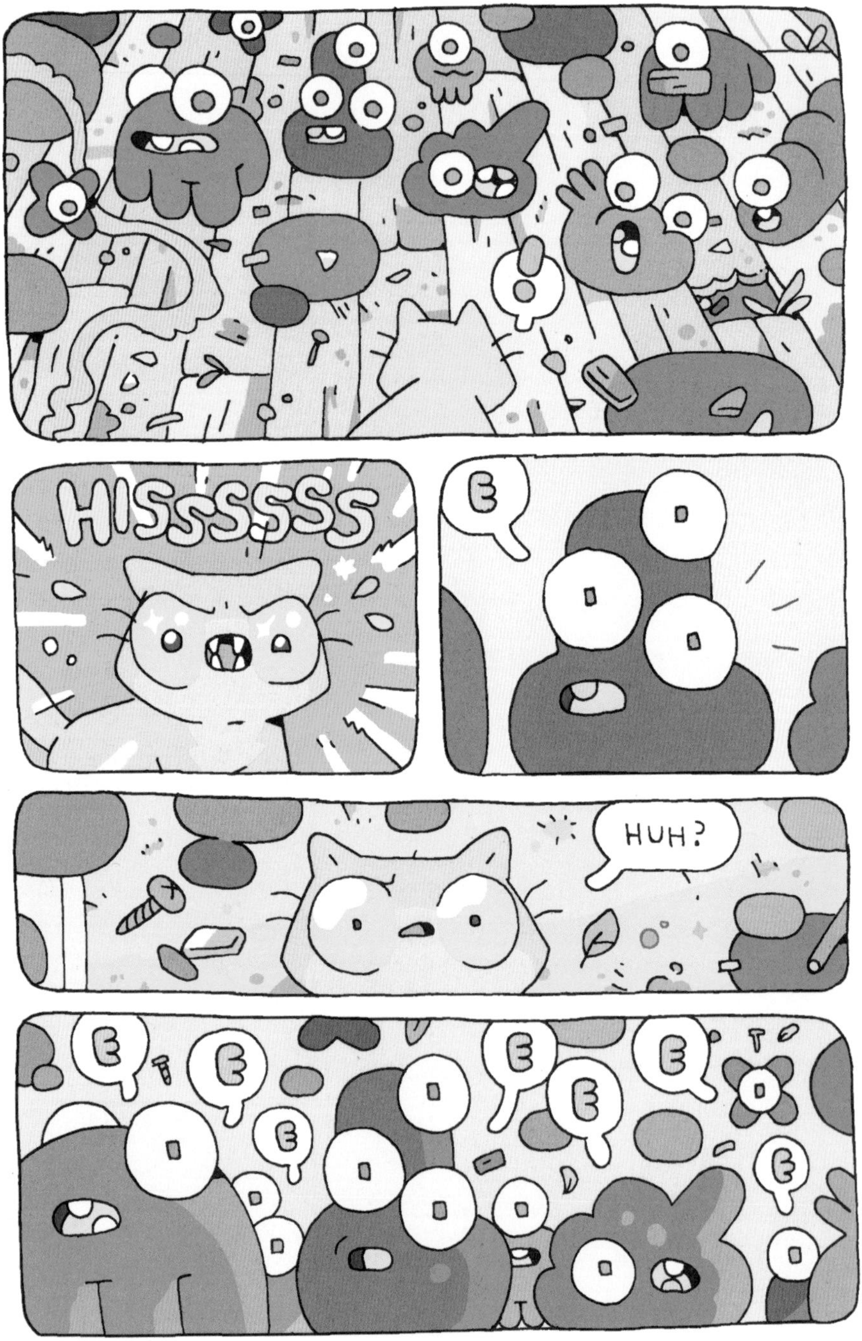
HISSSSSS
E
HUH?
E
E
E
E
E
E
E
E

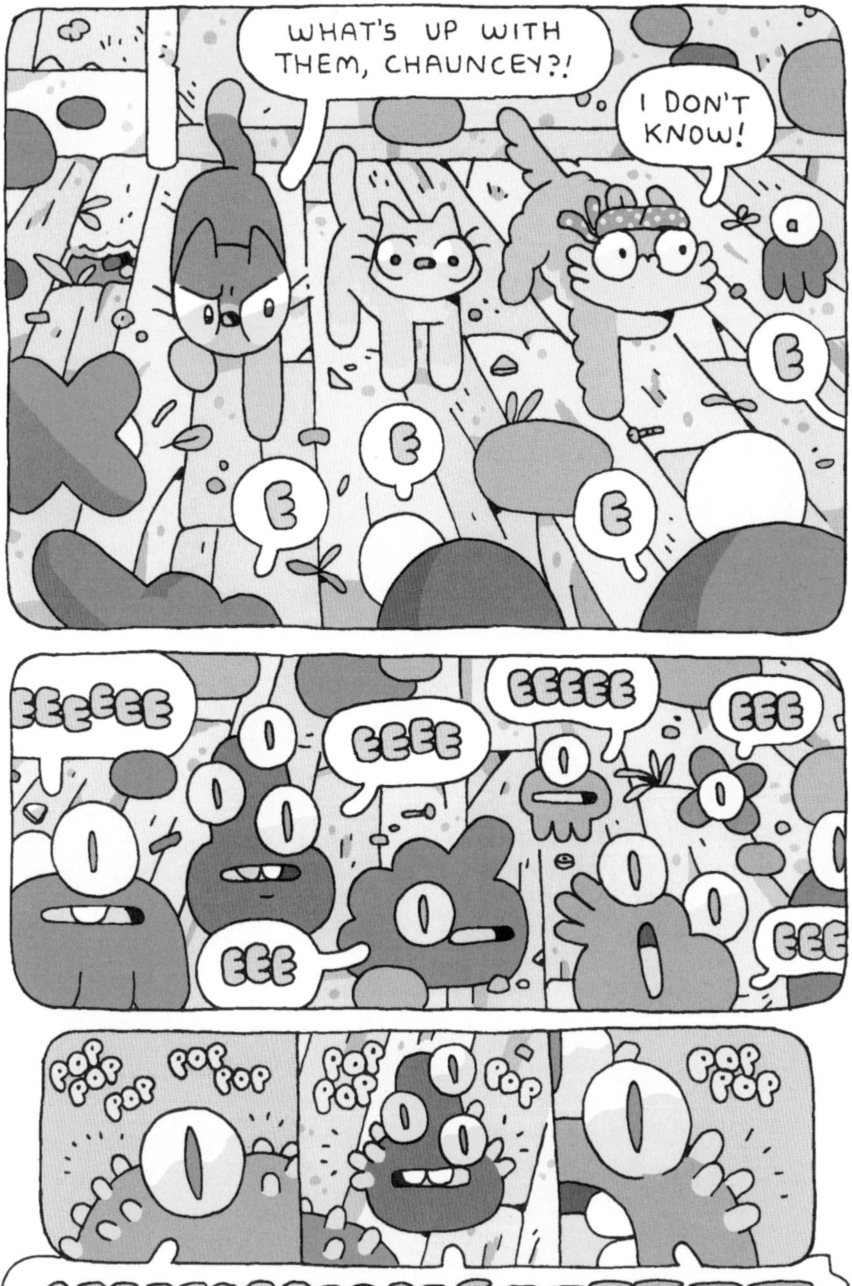
WHAT'S UP WITH THEM, CHAUNCEY?!
I DON'T KNOW!
E
E
E
E
EEEEEEE
EEEE
EEEEE
EEE
EEE
EEE
POP POP POP POP POP
POP POP POP
POP POP
EEEEEEEEEEEEEEEEEEEEEE

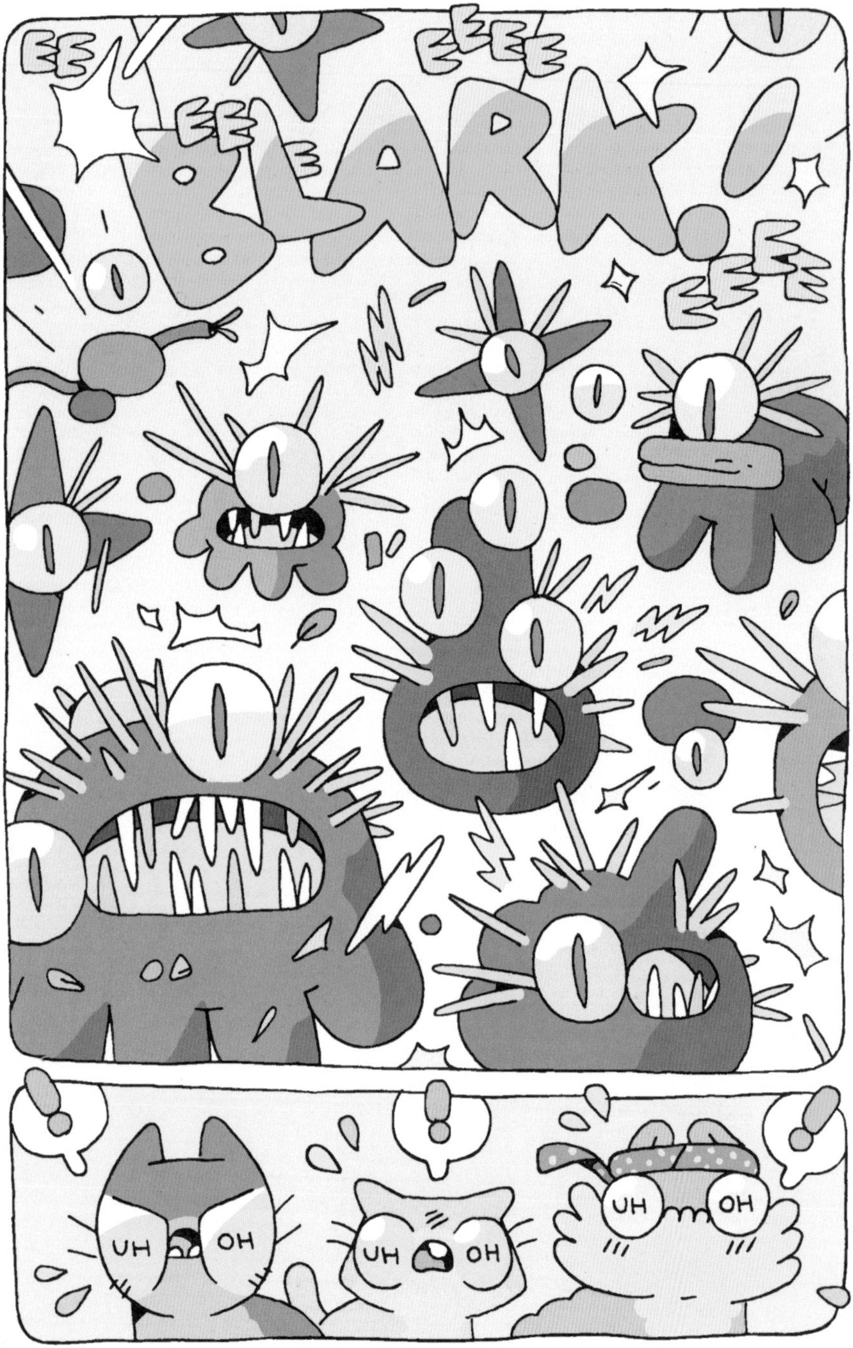
EE
EEEE
EEE
BLARK!
EEEE
UH OH
UH OH
UH OH

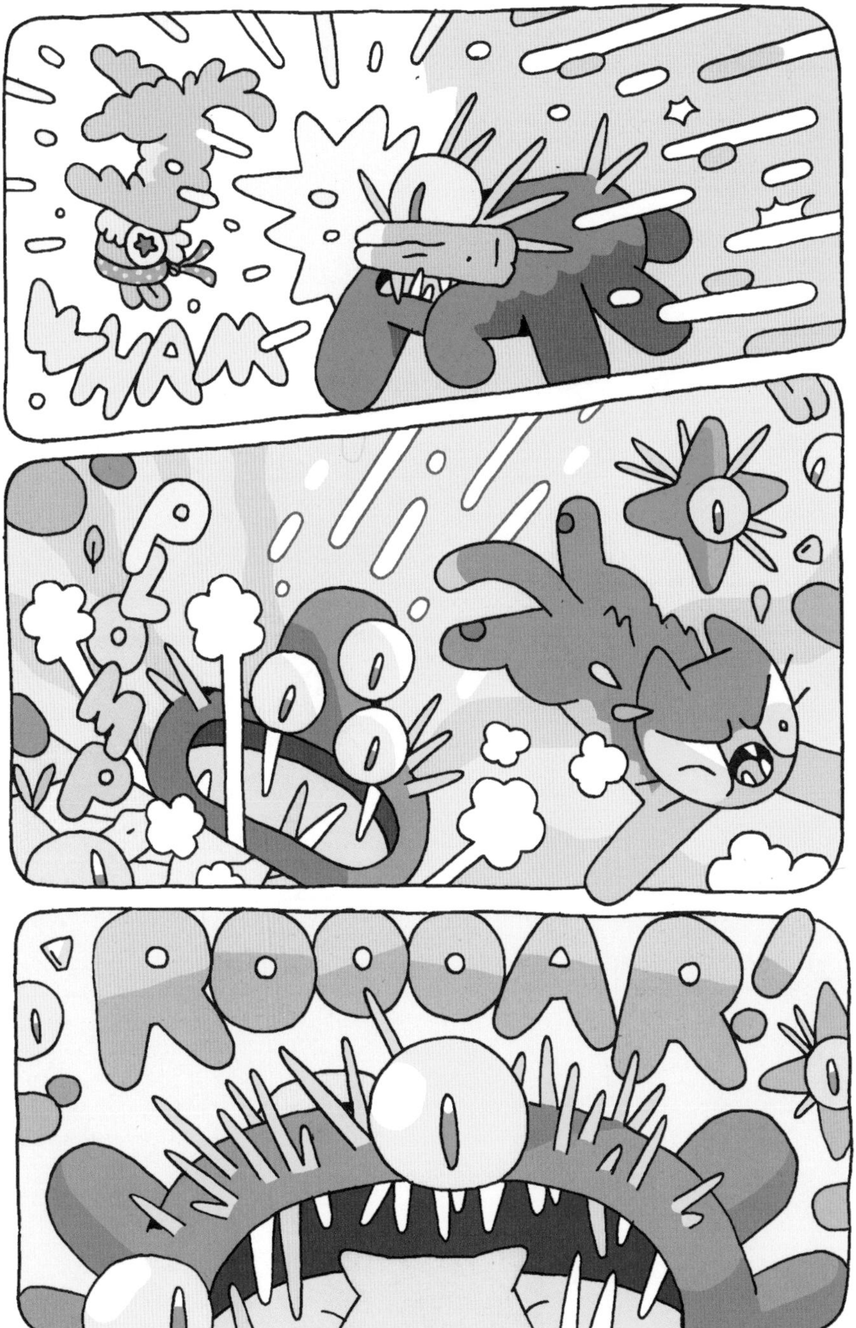
WHAM
PLOMP
ROOOAR!

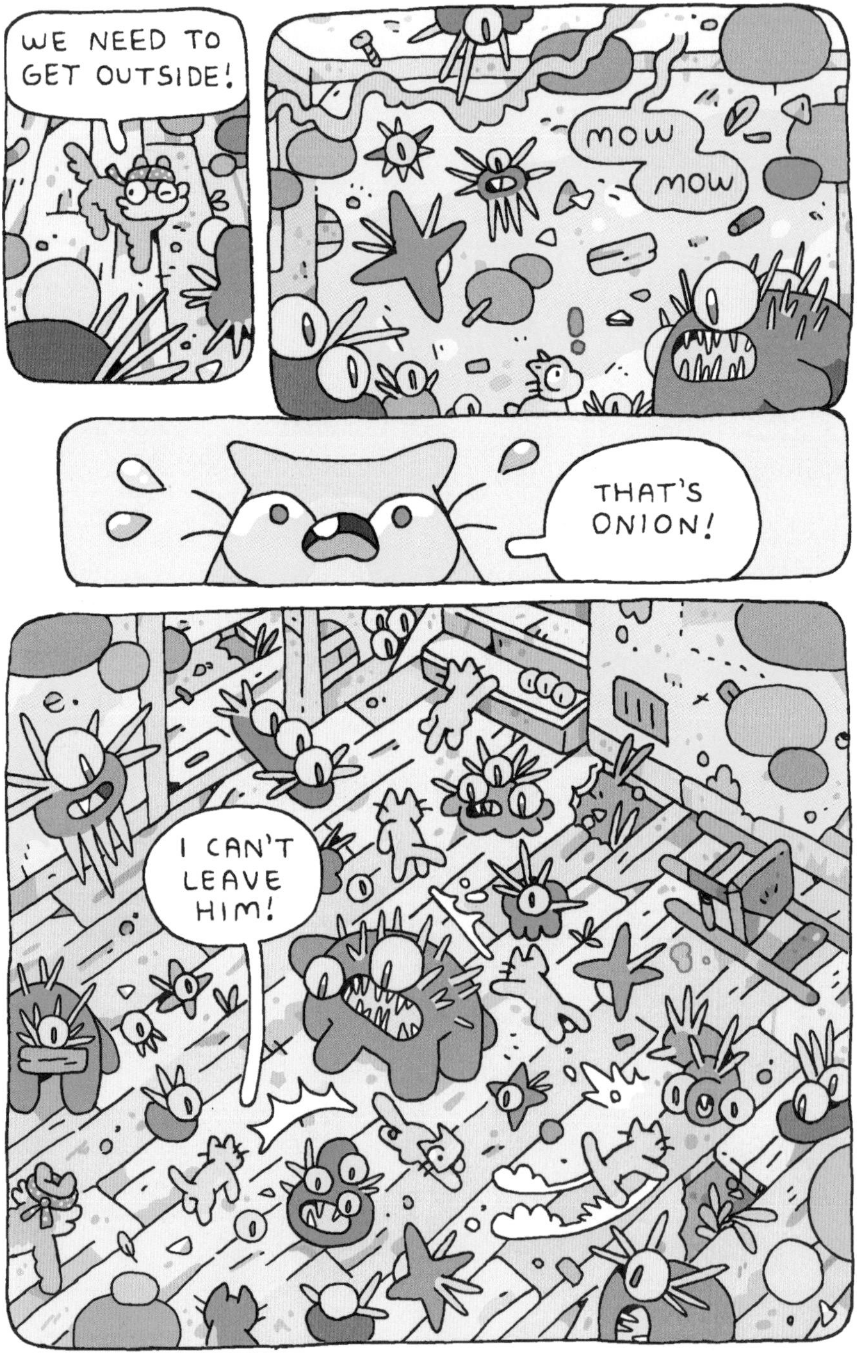
WE NEED TO GET OUTSIDE!
mow
mow
THAT'S ONION!
I CAN'T LEAVE HIM!

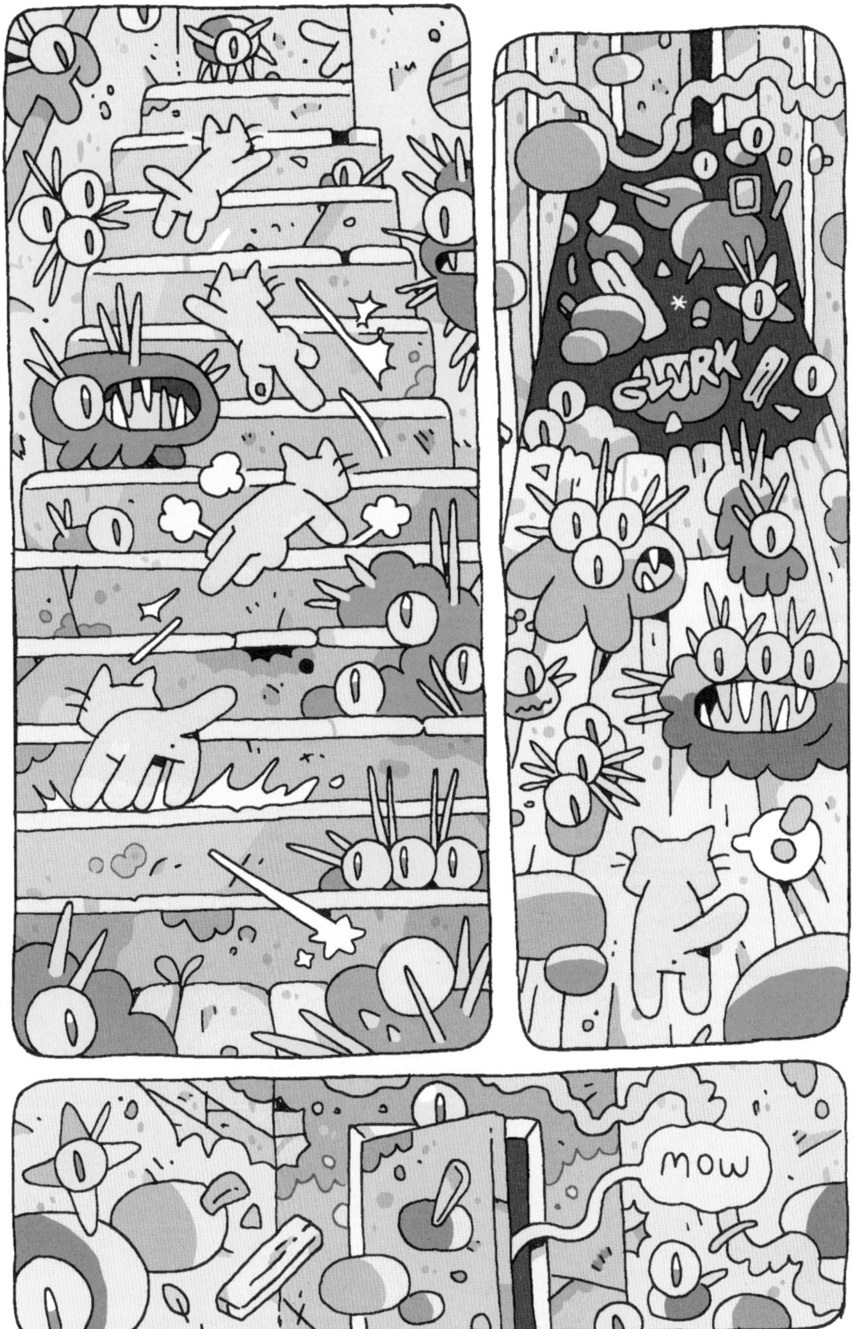
GLURK
mow

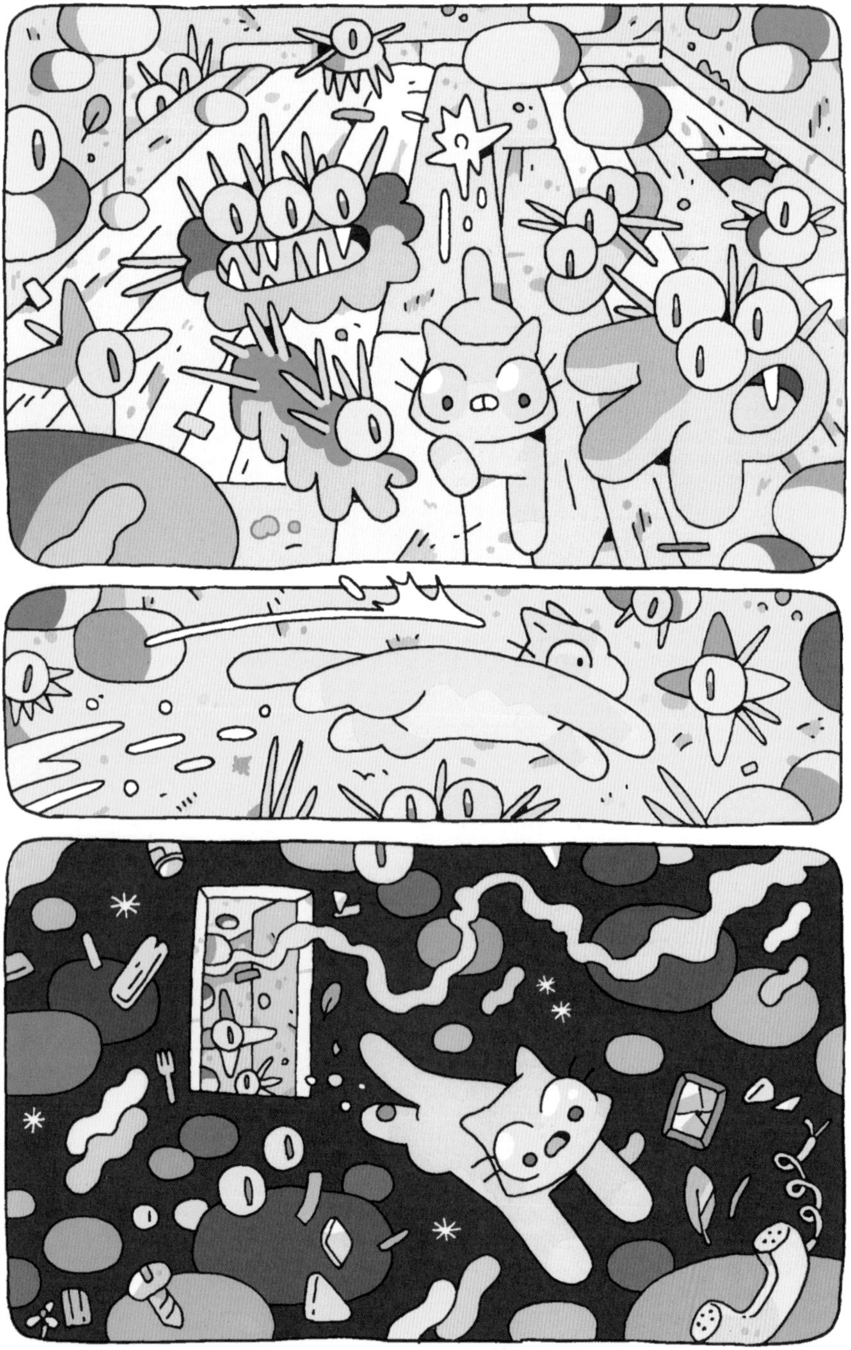

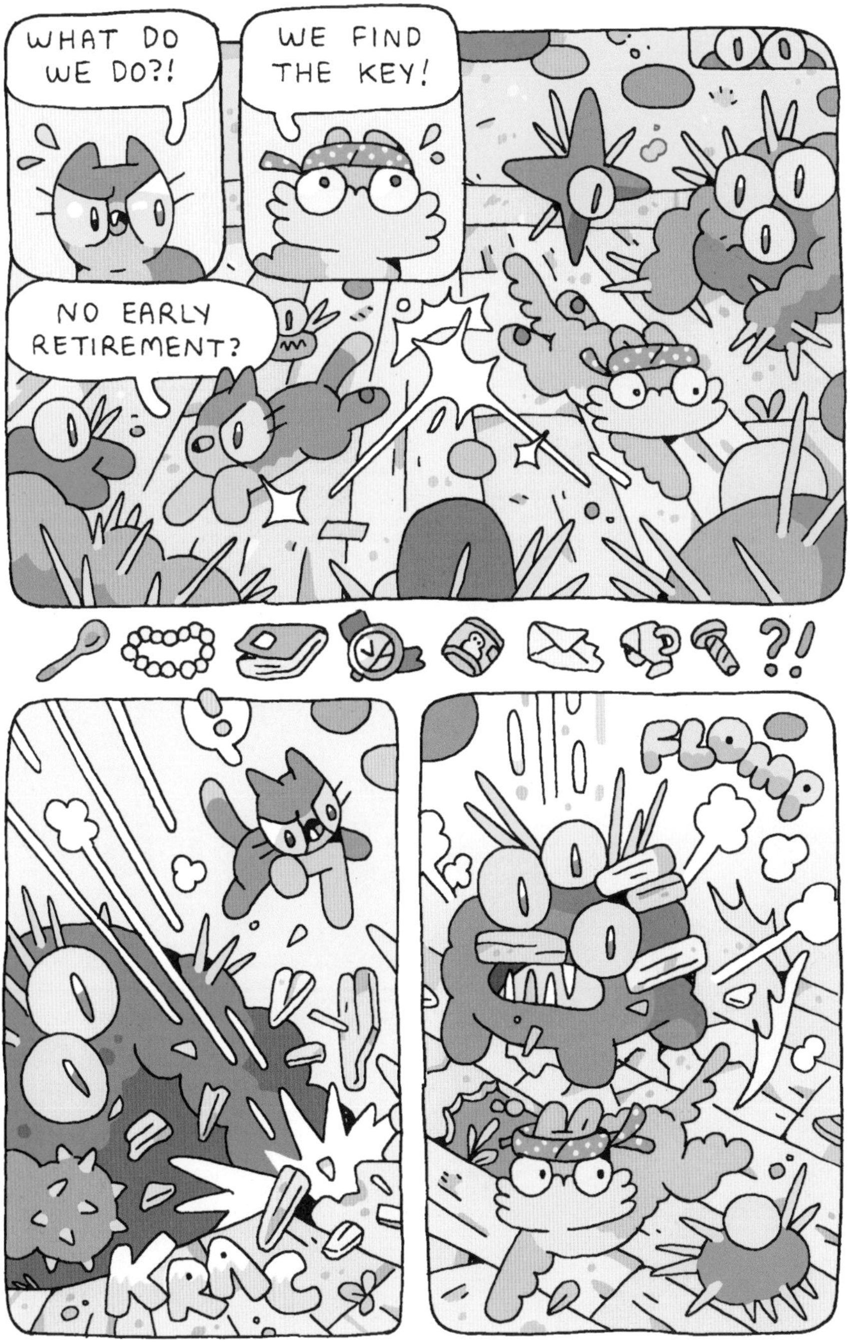
WHAT DO WE DO?!
WE FIND THE KEY!
NO EARLY RETIREMENT?
?!
FLOMP
KRAC

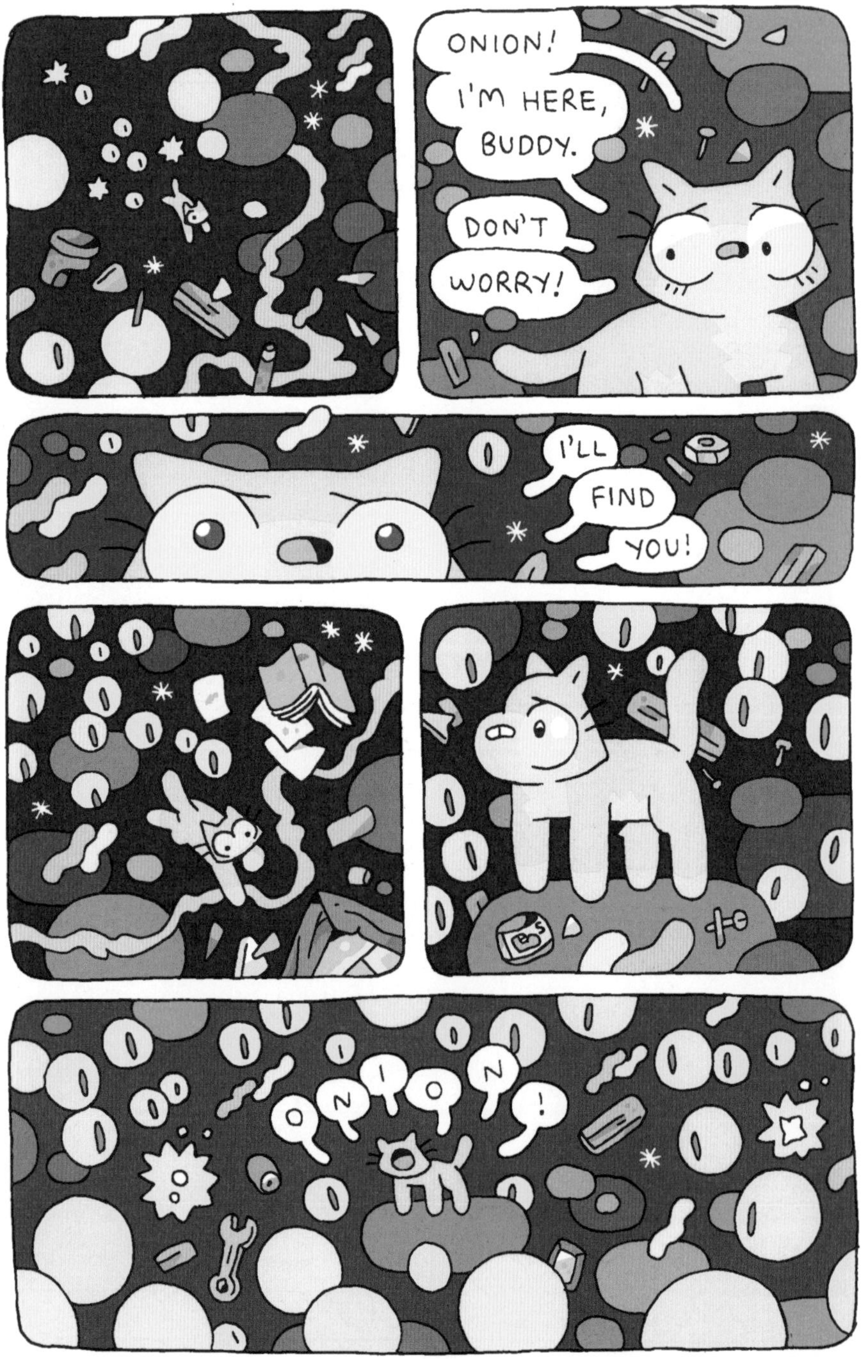
ONION!
I'M HERE, BUDDY.
DON'T
WORRY!
I'LL
FIND
YOU!
ONION!

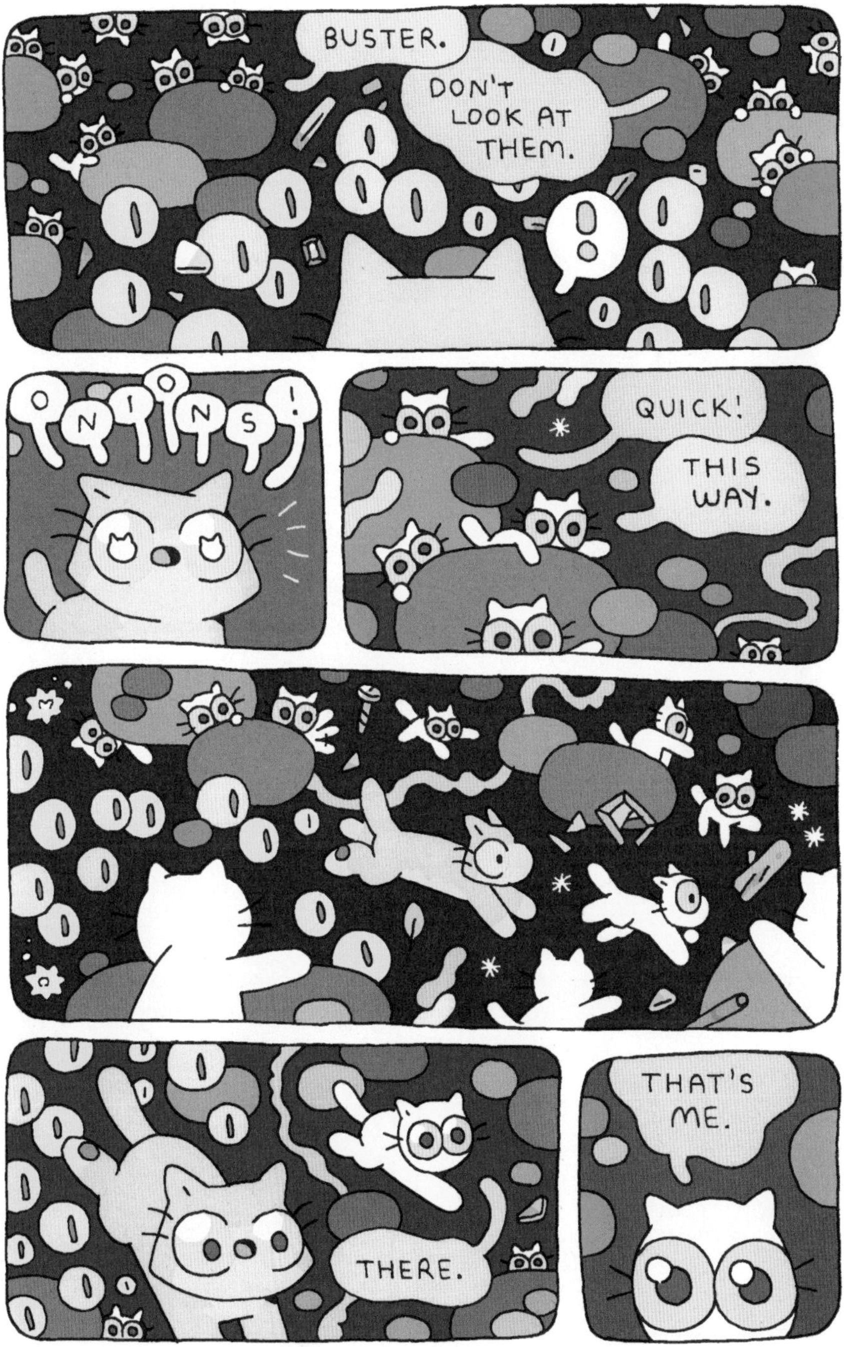
BUSTER.
DON'T LOOK AT THEM.
!
ONIONS!
QUICK!
THIS WAY.
THERE.
THAT'S ME.

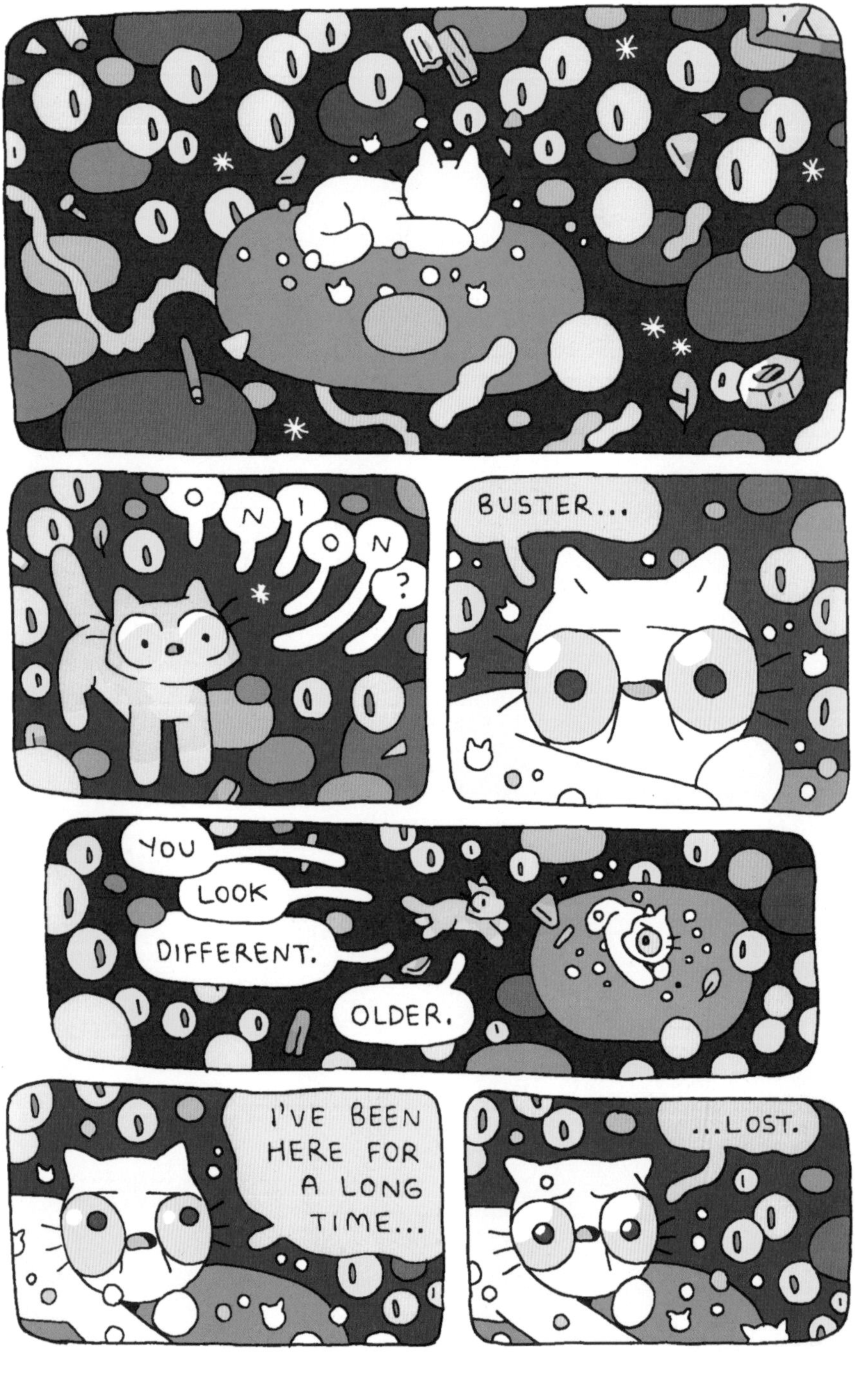
O
N
I
O
N
?
BUSTER...
YOU
LOOK
DIFFERENT.
OLDER.
I'VE BEEN HERE FOR A LONG TIME...
...LOST.

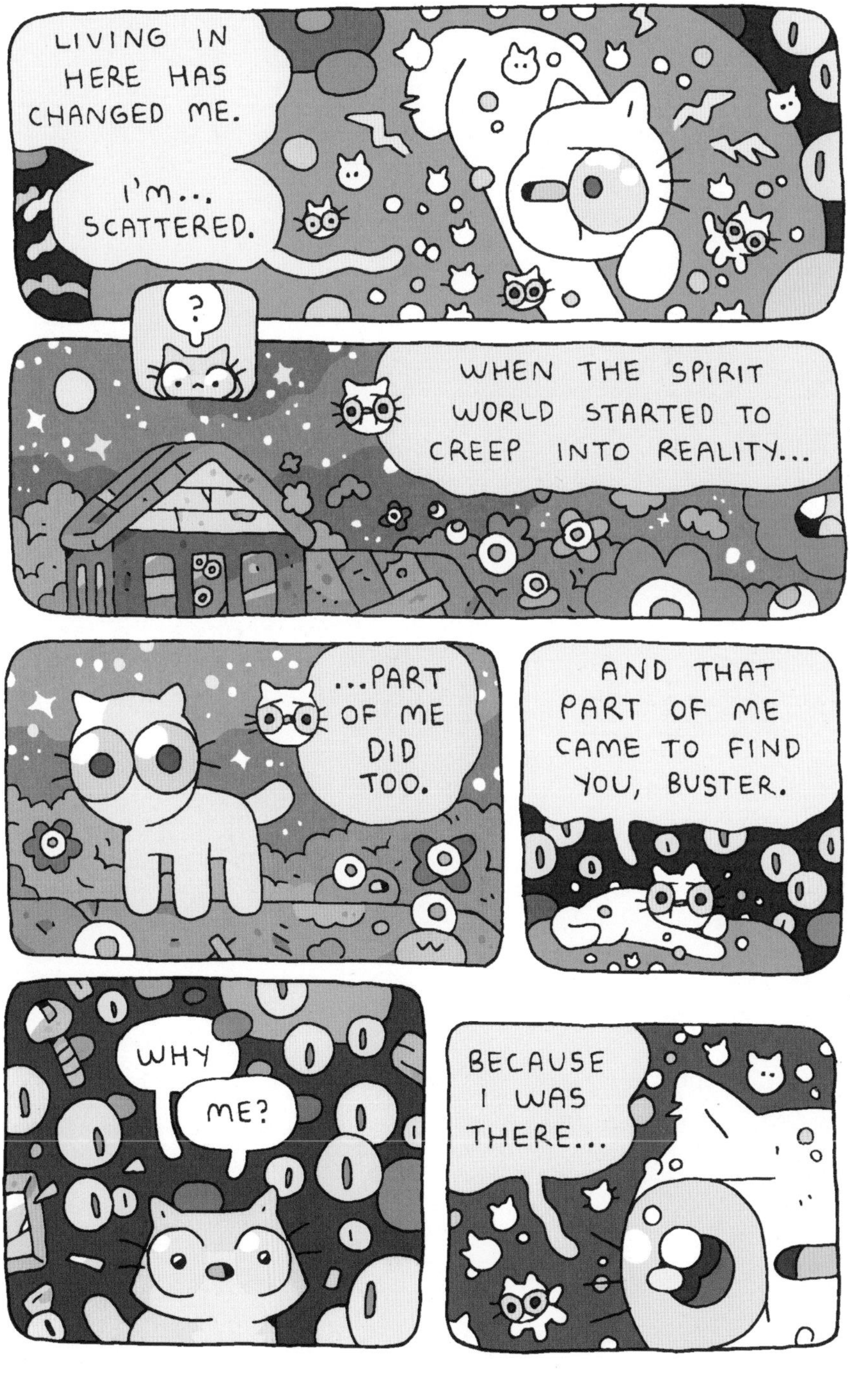
LIVING IN HERE HAS CHANGED ME.
I'M... SCATTERED.
?
WHEN THE SPIRIT WORLD STARTED TO CREEP INTO REALITY...
...PART OF ME DID TOO.
AND THAT PART OF ME CAME TO FIND YOU, BUSTER.
WHY
ME?
BECAUSE I WAS THERE...

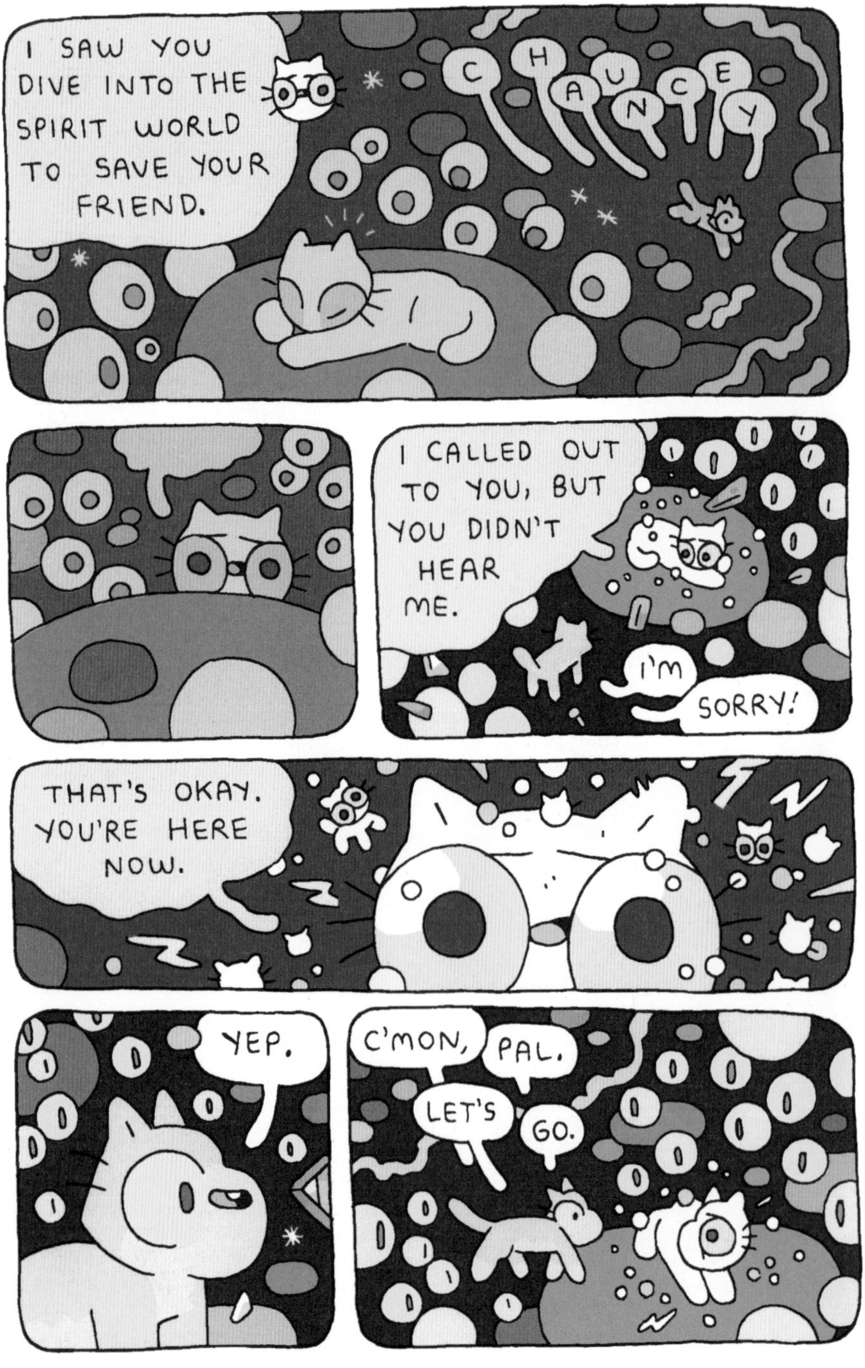
I SAW YOU DIVE INTO THE SPIRIT WORLD TO SAVE YOUR FRIEND.
CHAUNCEY
I CALLED OUT TO YOU, BUT YOU DIDN'T HEAR ME.
I'M
SORRY!
THAT'S OKAY. YOU'RE HERE NOW.
YEP.
C'MON,
PAL.
LET'S
GO.

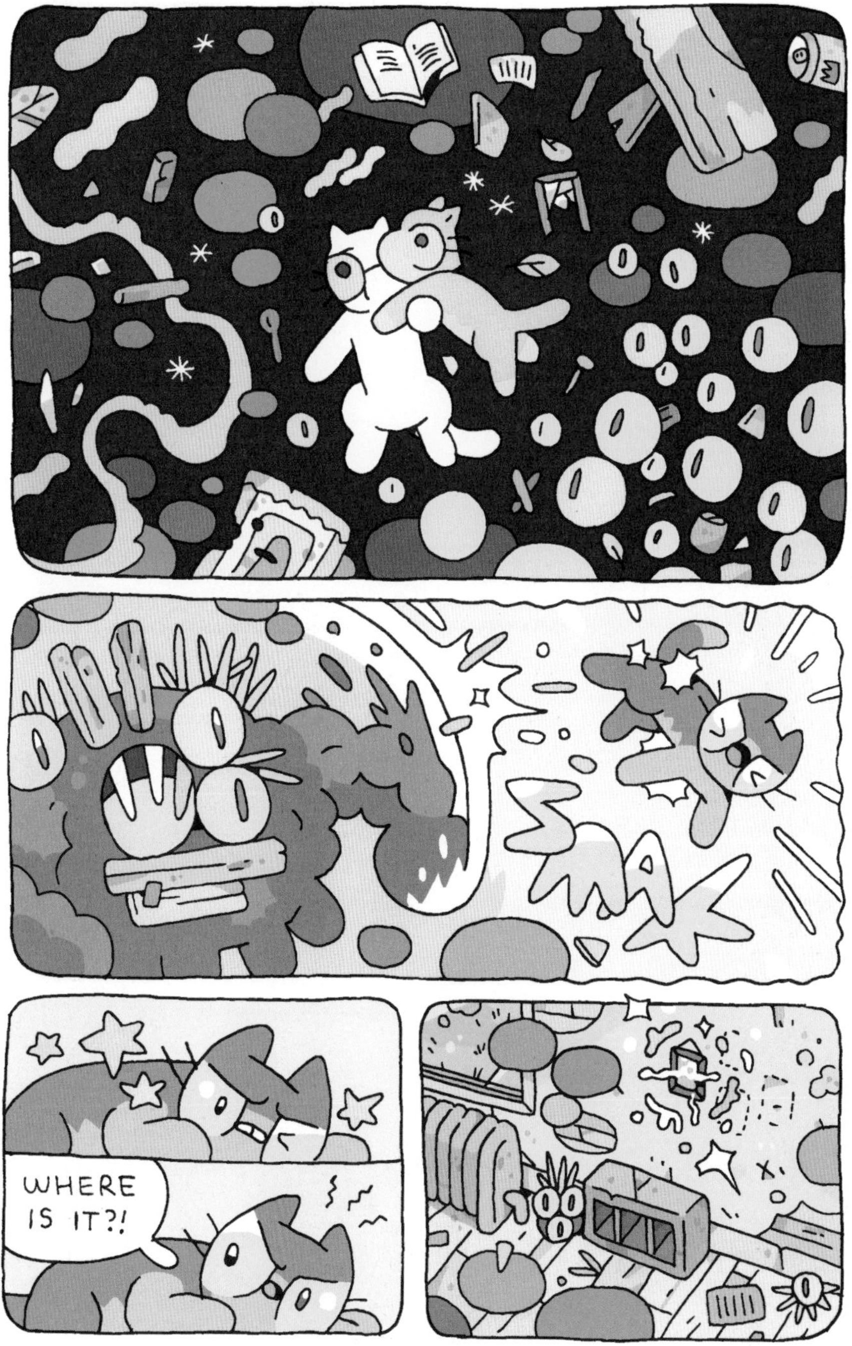
WHERE IS IT?!

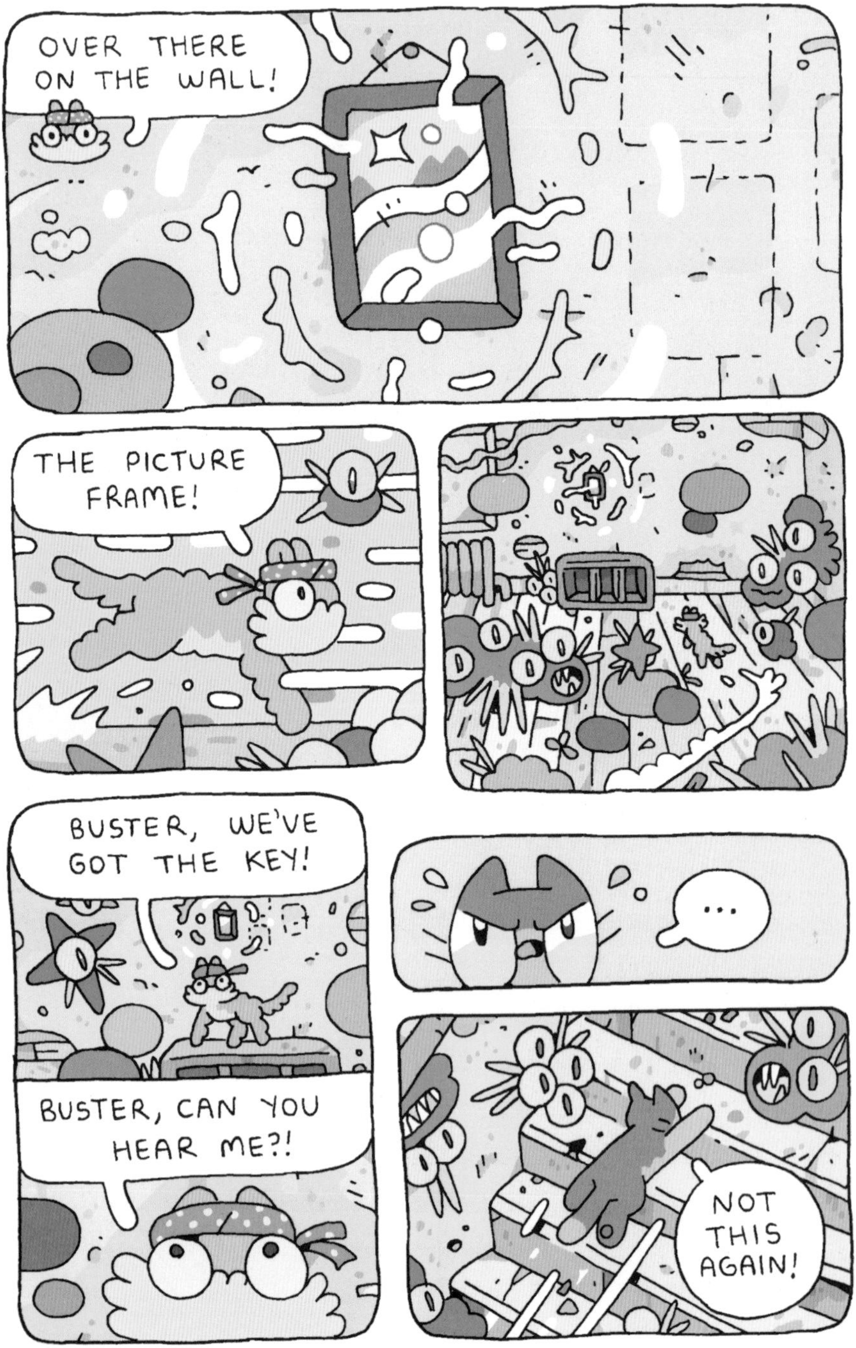
OVER THERE ON THE WALL!
THE PICTURE FRAME!
BUSTER, WE'VE GOT THE KEY!
BUSTER, CAN YOU HEAR ME?!
...
NOT THIS AGAIN!

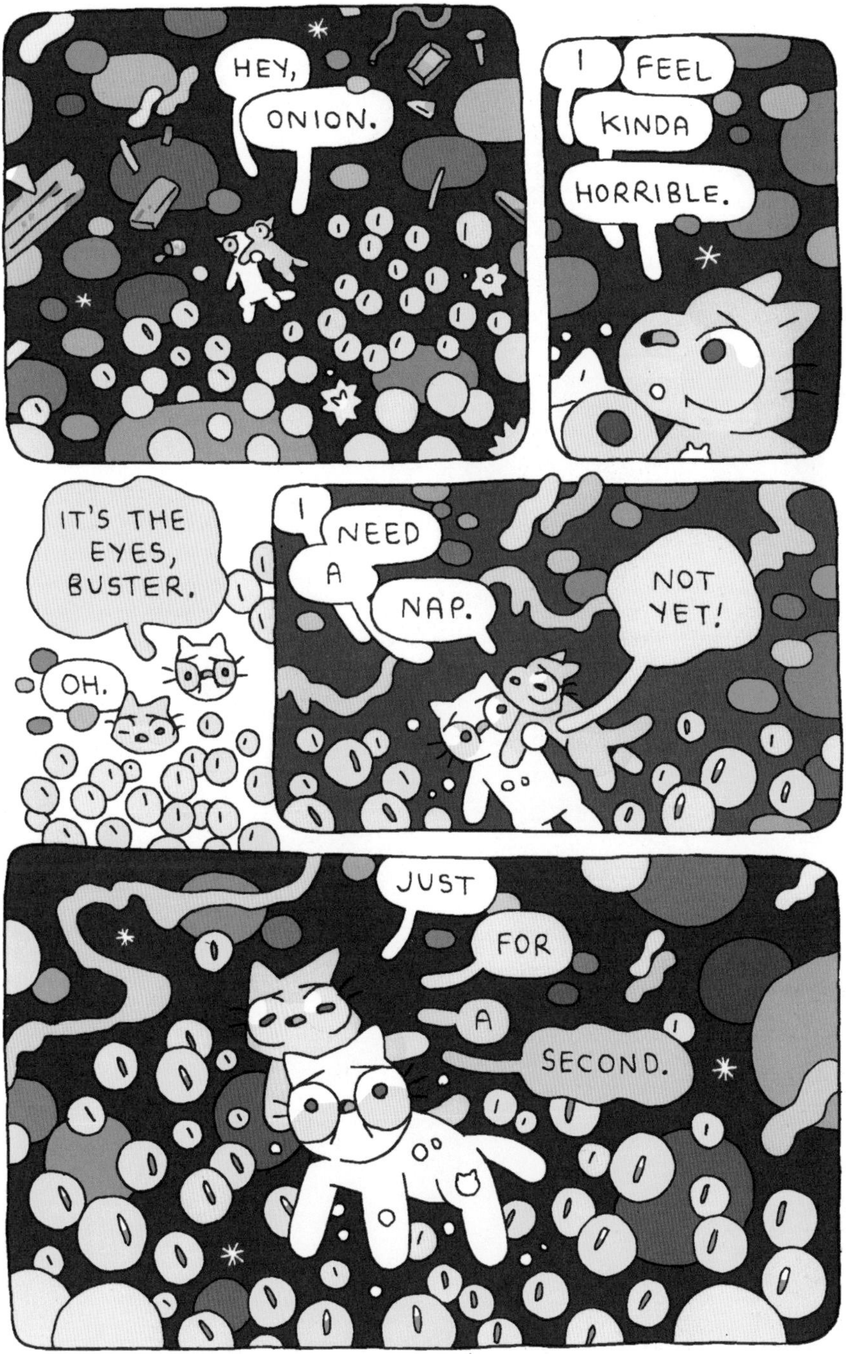
HEY,
ONION.
I
FEEL
KINDA
HORRIBLE.
IT'S THE EYES, BUSTER.
OH.
I
NEED
A
NAP.
NOT YET!
JUST
FOR
A
SECOND.

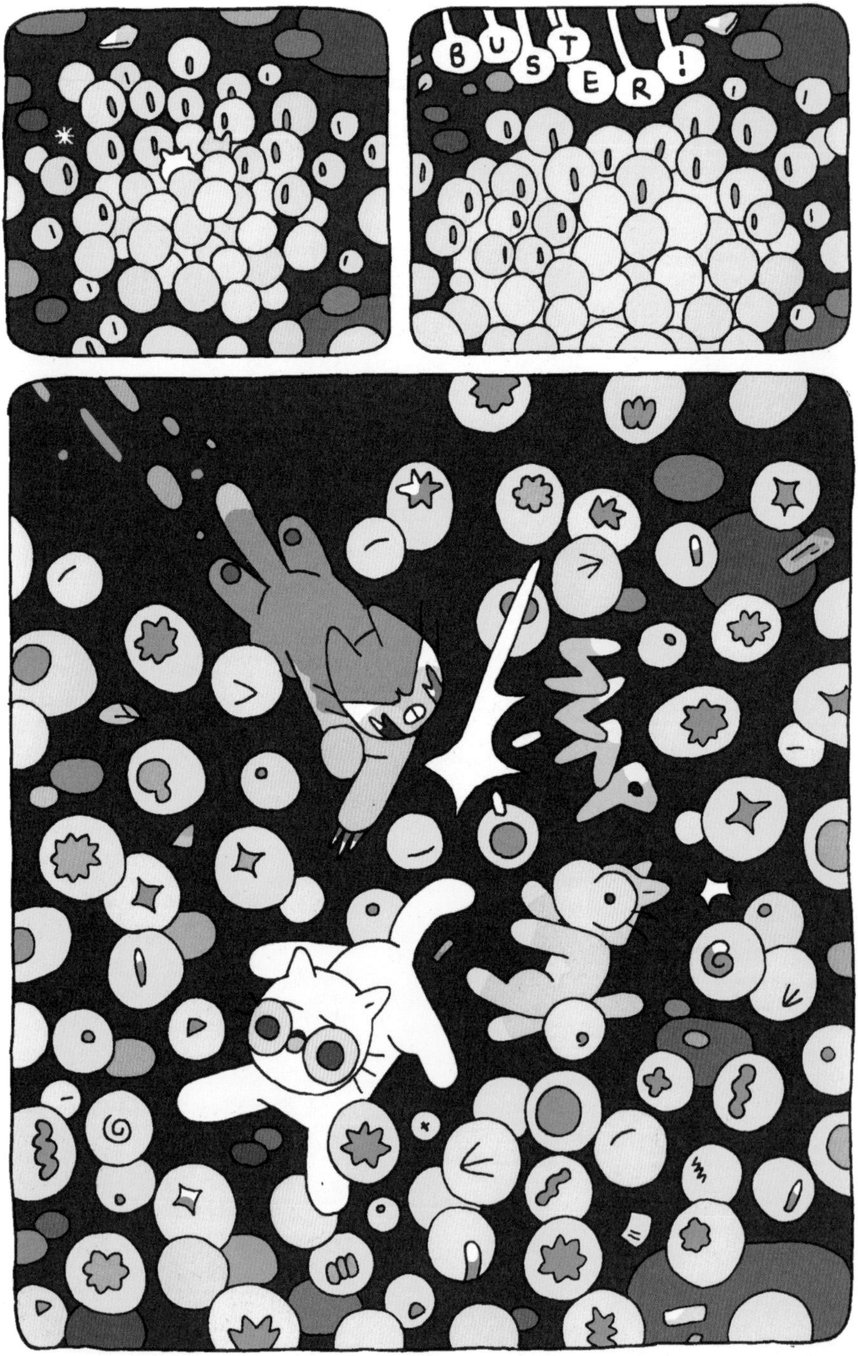
BUSTER!

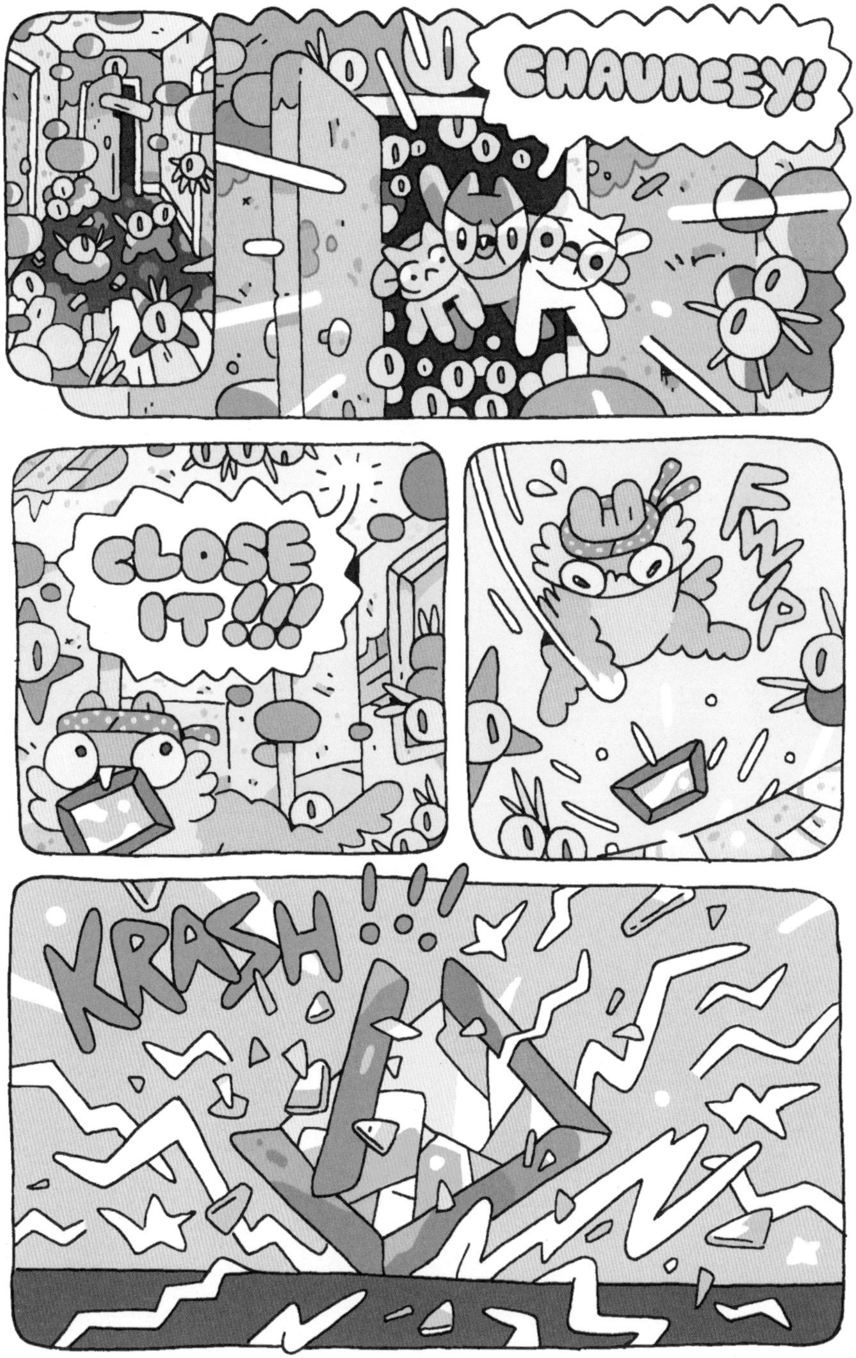
CHAUNCEY!
CLOSE IT!!!
FWIP
KRASH!!!

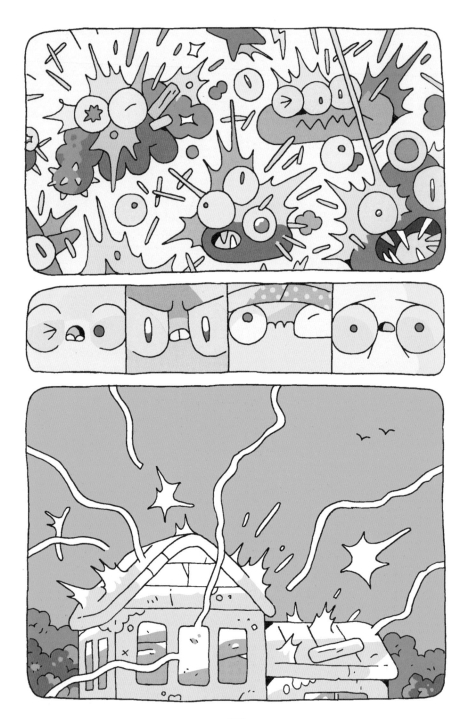

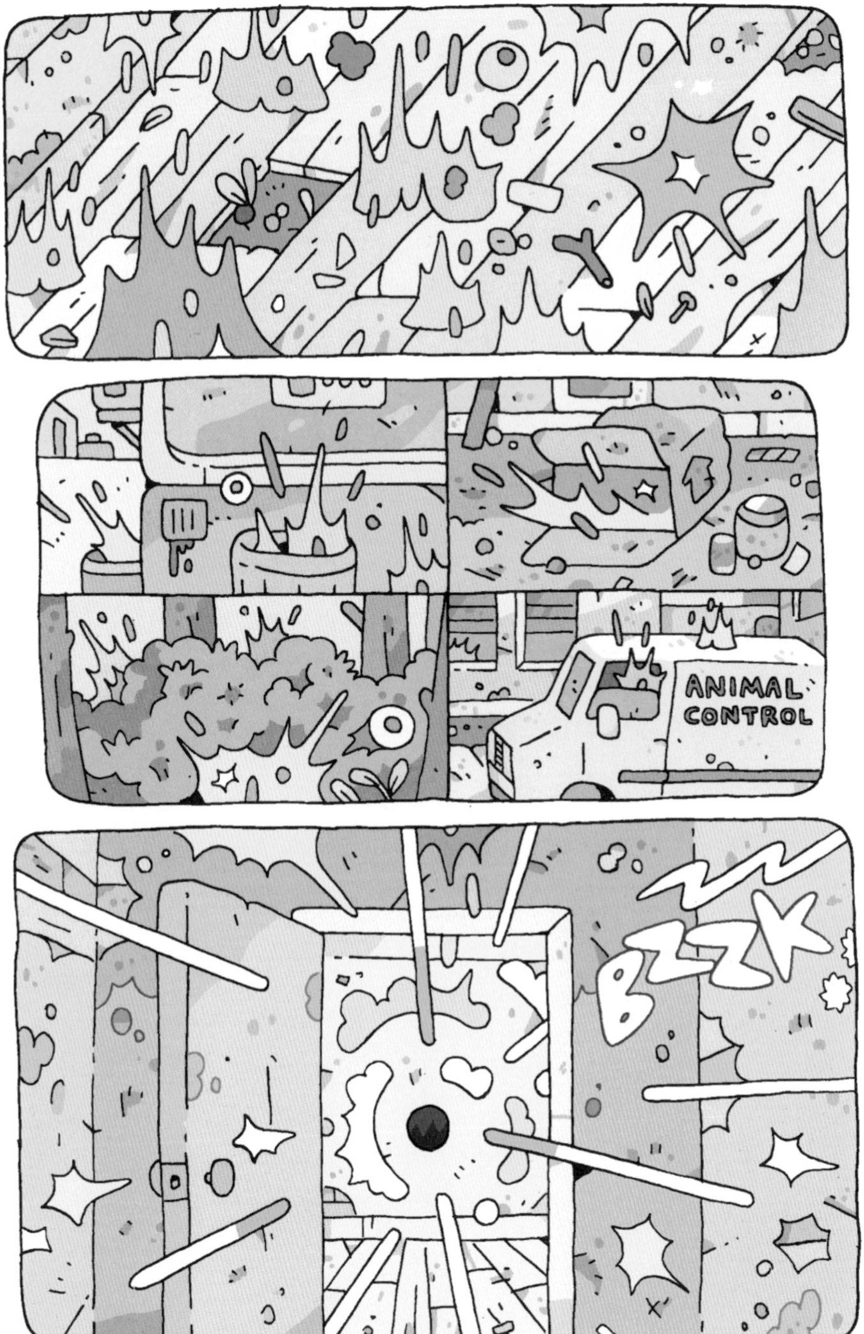
ANIMAL
CONTROL
BZZK

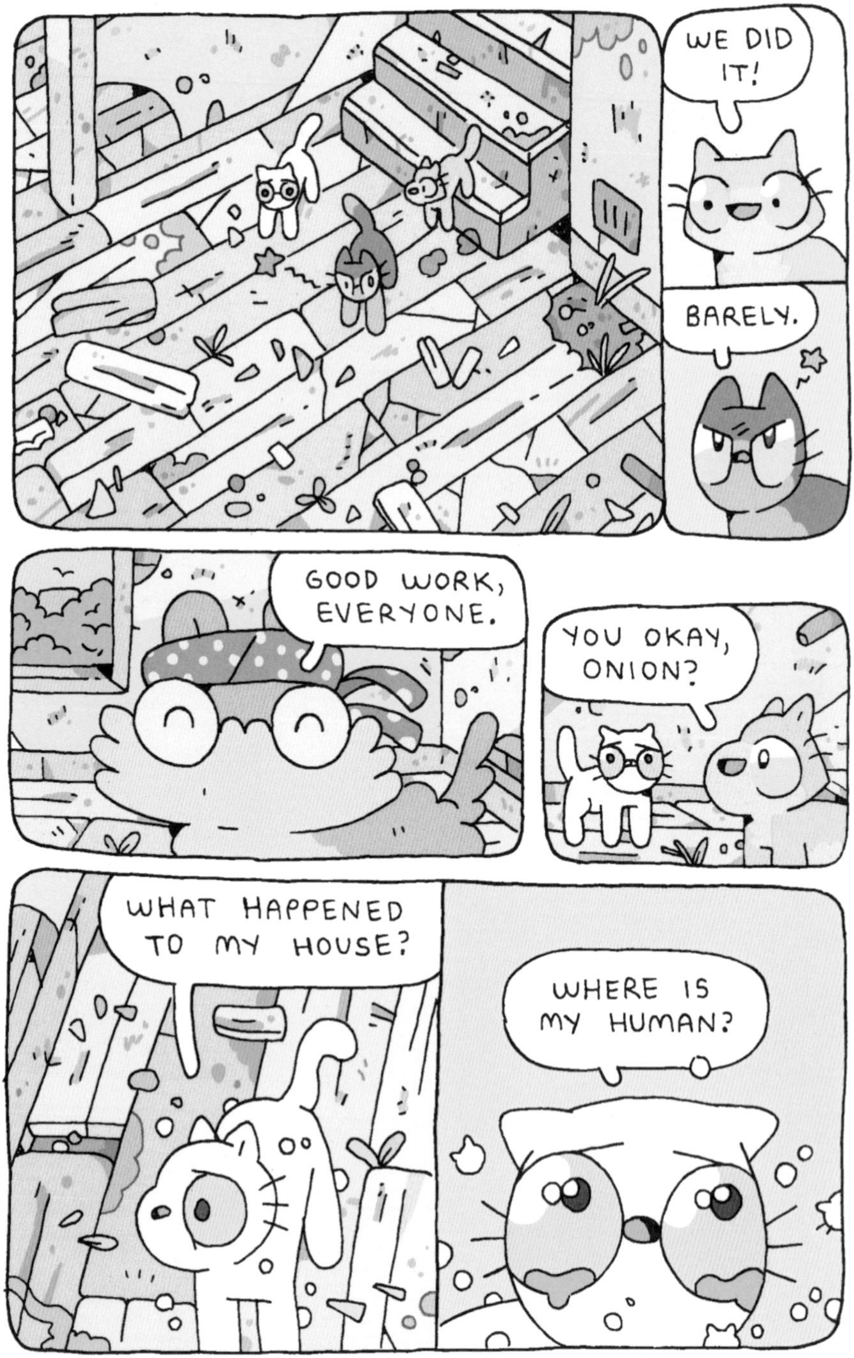
WE DID IT!
BARELY.
GOOD WORK, EVERYONE.
YOU OKAY, ONION?
WHAT HAPPENED TO MY HOUSE?
WHERE IS MY HUMAN?

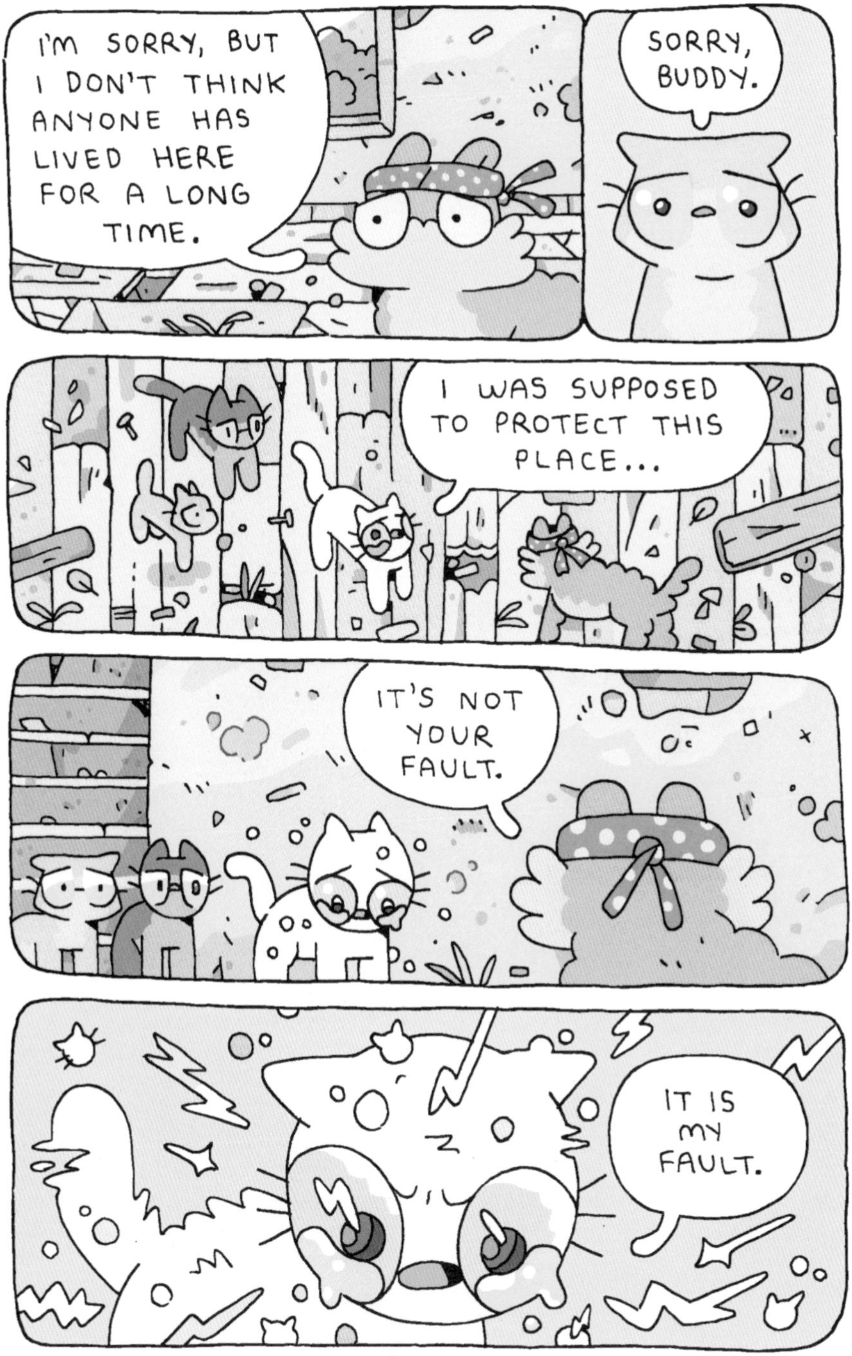
I'M SORRY, BUT I DON'T THINK ANYONE HAS LIVED HERE FOR A LONG TIME.
SORRY, BUDDY.
I WAS SUPPOSED TO PROTECT THIS PLACE...
IT'S NOT YOUR FAULT.
IT IS MY FAULT.

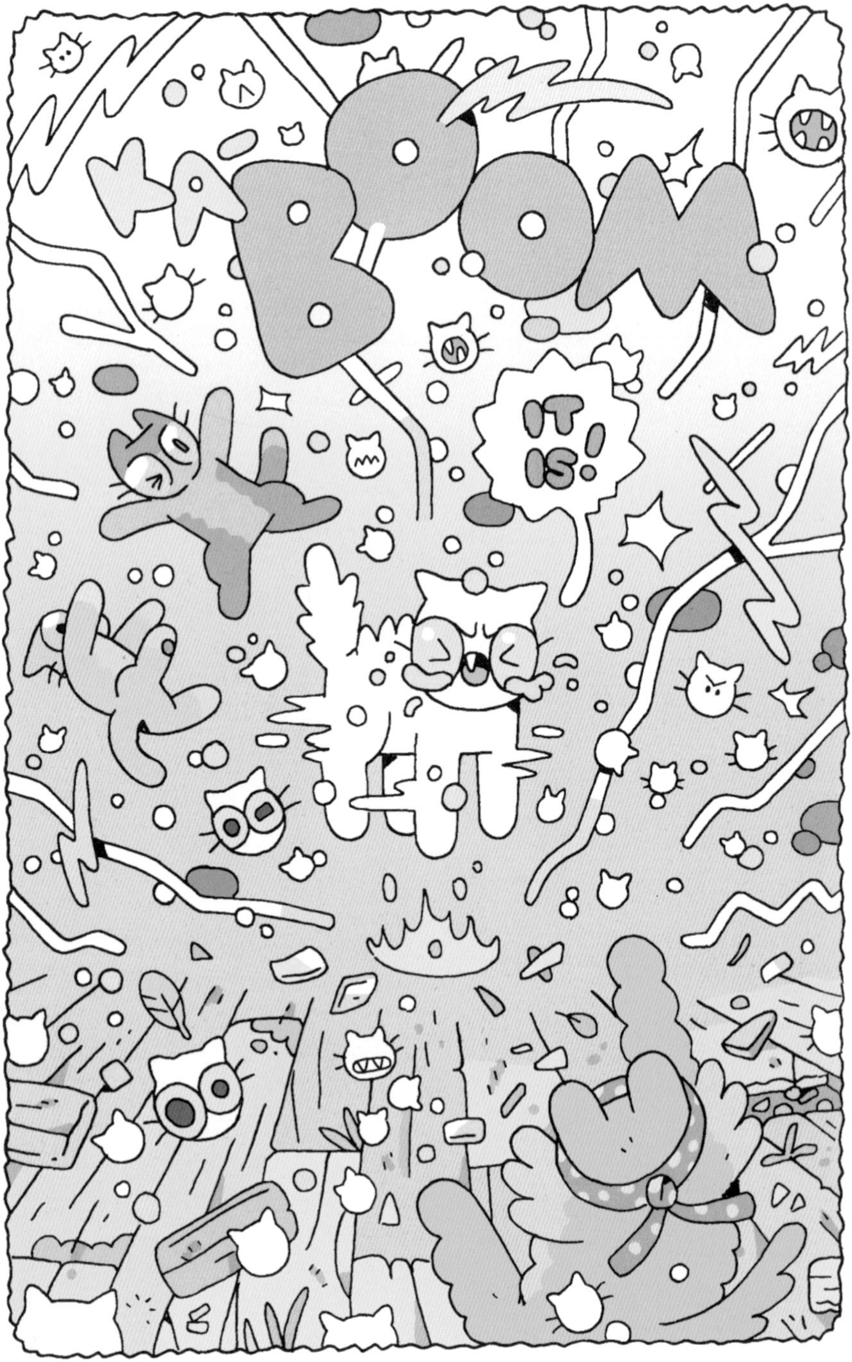
KA-BOOM
IT IS!

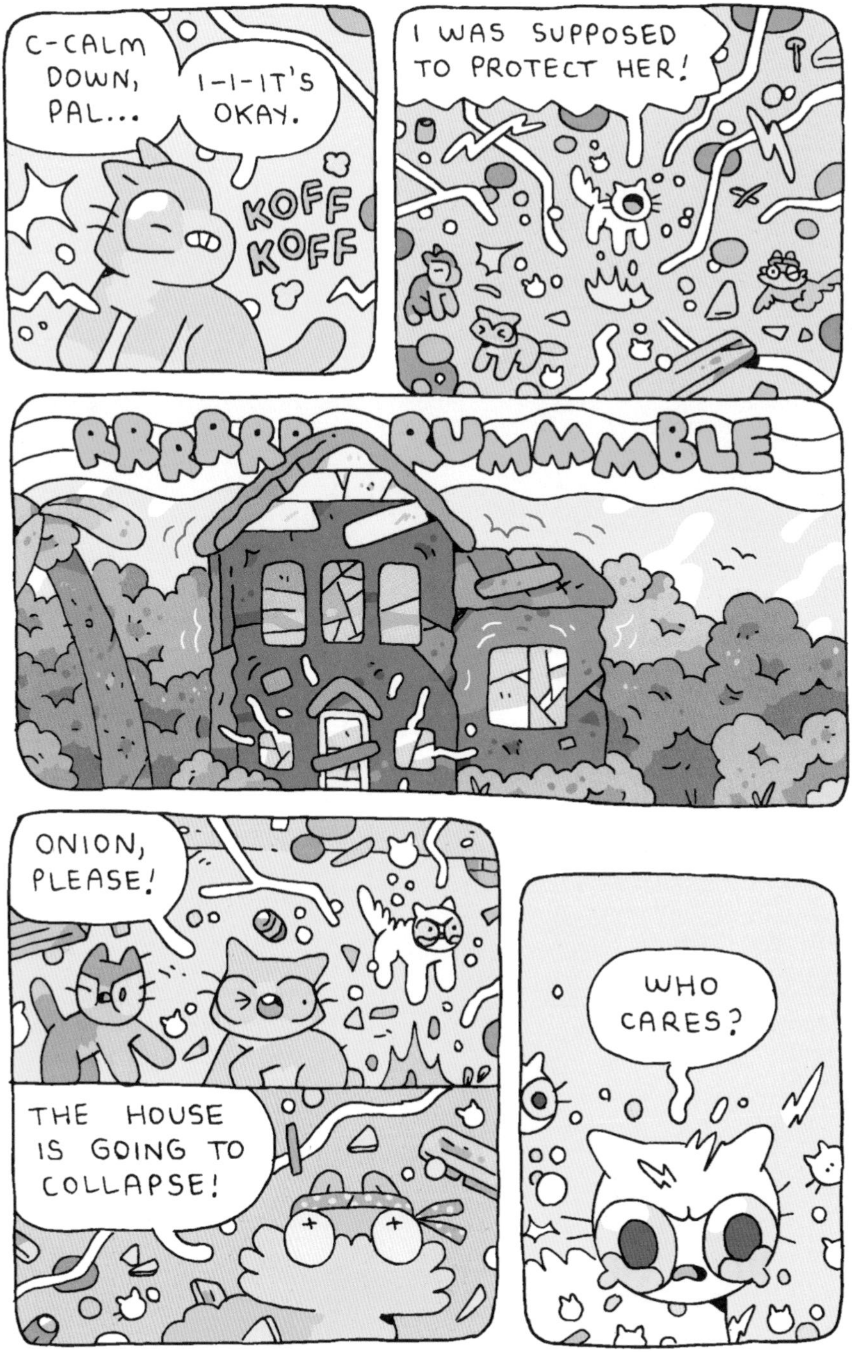
C-CALM DOWN, PAL...
I-I-IT'S OKAY.
KOFF KOFF
I WAS SUPPOSED TO PROTECT HER!
RRRRRR RUMMMBLE
ONION, PLEASE!
THE HOUSE IS GOING TO COLLAPSE!
WHO CARES?

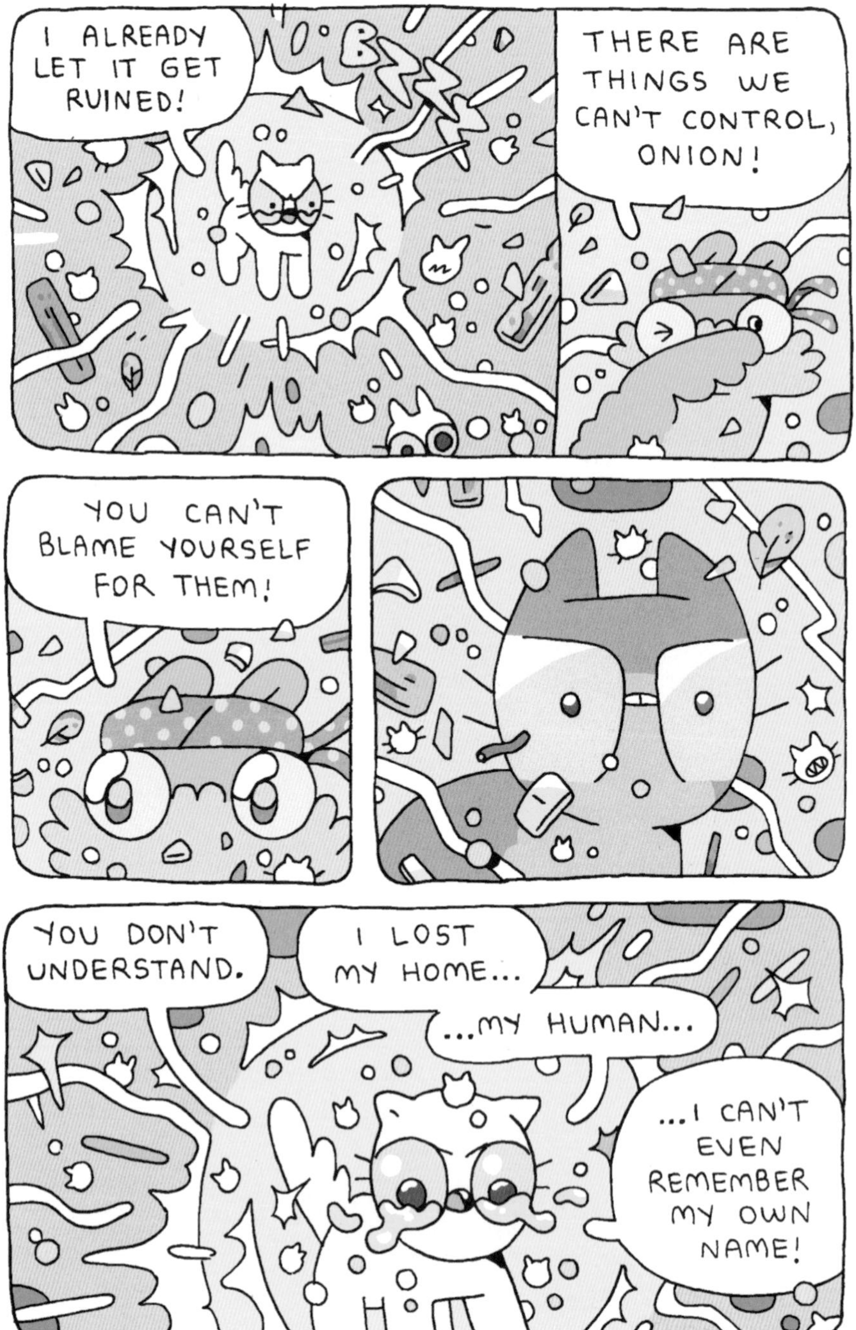
I ALREADY LET IT GET RUINED!
THERE ARE THINGS WE CAN'T CONTROL, ONION!
YOU CAN'T BLAME YOURSELF FOR THEM!
YOU DON'T UNDERSTAND.
I LOST MY HOME...
...MY HUMAN...
...I CAN'T EVEN REMEMBER MY OWN NAME!

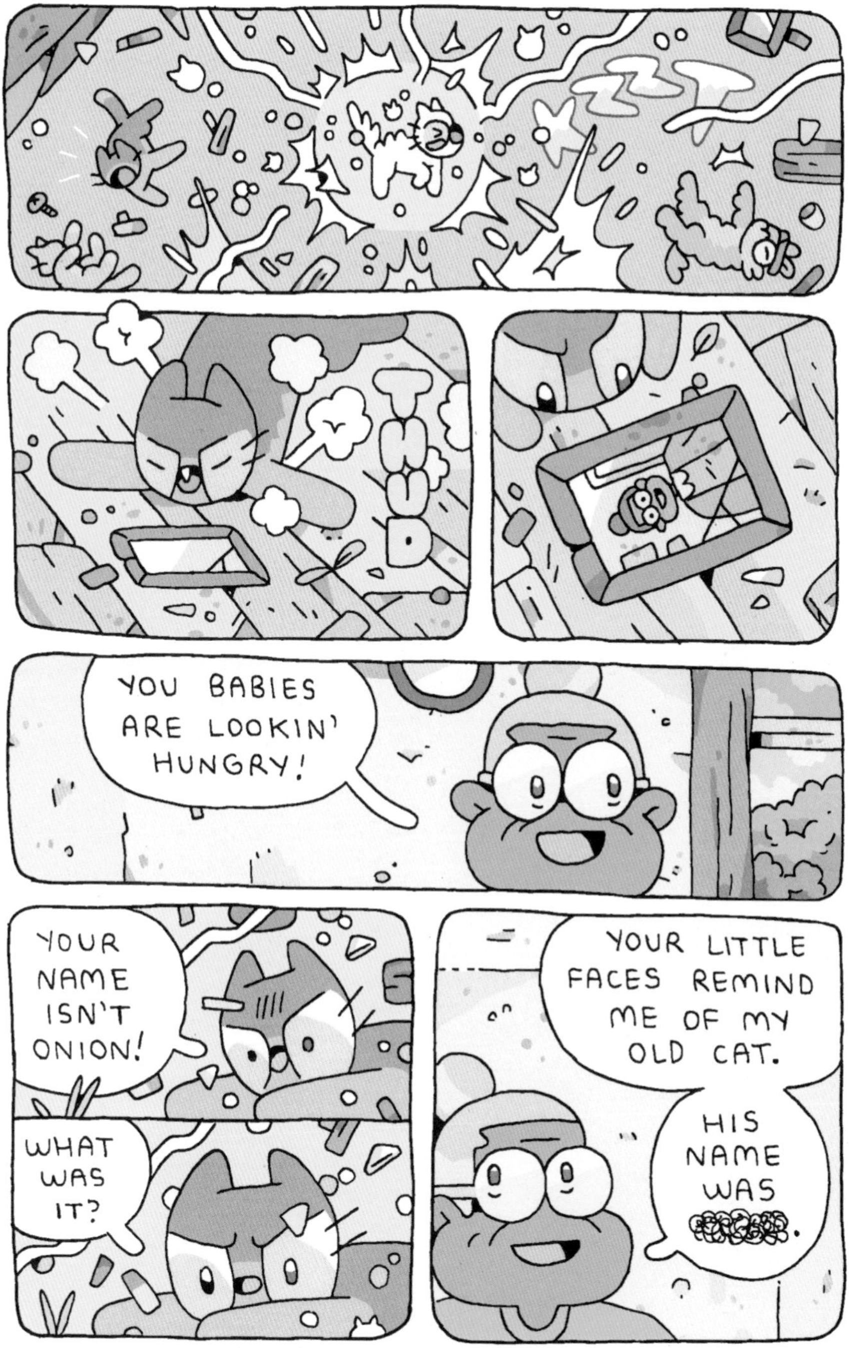
THUD
YOU BABIES ARE LOOKIN' HUNGRY!
YOUR NAME ISN'T ONION!
WHAT WAS IT?
YOUR LITTLE FACES REMIND ME OF MY OLD CAT.
HIS NAME WAS .

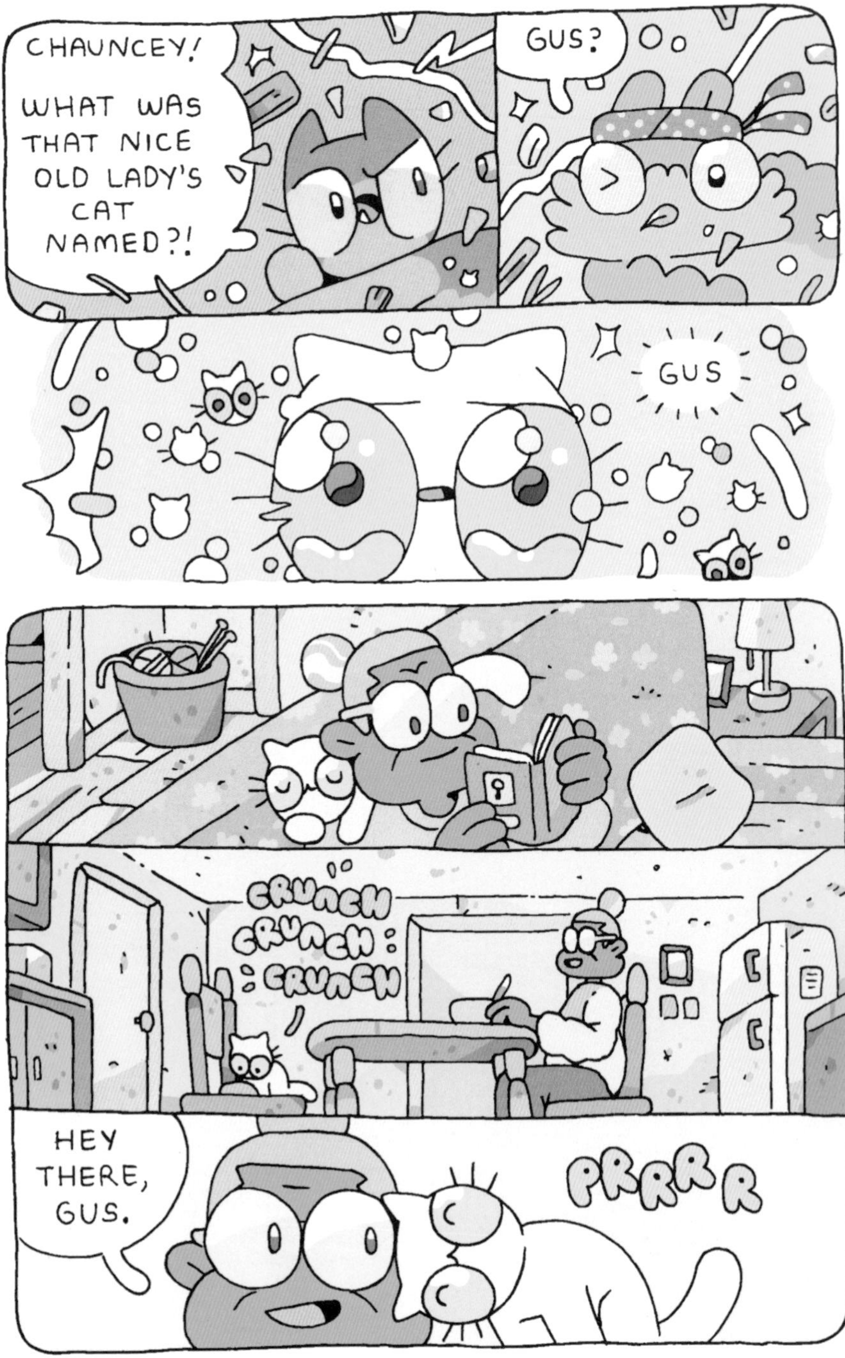
CHAUNCEY!
WHAT WAS THAT NICE OLD LADY'S CAT NAMED?!
GUS?
GUS
CRUNCH
CRUNCH
CRUNCH
HEY THERE, GUS.
PRRRR

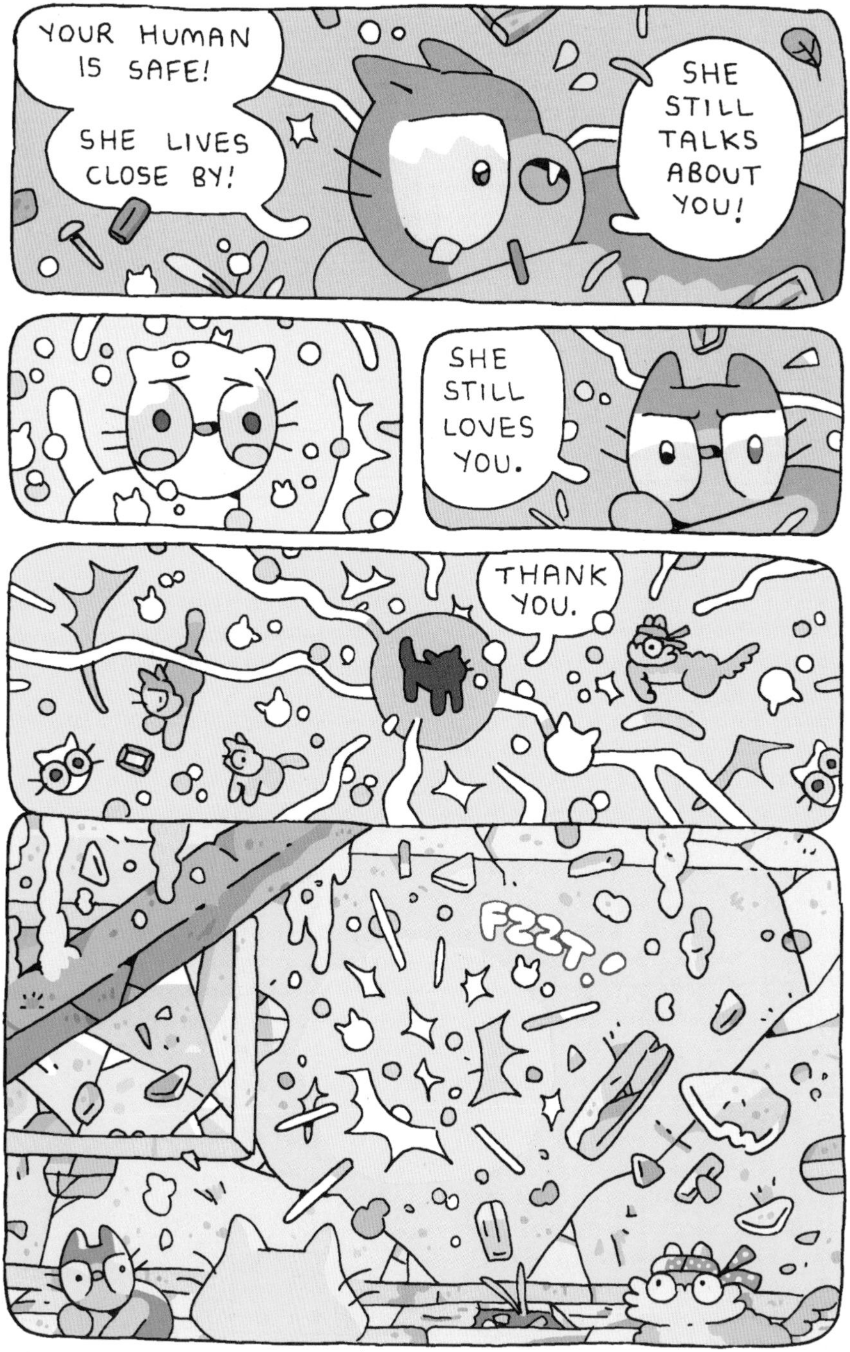
YOUR HUMAN IS SAFE!
SHE LIVES CLOSE BY!
SHE STILL TALKS ABOUT YOU!
SHE STILL LOVES YOU.
THANK YOU.
FZZT!

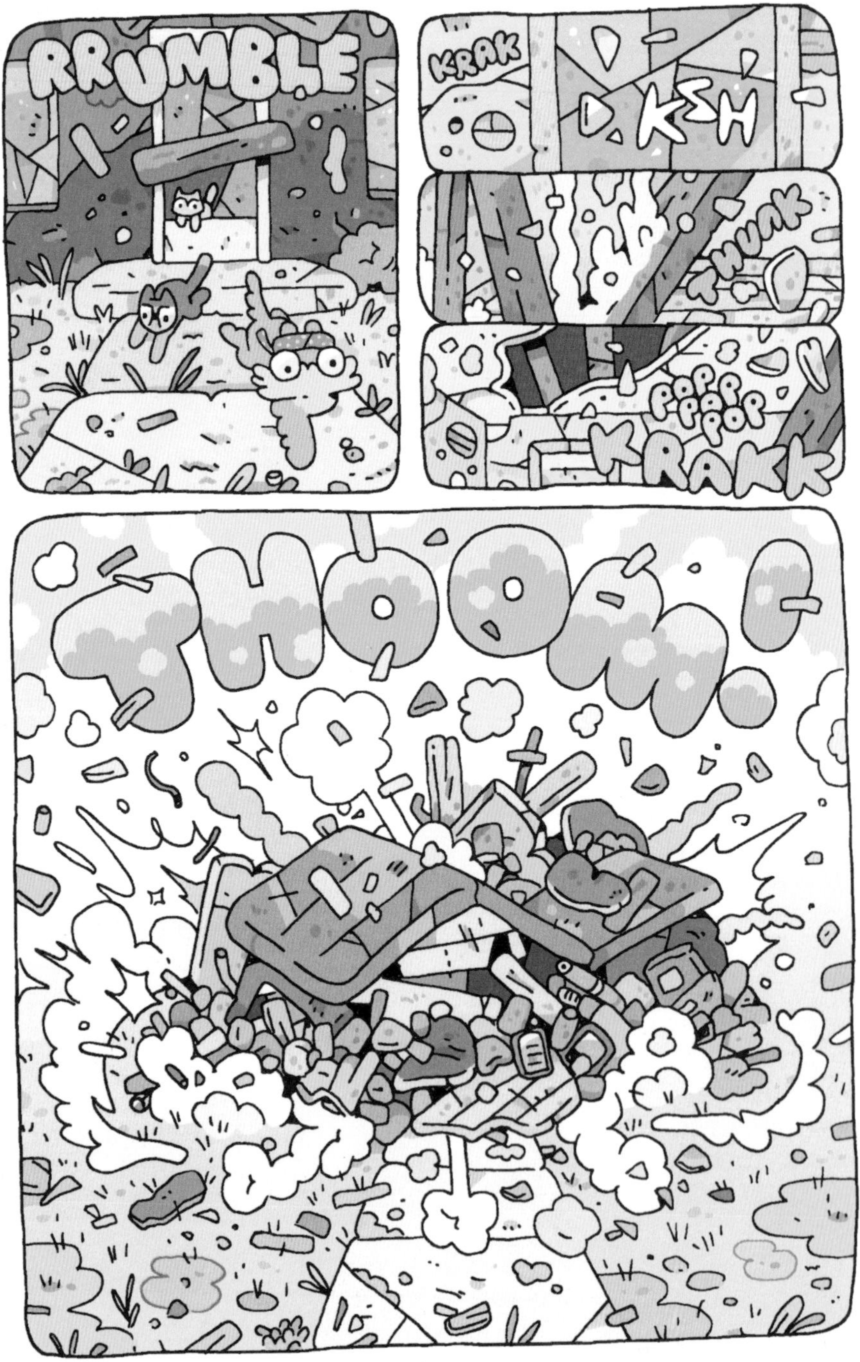
RRUMBLE
KRAK
KSH
THUNK
POPP POPP POP
KRAKK
THOOM!

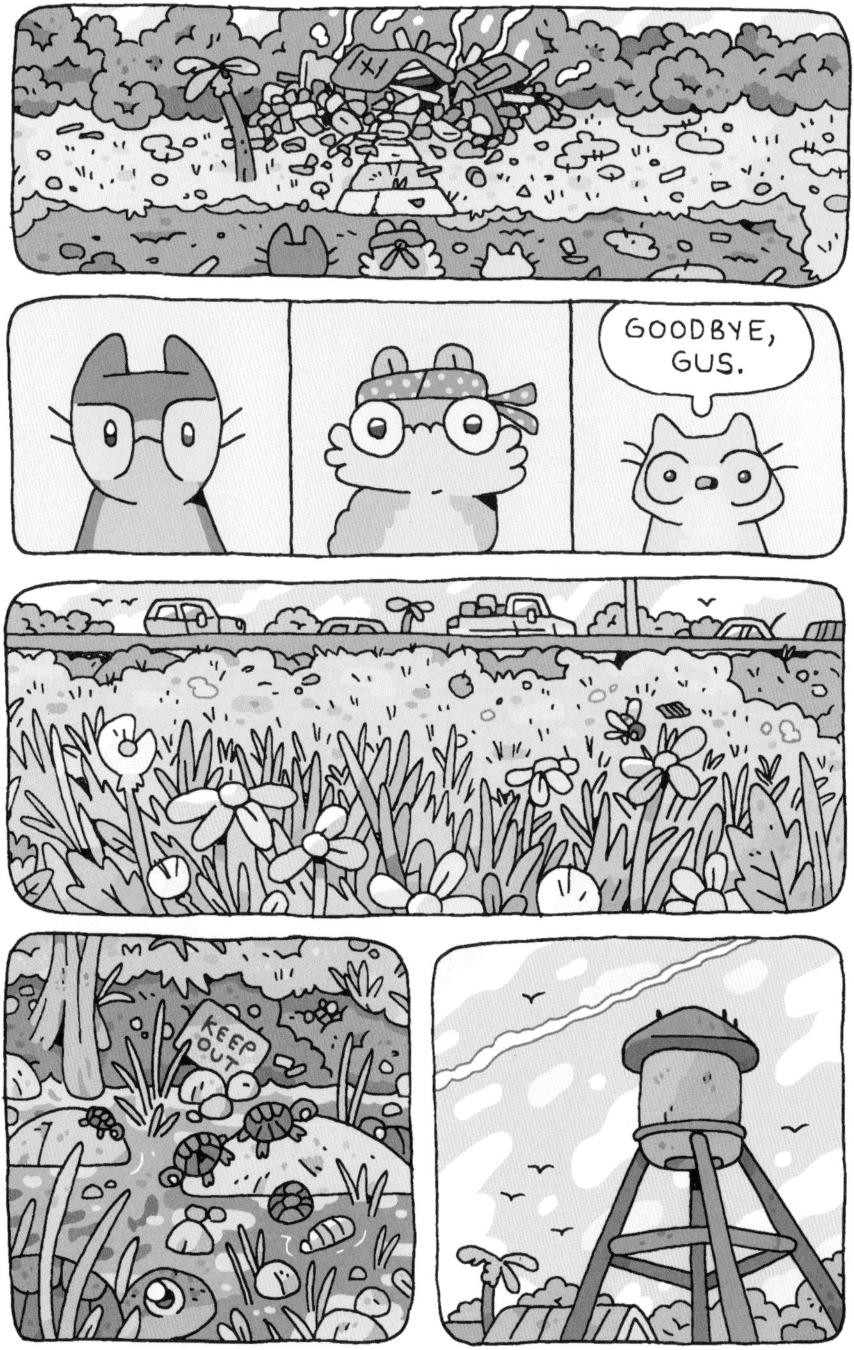
GOODBYE, GUS.
KEEP OUT

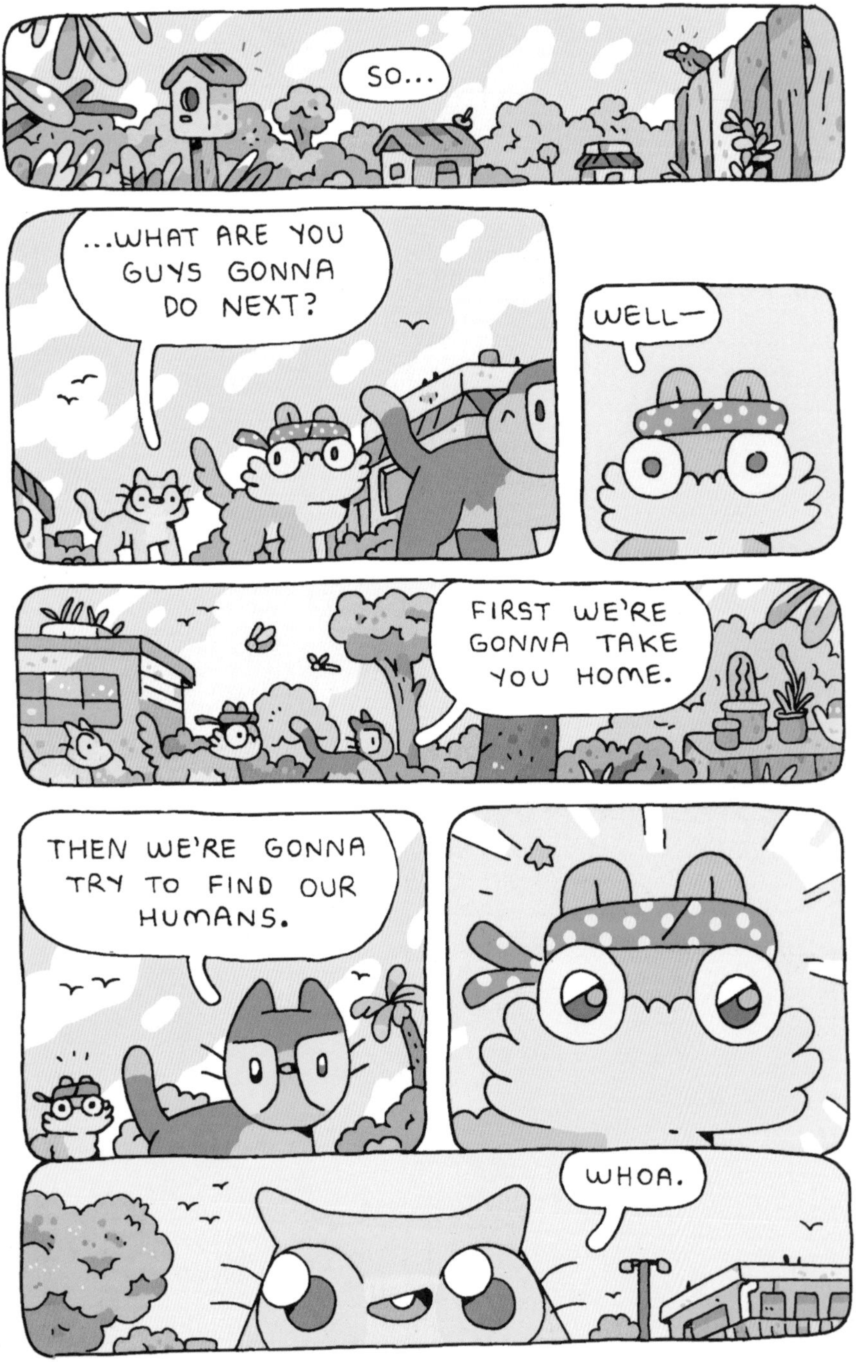
SO...
...WHAT ARE YOU GUYS GONNA DO NEXT?
WELL—
FIRST WE'RE GONNA TAKE YOU HOME.
THEN WE'RE GONNA TRY TO FIND OUR HUMANS.
WHOA.

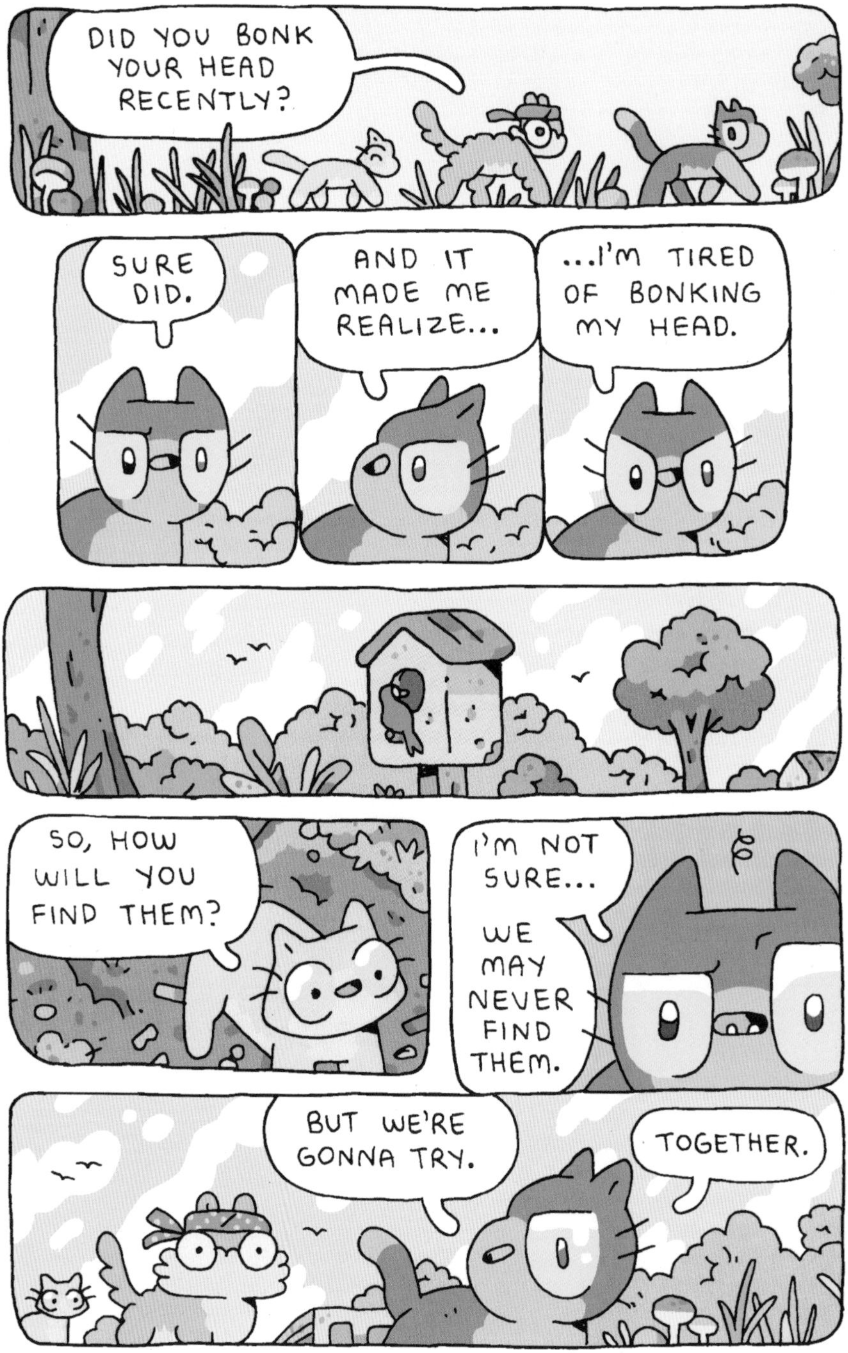
DID YOU BONK YOUR HEAD RECENTLY?
SURE DID.
AND IT MADE ME REALIZE...
...I'M TIRED OF BONKING MY HEAD.
SO, HOW WILL YOU FIND THEM?
I'M NOT SURE...
WE MAY NEVER FIND THEM.
BUT WE'RE GONNA TRY.
TOGETHER.

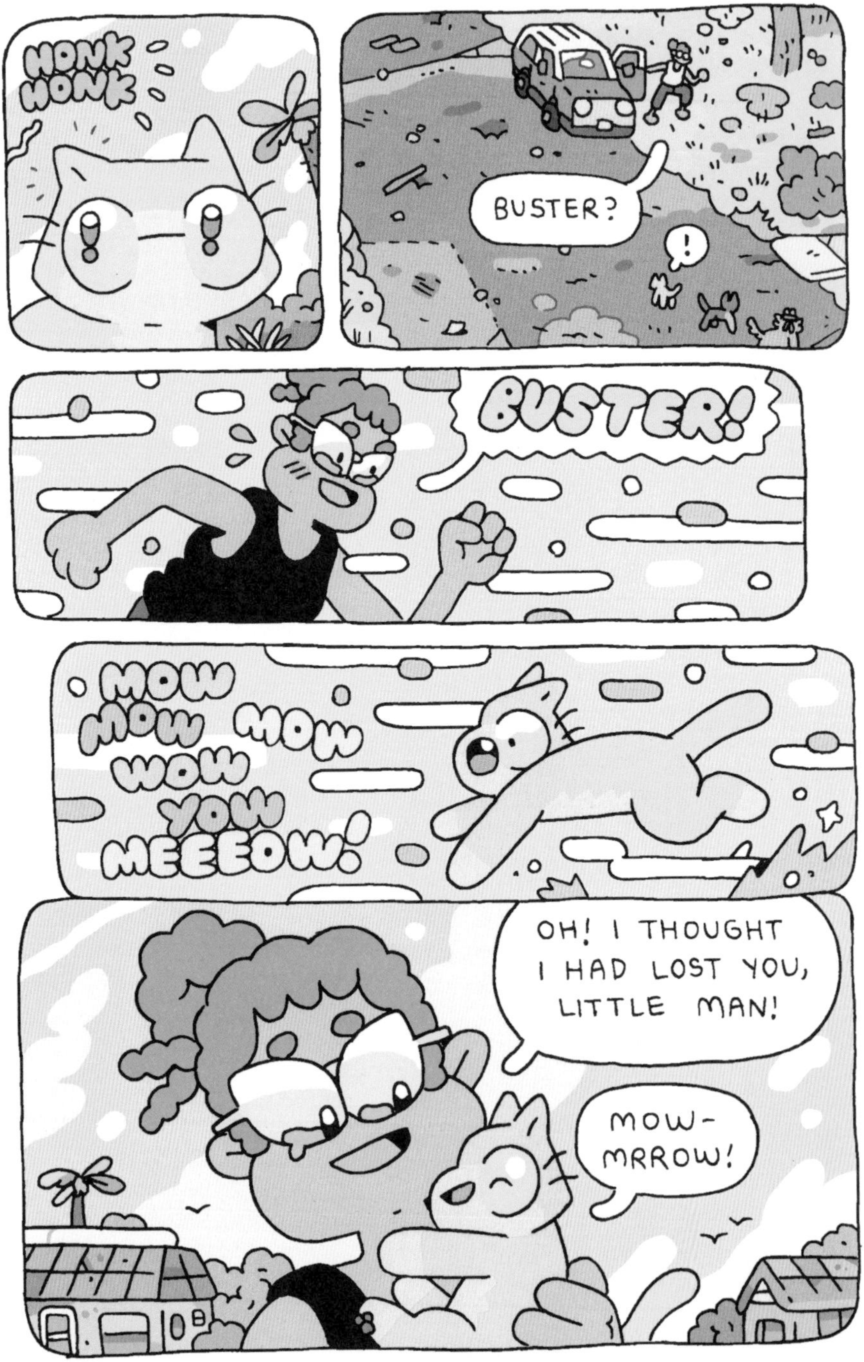
HONK HONK
BUSTER?
!
BUSTER!
MOW MOW MOW WOW YOW MEEEOW!
OH! I THOUGHT I HAD LOST YOU, LITTLE MAN!
MOW-MRROW!

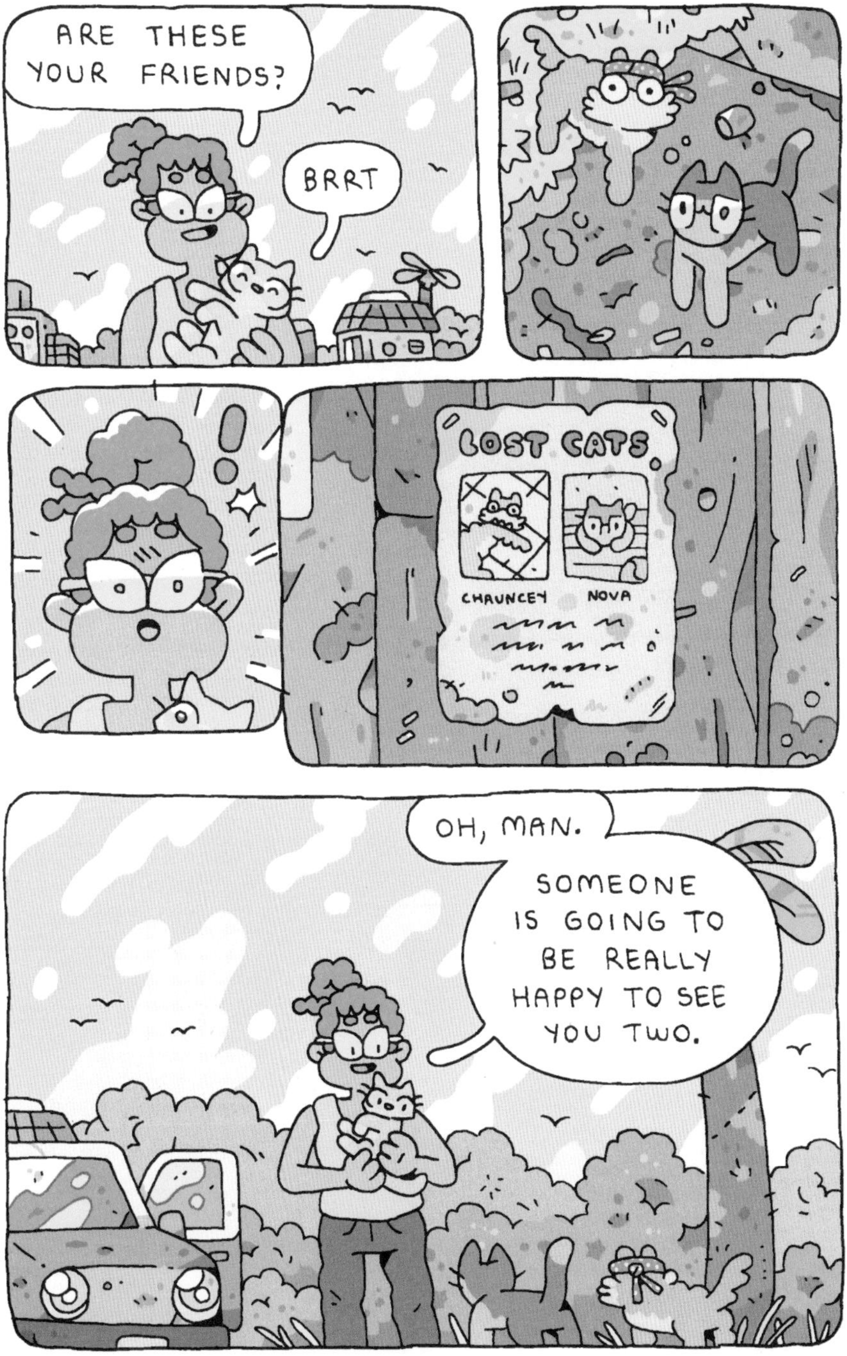
ARE THESE YOUR FRIENDS?
BRRT
LOST CATS
CHAUNCEY
NOVA
OH, MAN.
SOMEONE IS GOING TO BE REALLY HAPPY TO SEE YOU TWO.

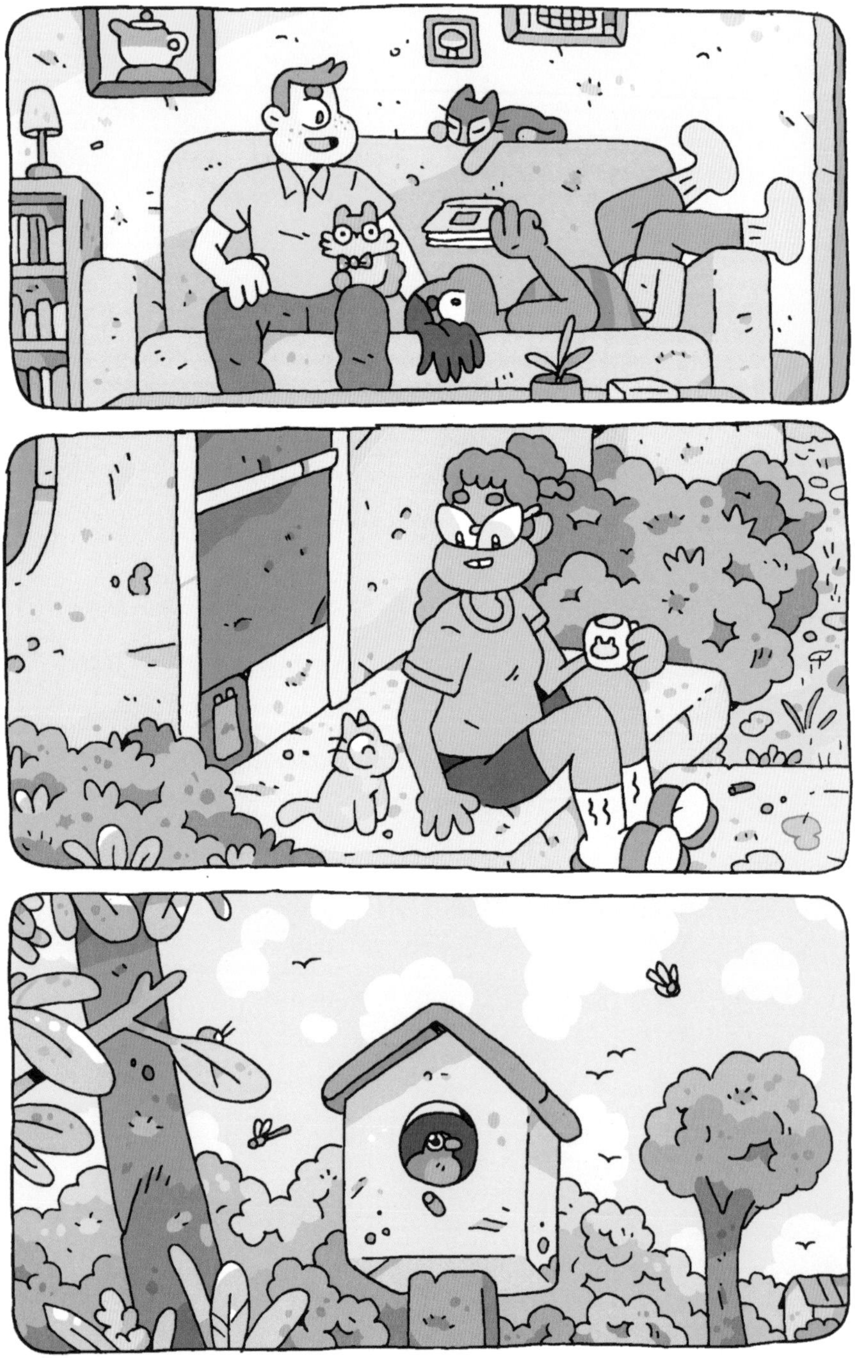

EPILOGUE

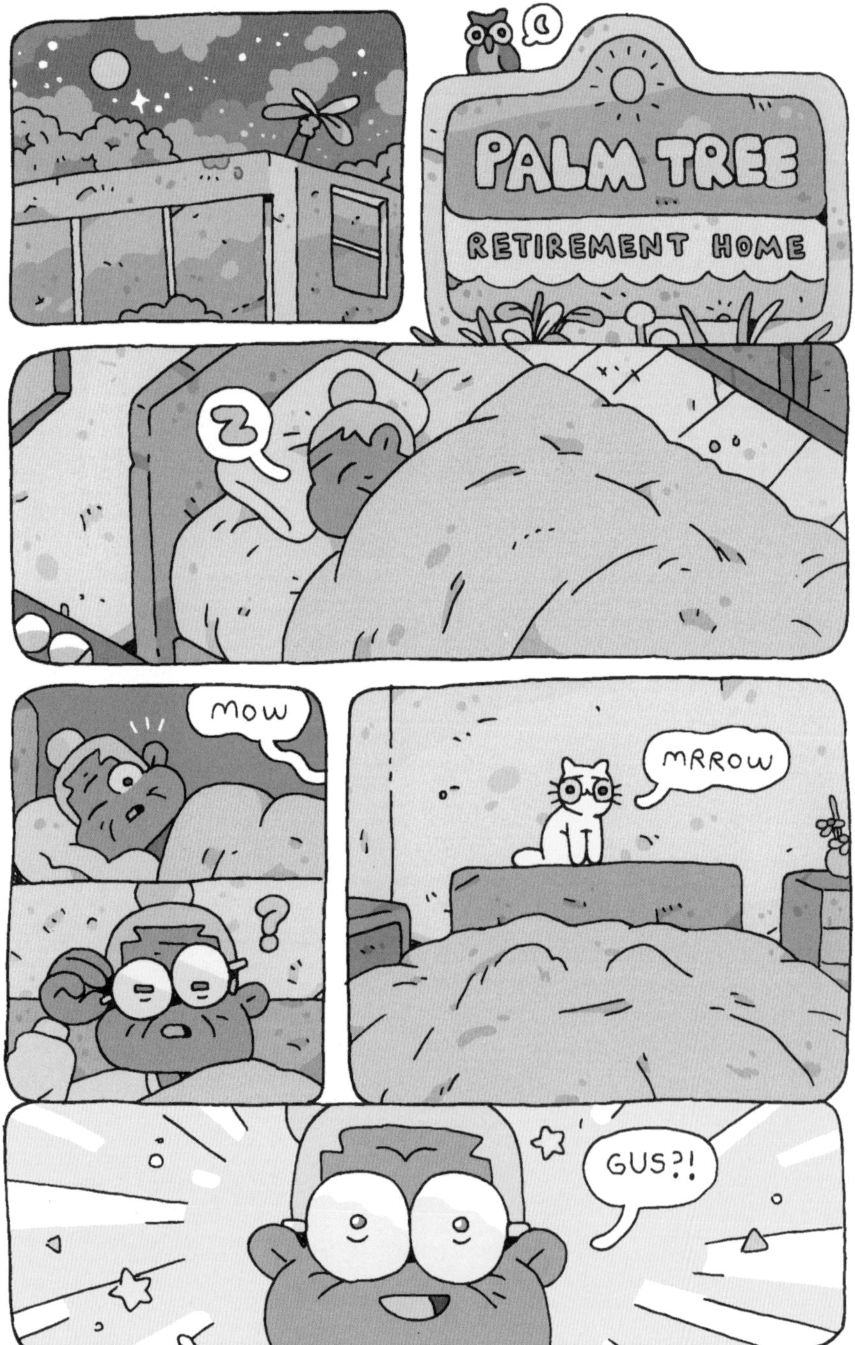
PALM TREE
RETIREMENT HOME
Z
MOW
?
MRROW
GUS?!

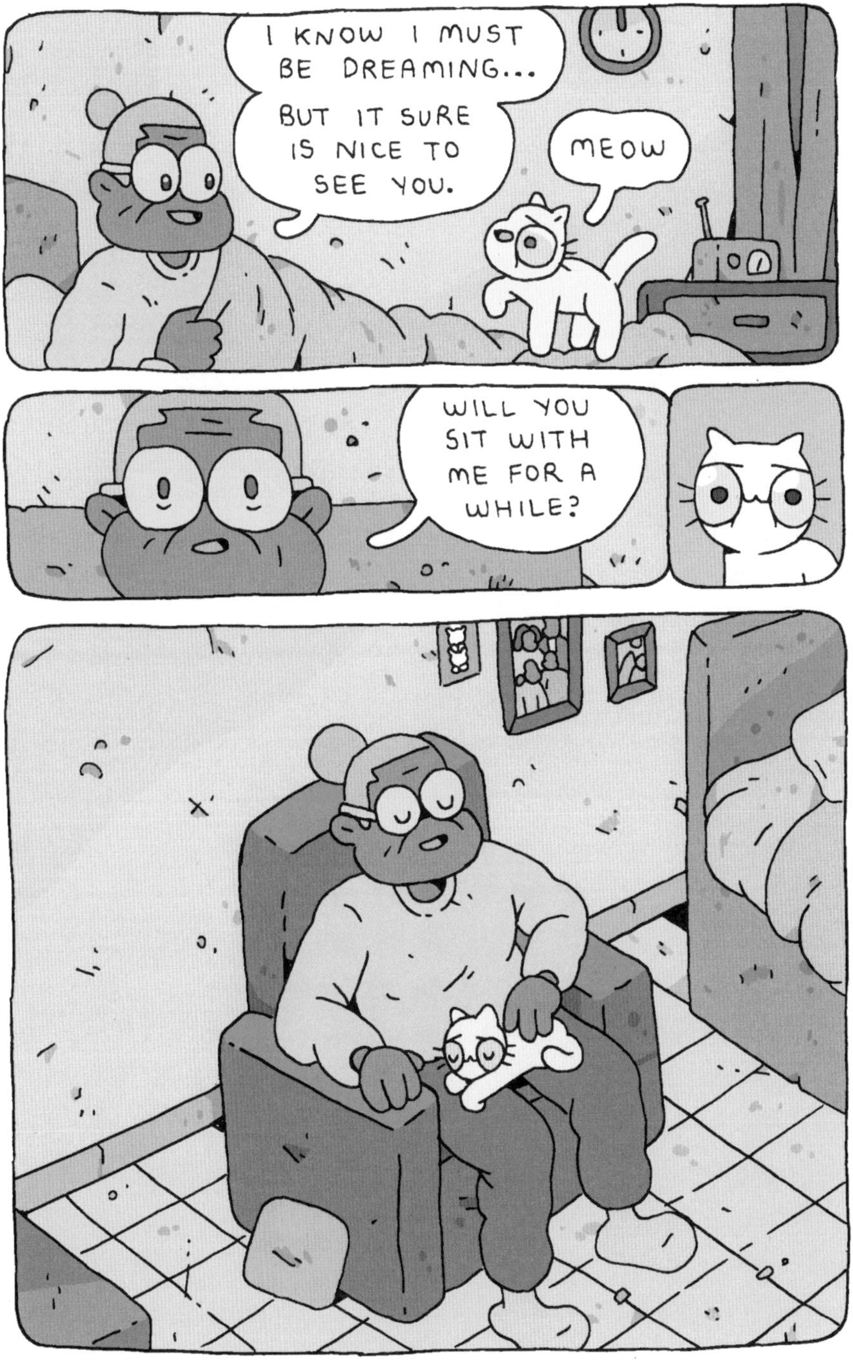
I KNOW I MUST BE DREAMING...
BUT IT SURE IS NICE TO SEE YOU.
MEOW
WILL YOU SIT WITH ME FOR A WHILE?

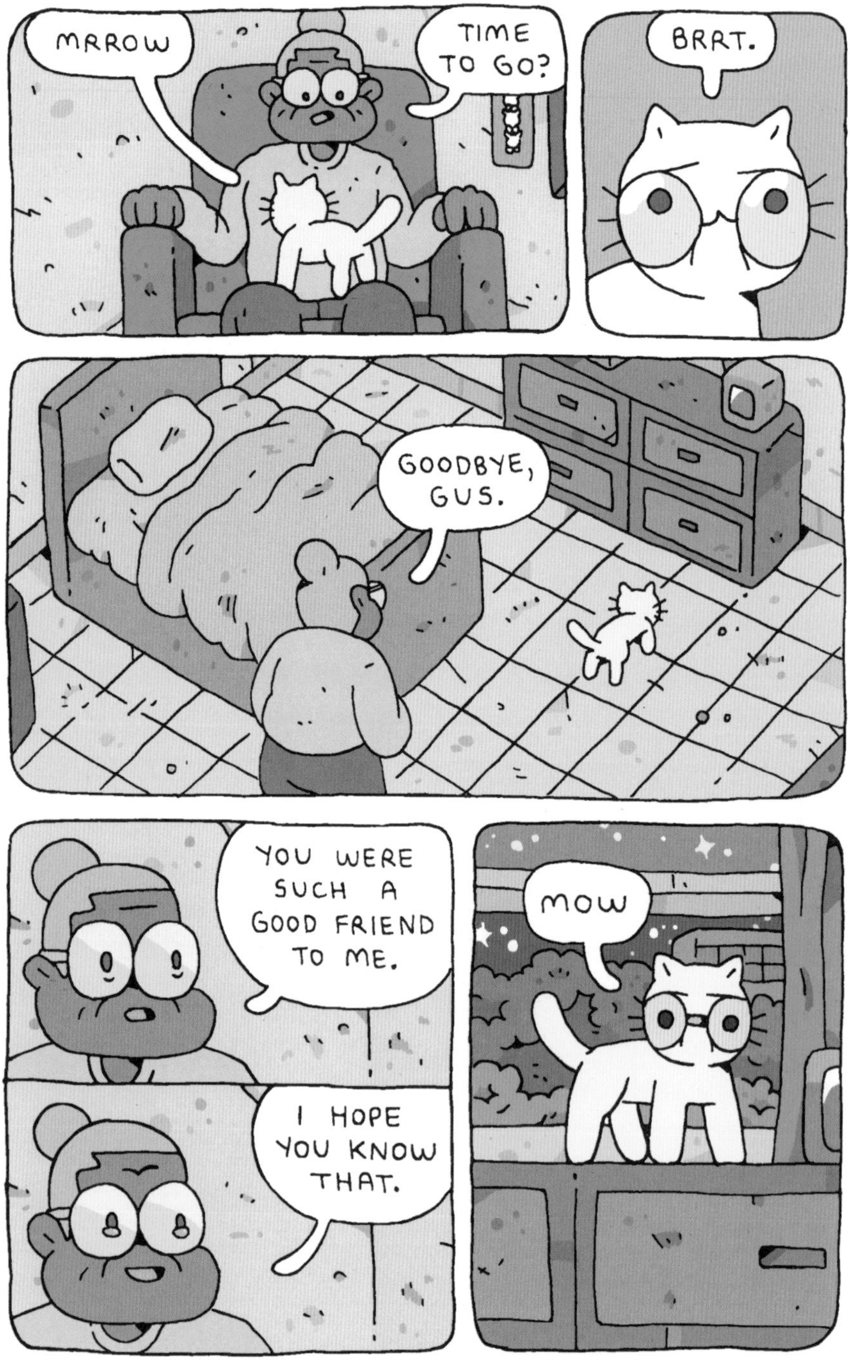
MRROW
TIME TO GO?
BRRT.
GOODBYE, GUS.
YOU WERE SUCH A GOOD FRIEND TO ME.
I HOPE YOU KNOW THAT.
MOW

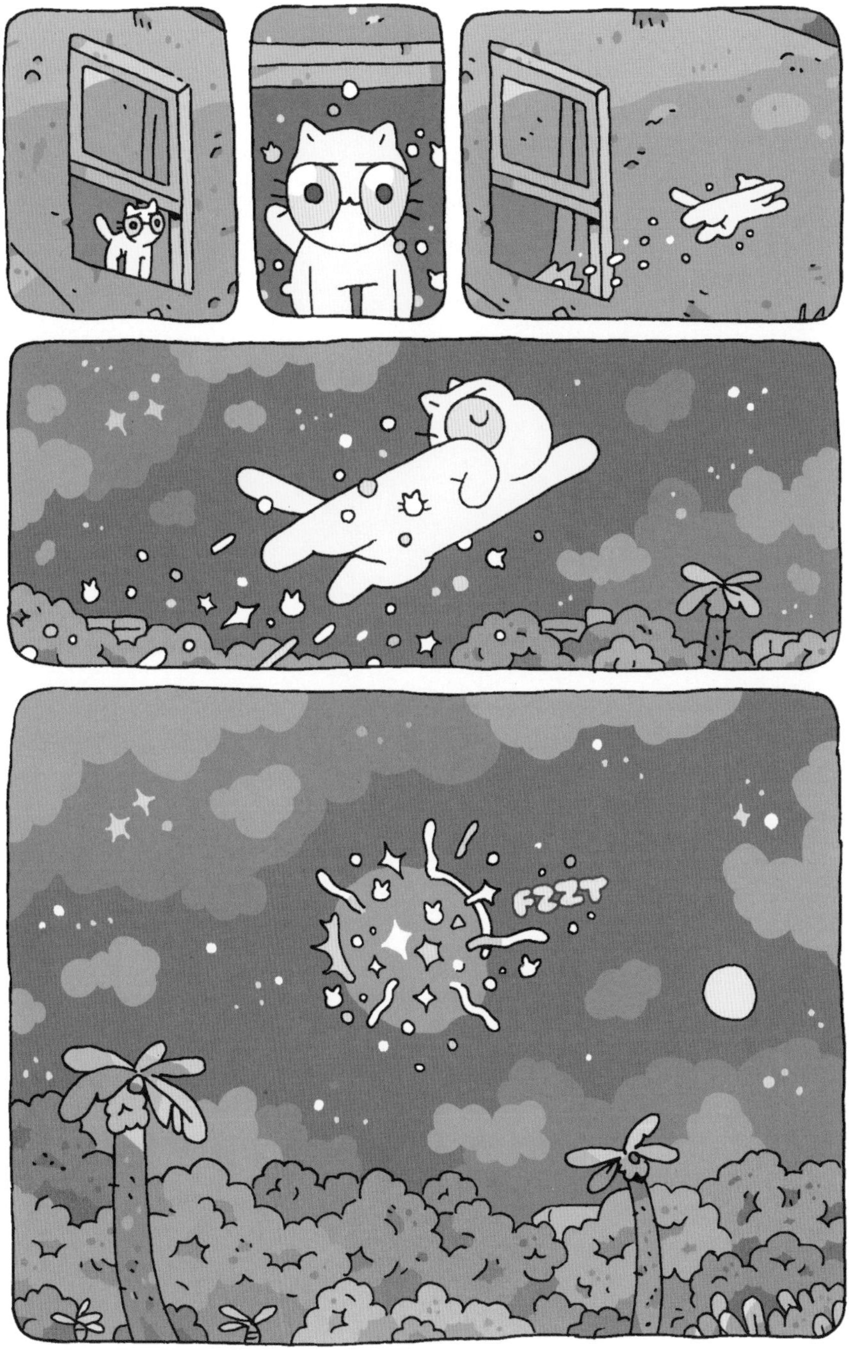
FZZT

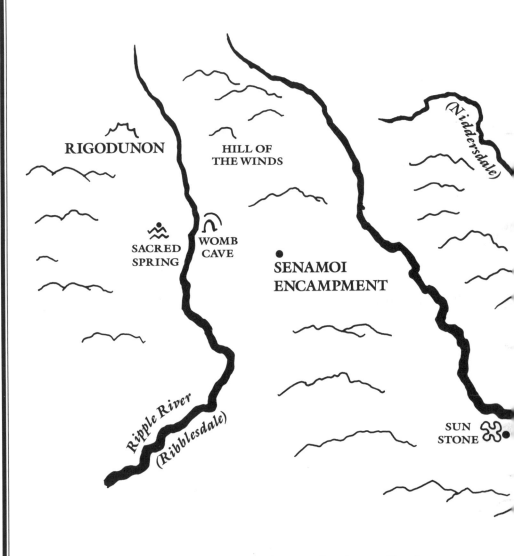

RIGODUNON

HILL OF
THE WINDS

(Niddersdale)

SACRED
SPRING

WOMB
CAVE

SENAMOI
ENCAMPMENT

Ripple River

(Ribblesdale)

SUN
STONE

THE DALES OF BRIGA